LP FIC REAY

Reay, Katherine

Lizzy & Jane

S

2/15

W9-AHA-982

Lizzy & Jane

Center Point
Large Print

Also by Katherine Reay and available from
Center Point Large Print:

Dear Mr. Knightley

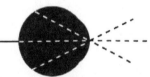

**This Large Print Book carries the
Seal of Approval of N.A.V.H.**

Katherine Reay

CENTER POINT LARGE PRINT
THORNDIKE, MAINE

This Center Point Large Print edition is published in the year 2014 by arrangement with Thomas Nelson.

Copyright © 2014 by Katherine Reay.

All rights reserved.

Names, characters, places, and incidents are either products of the author's imagination or used fictitiously. All characters are fictional, and any similarity to people living or dead is purely coincidental.

The text of this Large Print edition is unabridged. In other aspects, this book may vary from the original edition. Printed in the United States of America on permanent paper. Set in 16-point Times New Roman type.

ISBN: 978-1-62899-367-7

Library of Congress Cataloging-in-Publication Data

Reay, Katherine, 1970–
Lizzy & Jane / Katherine Reay. — Center Point Large Print edition.
pages ; cm
Summary: "A story of two sisters, bound together by family, food, and a passion for Jane Austen"—Provided by publisher.
ISBN 978-1-62899-367-7 (library binding : alk. paper)
1. Sisters—Fiction. 2. Large type books. 3. Domestic fiction.
  I. Title. II. Title: Lizzy and Jane.
PS3618.E23L59 2014b
813'.6—dc23
                                              2014033370

To Elizabeth,
Elizabeth,
and
Elizabeth.
In that order . . .
And to Mason—
Always. I love you.
Thank you.

Chapter 1

One misstep can kill a New York restaurant.

During cooking school we scoffed at Chef Palmer's warning, knowing it was true but equally certain it couldn't happen to us—and certainly not to me, Palmer's protégé. I shifted the spices back and forth in the sauté pan, dwelling over each word, each inflection, and my *many* recent mis-steps.

"Elizabeth? You good?" Tabitha, my sous chef, tapped my shoulder.

"Sure . . . just thinking." I glanced around the kitchen. "Palmer. We're slow tonight, even for a weeknight."

"Sounding the death knell?"

"Too soon?" I matched Tabitha's sarcasm with sincerity.

She pinched me. "Stop it."

"I was only kidding. Besides, we're up this week in reservations and walk-ins." I tilted my head toward the steel door leading to the dining room. "Is she here?"

"Just walked in." Tabitha paused. "I hope you know what you're doing."

"Getting a critic to disagree with the *Village Voice* review will diminish its power. We need that."

"Not if she reinforces it." Tabitha flicked my hand. "Careful."

An acrid smell struck me. I'd over-toasted the spices again. I shook the pan over the compost bin, wiped it with a rag, and tossed it onto the burner grate. The clank reverberated through the stainless steel kitchen, louder than the chaos around us.

I leaned back against the counter and closed my eyes.

"I'll do that," Tabitha said. "Go wander. Chat her up. Face time with critics helps."

"That's not a good idea right now." I waved to the pan. "You go. You're better at that stuff. I'll fix this."

"No one wants to see the sous chef." She started sorting more spices.

"Fine." I smoothed my hands down my apron and pushed through the door, glancing down at tables as I crossed the dining room.

A few customers tried to catch my eye, but the critic was somewhere, and I was afraid to see her selection, her eyes, her possible disappointment. Instead I focused on the dishes. The grilled sea bass with lime cucumber salsa caught my eye—on point and executed without flaw. Yet it lay lifeless and flat on the white china plate. What was wrong? A missing ingredient? Did it need something new? I chased the questions around the dining room before beelining back to the kitchen.

"Did you have fun?"

I rolled my eyes, and Tabitha's narrowed in response as she moved on to a balsamic reduction. "I need to tell you something else." She pushed a bowl of perfectly toasted spices to me.

"What?"

"Paul toured a man around your kitchen today." She waited until she had my attention. "He was in street clothes, but he was a chef. The way he inspected the knives, the stoves . . . either that or the health board."

"What time was this?"

"Around noon."

"But he knew I was coming in late today." I shrugged. "I'm sure it's nothing. I'll talk to him about it. Let's finish service."

The Wednesday evening progressed without another hitch, but I felt compressed and tight—so unlike long-ago evenings that were fun, vibrant, and flawless, when tough work energized rather than drained. Tonight my baseline required Herculean effort; a part of my mind couldn't stop puzzling over Paul's mystery visitor.

When the kitchen slowed, I gave up manufacturing a game face and headed to the alley. I propped the back door open with the broken stop and leaned against the brick wall. I was not stupid enough to close my eyes here—after all, it was a dark alley in New York's meatpacking district—but I was desperate enough to stand there alone

9

for as long as it took to regain a hint of equanimity.

A small movement at my feet startled me. "What are you doing here? I thought you'd gone." I knelt down and reached out as the cat approached cautiously.

She tiptoed, as if leaving her escape hatches open. I thought of it as "she," but the cat could have been a boy for all I knew. We weren't good friends.

"You need a home, silly. You need a name." I stroked her back and swept over a sticky patch. "Blech."

She curled closer. "Oh no, I'm not patting you after that, and don't get any ideas about me. We've been through this." She purred again. "I'll bring you some cream. Stay here."

I pulled the door open and saw the dishwasher fiddling with his phone. A spicy scent drifted toward me. One of my cardinal rules: no scent in the kitchen. It messes with one's palate—it also reminded me of my mom and divided my focus.

"Enrique?"

He almost dropped his phone in the sink in his haste to hide it. "Yes, Chef?"

"When you get a chance, take a bowl of cream to that cat out there."

"Yes, Chef."

"And, Enrique? Put the phone away and scrub off the cologne. You know the rules."

"Yes, Chef."

At eleven p.m., waiters collected the final orders. *The Feast is over—for tonight.* The mantra played through my brain as it did every night, supplanting Palmer's. My mother used to announce the end of the "feast" at each family dinner, as if wiping down the counters after one meal marked the moment to begin dreaming toward the next. I named the restaurant Feast in her honor, as a way to remember. And yet she drifted further away with each meal and each evening. My thoughts flickered to my sister, Jane. Did she remember? Did she say it to her family each night?

The kitchen door swung open as Tabitha returned from her nightly tour of the dining room. She caught my eye and mouthed, *Paul.* I sighed and crossed the prep area to the small closet by the freezer to check my makeup and hair. Blond and pale naturally—tired didn't help.

"Hello, Anne," I mumbled into the mirror.

"Who?"

I jumped. I hadn't realized Tabitha had followed me. "Anne Elliot. *Persuasion.* I've lost my bloom."

"Your what?"

A normal evening's work shouldn't sap me. "My glow? My *joie de vivre*?" I applied some lip gloss.

"Paul's waiting at his usual table."

I squeezed her arm, then pushed through the

steel door and surveyed the softly lit room, warm light playing against the dark wood of the bar and the floor, and I felt my mood lift. This was my sanctuary. But only about a third of the tables were still occupied. Palmer was right—one misstep *can* kill a restaurant. Mine.

I found Paul in a center booth with an open bottle of wine in front of him. He was leaning back against the wall, watching me, studying the room and absently fingering the bottle's label. Perfectly pressed, precisely dressed, with just the right hint of gray at his temples.

I slid in next to him. "Robert Craig? Howell Mountain?" I tilted the bottle.

"I hadn't tried the '07. Here's a glass for you." He slid a glass under my fingertips. "How was tonight?"

"Exhausting." I leaned back against the balustrade, swirling the wine in the glass. It picked up the light and glowed ruby red and warm.

"You say that every night."

"And it's true every night." I took a sip and let the wine rest in my mouth. "It didn't used to be," I whispered, then snapped myself awake. Paul Metzger, as much as I knew he cared about me, was still my boss. His venture capital firm owned Feast.

"I need to talk to you about that, dear."

I sat straight. "Dear? You only say that when you're annoyed."

Paul chuckled. "I keep saying you know me best. Lisa never caught on to that one."

"I'll be sure to prep your next wife."

"Very funny, dear." Paul's voice dropped, low and careful.

I turned to face him directly. "Out with it."

"Feast is underperforming." His glance swept the room. "You can see that."

"I can. And I'm sorry. I'll fix it."

Paul reached over and covered my hand. "I know you want to, but I've been watching. I don't think you know how."

"What do you mean?"

"Your hours are beyond reasonable, even for you. Your food . . . it's tight, not as expressive as usual. I called John to discuss it."

I narrowed my eyes in frustration. I wanted to scream, *I'm not a child,* but on some level, when it suited Paul and Chef John Palmer, I was.

"And what did you two diagnose?"

"Burnout? Stress? We're not sure, but I've got a lot invested in Feast, so I'm making a move. I hired you a new chef de cuisine." Paul raised his hand as my jaw dropped. "Before you say anything, Trent Murray trained at the California Culinary Academy in San Francisco and spent years under Dugar at Pot au Poulet. He's got seventeen thousand followers on Twitter, dozens of appearances on the Food Network, and he knows how to create the buzz we need."

"That's not what I'm about. That's show. That's not food."

"Elizabeth, John Palmer trained you and pushed me to back you. He's your biggest champion, and even he's concerned. It's a small culinary community and there's chatter. We need a rain-maker."

"It's just a slump."

"Call it anything you want, my dear, but it's real and it's affecting Feast. I'll call it Jane, if you don't mind."

I shot him a look.

"You can't multitask, Elizabeth—you never could. That's partly why you're so gifted in the kitchen; you're usually so focused. But right now you're divided."

"I don't mean to be. Jane's got her battle and I've got mine. I know that sounds horrid, but I've put everything I've got into this place. Don't hire somebody else."

"Two close friends fight breast cancer as I sit here. Don't tell me their friends and husbands don't feel that, don't fight beside them. And when Kara went through it five years ago, I dropped everything to help her, and we'd already been divorced for a decade. And your mother? I know you better than to think you believe what you just said."

I sat back and closed my eyes, letting Paul's words sink through me. I recalled a night three years before when he and I, flush with the excitement of a glittering launch, had sat in this very booth and chatted for hours. The empty restaurant, the soft leather cushions, the quiet after the chaos—we were in our own world. He shared stories from his marriages, his ex-wife management strategies, the woman he was pursuing for wife number three. Stories about his children, who were scarcely a decade younger than I. And I told him about leaving home for college, about cooking school, my early jobs, and, eventually, my mom. How her perfume smelled of gardenias; how she couldn't cook worth a darn but loved it nonetheless; how I'd started cooking at twelve to spend time with her and basically took over the kitchen at thirteen; how we had been so alike and created magic together; and how, when I was eighteen, all that magic died with her. Paul had never used that moment, that vulnerability, against me until now.

"I consider you a friend, Elizabeth," he said, "more than that on some days, and your personal decisions are your own, but this is business."

"I know. And I understand . . . I just didn't expect this." I leaned forward and swirled my wine as my eyes trailed from him to the huge mahogany bar that glowed deep brown and red across the room. It captured the gold radiance of the full-wall antique mirror behind it. I had designed it and paired its warmth with white walls and linen-covered tables that still looked crisp and cool after the busy night. Black-and-white photographs, all landscapes except the one of Jane and me near the front, made my sanctuary complete. I knew Feast, every quirk and every detail, and now I felt it slipping away.

Chapter 2

While it was unusual for a restaurant to open for weekday lunch but close for lunch service Saturday and Sunday, the decision had worked in Feast's favor. Weekend dinners glowed with an aura of exclusivity, and I relished the two peaceful mornings. I preferred to prep alone, and these times had long become my favorite moments— and the only days I entered Feast through the front door.

I turned the deadbolt and stepped into the small waiting area in front of the hostess stand. The day was cloudy and cold, and the dining room mirrored the distant coolness of the photographs, which had felt so warm and alive the previous evening. Yet the hush still whispered and soothed me in a city that usually shouted. I paused in the doorway to absorb it.

But something was wrong . . . It took a beat to isolate it. Silence. The alarm hadn't sounded. I turned to the panel and noticed the steady green light. I recalled my actions from the night before. I'd set it; I was certain. Had I forgotten a meeting with Tabitha? I caught a noise from the kitchen, soft but discordant, and hoisted my bag tighter as I passed through the dining room, hoping it was she—and questioning my sanity for hurling into the kitchen alone and unarmed if it wasn't. I swung the stainless steel door open, and rap music filled the air.

"Excuse me? Hello?" I yelled. All the lights were on, and music pulsed from the small dock on my desk.

I shouted louder. "Hello?"

Tabitha emerged from the freezer, her eyes wide. "You scared me," she shouted back. "You don't usually come in for another hour." She crossed the room and turned down the music.

"And you for another three. What's up?"

"I wanted to try some new ideas."

I dropped my bag on the small wooden desk. "You're worried."

"I am. This is a tough town and we've got a good gig. How many thirty-three-year-old women get a chance like this? Paul hiring a new chef isn't good, especially for me."

I dropped into the chair and held my head in my hands. "I know."

"Then fix it."

"If I knew what was wrong, it'd be fixed already." I looked up. "Paul said my food was 'tight,' and it's true. Maybe Trent Murray's 'buzz' will be enough distraction to lessen pressure on the kitchen, on me."

"And *my* job?"

"Paul said nothing about changes. He wouldn't do that." I cringed slightly, knowing that wasn't necessarily true. "At least not yet, not without talking to me."

"Show him some interest."

"Trent Murray?"

Tabitha slanted her eyes. "Paul. He's adored you for years. Use it."

"Tabitha!"

"It's not so wrong." She waited a moment, then pointed to something on the desk. "What's that?"

I sighed and tapped the small blue box toward her. "A new charm for the bracelet he gave me. It's a little silver colander."

She raised an eyebrow.

"Please, Tabitha. It's what he does. His assistant, Lois, sends the gifts. They mean nothing."

"It means you're on Paul's list."

"Stop it."

"My job is on the line here, Elizabeth." She ground out the words.

"Mine is too." I stood and faced her.

"Not in the same way."

"Hey." I pulled her into a hug. "We're going to get through this. We've survived three years because we can cook. Really cook."

18

"And what if we don't survive?" Tabitha patted my back. "You have to admit he's handsome."

I gently pushed her back. "And his three ex-wives are beautiful. We're not really having this conversation, are we?"

"But see? It's a sure bet. New York men never divorce the fourth wife." She shrugged at my glare. "No, we aren't really having this conversation. I just feel . . . I don't know. I stayed up till three reading Trent Murray's blog postings and credits. It didn't help."

"That's like looking up symptoms on WebMD. Didn't anyone tell you never to do that?"

"Lesson learned." She glanced to her board. "I'm prepping the sofrito for lobster risotto. Can we add it to the menu? Marco texted me he's got some beauties."

"Sure. I love that dish." I pitched my voice high and delighted. It was not a favorite dish of mine, but it was Tabitha's heart song, and she needed something of her own right now.

She nodded, pacified for the moment, and returned to her onions, celery, and carrots. I pulled out vegetables of my own. A hush fell over the kitchen; neither of us wanted to disturb our fragile peace.

"Chef Hughes!" A man with cropped brown hair pushed through the steel door from the dining room. He rushed forward, hand outstretched—

magnanimous and glowing, like a TV game show host.

Tabitha and I both jumped, and I heard her murmur, "Trent Murray."

He was lanky and strong and his arms were fully inked. "I'm so pleased to meet you."

"You're Murray?" I looked past him, expecting Paul to follow through the door. "How are you here?"

He stepped closer—too close—and I automatically leaned away. I was about to step back to reestablish my personal space when I caught myself. *Don't give any ground.* I forced myself a microstep forward.

"Paul told you about me, right?" He shoved his hand toward me again.

"Not that you'd be here. Today. How did you get in here anyway?"

Trent stepped back. "That's bad, isn't it? Paul insisted." He opened his hand to reveal a key and a scrap of paper. "I didn't need the alarm code, obviously. Give me five minutes and I'll have forgotten those numbers." He shoved both items into my hands. "I thought I'd come early and get a feel for the kitchen."

I stood there speechless, and he turned to Tabitha. "Trent Murray."

"Tabitha Philips."

"Great to meet you. You came with Chef Hughes when you opened, right? Palmer's famous duo."

I stepped into the silence. "Paul said you survived Dugar for three years."

"I did."

"That's impressive. I would think you could run your own restaurant after that . . ." I caught a flicker in his eyes. "And you know it."

Trent smiled broad but flat. "I could; you're right, but that's not what I want. This is a good fit for me." He looked as if he was about to say more, then stopped. I worked not to glance away. "Look, I'm sorry about Paul not getting to you first about today, but I'm ready to start tonight as your assistant, and I have no ulterior motives."

"*An* assistant." I gestured to Tabitha. "Tabitha, remember?"

As the first party arrived for service, I surveyed the kitchen. One would think Thomas Keller, or more on point, Ryan Reynolds, had joined the staff, judging by the overly warm reception that had accompanied introductions earlier, but now everyone seemed focused. Trent was overseeing meats and all seemed in perfect order . . . until something caught my attention.

"What is that?" I bellowed from the line. All heads turned to me.

"Your balsamic steak." Trent stepped away from his station.

"It never looks like this. Did you sear it and finish in the oven?"

"Yes, but don't you add a little sauce up front to caramelize? The sugars give you a better sear."

"I'm aware of that and choose not to. I don't like the texture change. Do it again." I passed back the plate and returned to the line.

"May I speak to you a moment, Chef?" I turned and found Trent directly behind me. He nodded toward the freezers.

The entire kitchen watched as we stepped out of the central space. Trent cupped my elbow. I wanted to pull away, but knew the gesture would look defensive and insecure—and all eyes were on us.

He whispered, "This is my first night. Give me a chance. I will learn your preferences."

I didn't trust myself to speak.

Trent sighed. "Paul approached me a couple weeks ago . . . I thought you were on board."

I bit my lip. "I am . . . I mean I will be." I couldn't risk my petulance reaching Paul's ears. "None of this is about you."

"Maybe a little bit about me?" He tapped his forefinger and thumb together.

I couldn't help but quirk a small smile before I brushed past him and back into the fray. Everyone, pretending not to pay attention, visibly exhaled, and the kitchen returned to its normal tempo.

I worked sauces, constructed and checked plates. As I moved through the evening, I listened to the light chatter, the calling of dishes, the banter between the pâtissier and Tabitha, and I began to relax. Then I noticed a new note—Trent chiming in on jokes and conversations. He had an easy way about him that brought him into the group seamlessly, like egg whites whipped to perfection, just shy of that single beat that hardened them. I felt a twinge of jealousy—I was that single beat. I didn't blend into the life of my own kitchen. But neither had any head chef I'd ever worked with—isolation came with the job.

The orders exited the line smoothly, and they included more small plates and appetizers than I'd sent out in months. I wondered if a party had escaped my attention.

A waiter returned. "A patron at the bar requested the beef tartar and bone marrow fritters?" He let his question hang above us.

"What? That's not on the menu."

"I know. I told him, but he said he was a friend of Chef Murray's."

Trent stepped beside me. "I'm sorry about that. It's a dish I used on a show last month, and it's gotten some play."

I crossed to the door and peeked through the dining room to the bar. It was packed. A lot of other restaurants commanded that atmosphere—a true bar culture—but Feast never had. It surprised me and, oddly, concerned me.

I turned back to Trent. "Your friends?"

"This is your kitchen. We can tell them no, or I can whip one up. We have all the ingredients."

I looked around the kitchen. *One misstep.* If I wanted Feast to succeed, there were concessions to be made, but like the steak, they had to be my decisions.

"Go ahead and make it." I turned back to the waiter. "Tell them we're delighted to prepare it, but it will take a few extra moments."

The waiter sighed with relief. "Thank you, Chef."

I turned away and worked a last vegetable dish—which felt odd as well. Starters were never ordered so late in the evening. This was the pâtissier's time, and as usual, she had just started her soft classical music and was gearing up for her grand finale. She was our own prima donna and we fed her ego—the kitchen usually grew quiet as we shut down and cleaned the main stations and constantly glanced in wonder at her delicate spun sugars and dustings of dark chocolate. But not tonight—every station was still active and bustling.

When the last orders exited the kitchen, I wilted against the counter. It had been our biggest night in months, and for moments I'd gotten lost in the food—and that hadn't happened in an equally long time. But rather than exhilaration, I felt pulled and displaced. Only his first night and already Trent hovered on the edge of every moment. I couldn't lay claim to the victory.

I looked to my knives. It was time to clean, sharpen, and lay them on my board to await tomorrow—my final ritual of the evening.

Tabitha came over and inspected a knife. "You get them sharper than anyone I know." She threw me a glance. "You okay?"

"It's all changing, Tabitha." I pressed my lips together to shut down any emotion.

She sighed and dropped her voice. "Maybe it's not bad. But we have to remain vital. I am, aren't I, Elizabeth?"

"Of course you are. We're in this together—always have been."

"Well, tonight felt good, even I can admit that."

"Almost like when we first opened."

Tabitha shrugged.

"What?"

"You were right before. It's changing, but it's not like it was."

"You're not pulling any punches today, are you?"

"You think you can control all this, but you can't. Your dad keeps calling about Jane; you're distracted; dishes are off, slow, whatever . . . It's not good."

"It will be."

"Ah . . . there's the Iron Chef I know." Tabitha shoulder-checked me.

"I'm working on it."

A waiter stepped in front of us. "Mr. Metzger is at table five."

"Thanks, Curt."

"You finish the knives. I'll be back." I pulled off my apron and ran my hands down the rough cotton of my jacket, straightening the wrinkles.

Paul sat alone at his table watching the group at the bar—a sophisticated set, more Prada, black, and silk than our usual crowd. They were clearly having fun, but I couldn't call them out of control. This type never crossed that line. They were the influencers, the movers and shakers, a restaurant's coveted diners. They ate well, drank well, and spent lots. I took a deep breath and wondered, *Are they just here for Trent? Will they come back?*

The chandeliers bounced light off the honeyed cracks and discolorations in the antique mirror, softening and warming the room. It created a flattering effect on the face of each person at the bar. I smiled. Maybe if I lived under those lights I'd get my bloom back.

I touched the chair next to Paul before he noticed me. He jumped to attention and pulled it out, settling me at the table.

"I ordered a bottle of Nickel and Nickel as we closed out." He poured me a glass. "Did Murray do well tonight?"

I took a sip and savored the wine. "You gave him a key to my kitchen and the alarm code. Do you know how I felt when he came barging through the door this morning?"

Paul cringed. "I didn't think of that. I wanted him to hit the weekend with a bang." Laughter from the bar caught his attention. "They're waiting for him."

"Trent?"

"He's been tweeting up his switch all week. Everyone's into it."

"Why didn't I know?"

"I keep telling you to get on Facebook, Twitter, Instagram . . . something."

I took a sip and pondered the bar. "So all this is part of the brave new world."

"Not part of. It *is* the world. The cooking matters, sure, but so do the vibe and the chatter. You can feel it in here. Three critics tweeted their plans to come tonight—expect some rave reviews tomorrow."

I clenched my teeth so tight I thought I might crack a molar.

"Paul?"

"Hmm . . ." He pulled his attention back to me.

I let a tear rest in my eye. "I'm a cook. I can't be a Trent Murray. I can't change like that."

He leaned forward and grabbed my hand. "Elizabeth, no one is asking you to change. That's why Murray's here. It's not a weakness to bring in experts. You're an amazing, determined, and gifted chef."

27

"But not right now . . . It's all I have, but it's not working."

"It will. Murray can help us recapture the momentum and give you time to focus on what you do best. This is meant to help, not add more pressure."

We chatted a few moments more before Paul stood to leave and I returned to the kitchen, now equally annoyed that I needed a Trent Murray and that I'd deliberately manipulated Paul for time, sympathy . . . my job.

I pushed the door to the kitchen so forcefully it banged against the wall. Every eye turned to me. Tabitha hurried over.

"What happened?"

"Nothing. Can you lock up?"

"Is everything okay?"

Her visible distress annoyed me further. "I need to get out of here. See you tomorrow?"

She nodded. "Tomorrow."

Chapter 3

I turned the key and unlocked my apartment door. It was dark and silent. I dropped my bag and headed to the kitchen, pleased that my roommate was still out for the evening.

I reached for my spice box and the eggs. *The perfect egg.* In school, Chef Palmer made us cook eggs a hundred different ways, believing that if you mastered the egg, nothing was beyond you. I always returned to it as a touch point.

I cracked two, whipped them with a touch of milk, and threw in dill, chives, and a few spices. Flipping and folding them in the pan, I then added a touch of Gruyère. Done.

I brought the dish over to the couch and sat eating in the dark. It had worked; it was good . . . but it wasn't enough.

A key turned in the lock.

"Elizabeth? That's freaky. Why no lights?" Suzanne, my roommate, flipped on the light and ambled into the room, dropping her bag near the couch.

"That new chef started tonight."

"That's fast." She plopped next to me and grabbed a throw pillow, crushing it in her arms. I took it as a sign of solidarity. Kill the pillow.

"What's worse, he did well. The waitstaff went gaga over Chef Dimples all night."

"Chef Dimples?"

"I overheard a couple servers call him that. And he can cook. No wonder they love him on TV." I groaned. "I don't have dimples and I can't cook." I held up my plate. "I also bought two new face creams on the way to work this morning."

Suzanne reached an arm around my shoulder and laughed. She knew but was willing to play along. "Do they smell good?"

"Heavenly."

"Eggs and lovely smelling creams? You *are* scared." She chuckled.

"What if I lose Feast?"

"It hasn't come to that." Suzanne captured my gaze. "What did Tabitha say?"

There was no way I was going to tell her what Tabitha said. "She's scared too. Feast can't afford two sous chefs, and we both know it. And because I'm close to Paul, Tabitha's sure she'll lose her job. And she may be right. Or we could both be gone tomorrow."

"Why *don't* you be gone tomorrow?"

"What?"

"Go see your dad. See Jane. Cook some meals in someone else's kitchen. Change things up a bit."

"Now is probably not the best time for a vacation."

Suzanne snuggled deeper into the cushions. "You can't do the same things and expect different results. You've been struggling for months, and if Feast is struggling, isn't it your job to find new solutions?"

"I've been trying."

"Then do something new—even ruthless dictators take time off."

"Hey—" I stopped. Going home hadn't occurred to me, but now I wondered if it was just the thing. Suzanne was right; Jane's cancer played constantly in my mind—consumed it really. And maybe going back to the very kitchen in which I learned to cook would inspire me. It could work. "Okay."

"Excellent." Suzanne added a perky note to her voice. "Now that that's settled, let's watch a movie. I left Grant and his friends at Blondie's Sports. I couldn't watch another basketball game. March Madness has got to end."

"Movie sounds great, but I need to blow my nose." I headed to our bathroom as Suzanne uncurled from the couch.

"Popcorn?" she called.

"Of course."

"I downloaded the PBS 2009 *Emma* last night. That guy who plays Sherlock on *Elementary*, Jonny Lee Miller—he's Mr. Knightley."

"I'm not really an Austen fan," I said. "Let's—"

"You always say that, but you know more about her than anyone I know."

I paused in the bathroom, tissue in hand. I worked hard to keep Austen quotes and references out of my communication—even though they still popped into my head as often as words like *salt, pepper,* and *sauté.* Clearly, I'd failed.

I yelled back, pretending not to have heard. "How about that new thriller? We saw the ad for it last night?"

"Okay. You do that and I'll make the popcorn."

"Forget that. You find the movie and I'll make the popcorn."

"Food snob."

"Tech geek."

As I turned the grinder on the stove popper, I thought about my last conversation with Dad just four nights ago.

"Jane didn't think I should tell you, but I think it's important."

"What? I'm not strong enough to take it?" Thirty-three years old, and I had gone right back to tweendom with a single comment.

"Elizabeth." Dad had sounded weary.

"Sorry, Dad. What's up?"

"She started chemotherapy."

"Why wouldn't she tell me? I knew she had to start sometime."

He paused for a moment while I regretted my harsh words. "She didn't want you to worry. She's afraid you're not handling this well."

"I'm fine. I'm sorry she's going through this, but you said it wasn't like Mom. You said Jane's prognosis is good."

"That doesn't mean she's not scared."

"I know, but—"

"No buts, Elizabeth. I wanted you to know. She goes in on Tuesdays, okay? It would be nice if you at least called your sister."

"I will."

But I hadn't. Every moment I wondered how she was doing, but I hadn't called.

I carried the bowls into the living room and handed one to Suzanne.

"What's that face?"

"Nothing." I nodded to the bowl. "You'll like that. Truffle salt and pasture butter." I curled up at the other end of the couch and reached for the remote. "But I don't think I should go home. I need to stay here and dig in." I grabbed a handful of popcorn and pressed Play.

Chapter 4

The next Saturday morning found me standing in the dining room at Feast, but this time I wasn't watching the light play across the wood or absorbing the peace of my usually quiet moment. I was staring at Jane. I couldn't pull my eyes from the photograph behind the hostess stand. We were laughing, her arms encircling me. To feel that young, that happy, that connected . . . It felt as far from my world as Seattle was from New York. I shrugged the memories away and headed to the kitchen, turning my thoughts to the night ahead.

Trent's aura had increased and mine had diminished in my own kitchen over the past week. His tastes had dictated the coming week's menu, and they were good—I hadn't fought a single one. He and Tabitha and I had reworked the menu Thursday, and the weekend offerings were edgy and vibrant, bursting with the new vegetables coming into season and offering a chance to showcase fresh flavors and innovative tech-niques.

My eyes caught the mortar and pestle sitting on the shelf above my knife rack. Jane gave it to me for my thirteenth birthday. My parents had laughed at what a strange gift it seemed for a teenager, but Jane had understood.

I pulled it down, relishing the smooth, cold marble beneath my hands. I set the mortar on the counter and pulled out my "secret stash" of spices—special ones I'd found at the smaller markets or that had been given to me by friends. I tried to clear my mind and breathe in the scents. I could feel my heartbeat—loud, staccato—in the gray quiet kitchen.

I reached for turmeric, soft and yellow, rich but not spicy—Paul. Trent, cumin seeds—fresh, ready to be crushed. But I knew. Mashing would not crush them, it would only soften their edges, crack their husks. Cumin was strong. It endured. Next I added coriander, which seemed to balance the mixture, then paprika, ginger, and a touch of cayenne. I picked up the pestle and ground the spices. The cumin seeds rolled over the others as I ground them against the stone. Scent wafted up. It was a very Moroccan mixture, and it fit my mood—spicy and aggressive, underpinned by subtle questions and hesitancy. That was the problem. It was holding back. Something wasn't right. What to add? Subtract? I smelled it and knew the proportions were skewed; it had lost balance.

I felt tears prick my eyes. I was tempted to hurl the heavy bowl, but that much marble would cause serious damage and require explanations. In my impotent anger, I brushed the mixture away, and as the last bit floated into the trash, I felt a tear follow.

"Darn it." I swiped it away with one finger, and the cayenne, and everything else, lit my eyes on fire. "Of course." I felt my way to the sink and rinsed out my eyes, then stood there with a towel pressed against them, wondering what else could go wrong.

I heard voices.

"Are you serious? I'd heard he has a nasty temper." Tabitha laughed, with something extra layered in the high notes. The last week had also created a new feeling in the kitchen, a camaraderie in which I was not included.

"That's not even the worst of it. One poor guy—"

Of course, it was Trent.

Tabitha pushed open the door and stopped when she noticed me. Trent bumped into her back. "Elizabeth?"

I lowered the towel and cleared my face of expression, though there was no getting rid of the red, blotchy eyes. "I got spices in my eyes."

Tabitha's gaze captured the mortar on the

counter near me. She gave me a look I interpreted as pity, and that made everything worse. I felt angry, betrayed—my heart pounded in my ears.

"You two having fun?" My voice cut the air.

"I was just telling Tabitha about Chef Dugar's temper. He can . . ." Trent's voice dwindled as he made eye contact. "Are you okay?"

"Of course I am. It's just the spices."

"Great. Say, Tabitha and I were talking last night about a few final tweaks to the menu. We wanted to see what you thought."

Trent reached into his satchel and pulled out his iPad.

"Tweaks? Without me?"

"We grabbed a drink on our way to the subway. You walk the other direction," Trent said by way of apology. He tapped on his screen.

I shifted my gaze to Tabitha, whose eyes held an expectant, almost challenging look.

She's chosen her side. As soon as the thought entered my head, I knew it was unfair. She was scared. And Trent certainly seemed the stronger champion.

"You know, I can't do this right now." I swiped the back of my hand across my eyes to clear them. "Can you two hold Feast down for a few days?"

"Elizabeth?"

"No, it's good. There's some stuff I need to take care of." I nodded. "You've got this." I pulled off my apron and grabbed my coat and bag.

Trent stood with his mouth slightly open, the iPad hanging from his hand. Tabitha ran after me into the alley. "Elizabeth! Wait!"

I took a deep breath and turned. "Don't say anything. Let me do this. That kitchen is not big enough for three chefs. And I don't want to go out like this. This is my restaurant." The tears filled my eyes again. "And I love it, and if I want to keep it, I have to change the losing game."

"What?"

"I'm taking some time off. Keep things running—because after I roam the food markets, get some rest, and clear my head, I'll be back and Feast *will* be mine." Without another word, I turned and walked away.

I leveraged the bags in one arm, unlocked my apartment door, and hip-checked it open. It slammed against the wall before I could catch it.

Suzanne, who was watching TV, jumped toward me to catch the falling groceries. "What are you doing here on a Saturday?"

"Taking your advice and a little vacation."

"You are? Why? What happened? I thought you said no."

"I decided you were right. So I'm changing a losing game."

"Good for you."

"I've been shopping. I've got a great dinner planned."

"Oh. I was about to go meet Grant." Suzanne hesitated. "Do you want me to cancel? Or you can join us?"

"No, you go." I smiled because, loyal friend that she was, I knew she'd do either if I asked. "I'm going to turn on some music, cook, and love every moment of it. You can have leftovers tomorrow."

"Excellent. What did Paul say?" Suzanne was collecting her keys and phone.

"I don't know yet. I left him a voice mail."

She squeezed my arm to say good-bye and walked out the door.

Silence filled our small apartment.

"Time to cook."

I finished prepping the navarin of lamb, suddenly overcome by the scents, the flavors . . . It was one of Mom's favorite dishes her final year. I hadn't even thought about it consciously as I shopped; I'd simply grabbed what spoke to me. Now memories wafted with the steam.

As it simmered, I called my dad.

"What's wrong?" He sounded winded.

"Can't I call without you thinking something's wrong?"

"Of course, but not on a Saturday evening at the start of dinner."

"Good point." I looked around my empty apartment, so removed from the bustle that now consumed Feast. "I needed to clear my head, so I'm off tonight and home cooking."

"What are you making?"

"I . . . I didn't even think, Dad." Tears started to form. "I made that navarin."

"Oh, honey. What's wrong?"

I pinched the bridge of my nose. "Nothing. I'm just tired." I switched tactics. "What are you up to this evening?"

"I was pruning the front bushes. Later I'm heading to the station for dinner. Since I retired, the crew has asked me every Saturday night. At first I thought they felt sorry for me, but it's fun for all of us."

"I bet they miss you. And no one could feel sorry for you, Dad. You're the most energetic guy I know."

"Thank you, sweetheart." I could hear the smile in his voice. "Do you want to talk?"

"No, you're busy. I just wanted to touch base." I felt intrusive. "You go and have fun. I'll call in a couple days."

We said quick good-byes, and the apartment settled into silence once again. I stood watching my favorite red Le Creuset pan on the stove—another gift, another reminder. Something had to be done.

I headed to my room and crawled under my bed. Amid the shoes, scarves, and general clutter, I found my suitcase.

My phone rang and I saw Paul's name flash across the screen.

"Elizabeth? What's up? I got your message."

I rubbed the top of the black canvas bag. "I need to head home."

"Is Jane okay? From your message I assumed you were staying here."

I hesitated. "I was, but . . . I need to go. Trent and Tabitha can handle Feast." I clenched my eyes shut, knowing the gamble I was taking.

"Of course they can. Grab a flight and take a couple weeks."

"A couple weeks? I was thinking a few days."

"A visit like this takes more than a few days. Trust me on that. Do you need help?"

I knew what he was offering, and even though I didn't think he would attach strings to a first-class airline ticket, I didn't want to test that assumption.

"No, Feast's paid me well. Thank you for that. I'll try to get a flight out tomorrow and call you within the week."

"Sounds good . . . And, Elizabeth? I'm glad you're going."

"I am too. Thanks." I hung up the phone and hoped I hadn't just made the worst mistake of my life.

Chapter 5

I pulled my rental into the driveway and sat for a moment, absorbing my childhood home—a small colonial, completely out of context in the Pacific Northwest. But its gray color helped it blend in, like a nod to the cloudy sky, asking if it could stay. It looked good. Fresh paint, trimmed bushes. When I left fifteen years ago, everything was tinged with sadness and death—the bushes, the paint, and the family.

Should I ring the doorbell? Knock? I laughed at my own questions. This was home. You don't ring your own doorbell. I stepped up the walk and tried the knob, and it turned in my hand. No one in Hood River locks the door.

"Dad?"

"Who's there?" he called from the kitchen.

"Me." The word caught in my throat.

Dad rounded the corner and stopped. I knew I had surprised him, but I was equally stunned at the changes in him since his fall visit to New York. His hair was grayer, noticeable even with his short military style, and the lines around his face cut deeper. I thought he had also dropped a few pounds, but his eyes looked bright—lit up, like a kid seeing fireworks.

"Lizzy, what are you doing here?" He rushed

forward. "You're home." His voice cracked.

"Dad, don't call me that." I laughed.

He crushed me to him, then immediately released me, holding me at arm's length. "Why are you here? You never come— Has something happened?"

"No, nothing. I just wanted . . . Isn't it time?"

"I don't know. I was waiting for you to tell me." He pulled me in again. Then he pushed me back out. "Are you tired? Are you hungry? You're on New York time."

He pulled me—again. I was beginning to get whiplash. "I don't know what to do. I'm so happy, so surprised."

"It's okay. I know it's been a long time since I was here."

"I didn't think you'd ever come." He pushed me back and released me. "Where are your bags?"

"In the car."

"I'll get them."

"No, let me." I followed him out the door and down the walk.

"Don't be silly." He popped my trunk and reached in to grab my black leather satchel and suitcase. "You carry this and I'll roll the bag."

As we walked back toward the house, I glanced around again. "It looks different than I remember."

He stopped and looked around too. "You probably remember everything a little shabby. Things were rough that last year with your mom, and they didn't get better for a while." He smiled, small and straight. "I've enjoyed working on it. It's a good house."

"It looks great." I passed him on the walk and held the front door open.

"Why don't you take a moment to freshen up or whatever you do, and I'll finish preparing dinner." He stood and stared at me, grinning. "I get to set an extra plate."

"Perfect." I smiled back. "I'll just be a minute."

He walked back to the kitchen and I stood there. I took a deep breath; it smelled the same: wood polish, books, and the odd tinny smell of the vacuum cleaner when you forget to change the bag . . . *Home*. But it didn't look lived in. The cushions were fluffed and stiff, and the books on the coffee table were stacked straight and sterile. And they were the same ones Mom had displayed years ago. *Oregon Wines. Jane Austen Country Living. Famous Homes of Europe*. And ancient copies of *Sunset, Shape*, and *Saveur*. I'd given her that last subscription for Christmas one year. I was the only one who ever used it.

As I hefted my suitcase up the stairs, I wondered if my bedroom would feel as empty and cold. It had been left behind by an angry, bereft eighteen-year-old girl. I was fairly certain Dad would never have touched it or redecorated it, but I hoped he had at least changed the sheets.

My door stood open. Even with only the light

from the hall spilling into its darkness, I could see the walls' blue tones and the white trim; the furniture, brown and traditional; and my bulletin board, crowded with pictures, notes, and clippings—signs of friendships long forgotten. I saw a picture of myself on the bedside table, my arms linked around two friends, grinning at the camera.

No one can be that happy.

I flipped on the light and absorbed the chaos of my bulletin board, trying to remember the names of friends who had once meant so much. There was a dried rose pinned to the corner. I crossed the room, coming up blank on its significance. I pulled it from its pin and crushed it in my fist, letting the dry pieces fall into my trash can.

The dresser was no better. Makeup in colors that never should have been manufactured rested in dishes. I pulled the wand from a completely dry and crumbling tube of blue mascara and tossed that into the trash can as well. My perfume, once tinted the faintest pink, was now dark brown in the clear bottle. I pitched it without bothering to smell it.

Dad called from the kitchen. "Come eat, Lizzy. It's ready."

Lizzy. I took a last look around. Maybe this was a mistake.

My heart pounded as I walked down the stairs and through the dining room to the kitchen, once Mom's sanctuary and the heart of our family. I took a deep breath and recalled every smell of my childhood: the cinnamon that dominated not only winter baking, but many of the tomato-based Italian dishes Mom loved; vanilla, always used as an undertone to her egg-based savories; and rosemary. When did she *not* use rosemary? And smoke—the woman could burn anything. Memories of us dancing around the kitchen swinging dish towels while she batted the smoke alarm with a broom made me smile. She had even flirted with the idea of removing its battery before remembering that Dad, the fire chief, would probably frown on that.

While letting the scenes and scents settle over me, more memories flashed before my eyes: Mom stirring sauce or peeling potatoes; Dad chopping an onion, complaining that it wasn't manly to cry; Jane filing her nails or reciting the latest high school gossip from her perch on the counter; and me, running around attempting to orchestrate it all—the cooking, the family, the magic—by stirring, mixing, adding . . . tweaking.

Trent's word. It made me cringe, but it fit—for that's what chefs do. If we have the gift, we take the ordinary and "tweak" it just so and just enough to make something more, something above and beyond. My heart hurt and I hesitated, weighing the cost of walking straight back out the front door and leaving all this behind.

The kitchen door swung shut behind me, and I

was pulled back to the present. The room felt as empty as the living room, and I wilted with relief. If it had been too close to my memories, I might have cried. But the white Corian counters stood stark and bare; the stove was clean, even new; the refrigerator door was devoid of artwork and photographs. And the smells—sharp, not sweet. Tomatoes without cinnamon.

"New stove?"

"I suppose it is. The old one broke about a decade ago."

I skipped over his remark and chirped, "What'd you make?"

Dad pressed his lips into a straight line. He was resetting the moment as well—skipping over the unpleasant, the difficult, and the unspoken. "Tonight we have a lasagna that Mary Flynn made for me a couple weeks ago. I've found they freeze well."

"Dr. Flynn's widow?"

"I complimented her lasagna at a church potluck a few years ago, and now I get the occasional pan." Dad grinned, then looked at me with a flicker of concern.

"Nice going," I reassured him.

"I think so." Dad's smile fell as he looked around. "Besides the stove, does it look the same?"

"Yes and no. It's clean and quiet. That's certainly different." I watched him cut the lasagna. The sauce ran between the layers of pasta, thick and rich, and the cheese slid from the top. "I've been gone a long time, and yet it feels as if I left yesterday."

"Fifteen years can't feel like yesterday." There was a hint of disappointment in his tone.

"I see you and Jane when I get to Seattle every couple years, and you come east lots . . ." A hint of defensiveness in mine.

"Seattle isn't home." He set the lasagna before me.

"Home was too hard, Dad." I reached for my fork as I looked around. "It still is. I expect to see Mom—"

Dad cut me off. "Would you mind if I said grace?"

I set my fork down. "Not at all."

Dad said a few simple words.

He picked up his fork, so I followed suit and took a bite. "This is good."

"Isn't it?"

I got up from the table and stepped to the cabinet above Mom's mixer, absently brushing off a layer of dust as I reached up. I found the jar I needed, musing that it was probably years old and tasteless—but still worth a try.

"What are you doing?"

"Hang on a sec." I clenched the jar in my fist and shook the spice into my hand, pinching a bit across his lasagna.

"What's that?"

"Trust me, it's just what it needs—a touch of earth and sweet to temper the tomato's bite. With fresh tomatoes you need less as summer approaches and they develop their own sugars. Taste it."

He took a bite. "It's fantastic. What'd you add?"

"Cinnamon." He didn't recognize it?

"Amazing. I'll have to tell Mary."

"Tell her a touch of milk tempers the acidity as well."

"Interesting."

We ate in silence for a few minutes.

"I'm headed to Seattle tomorrow, Elizabeth." Dad paused as if trying to choose his next best words. "It's really good you're here. You can come with me."

Elizabeth. Dad just used my full name. "I know I need to go see her, but can we wait a few days? I just got here."

"She has a chemo session Tuesday. I want to go tomorrow to help with the kids."

"You go. I'll follow in a couple days."

He narrowed his eyes, considering me, as he chewed. "You can cook at Jane's house for a couple days. Peter's going out of town, so she'll love the help."

I sat silent for a moment and let the truth wash over me. Dad and Jane were right—I wasn't handling her cancer well. I didn't want to see her. Jane acted like Dad, but she looked like Mom. Would that be magnified now?

"I need a little time here—as you said, fifteen years. And I've got to work too. I'll drive up Wednesday."

He didn't reply and I knew he wouldn't. He considered the discussion over. I pushed again. "Dad? Why can't I just rest here for a few days first?"

He caught my petulant tone and responded with appropriate chill. "This isn't about you. If you can't see that, you'll simply have to trust me. We leave at eight."

Chapter 6

I awoke the next morning disoriented. The light was wrong, the noises absent—except for birds chirping. I rolled over. *Birds chirping?* Moments passed in the haze between dream and reality before I recognized that New York did not charge by outside the window. Hood River, Oregon, with every one of its 7,300 citizens, yawned and stretched more slowly. I pulled a sweater over my T-shirt and pajama pants and went in search of coffee.

Dad sat, working a crossword at the kitchen table, and glanced up briefly as I ambled into the room. We had thawed in parting last night, but his directive still stung.

"Ooh, a crossword." I generated false enthusiasm as I glanced over his shoulder.

"Hang on a sec and you can take the next pass."

I pulled a mug from the shelf and poured a cup of acrid-smelling brew. Dad needed new, and probably better, beans. I leaned against the counter and tried to enjoy the stillness. Usually my split-second breakfast was spent mentally prioritizing to-do lists and the details of an evening's service. But now . . . there was only a crossword.

"What time do we leave?" I worked to keep my tone neutral.

"How about an hour?"

"I'll be ready."

"We'll leave your car here and take the truck. That way you won't get miles on it."

"No, let's take the rental. It's more comfortable, and the miles don't matter. Really."

"Okay." He turned back to his crossword. I took a sip and watched him. How was a four-hour drive going to feel?

We were still too quiet when we pulled out one hour, to the minute, later. I glanced over at him. "I'm sorry about last night."

He didn't reply.

"Dad?"

He sighed as if he'd been storing it up for years. "I wish it wasn't so hard between you girls. I feel I'm to blame. That's hard too."

"How are you to blame?"

"I'm the head of this family, and when one of our numbers went down, we fell apart. I didn't lead."

I concentrated on the road. For my dad, that was a tough admission. Fire chiefs lead. Dad's crew had respected his authority and followed him anywhere. But at home it had always been a different story. Maybe it was because we were all girls, or maybe he had used up all his energy at work—either way, Dad never led. Instead he had watched with detached contentment as Mom worked out our family rituals, gave the orders, and doled out the discipline and the cough syrup. Until the day she didn't.

After a few minutes of silence, I found something to offer. "You couldn't force Jane to come home. She was an adult. She made her own decisions."

"I let Jane drown in her own fear when I should have been pulling the family together. Peter would've helped if I'd insisted."

"Nothing swamps Jane, so cut yourself some slack. You lost your wife."

"And both my daughters."

"That's not fair. You haven't 'lost' me. You come to New York at least twice a year and you love it."

"But you don't come home, and you don't even speak to Jane unless forced. You both lost your mother. It hurts to see you lose each other." Dad paused, but I sensed more was coming, so I stayed quiet and focused on the highway.

The pause drew long. "And?"

"And it's time to let the past go."

I sighed. I should've stayed in New York.

Before I knew it we were turning into Jane's driveway. It had been a couple years since I had visited, and even then that Christmas break was more accurately counted in hours than days. I smiled when I saw the house. It was my secret ideal, though I'd never admit it to her. It was a 1930s Craftsman with style and substance, boasting higher ceilings than most and a front porch painted brick red—I loved that detail. The rest of the house was beige with white trim and black shutters. Impeccably maintained.

I loved the way the inside was decorated, too, kid art on the walls mixed with black-and-white photographs and strong oil paintings. Much the way I designed Feast's interior, but Jane's interpretation was warmer and more vibrant, with comfortable chairs, embroidered throw pillows, and books. Even the small entry hall was such an alive space . . . and it bugged me that it was hers.

As soon as I opened the car door, I saw Jane walking down the porch steps. She wasn't bouncing, but she didn't look sick. She looked good in her jeans and a fitted green sweater—thin, but not skinny; shoulder-length blond hair, not bald; color in her cheeks, not pallid. I hadn't realized that I had even made such a checklist until I felt my breath release. Relief was immediately followed by annoyance. *She looks fine. Why'd I come?*

"You're here!"

And she sounds happy.

"We are," Dad said. "The drive was only three and a half hours. Your sister has a lead foot."

"Excellent." Jane turned to me. "You're here," she said again. I caught an unspoken *finally* hovering above us.

"Hey, Jane." I pulled her into a hug. "I don't know what to say about all this."

She patted my back and stepped away. "Later. Come in and have some lunch and catch up. There will be time."

I clenched my jaw. "Of course."

"I've put you in the guest room and, Dad, you're in Danny's. He gets to sleep in the basement. Peter even bought an air mattress, so he's thrilled and not exactly roughing it."

"That was good of him—both hims." Dad chuckled.

"It's the least Peter could do."

Jane's dismissive tone surprised me. She'd always seemed softer, nicer around Peter.

She rushed on. "I made chicken salad and some soup today. We can have the salad now and the soup can stretch for a few days. I'm at chemo tomorrow, and then I'm pretty useless until Friday, so soup seems to work best."

"Sounds perfect," Dad assured her.

"I can cook, you know." I threw the lob before thinking.

A flicker in Jane's eyes indicated she caught it, but she stayed silent and led us into the house.

Her chicken salad was remarkably good. She had complemented the chicken with a good mayonnaise, slivered almonds, finely chopped celery, fresh tarragon, purple grapes, and a hint of Dijon mustard. I was impressed. I would've added more salt and pepper, but couldn't think of much else missing.

As Dad and Jane sat chatting at the table about a million things of which I knew nothing, I pulled out my phone to e-mail Tabitha and check on Feast.

"Lizzy, are we bothering you?"

I compressed a smile at Jane's irritation, but didn't look up. "Not at all. Keep talking. I'm finishing an e-mail."

"I gathered that. I asked if you wanted to go for a walk."

I glanced up. Dad looked expectant, like a kid awaiting a cookie. Jane looked ticked, like Dad got the bigger cookie.

I lowered my phone to my lap. "Sure, Jane, I'd love to go for a walk." I sounded perky and eager —an attempt to seize the high ground. "Dad?"

"You two go. I'm going to sit in the living room and read. I may even take a nap before the kids come home."

I shifted back to Jane. "Can you give me a sec to finish this? Then I'm all yours."

As I signed off on my message, I recalled the last time Jane had asked me to take a walk. I was ten years old; she was eighteen and soon leaving for college.

"I'm walking to town. Do you want to come along and get an ice cream?"

"Yeah." I had tried to match her tone, and the word came out like *Duh*. I mimicked all things Jane back then.

I raced to grab my shoes and flew out the front door, expecting to find myself alone with my gorgeous big sister. Instead I saw a few of her friends waiting on the sidewalk with her.

Molly, her best friend, turned to me. "I'm babysitting Will today. Why don't you walk with him, Lizzy, and hold his hand? You can be in charge."

"Okay." A wave of defeat had washed over me as Will Bolton's sticky, chubby hand slid into mine.

And that was my last real memory of life with my sister. She rarely came home from college, and years later, when Mom was dying, she never came home at all.

Lost in the memory, I caught only the end of

Jane's sentence. ". . . positive, invasive carcinoma."

"What?"

"The cancer. That's what it's called." She shot me a look. "Are you even listening?"

"Of course. Is it what Mom had?"

"Hers was triple negative, that's the most aggressive, and hers was advanced by the time they found it. But mine we caught early. I'll have one kind of chemotherapy cocktail twice more, then a different one four times, then I'll have surgery and radiation, but the radiation's not definite. If all goes as well as expected, I may not need it." She listed it so clinically. Quintessentially Jane.

"Okay, then."

She let a small sigh fall in tandem with her shoulders. Finally, there was the truth.

We walked in silence for a few minutes.

"I don't . . . you know . . ."

"Don't what?"

"Have confidence this will go as well as expected." Her voice cracked.

"Nothing ever does."

We drifted back to silence as we turned into the park. She opened her mouth to say something when we heard a voice yell her name.

"Bright smile, Lizzy." She pushed the words out of the corner of her mouth.

"Of course," I mumbled as a man more my age

than Jane's strode toward us. He was tall and good-looking in a loose, lanky, Seattle way. My gaze dropped to his shoes—flip-flops.

"Hey, Nick. Is Matt here?" Jane stood straight and boomed out a voice too bright.

Nick pointed across the playground. "He had a half day at school and Mom couldn't take him. So work is effectively done for the day." He shrugged.

"Nick, meet my sister, Lizzy. She's visiting for a couple days from New York."

Nick's gaze briefly surveyed me, and I felt overdressed in my black cashmere sweater, pencil skirt, and Prada boots. His bright green eyes danced, implying that he agreed. He reached out and we shook hands.

"It's Elizabeth." His hand was warm and, for some reason, that bothered me. I pulled away brusquely.

Nick threw a glance at Jane, who rolled her eyes.

"Jane didn't have a silly nickname to shed, so she keeps forgetting."

"Elizabeth suits you." He turned back to Jane. "I've talked with Gordon Holman and finished his website. Could I come by tomorrow to show you the new design and discuss next steps?"

Jane looked into the distance. "Tomorrow I . . . It's not great, Nick. Can it wait till Thursday?"

"Sure. I'll drop by in the morning." He glanced

back to me. "Nice to meet you, Elizabeth from New York." He added my name and city slowly and distinctly, accompanying it with a small bow. I couldn't help but smile before ducking my head, embarrassed. He loped across the playground, glancing back once, to where he'd left his computer and a bag on the bench.

"I can't believe that. He was actually flirting with—"

I cut her off. "Who's Gordon Holman?"

She sighed. "I had a consulting company. Not much, about ten clients—social media, website development, and stuff."

"Had?"

"Peter convinced me to step back, so Nick folded them into his business."

"It's only ten clients. He'll give them back, right?" I heard the panic in my voice—as if my story at Feast would parallel hers.

"Gee, Lizzy, why would I bother? It's only ten clients."

"I didn't mean it like that. I just meant he wouldn't sacrifice much to give them back when you're ready."

"You just meant it was small and insignificant. Not nearly as glamorous and important as what you do." Jane turned out of the park.

I followed, feeling ten years old and wishing for someone, even chubby five-year-old Will Bolton, to hold my hand.

Chapter 7

The kids got home right before dinner. I was exiting the powder room and stood stunned as they burst through the hall before me. I instantly rethought my stance on social media. I'd missed so many changes. I remembered short, cute, undefined children—a gorgeous mix of their fair-skinned mother and Korean father—but still on par with the amorphous small fry generally found at parks, malls, and behaving badly in restaurants. I was unprepared for these tall, leggy individuals. Almost thirteen-year-old Kate was just a few inches shorter than I, probably five feet five, with long, dark-brown almost black hair pulled into a high ponytail. Her dark complexion, as compared to her mother and to me, seemed exotic, but she had our smattering of freckles across her nose. Ten-year-old Daniel was not much shorter, and spunky. He was the spitting image of Peter but with lighter hair. They charged into the kitchen ahead of their dad.

"Mom, soccer practice ran fifteen minutes late."

"Dad was late. Mr. Shugart was not pleased."

The kids dropped their verbal bombs simultaneously and scurried to the basement without asking about me or Dad.

Jane looked irritated. Peter rounded the corner

in time to catch her expression. "I went to get Danny first. The coach held over practice."

"Did you call the piano teacher?"

"You didn't give me his number."

"You—"

Wisely or not, I stepped into the fray. "Peter, it's so good to see you." It took him a second to drag his gaze from Jane and rest it on me.

"Elizabeth? I didn't see Jim's truck. Weren't you coming tomorrow?" He glanced around for Dad.

"I told you today . . . Never mind." Jane turned back to her carrots.

"Today. Tomorrow. I'm just happy to be here." I sounded magnanimous, even to myself.

Peter quickly hugged me. "Good to see you. I'm sorry I won't be around. I head to China tomorrow, but I'm glad you're here. This week will be hard on Jane."

"Every day is . . . ," she murmured.

"We've got it covered." Now I sounded too bright. This was exhausting.

Peter smiled small and flat at me. "I'm going to go put down my bag and get out of this coat. Where is Jim?"

"I think he's in Danny's room reading. I bet he didn't hear you come in."

"I'll go find him." Peter threw one last look at Jane, who was concentrating on her carrots. "I brought you these." He laid two chocolate bars on the counter—Theo Dark Chocolate and Orange. He shrugged and left the room.

Jane glanced at the bars. She didn't look at me, but I could see her eyes soften and her lip tremble.

"I'm going to find my niece and nephew. I can't believe they didn't notice me." I took a last look at Jane as well—still focused on those carrots. Her movements were slow and laborious, and I tamped down the urge to grab the knife and finish the job.

As I walked down the basement steps, I absorbed a taste of the pressure squeezing Jane's family. When I was seventeen it had felt more cut-and-dried: Mom got sick and the world tilted sideways and never righted itself.

But was that the reality? For months, as Mom endured chemotherapy, she had kept up a cheerful prattle. She had moved more slowly; she was tired; she lost her hair; her skin changed color; hospice arrived . . . That was my story, and the memories had blurred to accommodate, but now I suspected there was much I had missed: nuances, pressures, despair, fear, angry words that never penetrated my world. Recalling those months, I would say Mom had been oddly joyful. I missed her all the more with that memory—real or not.

Kate and Danny were pulling books and papers out of their backpacks at a table in the center of the basement. It was a lively, cheerful space with calendars and maps on the wall, posters, computers, a printer—the perfect kid and home-work sanctuary.

"Danny, do your math first; the other is just drawing." Kate sounded bossy, like her mother.

"You two have a lot of work tonight?"

"Aunt Elizabeth?" Two heads spun around, two voices questioned.

"Oh come on, it hasn't been that long."

Kate frowned. "It's not that. Dad said you and Grandpa were coming tomorrow."

"Well, I'm here. Can I get a hug?" After a round of hugs and Danny-giggles as I mussed his hair, we turned our attention back to their work. Kate kept glancing at me.

"What's up?"

"Were you in the kitchen when we got home?"

"No, I was in the back hall. It was dark; you wouldn't have seen me. And I couldn't move; I was stunned to see how you've grown." I expected her to smile, but she pressed her lips together.

"I shouldn't have said Dad was late."

"Sweetheart . . ." I reached over and tugged at her ponytail. "You said nothing wrong. We grown-ups sometimes boil too hot. Do you ever do that?"

She nodded but seemed unconvinced.

I pulled her in for a squeeze as Peter came down the steps. He looked at me hugging Kate and furrowed his brows. "You work," I said. "I'm going to talk to your dad."

I crossed the room to the washer and dryer, where Peter stood sorting laundry.

"Packing?"

"I'll be gone a week."

"I'm sorry."

He threw me a glance as if trying to assess why I was sorry—there were so many options from which to choose.

"It's my job. We need the income, the health insurance . . ."

"Of course you do."

"I wish she could see that."

"I don't know my sister that well, but I bet she knows at least that." I tried to sound light and logical.

"Perhaps."

He gathered his laundry and I trailed him up the stairs. Halfway up he stopped and turned around. "She likes to be read to during chemo. The Adriamycin is red—you can see it—and when you read, she'll close her eyes to listen. She doesn't like to watch it thread its way into her. And make sure she drinks tons of water. Some people get nauseated and throw up. She's on tons of antinausea meds, so I doubt that'll happen. It hasn't yet, but she feels so sick that she doesn't eat or drink. Last time she got constipated and suffered horrible stomach pains. And the headaches . . . they're pretty bad. I think that's the antinausea meds, not the chemo. I've read they can do that, which is another reason she likes someone to read to her. She says it hurts to track the page."

"Got it."

Peter looked at me—hard. "I'll leave you my notes." And he continued up the stairs.

Chapter 8

The next morning I woke more easily. West Coast time made the kids' seven a.m. wake-up call feel luxurious. I could hear Danny happily howling about something, and when I peeked in, I found Peter pouncing on him.

"You go wake Kate." Peter grinned at me. "It's hilarious. Just poke her stomach."

I went into Kate's room and found her stretched on her back as wide as she could go. She looked so long and grown-up. With Peter and Danny standing in the doorway, I took one finger and poked her stomach. She crumpled in like a sea anemone, then splayed back out. Peter was right—it was hilarious. I couldn't believe she didn't hear all the snorting and chortling around her. Three more pokes and I couldn't take it anymore. I simply tickled her awake.

"Breakfast in a few minutes, kids," Peter said.

"Can I do that for you?"

"I'd appreciate it. I've got to finish packing."

Peter headed back to his room, and I lumbered down the stairs to scrounge around.

Danny bounced into the kitchen twenty minutes later. "What's for breakfast?"

"Oatmeal."

"Oatmeal?" He scrunched his face.

I started my sell job. "I've got brown sugar, almonds, raisins, and cut strawberries for it. I couldn't find honey—that's what I like—but you'll still love it."

Kate joined us. "What's burning?"

"Oatmeal!" I ran to the stove and dragged the pot off the flame. "Your breakfast." I lifted the lid. "It's ruined. I never do that."

"So what's for breakfast?" Danny asked in precisely the same tone he'd used before.

"How about toast? I bet there's jam."

"Toast?"

I wanted to ask, *Must we go through this?* but he's ten. Maybe that's what they do. I nodded. "Toast." I dropped two slices of bread into the toaster.

"Danny, we're late. Eat it on the way. The bell rings in ten minutes."

"Where's school?"

"Four blocks that way." Danny pointed.

"Go then. I'm sorry this is late." I pushed them toward the door, shoving the toast into their hands. "Am I supposed to drive you or something?"

"We run."

"Get to it then."

Danny rolled his eyes and took off. Kate had already dashed away.

"Late?" Peter said behind me.

I turned around. "Not sure. Are they?"

He looked at his watch. "Only by a couple minutes. Kate's a fast runner and Danny's a smooth talker. They'll be fine."

Dad came in and grabbed the car keys off the counter. "Peter, you ready to go?" He moved toward the back door.

"I thought I'd make the airport run and you'd take Jane to chemotherapy." I looked between the men, hoping one of them would agree.

"No, you'll do." Jane marched into the room.

"I'll do?"

"I didn't mean it like that." She dug around in a drawer for something.

Peter rolled his suitcase past me. "I left my notes on your bed."

"Got it."

"What notes?" Jane barked.

I looked between them. "Just some tips to keep you comfy."

Jane snorted. Peter shrugged and reached to kiss her good-bye. She turned her head, and he ended up kissing her temple. My heart hurt for him as I rolled my eyes at Jane. Then I noticed Dad watching me—my turn to tilt and duck my head away.

Peter and Dad went out the back door while Jane led me to the front hall.

"Tonight I'm cooking," I said. "You wouldn't let me do anything last night."

She pulled out her keys. "I didn't want to be shown up in my own kitchen. Besides, I felt good. You can cook tonight and tomorrow, even Thursday, if you want. I think Dad said you're leaving Friday. That's when I start to like food again."

"You won't eat until Friday?" We climbed into her car and backed out of the driveway.

"My stomach feels closed. Actually it's my nose and mouth that shut down. Nothing smells or tastes good."

"I'll make you something so yummy you won't be able to help yourself."

I started running menu options in my brain, mixing and matching until the exercise completely absorbed me. A few new recipes developed in my head, and I was pleased with my visualizations.

Before I knew it, Jane was pulling in to the hospital parking ramp.

"Welcome back." She wasn't smiling.

"Sorry. I was thinking about what might taste good to you."

"I told you, nothing does."

I pursed my lips together and got out of the car. The cancer center wing was large, looming, and intimidating. Mom's whole hospital had been much smaller. Jane gave me a hurry-up glare, and I picked up my pace.

Inside, the elevator doors opened onto a sterile cream-colored lobby. There was a sign reading Infusion Center pointing to the left. I followed Jane.

The Infusion Center was painted a deeper shade of cream—vanilla extract added to milk—with huge plate-glass windows looking out onto the city. Recliners sat squat and sturdy in pods, like staged living room arrangements, along the walls. Each had a curtain attached to a track in the ceiling that could surround it, but few were pulled. There were also straight-back chairs scattered throughout the room, some tucked up next to the recliners as if seeking protection.

Most of the recliners were occupied, each with a friend or relative sitting close beside. It felt like a strange dystopian library, with everyone reading or whispering. While Jane flashed some card at a reader machine, I surveyed the occupants. Two brothers sat quietly arguing. At least I assumed brothers by the antagonistic expressions and matching eyes. Next to them I saw a lovely looking older woman patting her husband's hand. Her face was soft and gentle and lightly wrinkled. His was not. A young boy, maybe twelve or thirteen, caught my attention.

Jane noticed my face and followed my line of sight. "That's Andy."

"He's too young to be here," I whispered.

"I know. He's probably a couple years older than Kate, but he's small. I don't know why he gets his chemo here rather than up at Children's."

We walked across the room, and Jane claimed a chair next to the brothers' pod.

"What happens now?"

"We wait. Cecilia or one of the other nurses will draw some blood, check it out, and then deliver Cytoxan and the Red Devil."

"The what?"

"Adriamycin. It's bright red. But I read a book by a doctor who was also a patient, and she called it Red Sunshine because it shone in and burned away all her cancer. I like that imagery better."

"I'll go with that too." I sat down. It felt stiff and awkward, like the moment before a restaurant health inspector reaches for his pen to approve or deny your permit.

A nurse came toward us, and I couldn't help thinking, *That's a nurse?* She had dyed jet-black hair pulled back into a bun with short, uniform pageboy bangs across her forehead. She was beautiful and neat, with flawless pale skin and high cheekbones, but the dark lipstick, tattoo ink peeking from beneath the sleeves of her uniform, and piercings traveling up her right ear slightly disconcerted me.

It occurred to me that I probably appeared just as foreign to her in my fitted Anne Fontaine tunic, so white one almost needed sunglasses, and my black wool leggings and heeled boots.

"Jane. Right on time. Good to see you."

"Thanks, Cecilia. This is my little sister, Lizzy." There was no point in correcting her. "She's visiting from New York."

"That's so nice. Are you here for long?" Cecilia smiled at me.

Jane answered, "A couple days. She never stays long."

I kept my expression completely bland until Cecilia turned back to Jane. She sat down and inserted a needle into Jane's chest, and I gasped.

"I gather Mom didn't have a central port?"

"I . . ." I wanted to say I was sorry. Sorry for being a jerk, sorry for ever insisting she use my full name and for never staying for long visits, and desperately sorry that she had to endure this . . . but I didn't. I caught my lip between my teeth, unsure I could watch Cecilia work.

Cecilia slid her glance to me. "It's hard the first time. I know this must seem really strange." She turned back to Jane and smiled. "You look good today, Jane." She withdrew the tube and laid tape over the needle. "I'll be back." She shook the vial as she walked away.

"You never do, you know." Jane turned to me. "Stay long."

"Drop it, Jane. I'm not biting."

Jane widened her eyes to look innocently doe-like. "Just saying." I knew that expression. I saw it plenty as a kid, watching Jane wheedle herself out of trouble.

We squared off in silence because, for once, I didn't want to fight.

"Hey, we're going to be late." Jane jumped from the recliner.

"For what?"

"I got distracted. I have to go see Dr. Chun now. It's like a two-minute visit, but Cecilia doesn't give me the good stuff until I do. Come on."

We headed down a maze of hallways and corridors until we found ourselves in the oncology suite. I waited while Jane stepped into the office and back out again a few minutes later. Her shoulders rounded forward and she wouldn't look at me.

"What's wrong?" I caught up to her.

She shook her head and kept walking.

"Jane, stop. What'd your doctor say?"

She glanced at me and swiped at her eyes. "She said my count's low. I can get this week's dose, but she'll have to step it back or even skip one if it doesn't come up." She stopped and leaned against the wall. "This is my program, Lizzy. They gave me over a 90 percent recovery rate with this plan." She wiped her palm across her nose. "It's supposed to work."

"Hey . . . it's going to work." She threw me a glance, letting me know I had no clue what I was offering. I moved on. "What does 'stepping back' even mean?"

"It means I'm not strong enough, my body is taking too big a hit from the chemo and not recovering well. So you tell me how this'll work if I can't stay on plan?"

Her question wasn't argumentative; she was pleading for reassurance. But she was right; I had no answers. "Maybe they can pick different drugs. Doctors switch antibiotics all the time. Maybe something else will work better?"

Jane rounded on me, all pleading gone. Her eyes still shimmered with tears, but now they flashed fire too. "This isn't a sore throat." She choked on a sob and caught herself. "There aren't other options. This is it."

"Oh . . ." I held up my hands. "I didn't know."

"Now you do."

"Thank you for explaining," I whispered to no one as I watched her walk away. I tapped the back of my head against the wall and let her go.

After getting lost twice, I finally reached the Infusion Center and found Jane sitting in the recliner with her eyes clenched shut. I sat and said nothing.

Cecilia came around the corner and approached us, fully dressed in a protective gown and gloves and sporting a serious expression—in her eyes, anyway, for that was all her face mask left exposed.

"Is this for real?" I whispered.

Jane opened her eyes. "It may be red, but it's not Kool-Aid. She's got to protect herself."

"And the face mask?"

"She says it's because she leans over so many of us in a day. We don't need any more germs. So I guess that's to protect us, not her."

"Still—"

"Are you okay, Jane?" Cecilia cut into our whispers with a concerned, muffled-sounding voice.

Jane minutely shook her head.

"Don't get discouraged. Counts bounce around all the time. Try to rest and eat more this week."

"I *am* trying. I can't try any harder." Jane bit her lip.

Cecilia's eyes softened. "I know. Just keep at it. Everyone reacts differently, but most go through this and are able to complete treatment."

"Really?"

"Yes, and I know Dr. Chun told you that." Cecilia's eyes crinkled. A smile.

"She did . . . I . . ."

"Unique as you are, Jane, you aren't remarkable in this area—everyone's counts bounce a bit."

Jane sputtered over a bit of laughter. I looked to Cecilia, part impressed, part jealous with how easily she handled my sister. She hooked Jane up to an IV bag and opened a valve. It was like dropping food coloring into a glass of water. The red color struck, contained and discreet, then spread through the bag, turning it bright red within seconds.

"How long . . . how long does this take?" I felt a stab of pain and looked down at my fingers. I'd shredded the cuticle on my left pinky without noticing.

Jane glared at me. Clearly I did not know how to handle my sister.

"It takes a couple hours, with both drugs and flushing. When Jane moves to the Taxol, that's over six hours long." Cecilia squeezed Jane's shoulder. "All set. I'll be back soon."

Jane glanced at the IV and I followed her gaze. It was obvious why they called it the Red Devil. The medicine was fire red and grimly mesmerizing. I remembered Peter's directives.

"Shall I read to you?"

"I'd like that. Peter sat there and worked on his computer last time. I read some but hated it. I kept watching that . . ." She pointed to the IV line.

I dug into my bag for my Kindle, wondering how Jane and Peter could see the same scene so differently. I looked up and found tears had gathered in her eyes again. Time to read.

"I've got about a hundred books on here. What would you like?" I started scrolling. "Oh, I've got *The Weird Sisters*. Have you read that?" *Yikes, it could be about us.* "How about a classic? I just reread *Catcher in the Rye*—so much better when you're out of high school. Or what about a sweeping romance? I've got Heathcliff and Cathy just waiting to cross the moors together. And I've got—"

"Grab *Emma* from my bag."

No Austen, please.

"It's beneath your chair." Jane pointed to her brown bag.

I leaned down and pulled out Tic Tacs, a wallet, and more receipts than I could crumple. "Do you ever clean this thing out?"

"Skip the commentary."

I dug again. "You sure it's here? I've got plenty of others." Then I felt it. "You must know this novel backwards and forwards by now. Don't you want something else?" I looked up and gently shook my Kindle. "One hundred books, right here at my fingertips."

"I'm working my way through Austen. I finished *Sense and Sensibility* a couple days ago." Jane blinked her eyes, trying to clear them. "What's wrong with *Emma*, anyway? You love Austen."

"Not really."

"Come on. You were as addicted as the rest of us. How many times did we watch all those *Pride and Prejudice* remakes? You were obsessed with Greer Garson in that 1940 one. Heck, you're Lizzy."

"Elizabeth."

"That's so formal. Was Lizzy not good enough for you?"

"I don't like it, and I've told you that for years." I started to put the book away. "Let's just find something else."

"I don't have anything else." Jane grabbed it. "Don't read. Sit there or go to the cafeteria; I don't care. I'll be done in a couple hours."

I yanked the book back. Jane was ticked—but she was scared too. I could see it in her eyes: her blood count, the central line, the Red Devil—everything boiled around her and it all glowed red. I sat back and held the book in my lap.

"I used to read to Mom that last year. At the end she only wanted Austen." I shrugged. "Who am I kidding? The woman only *ever* wanted Austen."

"She was singularly focused." Jane offered a small commiserating smile.

"She started with *Sense and Sensibility* too. Then we read *Mansfield Park*, *Emma*, and *Northanger Abbey*. *Pride and Prejudice* was her last . . ." I couldn't continue.

"Lizzy."

I shrugged. "It just seemed good to leave the nickname behind when I went to college. Besides, New York doesn't feel like a Lizzy sort of place."

Jane sat silent for a moment, then took a deep breath. I cringed because I knew that breath—it was her prelecture launch. *Don't do it, Jane.*

"That's an excuse. You changed it to leave us all behind."

"I'm not the one who left everyone behind," I mumbled, but Jane was just getting warmed up.

"You can't do that. Dropping your nickname and pretending Mom never existed won't work . . . That's why I want to read Austen right now. It reminds me of Mom and of one of the best parts of my childhood. Don't you want to remember?"

"As if you know anything about me or about that time." I leaned forward, angry. "Maybe I would want to read Austen novels and watch the movies and roll around in the romance of it all if it reminded me of Mom's life, and of good and whole moments, but it doesn't. I don't have the luxury of your memories. Each word is a death knell."

Jane snapped her mouth shut as if swallowing something bitter. I closed my eyes as the anger washed away and was replaced by regret. Jane was doing battle with cancer—a daunting opponent—and here I had picked another fight.

"I'm sorry." I turned to the marked page and started to read. " 'An egg boiled very soft—' "

"Don't. Please don't read. Just go," Jane whispered, her eyes again closed.

I spread my hand across the pages. "I can't. Please, Jane. I've nothing else to give you. I'm sorry."

She didn't reply or open her eyes. I continued to

read. " ' —is not unwholesome. Serle understands boiling an egg better than anybody. I would not recommend an egg boiled by anybody else; but you need not be afraid, they are very small, you see—one of our small eggs will not hurt you.' "

I chuckled. "I'd forgotten all the food references in *Emma*. This could be fun."

"Only you," Jane mumbled.

I pondered her comment. When I first started to cook, around age twelve, Jane was my staunchest supporter. She'd call home and ask what I was making and how it tasted. But as I became more confident in the kitchen, her ardor cooled. I believe she thought I pursued cooking to gain attention and form a special bond with Mom. She never understood that, when working with food, I never needed extra attention—I was whole and complete.

I returned to the story, and after about an hour of whispering the words, I needed a break. I looked around and found a water bottle sitting on the side table.

"Where'd that come from?"

"Cecilia put it there about ten minutes ago. I think it's for you."

"That was really sweet."

"She is really sweet." Jane's voice was dead and even. I wasn't forgiven.

I scanned the room to thank Cecilia and noticed that Andy's chair was empty. "Where'd the kid go?"

"They walked out about half an hour ago." Jane fixed her gaze on the far wall. "He's getting thinner."

I reached for something light, verging on ridiculous, to smooth away the conclusion she seemed to draw from that. "Maybe he'll grow up into a dashing and slightly misguided Frank Weston?"

"Are you trying to play Mom's game?"

"Thought it might help."

Mom used to point out people wherever we went, the grocery store, church, the dry cleaners, and ask us which Austen character they reflected.

"Maybe another time."

I reached for another distraction and nodded toward the brothers. "Those two are brothers, right?"

"Yeah, I sat next to Tyler last time. He's about your age. Brian's a bit older, maybe a couple years younger than me. He moved here from Chicago to take care of Tyler. Leukemia, I think."

"That's hard."

I looked around again, searching for someone or something new. "What about those two? She looks sweet; he looks like a curmudgeon—and yet he keeps patting her hand. It's cute."

Jane looked at them and her expression softened. "They're lovely. I sometimes wonder if Peter and I can become that."

"Aren't you already?"

Jane snorted. "We were . . . before this caught us."

I sat silent. If there is one thing I've learned as my friends marry, it's that you can listen to them dish about their husbands, but you never join in. An innocent "He sure has his opinions" froze a friendship for weeks—and a discernible chill still hovers. I could only imagine how Jane might eviscerate me if I crossed that line.

So I changed the subject again. "I'm all refreshed. Let's keep reading."

" 'Invite him to dinner, Emma, and help him to the best of the fish and the chicken, but leave him to chuse his own wife—' "

"Are you reading only the foodie parts?"

"You fell asleep. I can't help it if they're so interesting they wake you up."

"Look."

The last red flash of the chemo cocktail, as Jane called it, threaded its way toward her chest. It snaked down the line, up the line, and disappeared. Jane sighed, absorbing the last drop.

"Is that it?"

"That's it. Cecilia will be over in a minute to flush the line and unhook me."

"I'll clean up." I reached down to pick up a few stray receipts that had fallen out during my search and shoved them and *Emma* back into the recesses of Jane's bottomless brown bag.

"One more down." A perky, muffled voice chirped above me.

I looked up to find Cecilia, fully protected, opening another valve on Jane's IV. A few seconds later she disconnected her; then Cecilia stepped back and lowered her mask to reveal an open and cheerful expression.

"Still umpteen to go."

"True, but if you focus on the accomplishment, it helps. Each step is a big deal, Jane, and you're doing well despite what happened today."

"You don't know that." Jane reprimanded her for offering Pollyanna promises.

Cecilia paused. I wondered if she would launch a counterattack.

"You're right. Every case is as unique as every individual, but some things are more common than you think, like counts going up and counts going down with no rhyme or reason. I also know your cancer was caught at an early stage, and it's a type with good response rates. And you're strong, Jane. That's important too." She smiled and paused to let her facts sink deep. "Perspective can change everything." She added the last sentence as if it wasn't advice, but a personal reminder.

Jane closed her mouth. I pressed my lips together to stop a small smile from escaping. I knew she wanted to lash out but couldn't figure out how. Cecilia's gentle tone had ended any argument.

Cecilia seemed to understand Jane's struggle and squeezed her shoulder. "You did great today."

Jane looked up and her lip quivered as she whispered, "Thank you."

We gathered up our coats, our bags, and the clutter we'd created in our few hours and headed toward the elevator.

My stomach growled. "Time to eat. You hungry?"

"I should try. It may be my last meal for days."

"Don't say that. I'm going to Whole Foods this afternoon and I'll fix you something super yummy. You'll see."

"You'd be a miracle worker if you pulled that off."

"You may call me Anne Sullivan then, if Elizabeth is too difficult to remember."

"Cute. For now, let's go to Café Flora. They have the most wonderful egg dishes."

"Ah . . . 'An egg boiled very soft is not unwholesome.' " I grinned and pushed the button for the lobby. "Direct me home first and we'll pick up Dad."

After a quiet car ride, we found Dad pacing Jane's front hall so deep in thought he jumped when we opened the door.

"I didn't expect you for another hour or two."

"We didn't run any errands like last time."

I instantly surmised that not only had Peter

not read to her, but he took her on errands afterward—probably out to lunch. *Insensitive clod.* I felt a sudden kinship with my normally reserved and inscrutable brother-in-law. I needed a break. "We came back to grab you for lunch, but I think I'll stay here if you two don't mind."

"Why?" Jane snapped.

"We can all stay," Dad soothed.

"I want to get to the grocery store and work up a great dinner."

"I told you—" Jane stopped, noticing flowers on the dining room table. "Dad, did you buy me flowers?"

"No, they arrived about an hour ago."

She pulled the card from the holder and read: " 'Elizabeth told me today was important. My thoughts are with you. Paul Metzger.' Is this your Paul? Feast's owner?"

"Not mine, but yes, that's Paul."

"Very thoughtful." She put the card down.

I took a breath. *Thoughtful* was not the word that came to mind—it was my turn to get manipulated. And the message came through loud and clear: *Don't forget Feast; don't forget me.* I turned back to Dad. "Please, Dad. You take Jane to lunch. I want to work on the menus."

"We'll all—"

I cut him off. "This is my way to help."

That did it.

"Fine." Jane knew it too.

Dad gave me a quick pat on the back and ushered her out the front door. As it shut, I started to sigh. But the hallway felt empty and cold and far from relief.

Chapter 9

Looking around Jane's kitchen, I remembered that she had just finished reading *Sense and Sensibility*. I chuckled to myself, feeling a bit like Mrs. Jennings, hoping Marianne could be "tempted to eat by every delicacy in the house." And I felt as useless as Mrs. Jennings, for I knew as much about Jane as she knew of Marianne.

But Elinor knew. A true sister would and should . . .

What I knew was our mother. During her illness, Mom surrounded herself with anything safe, anything beloved—books, smells, clothes, movies, and friends . . . There was a blue cashmere sweater she insisted on wearing every day. She would hand wash it each week—or I did near the end—so that it would look fresh and others wouldn't feel we weren't taking proper care of her. She loved its warmth, the soft feel against her skin, and the color—"It's the sky in summer. You take walks around the garden or to Meryton under a sky this color. What could be nicer?"

So many things, Mom.

That was the place to start. Jane Austen. A quick Internet search confirmed what I assumed: a diet full of fricassees, puddings and pies (savory and sweet), and stews, but few vegetables and a strong prejudice against salads until later in the nineteenth century.

I looked up a Whole Foods nearby—a haven, albeit an expensive one, for fresh, organic, and beautiful produce—and then jotted down some recipes I thought would appeal to Jane's appetite. I landed on a green bean salad with mustard and tarragon and a simple shepherd's pie. She'd used mustard and tarragon in her own chicken salad. And I figured any good Regency lover would devour a shepherd's pie.

I noted other produce I wanted to buy: winter squashes, root vegetables, kale and other leafy greens. All good for sautés, grilling, and stewing. And fava beans, a great thickener and nutritious base, were also coming into season. And green garlic and garlic flowers, which are softer and more delicate than traditional garlic, more like tender asparagus. I wanted to create comfortable, healthy meals that cooked slow and long, making the flavors subtle—comfortably Regency.

I also listed pickles. I adored them and knew that fermented vegetables boosted the immune system and supported the digestive tract—both good for Jane right now. My excitement grew along with my list.

Finally ready to go, I grabbed my handbag from the guest room. As I headed back downstairs, I heard the front door unlock.

". . . your presentations at the high school, Dad. Those mean a ton to you. Please go back. This is a long road and I'm doing fine. There will be other times I'll need you more."

"I don't think you should be alone with Peter gone. You need help with Kate and Danny."

Something clanked. I envisioned Jane's car keys dropping into the bowl by the door.

"Why don't I ask Lizzy to stay? It would be nice for you girls. She could help cook."

"Please."

The sarcasm stopped me, and I stood perfectly still on the third stair down.

"Elizabeth's for Elizabeth." Jane emphasized my full name. "She can't see past herself to help me. Take her with you. We'll be fine."

"That's not fair, Jane. She was fantastic with your mom. I'll never forget how much that girl shouldered."

My eyes filled with tears. *Thanks, Dad.*

"Well, the little girl's all grown up, and she's a pretty cold fish in shiny scales. Don't leave her with me."

"You two girls . . ." The conversation continued as they headed to the back of the house and outside my earshot.

I slipped back upstairs to my room and then

stepped into the hallway when I heard Dad's footsteps coming up the stairs.

"You're back. How was lunch?" I plastered on a smile and hoped the dim light hid my eyes.

"It was very good." He sounded weary. "I think I'll read a bit before the kids get home."

"Sure. Jane downstairs?"

"Somewhere." He walked into Danny's room and shut the door.

I stood at the top of the stairs. Part of me wanted to go yell at my sister, the other part wanted to avoid her forever.

"I'm heading to the grocery store, Dad," I called out, sure that Jane could hear me as well from wherever she was in the house. I raced down the stairs and slammed the front door behind me.

"Kate, Danny, Dad, Jane . . . dinner," I shouted as I pulled down two glasses for the kids.

Pounding elephants rushed the stairs from the basement.

"Wow, you guys are fast—and heavy."

"We're hungry," Danny stated plaintively.

I glanced at the clock. Seven thirty. "In New York you wouldn't be caught in a restaurant so unfashionably early."

"I'm glad I live in Seattle." Danny flopped into a chair.

"Good point."

"Rude." Kate poked her brother.

"He's right, though. I didn't think about hungry kids. Sorry, guys."

"No biggie. I got all my homework done." Kate didn't smile.

"Okay then. 'Always look on the bright side . . . ,'" I sang out, then stopped. "You don't know that one, do you?"

They stared blankly at me.

"Someday get your dad to let you watch *Monty Python*—and don't tell your mom."

Danny grinned and Kate looked scandalized. She really was Jane's Mini Me.

"Where are our trays?" Danny canvassed the room.

"Trays?"

"We eat in the basement. I thought we only ate up here last night 'cause you just came."

"Why would you—?"

Jane blew into the room in a freeze that I'm sure chilled only me as she hiked an eyebrow, questioning our conversation. I threw back her signature wide-eyed doe expression before turning back to Danny. "Could you please pour two milks?"

I turned to the plates and scooped out the shepherd's pie. As I broke through the thin crust on the mashed potatoes, the most amazing aroma enveloped me. A similar version was one of Mom's favorites; it was one dish she never burned, never oversalted, and always made into a celebration. Jane and I used to fight over seconds.

But tonight it was mine—and it was better than Mom's. I always added a touch of oregano and cinnamon to the tomato base to give it extra richness. And for this pie I'd used more vegetables, mincing them super fine, and used a bit of grass-fed ground beef rather than relying exclusively on the lamb—the first naturally thickened the base, and the second softened the taste.

Everyone sat down, and Dad beamed. He loved Mom's cooking—and when shepherd's pie was on offer, he used to invite a few "boys" from his station over for dinner. You'd think I'd grown up with at least ten brothers for all the young men who hung around our house. In reality, it meant no one wanted to date Jane or me—ever.

"What's this?" Danny poked at his salad.

"That is a salad of blanched green beans and snow peas, with mustard and onion, tarragon, and a little fresh chili. That purple leaf is baby chard. I think you'll love it."

Danny looked skeptical but grabbed his fork as soon as I set down the shepherd's pie.

"Danny." Jane stopped him instantly. "Why don't you say grace?"

He brightened up quickly, as if she'd handed him a gift rather than a reprimand.

"Dear God, thanks for Aunt Elizabeth and her food. Please help Mom feel better and bring Dad home safe. Amen."

"Thanks, Danny-bananny. Dig in." Jane winked at her son.

Everyone took huge bites except for me. I watched to catch their first expressions. The kids lit up instantly.

"Aunt Elizabeth, will you make this again?"

"Mom, can you cook this?"

Jane laughed. "I can try." She reached for her fork and gently scraped it across her food. *Studying it or remembering it?*

I started to doubt myself. She scraped again.

After a couple seconds she scooped a small bite and chewed slowly, carefully. I wondered how ground meat slowly stewed in tomato sauce with mashed potatoes and peas could require that much work. I listed each ingredient in my head, noting the soft textures. A person could gum this dish. Jane chewed on.

Then she clasped her napkin across her mouth and lunged from the table and out of the kitchen.

Kate looked at me. "She doesn't eat anymore." Danny didn't even look up. I flickered my eyes to Dad, who blinked an attempt at sympathy, but I wanted none of it. I only tasted failure.

Dad kept up a cheerful prattle with the children as I listed the ingredients in my head, trying to figure out where I'd gone wrong. I didn't think anyone noticed me. I was wrong there too.

"It's okay, Aunt Elizabeth. Don't feel bad."

"Thanks, Danny. You're a sharp kid, you know

that?" I kissed him on the top of the head as he and Kate headed upstairs.

Alone in the kitchen, Dad touched my arm. "Are you okay?"

I slammed the leftovers into the refrigerator. "Anyone can make that dish, and mine was good. I know it. There's no way I can't cook a simple shepherd's pie—in my sleep! And what's with the kids eating in the basement?" I tossed the glass pan into Jane's porcelain farmers' sink and cringed at the loud clank. I glanced down, hoping I hadn't cracked the pan or the sink.

"Calm down."

"You don't get it, Dad. I needed that—" I looked at him and realized I didn't want him to get it. I couldn't tell him about Feast. I shifted tactics. "I needed to do this for her. She said she likes familiar things. Shepherd's pie was a favorite." I turned away to wipe down the counters. "It doesn't matter."

"Sometimes it's enough just to be there." Dad sighed. "I'm only learning that now. But you? You knew it back then. You were there for Mom, all the way." He stepped closer and patted my shoulder. "I'm proud of you, honey. You listened to your sister and did your best. Don't dwell on the fact that her stomach couldn't handle it."

"But . . ."

"It's the way it is right now." Dad shrugged, ending the discussion. "I'm heading to bed." He sighed again and pulled me into a half hug. "I think we should leave around eight again. I agreed to take a fire safety presentation off the station's hands, since we'll be back."

"I thought we were leaving Thursday, if not Friday."

"Jane says she'll be fine, and I don't want to push her right now . . . It's hard to know what she needs."

I remembered the conversation from earlier, and it dawned on me that perhaps we both felt dismissed. "I'll be ready."

Dad went upstairs, and I stood in the kitchen thinking about his words. *"You listened to your sister and did your best."* Not true. I never asked Jane what tastes good right now, what she thought she could eat, what repulsed her, or what she craved. I never asked what the medicines did to her tastes. I only knew what she read. And while it might constitute a start, it wasn't a complete picture.

Peter's notes told me that she could be suffering an endless number of side effects, most of which completely contradicted each other.

I threw the dish towel into the sink. I knew nothing.

Chapter 10

The next morning I didn't burn the oatmeal. Instead I took it off too early and served up cold oats al dente. The whole experience was getting too close to *Cold Comfort Farm*. If not for the kids' forgiveness and gentle teasing, I might have hurled the pot—regardless of the damage and subsequent apologies.

"You know," Danny said, "I don't like oatmeal anyway."

"Why didn't you say so?"

"You were so excited about the almonds and the strawberries."

I smiled. Then like the indomitable Flora Poste, he requested toast.

"That's not enough for breakfast, 'Robert Poste's child.' "

"Who?"

"She's the pragmatic modernist in *Cold Comfort Farm*, and she likes toast."

Danny looked lost.

"Never mind." I chuckled and dropped two slices of bread into the toaster.

"You laugh at your own jokes a lot."

His comment stopped me. "I guess I do. Most of them I say to myself. I'm at work most of the time, and I don't joke much there."

"Why not?"

"Hmm . . . 'cause I'm the boss, I guess." I snatched up the toast. "This is a little boring, but I've got just the thing for tomorrow."

"What?"

"It's a surprise."

"W—"

Kate cut across Danny's next question. "Aunt Elizabeth, we're going to be late."

I spread peanut butter across the toast and shoved it into their hands. "Move."

They both stared at the toast, then back at me.

"Come on. Eat and run." I turned them around and pushed them toward the door. I caught Danny throw Kate a look that shouted, *She does not know what she's doing!* He was right.

I stood on the porch and watched them book it across the blocks to school. Danny's backpack swung back and forth, threatening to topple him, and Kate snatched bites between strides.

With the kids out the door, I headed to the guest room and remembered that Dad had upped our departure. No breakfast surprise. My heart sank into my stomach. Danny mattered to me, and I was about to let him down. And Kate? She didn't smile much, and that made me sad.

I sat on the bed and absorbed the mess of clothing sprawled before me—mounds of flats, boots, sweaters, blouses, leggings, and indescribable junk. It reminded me of the day I had left home—I closed my eyes—almost half a lifetime ago. While all my high school friends celebrated at graduation parties, I headed home and packed —everything in my closet. I'd been admitted to a summer program at the Institute of Culinary Education and then to a college nearby. I told everyone I was going for the summer and I would return for the month before college started, but it was a lie. I knew that once gone I would stay gone. And as it turned out, the communication between the coasts was so terse and infrequent that I had no incentive to return. It felt as if Dad hadn't noticed my absence at all.

I snatched shoes and sweaters from the floor, feeling that same sense of loss. But it wasn't the same—couldn't be. I wasn't running away. This wasn't home, and Jane didn't need me. I'd done my duty, and now I needed to focus on Feast. Wasn't that the whole point of this trip in the first place—to feel alive about cooking again?

But where could I go to do that? Hood River with Dad? His life and fire safety presentations held no room for me. He loved me, I knew, but we didn't hold more than that between us. We didn't talk. We didn't relate. Return to Feast? Not yet. My one meal here constituted a complete failure. I needed to show Paul more.

Dad poked his head in. "Ten minutes?"

"Dad?" I flopped on the bed, defeated. "I can't go."

"Where? Home?"

"Anywhere." My voice cracked.

He looked at me for a long moment. Then he nodded. "I'll go back to Hood River and turn in your rental. You stay here."

"With Jane? That's not what I meant. I could find a kitchen somewhere. I just need to cook."

"You need to stay here." Dad's look disarmed me. "My girls are hurting. Both my girls."

I opened my mouth to protest and closed it again.

"It'll also give me an excuse to come back on Saturday. Jane needs more help than she'll admit." Dad leaned down, kissed me on the forehead, and walked out of the room.

I still had no words when Dad pulled out of the driveway minutes later. I tripped forward, perhaps to run after the car. I'll never know . . .

"Elizabeth, right?"

I spun around. Nick, the guy from the park, stood close behind me.

"Yes."

"Is Jane here?"

"She's still asleep. Was she expecting you?"

"No worries. We planned to meet tomorrow. I just wanted to bring her these." He stretched a brown paper bag in front of him.

I expected something light by the way he held it, but my arm dropped with the weight. "What is it?" I opened the bag, and the scent of apples, sweet and ripe, wafted up. They were brown and shriveled and resting in a Pyrex bowl. The sight was incongruent with the wonderful fragrant smell.

"I have a fantastic tree, cooking apples really—too tart to eat. But I freeze a lot. Jane mentioned last week that she loved applesauce, so I defrosted my last batch for her. They make the best applesauce I've ever had."

"Thanks."

"Do you know how to make applesauce?"

"I can figure it out."

"It's super easy; just add sugar and stew them over a low heat."

And cinnamon? You should also add nutmeg or a little chili, but not too much. I shrugged and simply said, "Thank you." I wasn't feeling much like a chef or like talking. I glanced down the road. Dad was gone.

"You're welcome." He paused. "Are you okay?"

I turned to find him staring at me. "Fine. Why?"

"You . . . you look lost."

"I'm fine." My words lacked conviction.

Nick smiled, and I noticed his eyes crinkle in the corners. "I almost didn't recognize you, you know?"

"Why's that?"

He wiggled a finger up and down, drawing lines from my head to my toes. I looked down. I was wearing jeans and an oversize sweatshirt of

Peter's I'd grabbed from the hall closet, and I stood barefoot.

"Yes?" I arched my tone, daring him to comment.

The grin disappeared. "You look . . . different." Nick paused and we stared at each other. His eyes softened, and I reinforced my glare until he shifted his gaze. He broke contact first as he turned to walk away. Four strides and he called over his shoulder, "Thanks for passing those along."

I turned and stalked back into the house, now angry—not about what he'd said, but about how I'd treated him. Then my next thought stopped me dead in my tracks: *Jane doesn't know I'm still here.* I pulled the apples from the bag, hoping they might ease the shock. I was also impressed at how quickly Nick must have frozen them last fall and how well he'd done the job. They still retained a firm skin and texture.

I set them to slow cook with salt, pepper, sugar, cinnamon, and a scant touch of nutmeg. Very traditional. Very English. I looked around the kitchen. The anticipation of confronting Jane, of nothing to do for a few days, of failure, made me jittery, and I tried to formulate a list. I came up with nothing, so I started straightening Jane's house: the kids' scattered clothing; Peter's books; Jane's keys, tissues, mugs, glasses . . .

It reminded me of our house growing up. Mom was cluttery as well—and I might be, too, but for

Suzanne, my dear borderline OCD roommate. I'd migrated her direction to keep the peace in our tiny apartment over the past four years, and it had worked—a serene apartment and a more organized kitchen at work. Now, faced with clutter everywhere, including my eruption in the guest room, I laughed at how foreign but comforting it felt.

I paused in the living room. The sun's rays shot over Lake Washington and ignited the room's beige walls, warming them from ginger to gold. New York had been cloudy this spring, and I'd been cloudy with it, but in this moment all my cloudy spaces felt ablaze with light. Jane's Red Sunshine comment bounced before me.

What will the blaze find in me? The thought came unbidden to my mind. In New York such thoughts didn't break in over work, traffic, and chaos, but in Jane's living room I had no list, no restaurant, no friends, and now no clutter. I sipped my coffee and snuggled into the couch as I watched the light bounce off flecks of dust in the air, making it look like fairy dust dancing around me.

I chuckled. This fairy dusting would upset Jane. She'd take it as a sign that her housekeeping, her work ethic, and her life weren't up to snuff. Just like when she said she was letting her clients down and had to give up her business. Jane was a pro at self-flogging.

Another thought crept in. *How different am I?* I knew how to hurt Jane because I knew what would hurt me. For years I'd defined myself by my work, my skills, my résumé, and my restaurant. Without that, what was left?

I reached for my phone and texted Suzanne: Jane is messy. You'd go nuts. I've picked up everything and now I'm bored. What are you doing?

She replied: It's noon. Market well underway. Super busy. Enjoy your boredom. It's called vacation.

Clearly I couldn't bug her. So I texted Tabitha: Vacation is too quiet. All good there?

She replied immediately: I'm heading to Feast now—preparing more broth. Keeping lobster risotto with saffron on menu for couple more days. Love that dish. Otherwise a typical day. Go have fun.

If I wanted out of exile, I needed to recapture my *zing*. So I quit pestering people and returned to the applesauce. It smelled delicious and comforting; the nutmeg played against the tart of the apple and the sweet of the brown sugar. Nick came to mind. Jane would appreciate the apples —his apples—as I had appreciated the flattering light dancing in his eyes and the tone of his voice . . . before I'd shot him down.

Chapter 11

Danny came home from school bouncing like a jumping bean. Jane had been up and roamed and moaned for a couple hours and watched a movie, but now she was down for another nap, and I was bored silly.

"What's up?" I pulled the last pan of chocolate chip cookies from the oven.

"Kai and Eric are going to the park. Can we go? Please."

"Do you want to, Kate?" I suspected the park might be passé for a teenager. I looked over at her as Danny tried to squeeze a yes out of me under the guise of a hug.

"Sure, some friends will be there." She shrugged.

"Okay then, grab a cookie and let's go." They each grabbed three cookies and headed back to the door.

We cut through a hedgerow down to the street below. It felt like we were tramping through someone's yard.

"Are you sure we can do this?"

"Of course." Kate smiled at me. "This used to be a street. Dad said in the thirties it washed out and the city didn't rebuild it, so now the houses get to plant gardens and stuff on the land, but it's public too."

"Cool." I eyed the houses on either side as we walked down the drive. "Hey, check out that kitchen. It's gorgeous."

"Aunt Elizabeth, you don't look," Kate chided. "You just walk."

"Is that bad?"

"Dad said it's rude."

"He's probably right."

Danny looked back at me and smiled. "She tells me not to look too."

"You never look, Danny. You do great," Kate said, and Danny smiled bright.

I touched Kate's shoulder. "You're a good sister."

We turned the corner onto Madison Street and headed toward the park. There were shops, small restaurants, a hardware store, and a few beauty salons.

"What was this?" I stopped in front of a small vacant storefront with a bright orange awning.

"It was a sandwich shop. It closed a couple months ago."

"That's too bad."

"Mom said it was overpriced and mediocre." Danny mimicked his mother's voice.

Typical Jane.

Then we turned into the park. Kate was right— her age group was here. Danny's too. And younger. And older. The huge park was alive and packed with kids and adults. The younger ones swarmed the monkey bars, the swings, and the swirly things—tons of cool playground contraptions that sported bright colors. The older ones stood in groups chatting or impressing each other on the balance beams or climbing stone sculptures. There was even a fifty-foot zip line that I knew I'd have to try someday soon.

But not today. Danny's comment about Jane reminded me of my own struggles with her. My mind still felt muddled with the fact that she had thrown up my home-run shepherd's pie and had also assumed I wouldn't stay, couldn't stay—as evidenced by her surprise at finding me in her kitchen this morning. It was another rejection, and I couldn't let it go.

I had been poking at the applesauce when she had walked in and jumped.

"You scared me. I thought you and Dad left." She glanced around as if trying to find Dad.

"He did. I decided to stay and help you out."

She narrowed her eyes. "I can't show you the sights, Elizabeth. I—"

"I'm here to help. Cook, I hope. I don't need to be entertained."

"I don't understand." Her look belied her statement. She understood; she didn't believe.

"It's true." I paused and felt my heart flutter. "Let me help."

She must have heard the plea in my voice because her eyes softened, flickering to question.

And she was right to do so—I wasn't sure myself why I had stayed. I shifted my eyes away and motioned to the stove.

"I made you a soft-boiled egg and a piece of twice-toasted bread. How does that sound?"

"Good." She sounded surprised. "Thank you."

"So we begin." I laid down the spoon and set out her small breakfast.

Neither of us spoke while she ate, and after she finished she headed to the basement to fold laundry. We'd spent the rest of the day carefully avoiding each other.

I now sat on a bench and wondered if the next few days would feel so formal and awkward. I watched kids loop across the monkey bars and spin themselves dizzy on some twirling thing. I looked up to see sunshine shoot around puffy marshmallow clouds. And slowly, slowly, I started to relax.

"It isn't right. It's not right," I mumbled. "I'm close. Stop trying. Just feel it. Don't think."

"What are you doing?"

I spun around. Kate watched me from the doorway to the basement.

"Salvaging my career," I whispered, then added, "Making soup. Come taste."

She blew on the spoon to cool it before she took a bite.

"It's good, Aunt Elizabeth."

"You like it?"

"It's okay."

"Then it's wrong." I sighed and returned to my mutterings. "It's close, so close. What's needed? Something . . ."

Kate stared at me with puckered eyebrows. I nudged her.

"All true artists are mad, you know . . . Last night we all loved the shepherd's pie, right?"

She nodded.

"But your mom didn't. She didn't even swallow one bite before she heaved it up."

"It's the medicine. She can't keep anything down."

"But what if she can? What if we can find something that sneaks past her nose and her mouth and actually gets to her stomach? See, that's the thing about last night." I warmed to my subject. "She didn't throw up because the food couldn't sit in her stomach—it never got there. She threw up because it triggered a reaction in her. So I think if *we* like it, if it tastes normal to us, then it will taste bad to her. It's a leap, I know, but your dad said that her mouth can feel sore, sensitive, taste like metal—all sorts of stuff we don't experience." I put another spoon into the soup and stirred; the rhythmic motion helped me think.

"Your mom mentioned the metal taste again today, so I'm trying to find something that reacts differently—a spice, a flavor that plays against the metal and lessens it."

"I don't get it."

"That's okay, sweetheart. I'm barely hanging on myself." But I needed this. It felt as if Feast's future depended on this meal. Maybe it did.

"Are you going to make the soup taste like metal?"

I laughed. "No, I'll make two dinners. If I'm right, hers will taste weird to us and ours not so good to her."

"She needs to eat more."

I looked down at Kate's steady sad eyes and squeezed her shoulders. "I know, kiddo. That's what I'm working on."

There's a scene in *Emma* when Emma sends arrowroot "of very superior quality" to Jane Fairfax—and Jane refuses it. Beautiful, self-satisfied Emma had probably never imagined such a thing—a rejection of her work as Lady Bountiful. And for Jane to tell her that she "was not at all in want of anything . . ." In other words, *Back off, Emma.* Who could fathom such a slight?

Did you? The question rose unbidden and unwelcome. I cringed at the link between Emma's arrowroot and my shepherd's pie. I took a deep breath to clear my mind and stirred the soup again.

After Kate returned to the basement, I separated the soup into two smaller pots. Time to experiment. I thought about Jane, and only Jane, and hoped that this offering might be welcomed.

The soup was a mixture of beans, root vegetables, and greens—a rich country stock. My frustration mounted as I couldn't think what to add, how to change her soup, how to make it work. I shook my head. I was again making this soup's success about me and not Jane—how naturally that occurred.

My sister walked into the kitchen just then and perched on the counter stool. "Hey, I just woke up. Did the kids do their homework?"

"We went to the park for a while, and they're doing it now." I turned to her. "What do you like to eat these days?"

"I'm not hungry."

"You haven't eaten since the egg this morning."

"And I won't."

I needed help—there was something out there, beyond reach, and for the first time in months I felt close to it. I needed the *zing* of getting it right and of food and meaning fusing.

"Forget trying to feed you. Tell me something you like right now. Anything."

Jane narrowed her eyes. "My kids, always. Peter, most days."

"Not good enough."

"My family's not good enough?"

"I didn't mean that. Can you use more senses? What do you like to smell? What's tasty on your good days? What makes you feel happy and secure? What do you like to touch?"

Jane chewed her lip. I turned back to the soup so I wouldn't keep adding questions. I closed my eyes, listening and waiting.

Jane never thought like this—at least as far as I knew. That was one of the reasons we never understood each other. There was the age gap, of course, but we also viewed the world through different-colored lenses. To Jane it was an ordered space along a linear line. To me—a chaotic mixture of sights, sounds, smells, and experiences to be fused together to make something new and different. Coloring outside the lines always unnerved Jane.

She started slowly. "I love the way Danny smells. I love Kate's hair, it's so soft and thick."

I glanced over. She raised her hand to her own. She didn't run her fingers through it; she simply patted it as if anchoring it to her scalp.

"I love the smell of clean-sheet day. I love to touch wool. My fingertips feel foreign, like there's a layer on them, and rubbing wool feels soft and comforting. It's a little scratchy too. I love the damp green smell of a sunny day when it's still wet but trying to dry, like the blueberries we bought the other day that weren't too strong in my mouth, not at all metallic and icky . . . I love reading Jane Austen and watching the movies and the smell of fires. All that makes me feel secure and believe everything is going to be fine, even though it may not." She swiped a tear. "There's a lot I love, Lizzy, and it all hurts. It's painful to see what may not be there soon."

I didn't think. I just walked around the island and pulled her into a tight hug. "It's all here and so are you. You're strong, Jane. You always were." I held her tight, and the years fell off me. She was that spectacular older sister who could do no wrong, and I was the kid who worshipped her.

She nodded into my shirt. I kissed the top of her head and stood back.

"Is that what you wanted to hear?" she whispered.

"It was perfect."

She smiled through her tears and gave a little shrug. I quirked a small smile. Neither of us was comfortable with vulnerability and emotion. "I'm going to find the kids."

She walked down to the basement and I knew. I knew exactly what to add to her soup.

I turned on the broiler to char some corn and added a touch of almond milk to her pot. I grabbed a handful of watercress and hovered over the pot. Maybe . . .

I looked toward the basement door, catching sounds of laughter. *Jane. My sister.* I scrunched my eyes shut. *Jane.* And I threw in the watercress and stirred. The corn had charred and an acrid smell assaulted me. I pulled it from the oven, cringed, and scraped it into her pot.

"Dinner, guys," I called down the basement stairs.

Kate and Danny emerged laughing and pulling Jane behind them.

"I should harness these guys," she teased and ruffled Danny's hair and plopped a kiss on top of Kate's. Both drew into their mother, and suddenly I saw my own within her.

"What?"

"You look . . . just like Mom."

Her eyes glistened and she pulled her kids a touch tighter. "Thank you." She then squeezed them with a tickle chaser and they bounced away. "See, guys, I'm the best, most gloriously wonderful mom in the whole wide world."

The kids laughed and pulled out their chairs. The *scritch scratch* of wood on wood brought us back to the business of dinner. And after a quick grace, given by Kate and featuring "the best, most gloriously wonderful mom," I watched Jane stir her soup. She took a whiff and looked up at me. A smile played on her lips.

"Mommy's soup smells weird." Danny scrunched his nose as he leaned over Jane's bowl. Steam rose from ours, but hers was cooler, as I thought heat might hurt her mouth.

"Rude. It's supposed to," Kate said.

Jane looked up.

"Not too weird." I smiled.

She slowly took a spoonful and swallowed. We

waited. She waited. She stared at me as she scooped another bite. We all exhaled.

"Well?" Danny demanded.

"I'm okay." Jane took another bite. She ran her tongue across her upper lip. "It tastes different, but I like it."

Zing.

I quit watching and passed around the loaf of heavy sprouted grain bread I'd baked. Jane dipped a slice into her soup and kept eating. The kids talked about their day and our walk to the park. The whole scene tripped toward normal.

"Nick dropped by this morning and brought you apples," I commented.

"Was I asleep?" Panic tinged Jane's voice.

I pursed my lips together, regretting my old habits and my thoughtlessness. *You know exactly what will bug her.* "No biggie. He said he'll come by again tomorrow. He'd frozen apples from his tree, so I made them into applesauce for dessert." Jane's face fell, and I rushed on, "We read it yesterday in *Emma*, remember? Mr. Woodhouse urged Miss Bates to eat the baked apples? Now you can."

"Only you remember food references. I forget everything." Jane leaned back in her chair.

"I love applesauce," Danny called out. I smiled at him, expecting a perky smile in return, but he looked upset, confused. He was watching his mom.

"You should have woken me, and he's a good friend, but he's doing too much." She looked down at the table. "I can't be this needy," she mumbled.

Danny looked to his bowl, and Kate threw me a quick glare.

"It's okay, Mommy." She reached out to touch Jane's hand.

"Thanks, sweetie." Jane took a deep start-over breath, but it sounded shaky.

"For goodness' sake, Jane. You don't have to do all the heavy lifting alone. You're not an island." I stopped talking, flashing my eyes between Jane and Kate.

"I'm not a charity either." Jane glared at me before she closed her eyes and didn't take another bite of soup. She left the table moments later.

The rest of us ate in silence until the kids drifted away to the basement to finish homework and I cleaned the kitchen.

Later I sat in the living room flipping channels long after Jane had kissed the kids good night. I was surprised when she came downstairs to join me. I tried again to be genuinely in her corner.

"You still tuck them in?" I pushed the remote's Pause button.

"They love it, and with so much else going on right now, it probably makes them feel more secure. It does me." She pulled at a thread in the throw blanket. "Thanks for tonight. We don't sit around the table like that. I'm not up to the cooking, the smelling, or sometimes the conversation. No one seems to be anymore. It was nice."

"Danny mentioned that they usually eat in the basement."

Jane pushed deeper into the armchair. "I hate that. In such a short time that's what we've become, and it's not just me. Sometimes it's too hard to even look at each other. And meals make it all worse. They're supposed to be happy, sharing times."

"Then I'll handle those for now."

Jane narrowed her eyes, assessing my sincerity. I held her gaze and said, "Can I ask you a few more questions?"

"What about?"

"What would you eat, if you could have anything in the world?"

"We've been through this. I'm not trying to insult your cooking, and tonight tasted good, but food isn't my friend right now." She pulled the blanket tight as if protecting herself from my questions, or from me, and said nothing for a few minutes, but I didn't restart the television.

"Fine. I love that beef stew Mom used to make. It sounds good to me, and I actually think about it a lot, but she added cilantro. I couldn't do that. And I love the idea of chicken potpie. And ham and mustard and a good strong cheese."

"A good strong cheese?"

"Doesn't it sound nice?" She pursed her lips. "I'd probably throw it up, but it might be worth it." She caught my eye. "That probably sounds provincial to you, doesn't it? You cook things far more sophisticated."

"Sometimes, but it sounds very Austen." I smiled. I hadn't been too far off.

"What's funny?"

"Nothing. It sounds warm and comforting and possibly nutritious. Why no cilantro?"

"There's something bitter about it now. It tastes like a fork soaking in lemon dish soap."

"Lemons, limes?"

"They clear out the tastes in my mouth. I like that."

"Cilantro bad, but citrus good. Tell me about vinegars."

"Blech. And I don't like lettuce. Thinking about the texture turns my stomach. I made a salad last week and ate all the stuff at the bottom of the bowl—the carrots, celery, avocados, beets, and pistachios. That was good."

"Tell me about spices."

She shook her heard. "Spices feel weird on my lips, and they get the saliva going and my stomach roils. That's when the metal taste is the sharpest. I think it's in my saliva." Jane rolled her head toward me. "That's all I've got. Can we talk about something else?"

"I'm only trying to help." *Help us both.*

"I know, but I'm tired. I'm tired of feeling this way, and I'm only at the beginning. I'm already tired of talking about it, thinking about it, living it." She sat up and stared at me. "This is why you shouldn't have stayed. I can't make this right for you. I can't take on another kid right now. You've got to stand on your own."

"You don't make it easy, do you?"

She raised her voice. "This isn't about you."

"I realize that. I was trying to make it about you. Maybe I didn't do it well. Maybe I don't know how . . . but I tried, Jane, so cut me some slack." I shifted in my armchair. "You know, despite how you feel about me and my ability to help and stick around and show up, you're not such a great role model. But I'm the one here, the only one. And I'm not another kid, or a cold fish in shiny scales."

Jane's lower lip dropped slightly as I stood and thrust the remote toward her. "Enjoy your show." She didn't lift her hand, so I dropped it in her lap and headed up the stairs.

Chapter 12

The next morning after the kids ran to school, late again, I cleaned the kitchen and started a stew while Jane and Nick met in the living room. Foreign words like "Google analytics," "behavioral targeting," and "search engine optimization" drifted to me. I turned back to my stew, wishing that good cooking, and not Nick and Jane's "optimization," was all that Feast needed to survive.

I needed out. I needed air and a little exercise. And I had an idea—one that excited me as much as search engines probably energized Nick and Jane. It had come in the fleeting moments as I awoke, during that in-between time when ideas, even brilliance, fill your brain before reality pushes them away. I had fallen asleep devising escape plans, but awoke to recipes and almond flour. I knew somehow that potatoes wouldn't sit well in Jane's mouth, but the beef stew she craved would. I only needed almond flour to thicken it.

So I dismissed my escape plans, cooked the kids scrambled eggs, sent them to school, and braised short ribs before setting them in the slow cooker —because for the first time in months, maybe years, a person, a food, a need, an answer, and an inspiration had melded together and become whole. This is what I was after and it felt close. I simmered with giddiness.

I stuck my head into the living room. "I need some almond flour. Is there a market nearby? I'd love to walk rather than drive."

Nick was packing his messenger bag as Jane replied, "There's one just past the park you went to yesterday, across the street."

"Perfect." I ducked back out to find a coat.

"I'm headed that way," Nick said. "I'll show you."

Jane then turned to Nick. "Thanks for keeping me posted on all this. You don't have to, you know."

"If you tell me to stop I will, but they're your clients and they feel pretty loyal to you."

"That's so nice."

"It's true."

Jane opened the door for Nick, and I silently followed, feeling as if both had forgotten my presence.

We stepped off the porch before Nick spoke again. "How's Jane doing, really?"

"Okay, I think. She's tired. Cranky. Jane. Hates to feel less than perfect."

"Oh."

"That was rude." I glanced over and presented Nick an off-kilter smile. "You must think that's all I am, too, after yesterday. I was so . . ."

"New York."

"Hey, it's a great city."

"I didn't say that. I simply implied it has a different vibe. Yesterday I meant that your outfit skewed more Seattle, but then your attitude was all New York." He chuckled and looked me up and down. "Now you're Madison Avenue veering to Village chic."

"I . . ." My brain completely blanked for a retort until I caught his grin. "You're teasing me, aren't you?"

"Slightly."

"Well, you certainly haven't caught me at my best. There's a lot going on right now."

"I can only imagine."

It took me a second to realize he was referring to Jane. How horrid that I hadn't been. "Yesterday, when you dropped off the apples, our dad was just leaving, and I'd decided to stay on to help out. Jane wasn't thrilled with my decision." I paused and reassessed the morning. "That's not exactly true. She just didn't understand it."

"You two aren't close?"

"She's eight years older and probably still sees me as ten-year-old Lizzy. That's the last time we ever spent any real time together. When she left for college, she left for good."

"It's good you're here then. Maybe this is your chance."

"To . . . ?"

"To get to know each other."

The thought pulled at me. It *was* my chance— my last chance. For Feast, at least. For Jane? I wasn't sure.

We passed a Starbucks and I stalled. "I think I'm going to grab a coffee. Thanks for walking with me, but I'll find it from here." I stepped in the door without waiting for his reply, and stalled again.

Nick chuckled behind me. "We Seattleites are hard-core about our coffee."

"I'll say." I looked around at approximately

three thousand square feet of coffee-infused glory divided into four sections, with leather armchairs, couches, a fireplace, tables, cool stools, a kids' play area, workbenches, a bar, wine, beer . . . an antipasto platter.

An antipasto platter? In Starbucks?

"Pick up your jaw and move that way." Nick lightly pushed me forward.

I ordered my latte and as I waited for it, I looked around. It was packed. People holding meetings, chats, and children; folks curled up reading books; others chasing kids or reading to them; patrons working on computers. I counted sixty people, and another sixty could fit.

"Do you want to sit a minute?"

"I can just go."

"I'm going to grab a table."

I vacillated just enough.

"Come on." He led me through the tables to a place near the window. "So how are *you* doing with all this?"

I bit my lip, unsure of what to say.

"Look, Jane and Peter are good friends, and I love Danny and Kate—she's my top babysitter—but this can't be easy on any of you. You won't betray her if you need to talk. I won't blab and I won't judge."

We sat and I pondered his offer. "Interesting word. *Betray.* That's the problem. We don't have any loyalty."

Nick's eyes widened.

"There I go again." I looked down to my lap. I'd begun to shred the napkin. "It's just that, like I said, Jane and I have a lot of . . . difficulty . . . between us."

He leaned back and nodded as if he had nothing better to do than listen to me—so I continued.

"I stayed yesterday only partly to help Jane. I also needed a kitchen. I have to work on my cooking."

"Women still do that?"

"Still do what?"

" 'Work on their cooking.' " He made quote marks with his fingers. "My mother said she spent the summer before she got married working on her cooking with her grandmother. It's sweet."

I raised my eyebrows.

"You didn't mean that, did you?" Nick scrubbed his hand over his eyes. "That was kinda medieval of me. Continue. You need to learn to cook . . ."

"Oh, I can cook. I mean I used to be good. Seriously good." I shook my head. "Anyway, I stayed to help and to cook, but I can't do either." I wadded the napkin bits in my fist and moved on to the brown wrapper on my coffee cup. "I saw some sisters at the park yesterday, and I loved the way they cared for each other and played together. They looked close."

"I can't help you there. I'm an only child like Matt."

"I wish," I retorted and clamped my hand over my mouth. Nick stared at me. "See? I didn't mean that, but I'm mad at her. I'm always mad at her, and that's horrible. She should get a hall pass, especially now, but I can't seem to give her one."

Nick laughed, letting me off the hook. "Did she like the applesauce?"

I cringed—as his question put me right back on it. "Not yet, but she will."

"Did you use enough sugar? I'm telling you, they're super tart."

"I think so, but I used brown. Do you do that? And I added nutmeg and a touch of salt. People sometimes forget the salt when they use sugar, but the two pair together. I also added a touch of pepper and let them steep in the skins. I think that way is more reminiscent of England's baked-apple traditions—you know, like the ones described in Austen, even Dickens. He loved his apples. Jane likes that stuff right now, and I thought, before serving it today, I might also add— What?"

Nick grinned so wide the corners of his eyes almost crinkled shut. "You *are* a cook. I simply add sugar and mash them."

"That works too." I looked down at the cup's wrapper. I'd killed it. "I get a little excited about food. I work as a chef in New York, a little restaurant called Feast, fresh farm to table, innovative—at least it used to be. It's small, and

I've got a tight menu that I keep close to locally available produce and organic suppliers. I get to play a lot, except for dessert. My pâtissier is a prima donna." I bit my lip and stopped babbling.

"Now I feel stupid. I must've looked like a complete fool trying to tell you how to cook the apples yesterday."

"No. You were being kind. I guess I didn't like getting caught without my armor."

"No one does," he said, so softly.

I glanced up. "I should go." I stood too quickly and lost my bearings.

Nick darted out of his seat and grabbed my upper arm. "Whoa there. Steady."

"All good. Sorry. I made breakfast for the kids this morning and forgot to eat myself."

"Grab something and join me. I think I'll work here awhile."

I wavered a moment. Fleeing felt wise, but staying felt right. "I'd like that."

I went to the counter, ordered oatmeal, and returned. Nick had pulled out his computer, but it lay shut before him. He watched as I stirred the oatmeal and added the toppings.

"It's pathetic when Starbucks can make better oatmeal than a trained chef. I've been trying this for Jane's kids and keep screwing it up."

"How much longer do you have to get it right?"

"A few days here, but another week away from

the restaurant." I took a bite. "How did you and Jane start working together?"

"Peter and I worked at the same agency until it shut its doors a couple years ago. He went on to Microsoft and I started my own firm—social media, PR, and marketing, like Jane, but mostly for small companies. When Jane was diagnosed, Peter suggested she cut back on work. I sense she's sad about it."

"Did she tell you that?"

"She's never mentioned it, but it must be hard. My hope is that she'll want her clients back someday, so I'm trying to keep her in the loop."

"Don't you want the business?"

"Not like this." He swung his head with each word.

"Of course. I didn't know exactly what Jane did—definitely not my forte." I scooped the last bite of oatmeal, chewing the nuts and raisins that had sunk to the bottom. "Ironically, that's what my restaurant lacks—a media presence, along with a few other things like inspired cooking of late."

"If it's not your forte, hire someone. We're a dime a dozen out there."

"We did. He just started." I pretended to be absorbed in cleaning my wrappers and mess. There was no way I was going to say more, especially not that Chef Dimples was singularly gifted as both consultant and cook.

But the pressure of Trent Murray and his giftedness crushed me, and I looked up. "Why? Why does it matter so much? If you've got a good product, do things right day in and day out, why isn't that enough?" My final note revealed my panic.

Nick leaned back and thought for a moment, his eyes never leaving mine. "Not long ago it was. But there's more chatter now, and oddly, we want relationships from more than just people." He leaned forward and spread his hands across to me. You could measure the space between us in inches, not feet.

"People want to know their movie stars, their artists, their breweries, their auto repair shops . . . their chefs." He paused and smiled. "Right now I'm working with a woman, one of Jane's clients, who teaches cooking classes. Those experiences are personal, and people expect to find her approachable, knowledgeable, trustworthy, even kind, before they'll shell out a hundred bucks for one of her classes."

"A hundred bucks?"

"And for that hundred bucks her customers demand not only a class but a personal connection to her. That's where I come in. I find ways for people to feel attached to her and the experience."

"Attached?" I snorted and covered my mouth to stop the sound. I suspected few people, even Tabitha or Suzanne, felt truly attached to me.

"Sorry. That struck me as funny. Sadly funny."

Nick's expression flickered.

"No. Not for her, for me . . . I put everything into my food, not necessarily into my customers, and it worked. But right now my cooking is off somehow, and the loyalty isn't there."

"Marketing is real and makes a difference, but you're right that the product is paramount. People expect more from their dollars today."

"I noticed."

Chapter 13

Saturday morning brought us a Cat in the Hat moment. Kate and Danny drooped like Sally and her brother looking out at the rain, waiting for something to happen.

"Okay, you two, into the kitchen."

"Why?" Danny and his one-word questions.

"I promised you a breakfast surprise and I got distracted. Today's the day."

I reached into the freezer and pulled out a glass container.

"Wha—"

"No questions. Sit at the table."

Both sat silent and wide-eyed as I scooped out breakfast and poured maple syrup on top.

"No way!" Danny cried as I placed the bowls in front of them.

Kate didn't say a word, just dug in.

"What's going on?" Jane called from the stairs.

"Breakfast," we all shouted.

Jane headed straight for the table and leaned over Kate. "Ice cream? Seriously, Lizzy?"

"Bacon ice cream, Mom, with maple syrup."

Jane raised her eyebrows. I almost laughed at her obvious struggle: *Do I yell? Or do I grab a spoon? Yell? Spoon?*

I waited.

She reached for a bowl. "This sugar high's all on you." *Right on the fence.* But her compressed smile soothed the sting from her words.

"I'll take them to Pike Place Market until they crash."

"Can I come?"

"Of course." I smiled, feeling a layer of ice thaw in the midst of our frozen breakfast.

Pike Place Market is a Seattle favorite, a national favorite, and cited in plenty of cooking magazines as the oldest continuous farmers' market in the country. And it lived up to the hype—packed with produce, meats, fish, flowers, handmade goods, and people. The guys at the fish market, who called out a chant before hurling large fish at each other, held us mesmerized. The ones working the crowd seemed oblivious to the shouts of their colleagues behind the counter, then reached out at the last second to catch a soaring twenty-plus-pound salmon or halibut or something else large and slippery right before it smacked a spellbound tourist in the face. There was even a monkfish sitting in the ice and tied to a string, which they pulled from behind the counter whenever anyone touched it. Danny screamed and jumped a foot off the ground.

And the flowers! Huge bouquets bursting with variety and color that would cost well over a hundred dollars in New York cost fifteen here. I bought two enormous ones and handed them to the kids to carry. Danny got completely lost behind his. And the honey! My knees almost buckled as I tasted blueberry honey, raspberry honey, wildflower honey, sunflower honey—I bought six jars without even thinking.

"What are you going to do with all that?" Jane asked.

"I have no idea, but I sense lots of baking, even some infusions. I can take what we don't use back to New York. Honey carries such local flavor; they'll be so fresh at Feast."

While we scoured the market the sun came out, hot and bright. The ground was drying, and I remembered Jane's list.

"Come on." I pulled her arm and called to the kids, leading them outside.

"What are you—" Jane stepped onto the pavement and smiled. "Oh . . . this is so odd for April. It feels wonderful." She took a deep breath and glanced at me, pulling in the corner of her lip as she lifted her face to the sun.

My mind flashed back to a Christmas break when I was about twelve. Jane had come home from college and done something wrong, broken something, I couldn't recall what, but I remembered that Mom had launched into me. Mid-diatribe I had looked over to Jane and found her pulling in that same corner of her lip—trying to say sorry, but lacking the courage to do it or to take the blame. I smiled as I now began to understand my sister, and I, too, soaked in the sun.

After a moment I opened my eyes and glanced at her. She looked pale. "How are you doing? Time to head home?"

"Can we go to the park?" Danny called.

Jane brightened and turned to me. "They can play, and I'll show you Madison Park's cooking store. It's a good one. You'll love it."

When we finally returned home, with honey and flowers from the market and a new silicone whisk from the cooking store, Jane and the kids drifted down to the basement to watch a movie. I wanted to give them some time alone, so I curled up in the living room with a copy of *Sense and Sensibility*. I felt nervous about opening it, but I couldn't deny that simply holding the book felt like coming home—and it didn't hurt.

I had pulled it from Jane's shelf because I loved the sisters, Elinor and Marianne. The two most famous Austen sisters, after whom we were named, portrayed too intimidating a relationship for me—always had. Lizzy and Jane Bennet understood each other, championed each other without fail, and possessed an unbreakable bond. Even Darcy could not find fault in their relationship or conduct—and he could find fault in most things. But Elinor and Marianne? They had more conflict, rubbed more, barked more . . . They felt more real, more flawed, and yet their bond was as strong, as enduring, and as beautiful.

My thoughts drifted. I had told Jane that I changed my name from Lizzy to Elizabeth in college—as if it was simply the time to grow up. That was a lie. I changed it the moment Mom died. I stood in our kitchen that very evening yelling at my dad about my nickname, my real name, and that it was ridiculous to have ever named us after Jane and Elizabeth Bennet in the first place. I yelled that we were merely derivative characters who were now left with nothing. I yelled that he was nothing. I wanted him to attack; I wanted a fight; I wanted a feeling. He had simply replied, "It was important to your mom." As if that was a good enough reason . . . for anything, for everything.

But to him it always was, and that commitment had enveloped our family. But when the object of his, and our, devotion was gone, so were the magic, the books, and "Lizzy"—all in a single black moment. I put it all away . . . until now.

The family of Dashwood had been long settled in Sussex. Their estate was large, and their residence was at Norland Park, in the centre . . .

I got lost in the story until I heard a soft tapping on the door. I glanced out the window to find my dad's truck parked out front.

I hopped up and pulled open the front door. "Welcome back."

"How are my girls? I've worried about you two."

"You don't need to worry about us. We're both still standing." I reached out to hug him.

He pulled me tight, then released me. "That's 'cause you're strong."

I pulled him out of the swing of the door. "Come in. Come in. Jane's in the basement with the kids watching a movie. Do you want to head down there?"

"I'd rather sit with you a moment."

"Sure, I was just in here reading."

I led him back into the living room and curled up in the chair. He looked at me, around me, then at the book. I felt as lost as he looked.

After a moment he found his voice. "Is she doing well?"

"She's been pretty wiped. Is that normal?"

"Your mom was during chemo. Do you remember that?"

"Not as well as I thought I did. I seem to remember her pretty upbeat."

"She was. She changed a lot during that time.

She found peace, but she was tired. She didn't cook like she loved. You did. We used to sit in the family room and read at night. Life got quieter." Dad pointed to my book.

"When you say it like that, I see it. I don't know how I didn't then."

"You were young, and perhaps we didn't share as much as we should have."

Dad had never talked this openly. Perhaps I'd not given him a chance. "Did you know right away? That she wouldn't make it?"

"The doctors weren't optimistic from the beginning. The cancer was aggressive, and treatments weren't what they are now. So, yes, we basically knew." He found a spot on the wall on which to focus—some things were too difficult for direct eye contact.

But I needed it. I waited until Dad shifted his gaze back to me before speaking. "Watching Jane, I feel like I missed a lot . . . I feel I misread or misjudged things."

"What you caught was enough."

"But I placed blame . . . I didn't know . . ."

Dad shook his head as if trying to stop my sentence, my sideways apology, so I let it fade away. He picked up the pause. "How's your cooking?"

"She's eaten the past couple days."

"I meant how it's going for you. Is it what *you* wanted it to be?"

I considered. I hadn't said much to him about Feast, but I suspected he'd seen more than I intended. "It's better. That's part of why I came home—I don't cook the same right now. It's a problem, but there have been moments this week when it's felt alive and I've felt like me." I closed my eyes, remembering. "I love those feelings."

"I felt that way at the fire station. It's powerful." Dad smiled, remembering as well.

I cringed as I recalled a phone conversation from four months earlier. He'd called to tell me the date of his retirement party, after thirty years on the force, and I had made excuses as to why I couldn't come. I claimed stress, busyness, the flu ravaging the staff, commitments with Paul . . .

I also remembered his reply: "Don't feel bad you can't come; it's not that big a deal. Folks retire every day."

Until now he'd never mentioned it again. Jane hadn't let it go, of course, and for a couple weeks I got lovely e-mails from her—cool and precise, the perfect layering of guilt and indignation. So I'd skipped my Christmas visit completely— petty, emotional payback maybe—but still Dad had not said anything or even given me guilt about missing Christmas.

"I'm sorry, Dad."

"About what?"

"I should've been at your party. I should've

come home then." I fidgeted, passing the book from one hand to the other.

"It's okay, sweetheart." He gripped the armchair, leaning forward and pressing his assurance.

I smiled and I knew; it wasn't.

Chapter 14

On Monday morning Dad and I sat at the kitchen table working a crossword. The kids had just left for school—on time—and Jane still slept.

"That's 'avenged.' "

"You're good at these." Dad filled in the word.

"I hate them."

"You hate crosswords?"

"You have to follow a pattern or a pun sometimes and it's too precise, but I'm happy to help."

"Such a sacrifice . . ." Dad chuckled.

I sat back and laughed, watching my dad work each grid of the puzzle. It had been a good weekend. Jane had slept most of it, so Dad and I talked more than we had in years. It was as if coming home, even for that one night, had opened some metaphorical gates and allowed things to be said and felt that weren't possible on his short visits to New York or mine to Seattle.

"Do you have to leave? It's been nice having you here."

Dad reached over and squeezed my hand. "I've enjoyed it, too, but it's time. There are no more lightbulbs to change or windows to clean or cars to detail."

"You can just rest, you know."

"I don't want to hover. Your mom hated that, and I don't want to do that to Jane. She wouldn't like it. But I'm glad you decided to stay till Peter gets back. That's good."

"It's not a big deal. I just switched my ticket to fly out of here rather than Portland."

"It is a big deal—for all of us." Dad paused, watching me. "You call me tomorrow about her counts, okay? They're looking at a lot of stuff, but her white blood cell count shows her ability to stave off infection. That's an important one. You call me."

"I will. Are you coming back?"

Dad folded his crossword and stood to leave. "Absolutely. I'll see you before you go." He crossed to the door and picked up his duffel bag.

I followed. "Why aren't you waiting to say good-bye to Jane?" I glanced at the clock. "I'm supposed to wake her up soon for a meeting with Nick. She made me promise not to let her oversleep."

"I often come and not say good-bye when I go. This feels more normal."

"And sometimes you need normal." I understood.

He pressed his lips in and nodded, pulling me in for a quick hug and an "I love you, kiddo" before he turned away.

I watched him pull out of the driveway before going to wake Jane. She was already awake and sitting up in bed. The light peeked through the woven shades, and she looked pale, almost ethereal.

"You look like royalty expecting breakfast in bed."

"You offering?"

"No." I sat on the edge of the bed.

"I've been sitting here reading. You know, I've never done this—relaxed in bed long enough to let the sun come up, and watch it move across the floor and change."

"I don't think I ever have. Most people don't have that kind of time."

"It's nice."

"It's a relaxing room." I scooted back against the headboard and looked around.

She had no rug on the floor, just the hardwood, and their bed, a dresser, and two chairs. All proportioned. The wallpaper was cream with tree vines trailing up every few feet, adding life but not clutter or chaos. And the bed coverings were the same cream as the walls. It felt clean, simple, quiet yet warm.

"You know, I will bring you breakfast in bed. This is worth savoring."

She looked around as well, then turned to me and smiled. "Tomorrow after the kids go to school, bring up coffees and we'll read before we head to the hospital."

"It's a date."

We sat a little longer; then she got up to shower, and I headed to the kitchen and to my computer. I needed to touch base with Tabitha and Paul, primarily. Feast seemed to be doing well, but I wanted them to feel my absence every day, to know I was working my way back and to believe I was vital to their happiness. So each day I sent recipes, reminders, touch points, and ideas. It felt slightly calculated and impersonal, but it was all I had to offer. Paul employed Lois, his assistant, for the same purpose—it was a game we both played daily.

After covering all my bases, I started a stew for dinner. I'd been studying Peter's notes each evening, changing my recipes as I came across new information and symptoms. And it worked. Jane had started to eat meals with more consistency and complimented me on the tastes. Her appetite seemed to increase daily. Even the kids had noticed, and mealtime had grown lighter, topped with bits of laughter and fun.

"It smells bad in here, Aunt Elizabeth." Danny walked in through the back door after school.

In our short week I'd begun to find Danny's

brusque honesty comforting. I knew where I stood with him.

"Bad?" I couldn't catch it. Different, yes, but not bad. "Kate?"

Kate dropped her backpack, looked at her brother and back at me. "He's rude, but right. It's kinda bad."

"Well, I made you more cookies, so grab one of those." I returned to my stew, stirring and thinking. The sudden silence turned me around again. The kids had vanished with the entire plate of cookies. *Oops.* I chuckled.

Jane walked in and looked around the room. "I thought I heard the kids."

"You did, but they stole an entire plate of cookies and bolted."

"You let them take the whole plate?" Jane scowled and yanked the basement door open.

"Oops again," I whispered.

"Hey, Elizabeth."

"Nick?" I spun around. "I didn't know you were still here."

The western light slanted in the windows and hit him straight on. It was like seeing someone in high-def. He had stubble across his jaw, and his dark hair curled slightly above his ears. His teeth were perfectly straight, and he had a scar across his chin. It was a good strong chin. And his green eyes laughed at me.

"We had a lot to discuss today." He smiled

and approached. "What are you making?"

"Another stew. I'm so close. I messed one up a few days ago—when I was heading to the Red Apple for the almond flour—but now I'm close. The kids say it smells bad. It's supposed to be different, but not . . ."

Nick opened his mouth to say something when we heard pounding on the basement steps. He backed away.

"Here are the cookies, Aunt Elizabeth. We only ate two each." Both Danny and Kate glanced at their mom standing behind them.

Kate spoke up. "We each ate four."

"I would've done the same."

Jane stepped forward. "Is this dinner? Can I taste?"

I handed her the spoon, and she blew on a bite, then swallowed. I flashed my eyes to Nick, sure that he would be focused on Jane, the moment's judge and jury, but he was watching me.

"This is for tonight?" Her voice sounded light, even pleased.

"You like it?"

"Nick, come taste this."

Nick raised his eyebrow to me and stepped to the stove. Jane handed him a clean spoon. He took one bite and stood perfectly still. "It's . . . interesting."

I smiled. *Interesting* is code for horrible—always has been.

Jane mistook his meaning. "I know. Do you want to stay for dinner?" She looked at the two pots. "We have plenty. Go get Matt and come back."

"I've got some work to do tonight, and Matt's been at my parents' all afternoon. We should head home, but thank you." He winked at me and turned to leave.

A wink? I'd received winks before—construction workers, my sixty-year-old cheese monger, the old man who plays his guitar on 57th and Lexington—but none ever made my stomach flutter. Suddenly I knew two things: Nick couldn't leave, and winks were better than chocolate.

"I'll walk you out." I fled the room while Jane raved about the stew and tried to force the kids to taste it. I got the impression that Danny had clamped his mouth shut.

"Are you sure you're a chef?" Nick whispered.

"Very funny. That pot was for Jane only. There's a normal batch, too, and I made a lot, so if you want to bring your son over, that's fine."

"Why is hers different?"

"Chemotherapy messes with your taste buds. I've been trying out new flavors. Mostly I'm messing up, but I paid more attention this time. To her."

"Good for you." He stopped and stared at me.

I shrugged and looked up—and found myself standing much too close. My eyes were level with his shoulders. I stepped away. "Do you want to come back?"

"You promise the other pot is edible?"

"It's a simple grass-fed, organic beef stew, fairly dry sauce-wise, with tomatoes and red wine, but moist, packed with al dente root vegetables and braised greens, the firmer ones that hold up to a slow cook, like mustard greens and chard, a little olive oil, almond flour to thicken, sea salt and pepper to finish off, and—"

"Sold." Nick put a hand on my shoulder, silencing me. "I'll grab Matt and be back in fifteen minutes."

He walked out the door, and I ambled back to the kitchen, grinning and thinking, *Zing*—and it had nothing to do with the stew.

Nick returned as I was setting the table. Matt immediately dove to the basement to find Danny. Kate passed him on the stairs, said a well-trained and polite hello to Nick, and headed to her room. Jane had gone upstairs to rest.

"I'm still skeptical about your stew."

"Given my track record lately, I don't blame you."

"So you flubbed a few meals. That's hardly a track record."

"Ah . . . that marketing consultant I told you about? He's a chef too. Sent to save me on multiple levels, I suspect."

"Ah . . . So it's not normal to have two chefs?"

"Not in a restaurant Feast's size, and I already had a sous chef. Three chefs make one too many."

"You're afraid he'll replace you." It was a statement, not a question.

I studied Nick for a moment and knew I could trust him. "I am."

He didn't reply or offer silly assurances, but instead grabbed the broad bowls off the counter and finished setting the table.

We heard Matt call across the basement to Danny, "Let's go find Kate."

"Why?" Danny sounded confused and annoyed.

Nick glanced at me and chuckled. "Matt's got a crush on Kate. Mom says he talks about her all the time."

Mom? What? I deflated. "How old is he?"

"Six." Nick laughed and, after laying down the bowls, came back to stand near me. "Friends tell me it's normal, but I think it's way too young. At least it's not some Disney actress."

"Kate is definitely a better choice."

"We all went out for dinner a couple weeks ago, and he held Kate's hand the entire evening. I think it bothered me more than it bugged her. She sits for him a lot, so she's probably used to the adoration."

"What does your wife say?"

"I'm not married." Nick's expression flickered.

"I didn't think you were, but you said his mom says he talks about Kate."

"No, *my* mom said that. She and Dad help me out. They live about a mile away."

I blew out the breath I'd been holding and turned back to the stew and added salt. "Do you want to grab dinner tomorrow night?" I clamped my mouth shut, shocked I'd asked.

"Dinner?"

"Forget I asked. It's just . . . I don't know anyone, and Jane will be in bed at eight o'clock tomorrow night along with the kids. Dad chastised me all weekend for not getting out, and I just thought . . . It's no big deal." I stole a glance at him.

"I'd love to take you out—not being married and all."

"Excellent. There's a restaurant in this month's *Seattle Met* I'd love to try. I can be ready around seven o'clock."

"Anything else I need to know?"

"No." I rolled my eyes. "I think I handled all that badly enough."

Jane's voice appeared from nowhere. "You're back. Is Matt downstairs?" She darted her eyes between us. "Did I miss something?"

Nick smiled. "I'm taking Elizabeth to dinner tomorrow."

Chapter 15

A different nurse took Jane's initial blood draw in the Infusion Center. She didn't speak; she didn't smile. I looked around for Cecilia, instinctively knowing her presence would calm me, as coming back felt more oppressive, real, and scary than the first time. It was ironic because nothing about Cecilia's look was calming—not the dyed hair, the piercings, the tattoos, the dark makeup, or the heavy shoes. But there she was across the room, holding hands with and leaning toward an older woman, looking as if that conversation held the only words that mattered in the entire world. I smiled—she was more than calming.

I focused on her because everyone else set my teeth on edge, clamped hard and driving through the back of my neck: a middle-aged man argued with yet another nurse; the older man from the time before was scowling over his crossword puzzle, his lovely wife nowhere to be seen; one brother looked like thunder, while the one hooked to the IV graded papers and darted furtive, unsure glances at his sibling . . . And Andy? His young presence jarred me regardless of his expression.

Following our jaunt to see Dr. Chun, Cecilia returned with Jane's IV bag and a genuine smile in her eyes. "Your color is better and your count is up. What changed?"

"I'm eating." Jane's eyes still held a glow of relief.

"It's working. Food, rest, and a good perspective." Cecilia squeezed Jane's hand as she set up the IV.

The first nurse hovered nearby. She was thin, older, and held a stern expression. I noticed her derisive eyebrow lift as she took in the scene before her. Neither Jane nor Cecilia noticed.

"Did you know Lizzy runs her own restaurant in New York?"

"I didn't. That's wonderful."

The other nurse coughed slightly, and Cecilia peeked over her shoulder before adding, "All set. Let's get you started."

Jane sighed and closed her eyes, preparing for the Red Devil.

"I'll be around again soon." Cecilia straightened and removed her mask as she and the other nurse turned back toward the front desk.

"Who's Nurse Ratched?" I whispered.

"That's not funny," Jane hissed. "She's not that bad. Her name's Donna."

"Are you sure? She looks like a Nurse Ratched to me."

"Shh . . . Don't call her that. Cecilia is coming back."

Donna stayed behind the desk as Cecilia

walked toward us. She hesitated and then pulled out a chair next to me and whispered, "Do you cook for other people?"

"I don't understand."

She turned to Jane. "Are you really eating? Do you feel better? Your count was strong."

"I can't tell you what a difference keeping food down has made."

Cecilia looked around furtively. "There's a patient. You know Tyler." She nodded across the room and lowered her voice further, forcing us to lean in to catch her words. "His brother moved here to take care of him, but meals aren't going well. Tyler hardly eats and Brian can't cook. He keeps ordering out and is terribly frustrated." Cecilia looked at me, pleading.

"I'm not sure what you're after."

"Could you cook some meals for him?"

"I leave in a few days."

Nurse Ratched moved in our direction.

"I shouldn't have asked." Cecilia stood and walked away, absorbing a glare from Donna as they passed but offering her no explanation or conversation.

I turned back to Jane, who was glaring at me. "What did I do?"

"Cook him some meals, you grinch."

"You can't be serious. I'm here to visit you, not start a soup kitchen."

"But maybe you can help. Mom always shared

food—that's all we ever did. We had so many strays and firefighters at our house you'd think it *was* a soup kitchen. Why wouldn't you want to help?"

I retaliated. "As if you'd know about helping or cooking. My memory's got you filing your nails at the table."

"No one needed me. Mom's little chef."

"Stop complaining. Daddy's little girl."

"Until you started cooking. Then you were just like Mom—and he always loved her best." She paused and then sighed dramatically. "Forget it. We're not kids. Can't we put all that behind us? It's petty."

"Never coming to visit your dying mother is not petty. It's unforgivably selfish." I dipped my words low and slow. "Sorry, Jane. Having trouble getting past that one."

Jane narrowed her eyes. She looked furious, but then her eyes filled and spilled over with tears. "You have no right to judge my decisions."

I grabbed my empty water bottle and stalked from the room. But there was nowhere to go, so I wandered down the hall and stood at the window watching the rain, watching the cars, watching . . .

Jane was right—on all counts. Food was relational to Mom. That was her gift. She wasn't a good cook; she was a loving cook. I can remember every food reference in literature I read, and for a while I had a living example before me, and yet I still forgot.

Great writers and my mom never used food as an object. Instead it was a medium, a catalyst to mend hearts, to break down barriers, to build relationships. Mom's cooking fed body and soul. She used to quip, "If the food is good, there's no need to talk about the weather." That was my mantra for years—food as meal and conversation, a total experience.

I leaned my forehead against the glass and thought again about Emma and the arrowroot. Mom had highlighted it in my sophomore English class. "Jane Fairfax knew it was given with a selfish heart. Emma didn't care about Jane, she just wanted to appear benevolent."

"That girl was still stupid. She was poor and should've accepted the gift." The football team had hooted for their spokesman.

"That girl's name was Jane Fairfax, and motivation always matters." Mom's glare seared them.

I tried to remember the rest of the lesson, but couldn't. I think she assigned a paper, and the football team stopped chuckling.

Another memory flashed before my eyes. It was from that same spring; Mom was baking a cake to take to a neighbor who'd had a knee replacement.

"We don't have enough chocolate." I shut the cabinet door.

"We're making an orange cake, not chocolate."

"Chocolate is *so* much better."

"Then we're lucky it's not for you. Mrs. Conner is sad and she hurts and it's spring. The orange cake will not only show we care, it'll bring sunshine and spring to her dinner tonight. She needs that."

"It's just a cake."

"It's never just a cake, Lizzy."

I remembered the end of that lesson: I rolled my eyes—Mom loathed that—and received dish duty. But it turned out okay; the batter was excellent.

I shoved the movie reel of scenes from my head. They didn't fit in my world. Food was the object. Arrowroot was arrowroot. Cake was cake. And if it was made with artisan dark chocolate and vanilla harvested by unicorns, all the better. People would crave it, order it, and pay for it. Food wasn't a metaphor—it was the commodity—and to couch it in other terms was fatuous. The one who prepared it best won.

Jane was right on the second count as well. I was a grinch and had no right to judge her—hadn't I made the same choices? Sure, I waited a little longer—but I left and never returned, shutting Dad out as completely and effectively as Jane had shut out Mom and us.

I knocked my head against the window glass. *How did I get here?* In the beginning I *had* believed that food was an offering, a vehicle to joy, celebration, communion. I came alive. The sum always swelled to greater than the parts. When had they equalized? When had they diminished?

I took a deep breath and suspected that the magic of cooking died long before I recognized its absence—perhaps the day Mom died. And I had lived and worked, and was working now, on nothing more than ambition and technique. *Enough.*

I headed back to the Infusion Center. In my periphery I saw Jane turn toward me. I didn't look; I marched straight to the brothers.

"I'm Elizabeth. My sister, Jane, is over there."

The brother in the straight-back chair shifted his eyes away, back, and said nothing.

The one hooked up to the Adriamycin laid *The Sun Also Rises* across his chest and smiled. "I know Jane." He nodded her direction before turning back to me. "I'm Tyler." He narrowed his eyes at his silent brother. "This is Brian."

I pulled over a chair and sat. "Cecilia mentioned that you're having trouble eating."

Brian stiffened and glared toward the desk. I followed his sight line and saw Cecilia catch his look. She dashed questioning eyes to me and I flinched, certain I'd betrayed her.

I rushed on. "It was just a comment. Jane's having trouble, too, and I'm a chef, a bored chef. Can I cook you some meals?"

"Thanks, but it'd be a waste of time." Brian returned to his magazine.

"Jane said the same thing, but she's eaten well this week. She's kept food down." I addressed Tyler, who sat silent, but by his tense posture I knew he was listening. He looked like he was about to fly off the seat. "I could try . . . I'm at a loss without much to do."

"It wouldn't wor—" Brian droned out.

"How much do you charge?" Tyler cut across him.

Brian looked up. His startled expression matched my own.

"Cost of groceries?"

"You've got time and labor." Tyler started scratching notes on the edge of his book.

"How about ten dollars per meal plus cost of groceries?"

"Times two of us. So groceries plus twenty bucks to feed us both per meal?" He raised an eyebrow.

"Sure."

"That'll work for now. We'll take ten each."

"Twenty meals?" I squeaked. "What if you don't like them?"

"I'm willing to take that risk."

It sounded more like a challenge than a risk—and I was up for a challenge. Maybe it was just what I needed. "Twenty it is. I can deliver them Thursday."

"We've got an appointment at ten. We'll meet in the parking lot." He tore a corner off a page. "Here's my cell. Call me and we can meet."

"Okay." I looked down at the scrap. *I can do this.* I shook the water bottle. It was still empty. "Excuse me. I'll see you both on Thursday."

"Why are you doing this?"

I jumped at Brian's harsh whisper behind me.

I glanced back but didn't stop until I'd reached the lobby's water fountain, certain he was trying to intimidate me. "It's simple. I found some things Jane can stomach, and maybe Tyler can benefit too."

"He eats nothing I bring in. Any restaurant. What makes you different?" Brian tapped the wall with his fist.

I capped the bottle and moved to the other side of him. "Are you the only one helping him?"

"His girlfriend dumped him when he got diagnosed last year. Our mom hasn't come once. Yeah, I'm it . . . and it sucks."

I was nodding my head in commiseration and sympathy until his last add. I pulled up short. Did it "suck" because no one else shared the load? Or did he feel imposed on? I understood both feelings, but recoiled from the second. It was a petty and ugly side of me—not one I wanted to acknowledge to myself, much less admit to others.

Brian watched me. I knew he expected agreement, but I only managed Jane's doe-in-the-headlights look.

"I don't need more on my plate, so I want to make sure you're not messing with us."

"Why would I do that?"

He studied me a moment. "People do it all the time. Everything requires payback. But Tyler, he's excited." Brian looked me up and down almost dismissively. "The kid thinks you can help."

"I'll do my best."

He narrowed his eyes as if to say *We'll see* and walked away.

I walked back to Jane, uncomfortable with Brian's comments, cynicism, and anger. I was also saddened that some of it registered with me.

"That was nice of you." Jane's tone bubbled with smugness.

"It had nothing to do with you."

"Of course not."

I took the book from her lap and searched for her bookmark.

"You're going to read?"

"If it'll keep you from talking to me." I struggled to keep a smile from my face, but I had to admit that I felt good. I was doing with food what I was taught to do, and somehow felt that could make everything right.

Hope danced in my periphery—as did Jane. She was working equally hard not to smile—and looking far too pleased with herself.

" 'How long it is, how terribly long since you were here! And how tired you must be after your journey! You must go to bed early, my dear—and I recommend a little gruel to you before you go—you and I will have a nice basin of gruel together. My dear Emma, suppose we all have a little gruel.' "

"Think I could make you and Tyler gruel?" I chortled.

"What is it anyway?"

"Think thin oatmeal. Probably better than the slop I've been force-feeding your kids lately."

"Do they like it? It sounds good."

I smiled and turned back to the page. *Only Jane.*

"Excuse me." Andy's mother, Courtney, tapped my shoulder. "Can you watch Andy for a moment? I need to call my daughter."

"Mom, where am I going to go?" the teenager murmured.

"I'll feel better."

Andy opened his mouth, but I cut him off. "Sure." I handed Jane the book and scooted my chair over before he could protest. We sat in awkward silence for a moment.

"Am I doing this right?"

"I'm not sure. Mom blinks less."

I laughed out loud and then pressed my lips together. Laughter might be forbidden in our dystopian library.

I noticed a deck of playing cards and a water

bottle on his side table. "Do you want to play cards?"

"Do you know gin rummy?"

"I do."

I shuffled the cards and dealt. I held three of a kind and two of another, the beginnings of a winning hand. About ten cards later, Andy slapped down a card—facedown.

"How'd you do that so fast?"

He laid out his hand and grinned as only a teenager can.

"You had what I needed!"

"I know."

"You did not," I countered.

"You discarded the four of hearts but not the five; you picked up the ten of spades but let the eight go by; you—"

"You count cards?"

"I don't think paying attention classifies as 'counting cards.' " He made quote marks with his fingers.

"You're right, and I never pay attention. It's always a surprise when I win or lose."

"You gotta respect your opponent more. I learned that from my brother. He crushes me in Halo every time."

"I'll remember that, young Jedi. Wanna play again?"

We played three more—very quick—games before his mom returned. I lost them all.

Courtney sat as I shuffled the cards and replaced them on the table. She opened her mouth to start a conversation. Shut it, looked around, and tried again. "Were you reading *Emma*?"

I smiled. "We were. Jane likes it, but her head aches when she reads. I hope we weren't too loud."

"Not at all. I haven't read it since college." She nudged her son. "Does him good to hear it too. I can't remember the last book he read."

"Mom."

"Well?"

"Harry Potter."

"You were ten!"

"I've been busy." He said it lightly as he flicked the IV line. Courtney blanched. "Mom, it was a joke."

"I know." She squeezed her eyes shut and pressed her hand against his leg. All small talk ended.

I quietly scooted my seat back to Jane, unsure if I'd caused the moment, contributed to it, or simply witnessed it. Nothing was light in our library; perhaps that's what made it dystopian—everything turned in a flash to its elemental base, and sometimes it skewed to a dark, frightening edge.

Jane tapped my arm and nodded toward her own IV line. We watched the last drop of red travel to her chest. I put away the book and we waited for

Cecilia, who was chatting with Andy. Courtney looked distracted, answering hesitantly and a beat late.

Cecilia came over to flush and unhook Jane.

"I'm cooking some meals for Tyler," I whispered.

"That's wonderful." Her eyes lit up. She held up her finger, instructing me to wait as she closed Jane's line. She then stood and removed her mask. "I can't talk with that on." She grinned for a moment as if the smile had been waiting for release.

"What are you cooking?"

"No idea yet, but Tyler wants twenty meals."

"Hmm . . . What'd Brian say?"

"Not much. Tyler took the lead, but Brian seems annoyed that I might actually help." I shrugged. I didn't want to say more.

Cecilia narrowed her eyes, watching me, as if I were telepathically relaying the conversation by the water fountain.

"It's hard for family members. Few realize that. They can't fix the problem or provide the one thing their loved one needs."

I knew that feeling and moved the conversation around it. "I'd better add tinfoil, Pyrex, and storage containers to my shopping list. I need—"

"Can I help? Tomorrow's my day off."

My head sprang up. "Seriously? Would you?"

My own enthusiasm surprised me. I shrugged to downplay it. "I could use the help."

Cecilia beamed, checked herself, and quietly whispered, "Text me what time and I'll see you tomorrow."

Chapter 16

On the drive home Jane sat silent. While waiting at a red light, I turned to watch her. She was a million miles away.

"Do you mind that I invited Cecilia?"

"Not at all. She's really nice."

"She is . . . Have you ever met someone and wanted to know her? Or is that odd?"

"It's not odd. That's how you make friends."

"Hmm . . . So that's how you do it," I quipped and looked back to the road, but Jane didn't laugh or comment. Quiet filled the car.

"You okay?"

"Peter comes home tomorrow." Her tone was flat.

"And?"

She sighed.

"I think this is really hard on him," I said.

"Hard on him? Are you kidding me?"

"Yeah, I mean no." I bit my lip, considering. "I mean he loves you and he can't fix you. He didn't protect you, couldn't protect you. Doesn't want to touch you for fear of hurting you but wants to make sure you're warm and close. He wants to provide for you, but the one thing you need is the one thing he can't give. It really is just like Cecilia said."

I glanced at her. Jane's jaw dropped.

"You weren't there. Dad was the same way. If you look at Peter, really look at him, you'll see it."

From the corner of my eye I could see her slowly shaking her head.

"Don't believe me, but it's true." Feast, Tyler and his meals, cooking . . . too much pressed on me to add Jane and our endless antagonisms to the list. "Just talk to him. Learn his perspective." Cecilia's comments about perspective still crashed through my brain.

"So how'd you get to be so smart about men?" she whispered.

I searched for sarcasm and found none. "I'm not. I guess I know men in this particular situation." I paused, debating how much to tell Jane. We needed new facts, new topics between us. So I dove in. "My most meaningful relationship of late is with my produce vendor—a stubborn sixty-year-old man with lettuces that melt in your mouth and language like a sailor, who calls his wife Sugar Plum and me Little Miss Hard-to-Please. But I adore him."

I turned the car down Jane's street. "And then there's Paul, and I don't know what we are. He owns Feast and I know he cares about me, but he calculates every move, and in the years I've known him he's gone through two wives. I'd rather not be number four even if he does decide to make a more overt play. And tonight? I have my first real date in over a year, and I had to ask him out. And since this is vacation, it hardly counts. How pathetic is that?"

Jane snorted. "You are Little Miss Hard-to-Please. I like that."

"That's your takeaway from all that? Why do I even talk to you?" But I was laughing as well.

"I'm kidding." Jane reached for my arm and tapped it. "I'm laughing with you, not at you. You asked Nick out?"

"Yes, and I did it horribly." I looked over to find her grinning. "It's not like that. Dad lectured me about getting out and getting fresh air, something about creative juices and all that, and Nick's the only guy around, so I asked him."

"Doesn't hurt that he's super cute."

"He is, isn't he? His eyes are so green, and I like his hair. It's got that cowlick sticking up in the front. I keep wanting to smush it down."

"Okay, part of me feels seventeen and the other part says this is weird. He's a friend of ours."

"It's okay to say another man is cute, Jane."

"Okay. He is sooo cute."

"I know."

We giggled the last two blocks home, forgetting

the years, conflict, and cancer between us. Jane, still a little jacked up on steroids, decided to clean the bathrooms, and I planted myself in her kitchen to develop dishes for Tyler. I'd almost finished organizing a week's worth of meals for him and for Jane when her soft tone interrupted me.

"Do you have any stew left?"

"I didn't hear you come in." I glanced at her. "Are you okay?"

"My head is killing me. I may have overdone it with the baseboards."

"Sit here." I pulled out a chair at the kitchen table and went to the refrigerator. "This'll take a minute to warm up. Would you like some apple slices?"

"That sounds good." Jane held her head.

I cut some apple slices, noting that the small breaks didn't keep reality at bay for long.

"Are you sure you don't want me to stay and help with the kids?" I stood over Jane's bed.

"You've already fed them and managed homework. There's nothing left. And I want to tuck them in. Go have fun."

"I really can stay."

"Are you nervous?" She scooted up against the headboard and laughed as I blushed and backed out of her room. "You are!" she called after me. "Are you changing again?"

"You Seattleites wear jeans and Hunter boots. I

can't do that." I looked down at my black dress. "But this is too much."

"Get those fancy black boots of yours and put them over jeans. You'll look great."

"The Manolos or the Pradas?"

"How should I know? The black ones."

"Exactly. And which jeans? The leggings? Or the boot-leg Joe's and leave them down?"

"Jeans and boots," she called. "You can't go wrong."

I grabbed a pair of skinny jeans, the Pradas, and a black sweater and quickly changed. I paced back to Jane.

"See? You look good." She nodded. "Where'd all this come from anyway?" She twirled her finger at me.

"All what?"

"We grew up in Oregon. I can't tell you leggings from jeggings or Prada from Converse— Okay, I can guess that one, but because I know Converse, not Prada."

"I don't know. I feel comfortable in specifics. I . . ."

"That sounds more like me. Mom always said you were the creative one, and look at your job— you are."

"There's a lot of technique and precision in cooking . . ." There was a hint there—an uncomfortable truth hiding just beyond reach. I flicked it further. "Maybe it's a New York thing."

I swung my hair over my shoulder. "Do I look satisfactory?"

"You look great." Jane offered a small smile. "I love your hair. It's so full and thick. It's darkened too. I like that."

"It's not still blond?" I lifted the ends to look at it. I'd always loved the color; it was the waves I hated. In fact, I once paid hundreds of dollars for thermal straightening and ended up looking like someone had stapled plywood boards to the sides of my face. So now I just tamed the waves as best as I could and remained perpetually disappointed. But the color . . .

"Dark blond. It's better deeper, shows off some highlights and doesn't make you look so bland." Jane touched her hair. "I'm bland, and now it's thin and . . ." She lifted a section above her ear, revealing a bald spot the size of a baseball.

"Oh."

"Will you help me shave it?"

"Now?"

"Tomorrow." She trailed two fingers through it, and the motion's light tug pulled a surprising amount away. "It's done."

"Tomorrow," I agreed, perching myself on the bed. "I'm sorry about dinner tonight."

"It's no big deal."

"It is. You need to eat. What'd I do wrong?"

"Nothing. My stomach didn't feel right. Stop stressing about it. You had a lot to do."

I realized she was right, but not about having too much to manage. I had let minutia steal my focus: I was texting Suzanne, checking on Tabitha, planning Tyler's meals, managing Paul, daydreaming about my date, joking with the kids . . . I didn't put any thought or preparation into dinner, but had whipped up a standard favorite and assumed it would fly.

Jane caught my expression. "Please don't beat yourself up over— There's the doorbell."

I stood up and smoothed my sweater. "Don't wait up," I teased.

"You have to wake me. I want to hear all the details."

"It's dinner, Jane, not prom."

"It's a first date. I haven't had one of those in eighteen years. Please?"

"I'm not even sure it's that, but sure, I'll wake you."

I bounced down the stairs and opened the door.

"Wow." Nick's face lit up.

I beamed. "Can you do that again?" I shut the door and pulled it right back open.

"Wow." He laughed.

"Yeah, that still felt good."

I shut the door behind me and led Nick off the porch. His car was an older-model Audi station wagon. It fit him—sporty, nice, and clean, quintessentially Mr. Mom.

"Is it okay if we go to La Spiga?" I asked.

"Definitely. It's one of my favorite places."

I circled his car to the passenger side. "I read an article that touted their craft cocktails and food pairings. I haven't done any of that yet at Feast."

I stepped back as I realized Nick had followed me around the car and was reaching to open the door.

"You'll love it."

I smiled and settled in to the seat. He stood guard until I was fully situated. Then he shut the door. *Zing.*

La Spiga was large and open and exciting. It was housed in what looked like a converted warehouse, with high ceilings, dark wood walls, high-backed booths, and a bar to die for. The lighting fixtures were 1930s industrial with vintage bulbs that showed the filaments and threw off that warm light that makes everyone look better. But the lighting was the only similarity I could find to Feast.

Feast was small, employing the stark white walls and tables to give it some sense of space. La Spiga was huge, playing on mixtures of textures and woods to create warmth. And where I'd put an antique mirror behind the bar, La Spiga had installed clear glass. You could see beyond the bar, beyond the displayed bottles. It gave the sense that if you looked hard enough, long enough, you could see through each bottle into the kitchen and into the magic beyond.

"Are you taking a picture?" Nick whispered.

"I know it's tacky, but this is too cool."

"I'm glad you like it." Nick pointed to the bar. "Do you want to get a table or sit up here and enjoy this?"

"Can we sit here?"

"Definitely." He held out a stool for me. "I think it's the best place."

"What do you recommend?"

Nick shrugged. "To be honest, I don't get out much."

I was about to question him, but the bartender came over to take our orders.

"What's your favorite?" Nick asked him.

"I think my lemon gin infusion is just right. I use it in a French 75 with a hint of basil. Or I've got another favorite, a twist on a Manhattan with rye that's not too sweet. I love that one."

"Oh . . ."

Nick turned to me. "Do you want to try one of each? You can taste both and pick the one you like best."

"You sure?"

"It's your night out."

I nodded.

The bartender smiled and walked away.

"What if you don't like the other one?"

"Of course I will, and they were his favorites. When someone shares like that with you, you go along."

The drinks soon arrived, and after a sip of each I started to break them down. "Taste this. The basil is fantastic, and do you taste the lemon? He's right; he didn't over-infuse. And his simple syrup brings out the fresh note of the basil. You often need a touch of sugar to do that." I reached for the other drink. "He used good cherries; they're not too sweet. Do you think he grows his own? They cut the bite, but . . . Taste this."

Nick smiled. "Do you know your face lights up when you talk about food—or drinks?"

"It does?"

"It does. You lit up like that talking about the apples the other day and then about your stew. It's beautiful."

I smiled and ducked my head. I was unused to compliments, and Nick's perspective—there was no artifice or protection. He listened to people's opinions, gave of his own apples, took Jane's clients fully intending to give them back, and now sat looking at me like I was the most beautiful and enchanting woman he knew.

Over starters of Affettati Misti, a cured meat platter, and the Crostini del Poggio Rosso, crostini topped with beef tenderloin and truffle pâte, I found myself interested in Nick beyond just a means to escape another evening flipping channels on Jane's couch.

"Does Matt live with you full time?" I wondered

about his ex-wife, but wasn't sure how to ask.

"He does. He's never even met his mom."

"Never met her? Doesn't that usually work the other way?"

"We weren't married. We didn't even date." Nick paused and took a deep breath. "We met in a bar and had one night. We didn't even exchange numbers." He looked over to catch my expression. I revealed none. "About a month later, she tracked me down through some friends and demanded I pay for her . . ." His voice trailed off.

"Abortion?" I asked gently.

"I told her I had to think about it. I didn't even know if the kid was mine. She assured me it was, but . . ."

"You didn't give her the money."

"I called my mom."

I blinked. That was not the answer I expected.

"Isn't that what you do when you screw up?"

I shrugged.

"I expected the riot act, wanted it. Then I would have gotten what I deserved—or the beginnings of it—but she didn't yell. She was silent for the longest time, and then she said, 'Do whatever you must to keep that baby. There's no other option.' And I knew she was right. I wanted to run, bury my head in the sand, or do anything else to make it go away. But she was right."

Nick rubbed his chin. It was free of the five o'clock shadow I'd noted every other time we'd met. He'd shaved for our date—that made me smile inside.

"So I called Rebecca and I begged. She was furious, said it was her body and I couldn't control her, but I kept begging. She actually took a paternity test to get me off her back. I love the irony of that." He paused. "Did you know they stick this huge needle into the uterus to do that?"

I cringed.

"Too much information. Sorry." He took a bite of crostini. "Anyway, I was the dad so I kept begging. Time ticked away and she didn't get an abortion. I moved into a cheaper apartment, got another job, helped her with the medical bills, and a few months later she handed me Matt."

"You don't know where she is?"

"Sorta. She showed up a couple years ago. She'd lost her job to downsizing and came to check us out. I got the impression she wanted to stay with us, but my agency was shutting down, Matt had the flu, and I was pretty stressed. I wasn't all that nice to her, and she didn't even stay to see Matt. That was the last I heard, so I expect she's still in San Francisco. I have no desire to keep in touch."

We sat silent for a moment.

"That was a lot, wasn't it?" Nick chuckled lightly.

"More than I expected."

He ran his hand over his eyes and took a deep

breath. "I've got to stop doing that." He opened his eyes. "I can't tell you how many first dates I've ruined with that story."

"I'll be gone soon; you're okay with me. But why tell it if it's uncomfortable?"

He sat still, considering. "That's why. I don't want to forget what I did and the cost. I love Matt, don't get me wrong, and I wouldn't change a hair on his head or a second of his life. He's the greatest blessing ever given me, but just because he's a blessing doesn't mean I didn't screw up."

"You might want to let yourself off that hook. Seems you did good to me."

"Maybe." He shook his head. "How's Jane doing?"

I suppressed a smile because I would have changed the subject too. "Okay, I think. She ate some this past week. I didn't screw up every meal. And her numbers were up today. She was so relieved she almost cried. I didn't realize how much that pressed on her until she walked out of the oncologist's office. When our mom was sick, she never shared that kinda stuff. I'm beginning to think I missed a lot back then."

"Your mom had cancer?"

"She died in the spring of my senior year in high school."

"I didn't know. This must be horrible for Jane."

I nodded and took a sip of my drink. The moment should have been spent feeling sorry for

Jane, but I was struggling. I was jealous that Nick thought of Jane first; I didn't want to share that link to our mother. I felt again like that seventeen-year-old who kept calling, wanting to talk, wanting to reach out, wanting an older sister and a guide. The return call never came.

"I'm so sorry," Nick whispered across my thoughts.

I shook my head. "It's okay. I got lost there a moment, didn't I?" I popped a piece of salami into my mouth to end the moment and collect myself.

Nick parked his car in Jane's driveway.

"Thanks for taking me out tonight. I'm actually embarrassed I asked you. I hope I didn't put you on the spot."

"Not at all. As I said, I enjoyed it." Nick settled back in to the seat. "I don't date much because I don't want to introduce Matt to women who aren't going to be in his life. But he knows you through Jane's family, so it was an easy evening out with no worries or expectations." Nick chuckled. "For me or for him."

I nodded. "Well, thank you." I got out of the car, knowing I should feel pleased but trending toward disappointed instead.

Chapter 17

The next morning Jane and I sat at the counter arranging the day and forming a schedule to best utilize her ovens and burners. As I cut an apple, my cell phone beeped with a text: Want to take a walk?

Jane looked up. "You're blushing. Is it Paul?"

"I am absolutely not blushing."

"Well?"

"Nick."

She laughed, small and careful. "Nick? You just went out last night."

"He was easy to talk to. I had fun." I looked at her smug expression. "I'm just glad he did too. He wants to take a walk." I focused on my phone and texted back: Going to the grocery store. Do you want to come?

Yes. I'll drive if you want.

See you in ten?

I'll be there.

I'll be there. I smiled. *I'll be there*—when you call, when you're hurt, when you're sick, when you're lonely, when life is overwhelming, when you're scared. *I'll be there.* What an amazing thought. I chuckled—he'd only offered to drive to the grocery store.

"What's funny?"

"My imagination." I didn't elaborate. "He's coming in ten minutes to take me to the grocery store, so I've got to finish. What have we not considered? Anything you want to add?" I crossed the kitchen, pulled a soft-boiled egg out of the water, and put it in front of her with a spoon and the apple slices.

"No. I'll put all your Pyrex in the dishwasher while you're gone."

"Thanks." I went to the hall to grab a coat.

Jane called after me. "He must like you. I can't drag Peter to a grocery store."

"Nick's a single dad. Doubt he has the luxury of avoiding it."

"I'm sure that's it."

A blush warmed my cheeks. The last boy I had felt giddy over was Spencer O'Neil in the fifth grade. Nick had made his intentions, or lack thereof, crystal clear. We were friends. He was hardly worth a blush.

Nevertheless he arrived right on time, and I still dashed for the door like a fifth grader. Jane trailed me into the hallway.

I swung around. "What are you doing?"

"I want to see Nick."

I raised an eyebrow as I yanked open the door. "Hi, come on in." I turned back to Jane, slightly amused and thoroughly annoyed. "Do you need something, Jane?"

She ignored me. "First my consulting business,

then dinner with my sister, and now the grocery store. Are you coming to cook with us this afternoon too?"

I caught the edge in Jane's voice and glanced at Nick. If he'd caught any undertones, he was ignoring them.

"Holding down the fort for a good friend, enjoyed dinner with a new friend, and I'm out of milk. But I don't have time to cook today, so no, I won't be joining you."

Jane's expression clouded. "Sorry. That was rude."

"Bye, Jane." I grabbed my bag.

"I'm going to eat." She padded back to the kitchen.

I turned and gently pushed Nick out the door. He called behind his shoulder, "Bye, Jane." As we walked to his car, he touched my arm. "Is she okay?"

"She coming down off tons of steroids and is full of chemo drugs, so I doubt it. I suspect she can't decide if you're the enemy, competition, a friend, or my new boyfriend."

"That was fast."

"What?" I stopped. "Don't flatter yourself. I was talking about Jane."

"Because you couldn't possibly like me, right, New York?"

"Not in a million years." I laughed.

"I'll remember that."

His mood was light and playful, and the banter lasted a few moments before we veered off into Jane's chemotherapy treatment. I found myself telling him more than I usually share—not just about what happens in the Infusion Center, but how I felt about it. I described reading to Jane, losing at cards to Andy, talking to Tyler, Brian's attitude, offering to cook . . . everything.

As I recounted it, I felt myself shift. Andy and Tyler seemed to matter more to me than our time spent together warranted, and I recognized a bubbly anticipation welling up inside me, the same feeling I'd had when I opened the door for Nick the night before, the same feeling that carried me through opening Feast.

"That's an amazing thing you're doing for him—and what an idea for a business. Cooking meals for people in difficult circumstances, like illness, chemo, or injuries."

"It's a favor, not a business."

"For you. But someone should do this. This town has the medical community to support it, and that's if you concentrated on cancer patients alone. If you expanded—"

My tingling anticipation cooled as my heart launched into my throat. "Hey, it's mine. Besides, it may not work."

"It will because it's a way to meet people's needs, reach them through food—and not just anyone, but people who are vulnerable. It's a gift and it's all there—an unmet need, an untapped market in an affluent town."

I could feel him crunching numbers and devising marketing plans beside me as I considered his word *gift*. The idea suddenly felt different, new and terrifyingly close—like my nerves were on fire.

"You okay? You've gone all still."

"I'm fine." I sat there feeling a foreign wonder, hoping it would stay. "I can do this. I can cook something he'll eat."

Nick glanced over. "I'm sure you can." He pulled in to the parking lot. "Do you want to give me some of your list or wander together?"

"Let's wander together, if you have the time?"

"Definitely."

We started in produce. It's my favorite section, but it can be the hardest too—because vegetables carry a whole variety of tastes, aftertastes, acids, sugars, textures . . . Nothing can make you gag faster than a vegetable turned sour in your mouth or your stomach.

But I needed tons of them because nothing delivers vitamins, minerals, fibers, and nutrients in such digestible ways. Beets, radishes, carrots, kale, and spinach had worked for Jane. I wanted to expand my list to broccoli, red and green cabbages, and other dark greens. I even played with the idea of baby roasted brussels sprouts— strong taste, even sometimes bitter, but if prepared right, that very element could appeal to Jane and Tyler. Olive oiled, salted, peppered, and broiled—it might remind them of popcorn with a sharp tang and a nutritional wallop on the side.

I also wanted to welcome Peter home with a cake. The family needed a celebration. I bought coconut and almond flour and selected a fresh coconut, thinking the kids could help shred it. And finally a brick of dark artisan chocolate—one I could shave myself. It was one of my secret pleasures and one my pâtissier never let me indulge.

An hour and a half later, we found ourselves in the checkout line. My mind raced with the logistics of getting everything done and of how to include Kate, Danny, and even Cecilia.

"Elizabeth?"

"Hmm . . . sorry. My head's already in the kitchen."

"I can understand that. But . . . can I take you out again?"

"I'd like that."

"I'm busy with a school function for Matt tomorrow night. What about Friday?"

"Peter'll be home. They could use the time alone."

"Good. Seven p.m.—again."

Chapter 18

Jane's kitchen faced west, so it felt cool, with no direct light yet, and its huge glass doors opened onto a patio, making it feel open and expansive. I unpacked the groceries, sorted them, emptied the dishwasher, and turned the ovens to four hundred. I was ready.

"This is beautiful." Cecilia looked around. "My apartment's kitchen is a bloated hallway, but I don't cook so it doesn't bug me."

"You'll cook today."

"Where's Jane?"

"She went up for a nap right before you arrived."

"Good for her. What are we making?"

"I thought we'd repeat what worked for Jane this past week. Some of the flavors are altered, so I think we'd better put Brian's portions in separate containers before we add the final seasonings."

"You're cooking for Brian too?"

"Tyler asked for meals for both of them."

"Good." Cecilia looked down at the recipe in front of her and started cracking eggs. "It's nice he's working remotely to be with him, but—"

"He's a jerk, Cecilia."

She threw me a startled glance. "I think it's more than that. I think Brian hurts in deeper ways than Tyler."

"Well, Tyler looks nervous around him. Brian kept casting him glances while we were talking, and he's so angry. Do you think you could talk to him?"

"About what?"

"The first time I came with Jane, you said something about perspective, and it helped. She stopped fighting with you. And it bounced around my mind for days. Maybe that's what Brian needs—a change in perspective. He can't be helping Tyler always scowling like that."

"I just shared my experience. And maybe he doesn't scowl when it's just the two of them."

"I bet he does. You should talk to him."

"I can try . . ." She whisked the eggs. "He may not hear me. He has this idea that Tyler's his burden rather than a blessing, that his cancer is an aberration in their lives rather than a part of them, and that it's all somehow directed at him . . ."

I didn't reply because she wasn't talking to me. She was sorting Brian, his motivations and his needs—very much the way I dissected recipes. I walked over to the island where I'd splayed Jane's cookbooks and printouts from the Internet.

Cecilia motioned to the recipe. "What am I making anyway?"

"It's basically a quiche without the crust. I got the idea from *The Pickwick Papers*. Dickens loved his breakfasts; he put a good one in almost every book. I figured he wasn't too beyond Austen to be relevant."

"Austen?"

"Jane Austen. Jane the sister, not the author, likes things that feel comfortable and safe. Right now she'd live in Regency England if you'd deliver the Red Devil there. So I've drawn my food inspirations from that cuisine, as mentioned in the books. She downed a bowl of gruel yesterday afternoon like it was her heart's greatest desire."

"That's horrible."

"It's just thin, almost pureed oatmeal. I added some spices and flavors to counteract the metal taste in her mouth and some ground almonds to up its nutritional content, and she ate every bite."

"Wow. I never thought about food like that, but it makes sense. You aren't a different person when you read versus when you eat or do anything else—everything in us does intersect, I guess . . ." Cecilia's voice drifted away as she thought, and a blush suffused her face. "Put it that way, I see why I eat terribly. I love American teenage food, and it fits with my soft spot for eighties teen movies. You know, *Breakfast Club*, *Sixteen Candles*, *Pretty in Pink* . . . I even dress like that when I feel sad. Austen's much more intellectual."

"That's Jane. If it makes you feel better, I read

only cookbooks, and they really shouldn't count as real books." I thought for a moment. "But I never forget a food reference."

"Never?"

I shrugged. "It's a gift."

"*Sixteen Candles*?"

"The cake, of course. Oh, but there's that quiche dinner too. See? *Sixteen Candles* and Dickens—all about breakfast."

"*Under the Tuscan Sun*?"

"Never read it, but I'm assuming a ton of Italian?"

"That was obvious." Cecilia smiled. "What's your favorite food reference?"

"I've got two. I think the best opening line in literature is Peter Mayle's *A Year in Provence*. 'The year began with lunch.' All books and all years should begin that way."

"And the other?"

" 'Coldtonguecoldhamcoldbeefpickledgherkins saladfrenchrollscressandwhichespottedmeatginger beerlemonadesodawater—' "

"That's too much!" She laughed.

"That's exactly what Mole said. But Rat said, 'It's only what I always take on these little excursions, and the other animals are always telling me that I'm a mean beast and cut it VERY fine!' " I grinned. "I love that line."

"What's that even from?"

"*The Wind in the Willows*. It's the best picnic ever." I pulled the meats from the refrigerator.

"I like a good picnic." Cecilia checked the recipe in front of her and added the cheese and dill. "So what else are we making?"

"I altered a wonderful chicken curry recipe that came to England in the early 1800s—it's now got more vegetables and should freeze beautifully. Right here." I pointed to a recipe. "And let's add broccoli. Great nutrients and carbs."

I moved down the island, pointing to another recipe. "These are smoothie recipes for snacks. I've got melons and other fruits to soften the greens in them. We'll blend them thick and vacuum-seal them. Then Tyler can add water, remix, and they'll be perfect."

"How many different things are we making?"

"About twelve."

Cecilia giggled. "I haven't made twelve meals in the last year."

"We'll be fine. I make more than that in ten minutes."

"If you say so . . . You're the chef."

I grinned again. It felt right—I was the chef.

We were whipping more eggs for a second breakfast dish when Jane joined us. "Are you two cooking up a storm?"

"We're cooking up something." I reached over to stay Cecilia's hand. "I think all the air's gone back out."

She shrugged. "I told you I don't know what I'm doing."

"No biggie." I set her to chopping a slaw while I finished the eggs.

Jane sat at the island, and we worked quietly and comfortably for the next few hours, sharing tidbits of our lives and snatches of food.

Near four o'clock the kids arrived home and chatted with Jane in the basement while Cecilia and I cleaned the kitchen and labeled the last dishes for the day. Stacks of sealed food containers, green for vegetables, red for main courses, and blue for starched sides, plus a box full of sealed pouches of smoothies, filled Jane's refrigerator, freezers, and a couple ice-filled coolers.

"I can't believe we did it." Cecilia labeled the last container.

"I've only got a little left to do tomorrow; then I'll deliver around eleven. Are they still there then?"

"Usually. Tyler sees his doctor and then comes up to chat with me so I can help him interpret it. It's remarkable how much patients don't hear or even say to their doctors." Cecilia shrugged. "Then I go to his doctor and tell him what's really going on with Tyler."

"Isn't that violating doctor-patient confidentiality?"

"Not at all. Nine times out of ten, that's how the doctors learn the soft stuff." At my blank look, she continued. "You know . . . if a patient is depressed, sad, uncomfortable, anxious . . . Like all this."

"This?"

"Isn't that what you did here? You looked at Tyler and Jane's totality. You're creating more than a meal; you're creating sustenance and meeting needs that are way beyond nutritional."

I dropped onto the kitchen school. "You think?"

Cecilia's face lit up into a bright smile. It seemed incongruent with her harsh hair and coal-black eyeliner—but it also looked natural and radiant and perfectly Cecilia. "You don't see it, do you?"

"See what?"

"The blessing you are." She stepped around the island and stood in front of me for a heartbeat, smiling. Then she pulled me into a big hug, squeezing me tight. It was my first real hug in years—not like Dad's pushing and pulling until your molars loosen and not like Jane's perfunctory squeeze with an added obligatory back pat, but like my mom's—who was the greatest, most thorough hugger in the world.

"Thanks for letting me in on this. You're wonderful." She pulled back after a moment. "Now I am going to leave all this deep and meaningful work for something more frivolous . . . I'm going boot shopping."

"You are? I love boot shopping."

"You wanna come?" She looked down at my

outfit. "We may have a different style, but I bet you know your way around a store."

"That I do." I laughed. "What type of boots are you looking for?"

"Brown."

I smiled. Jane would've said the same thing. Perhaps all Seattle would. "You know, as fun as that sounds, Peter comes home tonight. I want to help the kids with their homework, then bake a cake for him."

"That's so nice. See? Blessing." She lilted the last word as she walked toward the hallway and raised her hand in a half wave. "See you next Tuesday."

I lifted my hand to reply and stopped cold. *I'll be gone by then.*

Chapter 19

Peter's homecoming did not go as anticipated.

The kids and I had made something special—cake and memories. Danny burst with energy as we grated coconut and chocolate, and Kate learned how to sift and fold and test the cakes with determination and fascination. We sang and danced around the kitchen.

Peter's flight landed on time, but he texted that he had a meeting with a colleague in the Admirals Club. The time grew late and Jane grew tense. He didn't answer her text, and she eventually sent the kids to bed. After she tucked them in, she joined me in the kitchen.

"Where is he?" she asked.

"He said he was meeting with his coworker in the Admirals Club. Just text him again."

"Forget it." She bit her lip. "Maybe he doesn't want to come home . . . Maybe he's having an affair."

"You can't be serious."

"Maybe I am." She sat at the counter and pressed her fingers to her lips.

I stood in front of her, unable to move.

Her fingers trembled. "You don't understand. This is so hard. Maybe it's too much. Maybe he's given in."

"He has not given in. Peter adores you, and he said he was at the airport. Who makes that up?"

She shrugged in protest.

I opened my mouth to tell her she was ridiculous, but I caught her expression and stopped.

"I'm going to bed." She hurried off the stool as if going to bed would make it all go away.

"You're not waiting up? He'll miss seeing you, just like you miss him." I stumbled forward to cut her off.

"It's late." Jane looked at the clock above the door. "And I'm tired. I'm too tired."

She pulled the sleeves of her sweater over her

hands and tucked her arms across her body. There was no way she could have looked smaller or more vulnerable. She turned and shuffled out of the room.

The cake and I faced each other—the last two elements of a discarded celebration. I covered it, shoved it into a corner, and started to wipe down the counters.

An hour and two cups of chamomile tea later, Peter walked in the back door. "What are you doing up? Is Jane still awake?" His tone was soft and concerned.

I sighed, knowing I'd been right. Jane wrong. I set my cup down. "She got too tired about ten thirty."

"I knew the meeting was going too long . . . Ben is headed to Malaysia, and we needed to cover some stuff." He laid down his bag and shut the door.

"She knew that, but she was still upset."

"But I often do that to wrap up business. That way, when I'm home, I'm home." Peter narrowed his eyes fractionally. "What's wrong? Why would that upset her?"

"Because she's not herself right now and she feels vulnerable." I put my cup in the dishwasher. "The kids baked you a cake. Do you want to see it?"

"Of course."

I slid out the cake and removed the lid.

"What is it?"

"Kind of a Devil's food. I tweaked the recipe a bit."

"I love coconut. Can I have a slice? Or should we wait?"

"Totally up to you."

"We'll wait. Jane and the kids should share in it. We'll have it at breakfast." He started to walk out of the room, then turned back. "Thank you, Lizzy, for the cake . . . and for waiting up for me. I know it's not easy, but thank you." He flicked his gaze to the cake. "I bet they loved making that." He sounded disappointed.

"They did."

He nodded and left the room.

Cecilia had already texted me three times to find out the transfer time. Now she wanted to know which parking lot. One would think we were swapping state secrets.

As I watched Brian stalk across the parking lot, I texted her back and realized she understood him better than I did. He was trying to do the impossible—carry the weight of all that was unable to be held and pull his energy from sheer frustration and anger.

I stepped out and waved. "Hi. I've got three boxes in the trunk. Do you want me to follow you to your car?"

"I'm in the next row back. Let's just grab them."

I popped the trunk and met him around back. He looked thunderstruck.

"I had no idea. My cooler won't fit all that."

"Let's just get these in." I pointed to the box of smoothie pouches. "These eight you can dig through this week. These I started to freeze for the future, but they'll be fine out of your cooler until you get home."

"How much do I owe you?"

"It was $240 in groceries and $120 for labor."

"And the containers?"

"Forgot those. How about $60? I wanted something you could heat and reuse."

We carried the boxes over, and I sorted them between freezer and refrigerator piles.

"Cecilia put labels on so you have cooking instructions for each, and I added suggestions about what pairs well together." I handed him a sheet I'd typed out.

"Cecilia? Tyler's nurse?"

I flicked a glance up to the window. "She offered to help."

"I don't know how I feel about that. She's Tyler's nurse and knows private information."

"She doesn't talk; she's more professional than that. She wanted to help cook for you. I couldn't have done all this without her."

"Well . . ."

I stepped forward. "Well, nothing. She's a super caring woman who has gone out of her way to help you. Don't imply that she's unprofessional."

Brian stepped back. "Okay."

I pressed my lips together to stop my next sentence. I couldn't believe that I'd yelled at him, but I knew his type, ran into him every day—and *was* him on my worst days.

Brian slammed his trunk and pulled out his wallet. It was stuffed with twenties. He peeled off twenty-one. "Can we get ten to fifteen more?"

"You haven't eaten these yet."

"Do you want the business or not?"

His comment made me feel cheap.

"No, I don't want the business. This wasn't about that. I leave in a couple days anyway."

He shoved his wallet back into his pocket. "Got it." He nodded and headed back toward the hospital.

"You're welcome," I mumbled. Then I yelled, "I hope Tyler enjoys the meals." I let my opinion of Brian fall between us.

He stopped a few feet away and glanced back. I expected to catch an angry glare and was stunned by his fleeting expression of loss and despair. It vanished in a blink.

He continued his walk, but I stood frozen. What I had thought was an angry stalk looked different now. It looked like a walk tinged with desperation—a suppressed, scared gait that was fast because slow would make him too vulnerable; he might get caught. I walked the same way through New York and around Jane, every day.

I turned back to Jane's car, ashamed that I'd yelled at him and had assumed that I knew him. My phone rang.

"Were you watching us?"

Cecilia laughed. "Maybe. Was he pleased?"

"More surprised by the quantity than anything. Is he near you now?"

"No, I took my cell phone to the staff room. Why?"

"I sorta yelled at him. I thought he was being critical and needed to come down a peg. I was wrong."

"Is he okay?"

"I don't think so."

Cecilia was silent.

"Now I feel bad. What should I do?"

"Apologize if you need to. And pray for him."

"That's not going to help."

"Really? I find it works best, especially when I screw up."

"Can you go talk to him?"

"I can try, but Brian's tough for me. There's something so hurt and angry about him."

"Then he needs you. You can reach him. I know you can." I knew I was pushing, but there was something in her manner that made me trust her.

"I'm hanging up now," she whispered. "Donna walked in." The phone clicked off.

There was one more call to make.

"I just made $420!"

"Elizabeth?"

"Sorry. I wanted to let you know . . ." I felt like a fool.

"I thought that was your number, New York. I just hadn't put a contact in yet. Doing it right now." Nick's voice was bright and cheerful.

"I made $420. Well, not really. Net $120, but it still feels good."

"As it should. I told you it's a business."

"Stop trying to steal it."

"I'm messing with you . . . We should celebrate when we're out tomorrow night. I'll have to think up a new place you'll love."

I grinned. "That sounds wonderful."

Chapter 20

When I got home, I found Peter sitting at the kitchen counter, eating yogurt mixed with granola.

"I've got some strawberries if you want to add them." I reached into the refrigerator. "I told the kids not to wake you this morning. Sorry if that was wrong. We've just gotten used to letting Jane sleep in."

"No, it's good for her. We had a long talk, and then I went for a run. I needed to clear my head."

"Are you okay?" I rinsed the berries and, at his nod, tossed them into his bowl. He looked wan, his eyes puffy and his shoulders slumped.

"I'm a little tired, but okay." He stirred in the fruit. "Thank you again for being here."

"You're welcome. You've got a great family. I'm going to miss you all." I paused as my quiet apartment and solitary life rose in front of me. "Where's Jane?"

"Doing laundry." Peter closed his eyes for a beat. "I have another trip."

"Where to?"

"Shanghai."

"That's far and long, Peter. They need you here."

"Don't you think I know that? What can I do?" He swung his head around the room. I sensed he was not talking about his job. He glanced back and whatever he saw hardened his expression. "Don't look at me like that."

"Whoa." I threw up my hands. "That's not fair; I don't have any skin in this game. It's all yours, but . . ."

His eyebrows flattened straight as he narrowed his eyes, waiting for my next words. I held eye contact. "Peter, it's your family, and I'm the one here."

He deflated and flickered his glance away. He laid both hands, held in fists, on the counter on either side of his yogurt. "I know." He paused for a moment. "Sorry about that. You are the one here. It's just . . . She hates me."

"She's scared, and anger is her default mode. Always has been. You know that."

"But it's not usually directed at me. She hasn't been like this since your mom died. Take cover when your sister gets scared or can't control something." He looked at me, and his eyes lost their fight. "She accused me of having an affair. Did she tell you that?"

I stood perfectly still. It was too intimate a topic and not one I thought I could survive if I stepped into the middle.

"It doesn't matter if she voiced it or not. She thought it." He ran his hands through his short hair, the tips barely reaching over his fingers. "I'm not. But something's got to change."

"What does that mean?" My voice sounded high and panicked.

"It means I have a favor to ask." Peter reached his hand across the island to grab mine.

"Oh no."

"There's no one else. I don't think Jim can handle this. You know your father."

My heart dropped.

"I agreed to this trip, so I have to go, but my assistant is working this morning to reshuffle my schedule for the next several months. This is the last one." He reached for my arm. "Please? Then I'm home. Just give me two more weeks."

"Peter, I've got a restaurant, a job, a life . . ." I clamped my mouth shut. It sounded petty, and to be fair, I didn't have those things—not really.

"She starts Taxol next week. It could be easy or it could be tough on her. Some of the stuff I've read says it's worse than Adriamycin, if you can believe it. Please?" He let go of my hand and crossed the kitchen to dig around in his briefcase. "Here, I did some research. Some side effects are pretty bad." He shoved them into my hands.

I looked down at the pages and pages of handwritten notes, typed notes, spreadsheets, and hand-drawn pictures. "More?"

"I do it on the plane when I'm not working. It's all there. She should get through this fine, but keep an eye on her hands and feet. Keep asking her if they tingle."

"Peter." I wasn't angry. I wanted to cry. "What if I don't have two weeks? What if *my* boss says no? And did you tell her you did all this? Did you show her?" I grasped the pages.

"Please ask. And she doesn't need to know about all this"—he motioned to the papers. "Most of it would worry her, but you need to read them so you can watch her."

"She needs to know. She thinks you're having an affair, but instead this is how you spend your free time."

"Just say yes, Lizzy, please?"

I sighed. "I've never been able to figure you out."

"I'm a problem solver. This is my problem."

I leaned against the counter, considering the pages and what I might say to Paul. "I'll ask, but this is big, Peter. I don't mean to sound petty, but I'm risking Feast here."

"I know. This is huge. Feast revolves around you."

"I can ask." I felt the edge of the knife again: he thought I risked Feast because they couldn't survive without me; I knew it was a risk because they could.

I carried the pages up to my room and sat on the bed. I couldn't believe the mass of scribbles, notes, and diagrams. This wasn't the work of a seasoned business professional; this was heart stuff—an attempt to make the unthinkable manageable, an attempt to help, heal, relate, and empathize. And he refused to show her or discuss it with her . . . How was I to survive in the middle?

I pulled out my phone and texted Tabitha: Jane isn't great. How are things there? I paused and then typed my real question. Am I needed?

I started pacing. It was three p.m. in New York. Tabitha would be prepping at the restaurant. It wouldn't be hectic yet, and if she heard her phone she'd text back. Nothing.

I decided to call.

She picked up on the first ring. "I was just reading your text."

"What do you think?"

"Things are good here." She took a deep breath.

"I'll be honest—business is up. Trent has moved into the kitchen well." She paused, and when I didn't say anything, she continued, "But it's not his kitchen. He makes that clear. You'd like him. Every time we have a great night, he says, 'Thanks, guys, you made Chef Hughes proud tonight.' "

"He does?" That floored me. "What's his angle?"

"I've been trying to figure it out. I don't think he has one."

"Impossible."

"Regardless, you should be thrilled, especially if you're extending your vacation."

"It hardly feels like vacation, but you're right and I'm grateful. I didn't expect that much respect." My turn to pause. "I could leave here, Tabitha. I could fly home Saturday as planned."

She knew I wanted her advice.

"Is that what you want?" Her tone struck at the deep question.

"I wish I knew. Part of me says yes. Life at Feast is easy, despite the mess I left. But I'm needed here. I . . ." I couldn't say anything more. Peter's expression flashed before me. I felt as alone as he did. I fingered the pages spread before me and heard myself say something I didn't expect, "If I walk now, I doubt I'll ever come back."

"Stay." She paused. "This is about more than a

restaurant, more than cooking. Please, stay." Tabitha's voice sounded soft and pleading.

I chuckled lightly. "What do you know that I don't?" As I said it, I felt my heart trip—maybe she was lying; maybe Feast was already gone.

"I feel awful about what I said about Paul. I can't believe I even suggested it. And Feast aside, you're my friend and I want you to be happy. I'll keep up the fight here, and you stay and help your sister. You'll never forgive yourself if you don't."

I recognized her wisdom. "You're a good friend, Tabs."

"The best."

I took a deep breath. "The best . . . I'll ask Paul for a couple more weeks."

"We'll be right here when you get back."

"You think so?"

"We'll be 'tweaked' beyond recognition, but we'll be here." I could hear a smile in her voice.

"Send me some of the new recipes you're using." She didn't answer. "I just want to see them."

"Don't microfreak from Seattle."

"Is that like micromanage?"

"More futile."

"Fine." I tried to laugh, but it became a sigh. "Call if you need me."

I hung up and called Paul. He picked up on the first ring too—all these people waiting to hear from me.

He didn't say hello. "You're on a flight home Saturday?"

"That's what I called to talk about. My sister isn't doing well. I need two more weeks."

"Elizabeth, Saturday marks two weeks already."

"I know and I'm so sorry, but I'm needed here. You pushed this trip."

"You're needed here too."

"Paul . . ." I tried to form my next words.

He cut in. "How'd your cooking go?"

"I have no idea. I didn't see Tyler, and Brian was hardly complimentary. Nick said it's got potential for a business. He's a hair away from selling off the idea."

"He's the guy who took you out Tuesday?"

"Yeah, he helped with the shopping, too, but Cecilia helped with the cooking."

"You mention him a lot."

"I do?"

"Come home, Elizabeth." It was a whisper.

"I can't yet. My family needs me. They really do." The pause stretched. "I got the Moleskine notebooks yesterday. Thanks for sending those. That was really thoughtful."

"You use them to develop recipes."

"You noticed?"

"I notice everything." He sighed and changed his tone. "Except how letting you roll vacation time was such a liability."

"I agree." I smiled; Paul was giving me my time.

"Very poor planning. I think I've got twenty weeks of paid vacation ahead of me."

"Oh no you don't."

I laughed, slightly forced but genuinely grateful. "I wouldn't think of it. I want to be back as much as you want me back. Thanks for this."

"You're welcome and I doubt it." He hung up.

From the top of the stairs I could hear stern tones and biting words. I couldn't make them out, but I could sense that nothing good was being said. I didn't know what to do, so I went back to my room and stayed there until I heard the door slam.

I then wandered to the kitchen and found Jane sitting on the same stool where Peter had been, staring at a glass of water.

"Are you okay?"

She didn't look up. "Nothing is okay. This wasn't supposed to happen." She pressed her fists against her eyes. "I do everything right. I eat right. I exercise. I take care of my kids and my husband. I ran a small business that helped people. What more was I to do? And now, now this . . ." Tears started streaming down her face.

I rubbed her back. "This has nothing to do with what you did or didn't do. It just happened."

"That I can't accept."

"What?"

"That it just happens. It can't 'just happen.' What is the point of all this? Why do anything, if nothing matters? Everything I ever worked for—it's falling apart. What if I survive this and there's nothing left?"

"Don't let that happen."

"How?" Her anger had died. She wanted to know.

"Fight *with* Peter, not against him. I get that it's a fight, but you need him beside you, and Kate and Danny need to see that too. Don't let a little lump come between you."

"A little lump." Jane smiled through the tears. "That would be silly, wouldn't it?"

"Very."

Chapter 21

Nick arrived at the front door ten minutes late. "Thank you so much for understanding about tonight. Not quite the celebratory dinner I'd planned."

"I think an evening out with Matt will be fun."

Nick tilted his head into Jane's house. "You said Peter's home? Why don't we take Kate and Danny with us too? We'll make a party of it, and they can have a quiet evening."

I paused, wondering if Jane and Peter would appreciate that or want the normalcy of family. Then I thought about Danny and his radiant smile. I needed a few of those myself. "Let me go check."

I found Jane and Danny playing a video game in the basement. He was thrilled and she equally pleased he'd get to have fun, especially since Kate was spending the night at a friend's house.

"Where are you going?"

"To some restaurant, Stone Gardens."

Danny grinned and glanced at his mother, who winked and replied, "You'll love it." She looked me up and down, appraising my comfortable pencil jeans and sweater. "You're dressed fine too."

"What kind of a place is it?"

"You just want to be able to move."

Danny glared at his mom. "Come on, Aunt Elizabeth. Let's go."

Stone Gardens was not, in fact, a restaurant, but a huge warehouse divided into two large rooms, completely covered in fabricated rock walls full of colorful handholds, like M&M's scattered across a chocolate cake. It was a climbing gym. The larger room reached four stories high, with ropes hung every few feet, and the other room had lower walls that bent in at odd angles, some even running parallel to the floor. I felt as if I was in Willie Wonka's candy factory.

"Now I know why Jane was checking out my clothes. Why didn't you tell me?"

Nick laughed and grabbed my hand. "I thought you knew." He looked down, and I realized I was biting my lip. "Are you nervous? You'll love it. You can rope climb or boulder. You choose."

"And the difference is?"

He pulled me in front of him and held my shoulders, turning me to face the smaller room. "Bouldering walls aren't as high, but there are horizontal surfaces, so it's more like Spider-Man. No harness, just big mats to soften your fall." He shifted me forty-five degrees. "For rope climbing, you're hooked to a belay and you climb higher. See?" He pointed to the top where the ropes were anchored.

I watched several people going up and down—alive and laughing. "Can we do both?"

"Definitely."

Danny and Matt opted for rope climbing first. And even though my legs are twice as long as Matt's, he or Danny won every race. They had no fear and they didn't think. They simply climbed and I trailed them. But I still felt like the victor, for every time I touched down, Matt was right there to hug me.

After one climb I glanced over his head, expecting Nick to be smiling at Matt's joy, but instead I found a contemplative frown. It disappeared as soon as Nick noticed my gaze.

I shook it off and followed the boys to the bouldering side of the gym, where they scampered around like spider monkeys. I watched Danny first help Matt, then climb along beside him. I smiled and a sigh escaped.

"What's that for?" Nick came beside me.

"Danny's a good kid. I love seeing him laugh."

"Kate's changed a bit lately. How's she doing?"

"She knows more, and that makes it harder. She's also at that age where your friends mean everything and you want to fit in. Having your mother so sick makes you feel alone."

Nick reached for my hand and squeezed it. "From experience?"

I nodded.

"I'm sorry."

"Shall we climb?" My voice cracked. I cleared my throat to hide it and reached for the closest hand pull. Within a couple seconds I had made it five feet up, but then—as had been the case on my previous four attempts—I was stymied.

"Grab the red one right here."

"This one's closer." I reached for the blue.

"You won't—" and I fell. Nick reached down to help me up. "Are you okay?"

"Got the wind knocked out of me, and I think I bruised my ego."

He hauled me up and leaned toward me as if to whisper something . . .

"Dad!" Matt called. "Can we go eat?"

"Give me a sec, kiddo." He turned back to me and reached for my hands, rubbing them. "These will really hurt tomorrow. Along with a lot of other muscles you never knew existed." Nick smiled, and I again noticed the scar that ran along his chin.

Without thinking I trailed it with a finger. "What happened?"

"A bed, a Tonka truck, and a rough landing. I was two."

"Ouch."

"I'm hungry, Dad. Can we go to Lockspot?" Matt pulled Nick's shirt.

"I thought we might end up there."

Danny pumped his fist in the air. Matt watched and quickly followed suit.

Nick turned to me. "Fish and chips good with you?" At my nod he said, "Lockspot it is then. Let's go return our shoes, team."

After we handed in our shoes and washed our hands, which were black from the walls with a sore red undertone, we crossed the parking lot to the restaurant.

Nick pointed slightly beyond it. "We're on the Ballard Locks."

"I came here with my parents once. I remember the ladders. Haven't seen them in years—no salmon ladders in New York."

Nick's face lit up. "I'll have to bring you back—" Then fell. "You won't be here."

"I've got two more weeks."

He stopped. "I thought you were leaving tomorrow."

"I was, but Peter's got one more trip and he asked me to stay."

"Two weeks, huh?"

"Two weeks."

Nick reached for my hand. "We'll have to find more things to celebrate."

Lockspot was fully busy and completely fun. We got the last booth and piled in. It was dark, wood paneled, with red-and-white plastic tablecloths and vinegar in the condiment basket.

Danny laughed about school and Kate, Nick told hilarious stories of his childhood, and I shared some of my early teenage cooking disasters, like the brownies that had exploded in the oven because I'd used one cup of baking powder versus one teaspoon and then set the heat too high. We were so engrossed no one noticed Matt snuggling into my side.

"He's asleep, Aunt Elizabeth."

I looked down. "How is that possible?" I looked down at Matt's angelic face and reached my arm around him to pull him closer. "What a guy."

Nick smiled. "He is." Then he turned to Danny and cupped his shoulder. "You are too. Thanks for being so nice to Matt tonight."

"He's fun. Do you think I could babysit him sometime?"

"Ah . . ." Nick's eyes caught mine a beat before focusing back on Danny. "I guess it isn't really fair to hire only Kate, huh? I bet you'd do a good job."

Danny looked down at his plate, but I could see his delight.

"Tell you what, let's ask your parents, and maybe you can come play with him when I've got work to do on the weekends. Could we do that?"

"Yeah." Danny brightened, then glanced around the room.

Nick pointed to a pinball machine in the corner of the restaurant. "Do you want to go play?" He offered a couple quarters, and Danny shot from the booth.

"You just made his day. Pinball and babysitting. I think he likes to feel grown up."

"All guys do, but we don't admit it much." Nick motioned to his son. "He's not usually like that. He's only that affectionate with my mom." Nick studied Matt a moment. "And even then, it's not so . . . free."

"I love kids." I kissed the top of Matt's head. "They're open and straightforward. It's later that we don our armor and screw it all up."

"Experience again?"

I snorted and covered my nose. "Definitely. I may be bristly, rude, and terribly self-absorbed, but at least I'm self-aware."

"That's something, I guess." He laughed and I almost let it go, but I couldn't.

"It's okay, isn't it? I thought I caught a look when Matt grabbed my hand earlier."

"You did. I didn't expect him to latch onto you like that."

"I won't hurt him."

"I don't doubt that, but you're still leaving. I don't know that he'll understand when you're gone."

"Can't we just lump me into Jane's family? I really like him." I heard the plea in my voice.

"He really likes you too."

Chapter 22

My Monday started with closets but soon advanced into much more dangerous territory. I returned to the kitchen after my shower to find Jane with her head in the oven.

"You could just let the cancer get you."

"You're so funny." Her sarcasm was back after a few very deflated and depressed days.

"I thought chemo gave you less energy, not more. What's up?"

"More steroids. I took ten Decadron tablets to prep for tomorrow. Taxol requires more and earlier, I guess." She pulled her head out. Her hands were covered in grease and soot, and her cheeks were flaming red. "I feel great."

"Ten?"

"Welcome to Taxol." She dove back in.

"Get out of there. I'll do that." I pulled her shoulder to remove her from the oven once and for all.

"Perfect. You do that and I'll go vacuum my

car." She stood and wiped the grease from her hands onto her jeans.

"It's raining."

"Drizzling. Hardly anything."

I rolled my eyes, hoping this would end soon. I'd awoken to find her cleaning closets, the kitchen already scrubbed down and the kids completely frayed—all before school. Now the ovens? Next her car?

"Did you know you can actually unhinge car seats to vacuum under them? I looked in the manual. And I watched a YouTube video and learned how to clean my mass airflow sensor, but we'll have to take off the engine cover to get to that."

"Forget it. You are not taking apart your car to vacuum, and we are not opening the hood for any reason."

"We should."

"Jane, you're a freak."

She opened her mouth to protest and then shut it like a fish. "You're right. I'll stop. Too bad Peter's car's not here."

Soon her pantry distracted her, and I wandered to the basement to do laundry and then upstairs to make my bed. Finally, unable to take her manic cleaning and off-pitch singing any longer, I wandered outside. The sun was out and April was in full swing. It had been Mom's favorite time on the West Coast—the winter and spring rains made everything come alive and grow faster than Jack's beanstalk.

I was squatting in Jane's yard trying to identify anything in her overgrown jungle of an herb garden when I sensed someone standing behind me.

"I didn't know you were here." I stood up, wondering how much of my backside Nick had seen. I tugged at my T-shirt.

"Jane called this morning and asked if I could come over. She's been talking a mile a minute and is now revamping her website."

"Steroids. Lots of steroids."

"Ah . . . How long does it last?"

"I doubt past tomorrow."

"How was—"

"Did you—"

We spoke simultaneously.

"You first." I clamped my hand over my mouth.

"I was asking how your weekend was."

"Very nice. No major conflict. Jane ate and I took the kids to the park twice. Jane rested and Peter stayed close until he left yesterday morning. You?"

"Our weekend was quiet too. We went to the park once and to Costco." He looked around as if fishing for a topic. "Do you like Jane's garden?"

"This isn't much of one, but I love gardens. I wish Feast had one. I don't even have a window box at my apartment."

"I have a garden . . ." He stalled. "I feel I owe you an apology."

"What for?" I tried to keep my expression clear, but I knew. After our dinner at Lockspot on Friday, Nick had mentioned getting together again over the weekend, even thrown out possible plans, but then had not called or texted.

"Matt talked about you a lot this weekend." Nick rubbed the back of his neck. "It threw me."

"I completely get that. Just don't punish Danny and Kate because of me." I passed him and headed back to the house.

He reached out and grabbed my arm, immediately releasing it as I turned. "I wouldn't do that, and I came to the conclusion this morning that I was overreacting. I can't keep every attractive woman out of Matt's life. Fear like that isn't healthy, for him or me." He pointed to Jane's house, then looked back to me. "Some of my closest friends live in that house. It took me a moment to remember that."

"So I'm attractive?"

"Yes. And I bet I'm not the first to tell you that." He smiled and looked over my shoulder into Jane's garden. "She's not a good gardener, is she? I, on the other hand, have a great garden." He said it like he was tempting a small child with a lollipop.

"You do?" I said it like the kid who wanted that lollipop. "I must see this garden."

"Let's go." He flicked his finger conspiratorially toward Jane's back gate. "She'll be fixing that website for at least an hour."

We cut through the hedgerow again and soon found ourselves on Madison Street. Another block and we turned into his driveway. It was a shingled Craftsman house like Jane's, but it was dark green with white trim. It was so neat and perfect and masculine and Nick. Inside, it felt the same. There was a bright patterned area rug in the living room, with brown leather furniture that looked worn and soft. The rest of the downstairs had cream walls and hardwood floors that shone. Bookshelves lined the walls around the windows. There was very little clutter, but tons of personality and warmth.

I smiled, and he looked at me, questioning. "I love your house."

"Come on. I'll show you the garden."

Outside it was still misting, and everything looked fresh and vibrant. I stood perfectly still, absorbing Nick's backyard. It was small, and a full third was divided into raised beds full of neat rows of plants and herbs. He had small patches of grass between them, and bushes lined the back and side fences. But not just any bushes—roses, rosemary, wild strawberries, lavender, and fennel.

"This is amazing."

"I thought you might like it. I started it when Matt was two. Messing around out here is a good stress reliever for me, and he loves it. I don't know where I'd be without this haven."

"When will it all bloom?"

"Some is starting now. You can see new growth over here. All the herbs are filling out. And there . . ." He pointed to a tree nearby. "That's my apple tree. It's just starting to bud."

"I love it." I stood there absorbing the chaos creatively formed, cultivated, and maintained. To me, gardens represented a perfect and active creative experience—and I suddenly understood why Jane didn't have one. It would be another area in which she would need to impose order from chaos, and it would always defy her. I let the insight settle over me, not as a point of contention but of understanding.

"There isn't much to take right now, but there will be soon." Nick looked around, assessing his sanctuary.

The mist picked up, and we turned back to his surprisingly well-equipped kitchen—a Vitamix, Santoku knives, a La Pavoni espresso maker, a marble mortar and pestle . . . I walked over to it and lifted the wood pestle. Good weight. The wood was ground smooth, well used.

"This is an impressive kitchen. It would seem you cook."

"I've learned to, but not like you do."

"I like this." I held up the pestle. "Jane doesn't have one of these."

"I make a chicken rub that would knock your socks off."

"Will you make it for me?"

"Now that you're here for another couple weeks, I might."

"Okay then." I glanced away, embarrassed as I realized what my question implied.

Nick's eyes drifted above my head. "I've got a client call in about a half hour."

I twisted around and looked at his clock. "It's late. I gotta go too."

"It's raining. I'll drive you."

"I'd rather walk."

"Take an umbrella?"

"And let everyone know I'm a visitor? I don't think so."

"A baseball cap?"

I stopped. "That I'll accept."

"I'll be right back." Nick dashed up the stairs. I moved into the living room and migrated toward his bookshelves.

The bottom shelves were full of kid books. I smiled at a whole series of early readers based around Thomas the Tank Engine and Star Wars. There were others I recognized as well: Beatrix Potter, the Magic Tree House series, and *Where the Wild Things Are.* My eyes traveled up to Nick's choices. Lots of American history books:

Steven Ambrose, David McCullough, and John Meacham. Tom Clancy, Erik Larson, and Hemingway. Tons of Hemingway. *The Sun Also Rises*, *For Whom the Bell Tolls*, *A Moveable Feast*, *The Old Man and the Sea.*

I smiled, recalling his chicken rub. I would bet money it had a Spanish flair. I was so absorbed his tap on my shoulder startled me.

"You like Hemingway?" he asked softly above my ear.

"I do. I once had an English teacher who put him on the other end of the spectrum to Jane Austen and said you couldn't like both. I don't think that's true."

"So it's not just your sister who likes Jane Austen?"

I smiled and conceded, "I do too." I took a deep breath. "She was my mom's favorite, absolute favorite, to the point of naming her daughters after Austen's most famous sisters."

I slid *The Old Man and the Sea* back into its slot. "I put them away after she died, but they don't hold painful memories for Jane, and she's got me reading them again. It's good."

I tapped *A Moveable Feast*. "But I like Hemingway too. Both are very direct in their observations. Austen uses prose differently, but she doesn't pull any punches either." I tapped books on the shelf above Hemingway. "You've got a lot of Greek literature too."

"Ah, there's my weakness. Great lyric tragedy. Homer's the best. Have you read *The Odyssey* or *The Iliad*?"

"Never considered it."

"You should. 'The *Iliad* is great because all life is a battle, the *Odyssey* because all life is a journey, the Book of Job because all life is a riddle.'"

"Whoa. I've underestimated you."

"Not really. G. K. Chesterton said that. I saw that line after I read those, and I agreed with him—so it stuck." Nick handed me a hat.

"Mariners? This symbol always makes me hungry for shrimp cocktail."

"I don't think I've ever heard anyone say that." He quirked a smile and fitted the hat onto my head, drawing my ponytail through the back. "Perfect."

"Thanks." I ducked and stepped away, embarrassed that I'd noticed how he smelled—soapy, pine and something citrus—and that I'd not only liked it but had even leaned in to catch more of the scent. "And thanks for showing me the garden." I opened the door.

"I'm busy the rest of the day, but I can make some cuttings tonight and bring them over tomorrow. Jane might find gardening relaxing."

"I'm not sure, but maybe. Digging my hands into ground meat relaxes me. Maybe she could feel the same about dirt."

"Again, I don't think I've ever heard anyone say that." As I skipped down his steps, Nick called after me. "Elizabeth?"

I turned back. He followed me down the steps and paused. "I'm really glad you're here a little longer." He leaned down and hesitated mere inches from my face. I held my breath as he brushed his lips with mine, then kissed me again, lingering several heartbeats.

"Until later . . . ," he whispered.

"You said I was just a friend."

Nick smiled. "I know, but you don't feel like one. Or taste like one either. You're too attractive, remember?"

I hurried down the walk.

Chapter 23

Tuesday began more slowly. I found myself dwelling on certain more agreeable Monday moments just to avoid my unease about Taxol. I'd read and reread all Peter's notes, and as we settled in to our chairs in the Infusion Center, I was the nervous one.

"Hello?" Jane said. "You're so distracted today."

"I am?"

"Kate said you forgot breakfast completely."

I shook my head. "I started it, but then . . . You're right."

Jane smiled, but then turned her mouth downward at Cecilia's approach. Moments ago she'd been friendly and light, the Cecilia who drew people to her like a magnet; now her eyes were tight and strained and her movements stiff and compressed.

I quickly scanned the room and found myself looking straight into Donna's eyes. *Ahh . . .*

Jane whispered, "This should be fun."

"Always is."

She reached for my hand, and I knew she was nervous too. Taxol wasn't supposed to be as rough as the Red Devil, but who knew? That seemed to be the only certainty—there were no certainties.

"Sorry that took so long." Cecilia threw a glance over to Donna. "She's irritated today." She looked at me. "I asked Brian how Tyler fared with your meals. He didn't like my asking and got loud. It upset a few other patients."

"I'm sorry I encouraged you to talk to him at all."

"You didn't make me, and I haven't reached out to him as I should. I don't know why. I've certainly met tougher."

Out of the corner of my eye I saw Donna approaching. I put on a bright face and an even brighter tone and addressed Cecilia, hoping that she'd catch on as I changed the subject.

"Why all the steroids yesterday? Jane was a nightmare."

Cecilia smiled. "It's in case her heart stops, then we're ahead of the game. That's why Taxol takes so long. We go slowly."

Jane's mouth dropped open. Mine followed.

Cecilia compressed a smile. "I probably could've said that differently."

I found my voice. "Honesty works." Jane still looked like a guppy. "You okay?"

"Just appreciating the honesty." She pressed her lips together.

As Cecilia started to hook up the IV, Jane turned to me and whispered, "I don't think this is going to be so much fun anymore."

I dipped my head to hide my expression, which vacillated between humor and horror, and dug around to find our book. "Me neither."

I felt a shadow and looked up to see Brian looming above me. I shot a quick glance to Cecilia and sensed she was pretending that none of us was present as she flushed Jane's line and started the drug.

"Hey." I gestured to the chair next to me. "How was the food?"

"It was a disaster." Brian spoke too loudly. Several heads, including Donna's, turned our direction. "He can't eat. I shouldn't have let him get his hopes up."

"Really? I'm eating. Nothing was palatable to him?" Jane took up my defense, and I almost hugged her for it.

"Total waste. I know I asked for more, but don't bother." Then his eyes narrowed. "Hey, you said you weren't going to be here."

"I took another couple weeks off. But why? Why couldn't he eat?"

"He just doesn't, so don't raise his hopes again. Don't even bother him." Brian stalked away.

I turned to Jane, panic rising in me. "I thought I had this figured out. You've enjoyed my cooking. Right? What went wrong?" In my mind, Feast slipped further away. Everything slipped away. It was all contingent on my ability to cook, and if I didn't have that . . .

Cecilia's surgical glove clamped the hairs on my arm as she squeezed right above my wrist. "Stop it. You did a good thing. That's all you can do. You can't control the outcome or Brian's behavior."

"But—"

"There aren't any buts, so stop."

I took a few deep breaths and glanced over to Tyler. Brian had left the room, so I gently twisted my arm free and hurried over.

"I'm sorry about the meals."

"Don't worry about it. Eating's tough right now, but thank you so much for all the work."

I waved away his gratitude. "I want to make you some more meals. On me. You can't pay me."

"It's not a big deal."

"I need to . . . Please."

Tyler turned his book over on his lap and studied

me for a moment. I wondered what he saw. "Okay."

"Can I ask you some questions?"

"Anything."

"What kind of cancer do you have?" As I asked, I realized it didn't matter. I only needed to know about how his medications made him feel. And that was what I hadn't bothered to find out the week before.

"Progressive chronic lymphocytic leukemia."

I shook my head. "I don't even know what that is. What I really need to know is what you like, what you dislike, what tastes good and feels good, safe, and comfortable."

Tyler looked at me, confused.

"When I started cooking for Jane, I cooked dishes from our childhood. It was all I knew about her, and it crashed and burned. She threw up my first meal and a few after that. Probably like you did. But once I started asking questions and listening to her about what she liked and how she feels right now, I began to get it right. I didn't do that for you."

He nodded to me. "I've been on one drug or another for eight months, and I don't go up and down anymore. I'm just down. I have sores in my mouth, everything tastes like rusted metal, and I've been dosed down three times in two months."

"What does that mean?"

"I'm losing weight." He raised his arm like a

weight lifter and flapped his tricep. "I used to have muscles."

I immediately thought of proteins and calories. "Can you eat meats, dairy?"

"Not dairy. My gut is so tight, cheese is probably not best . . . Sorry." He looked to his lap.

I waved my hand again. No way were we going to get embarrassed by a little constipation. "What about yogurt, ice cream?"

"Maybe. I like cold things."

"Then the smoothies worked?"

"Some."

"Tell me about vegetables."

"I like peas, green beans. I can't eat broccoli, can't think about broccoli." He turned the shade of broccoli.

"Oh . . . the slaw and the chicken dish. That must have been torture. What about meat?"

"I like chicken, salmon. Beef tastes good. Never been a pork fan, but I like bacon."

I smiled, thinking I'd found a perfect candidate for my bacon ice cream. "Fruits?"

"No citrus. Oranges sting."

I cringed, realizing that was why only "some" of the smoothies had worked. Mouth sores. Half the smoothies had been packed with citrus and were probably torture.

I was ashamed that I had never asked these questions, never thought about Tyler as different from Jane. I had treated him like a nameless, faceless person who merely needed to be fed. Cecilia was right—everyone was unique, every experience unique. When would I understand and respect that?

I noticed his book. "Are you enjoying that? You were reading *The Sun Also Rises* last time."

Tyler shot me a startled look. "I was, but I like this better." He waved *A Farewell to Arms*. "I like Hemingway. He's direct, like math."

I chuckled. "I think all guys like Hemingway, but I've never heard him compared to math."

"I think of almost everything in those terms. I'm a math teacher at Garfield High School. Hemingway doesn't hide, and he writes at the pace of a Ping-Pong game. Everything runs with a strange, if not dark, sense of quick logic."

"You are so right." I laughed.

From the corner of my eye I saw Brian coming back. I didn't want to confront him or instigate another scene. "Thank you for letting me do this. Just like last time, I'll meet Brian here Thursday. Will you be here?"

"It's my weekly appointment."

"Great. I mean . . ."

"I get it. Thanks."

By this point Brian stood above me. I darted away. Tyler could explain everything if he chose.

"We've got cooking to do." I tapped Jane's leg to get her attention.

"I thought he didn't want any more."

"Brian doesn't, but Tyler's letting me make him more meals. My treat."

"Why do you care? Let it go."

"I can't. I feel . . . I feel like if I do this, I can break through—everything. And I need that. I need to help, to do something good." I looked down at my hands. I was shredding my cuticles again. "You were right. Food is communal. Mom once told me that it was no accident that Jesus's first miracle was at a wedding. It was a sign that he was the Master of the Feast—and all celebrations involve a feast. Some of the best, most thankful moments of our lives involve food—almost all, really."

I tapped *Emma*, resting on Jane's lap. "You see it in Austen. She only mentions food as a means to bring characters together, reveal aspects of their nature and their moral fiber. Hemingway does the same, though he skews more towards the drinks. Nevertheless, it's never about the food—it's about what the food becomes, in the hands of the giver and the recipient." I pressed my hands together. "I forgot that . . . and I hurt Tyler."

Jane stared at me in silence for a long moment before whispering, "How can I help?"

We spent the next few hours planning Tyler's meals.

"You know they drink a ton in that book, but they don't eat much." I racked my brain for all

Hemingway's food references in *The Sun Also Rises*.

"Maybe it's not something to focus on."

"It is. It's an aspect of Tyler that he's focusing on right now. He's a math teacher who likes clean, direct things. Hemingway reminds him of math. He's sparse, clean . . . it's right."

"Okay, what else do we have to work with?"

I shot her a look.

"Think harder. Every meal he wrote is somewhere in that brain of yours."

I smiled. "*The Sun Also Rises* takes place mostly in Paris and a little in Spain. Tons of wine, Pernod, villagers' wine . . . but the food is spare like the writing: a suckling pig, a roasted chicken, shrimp, bread and olive oil. Simple food, uncomplicated tastes."

I chewed my lip. "That's it. Let's stay with simple food. Hemingway loved Spain, so let's drift toward those flavors, but no spice. And we can make them mix and match like tapas. Tyler will have flexibility."

It felt good to collaborate with Jane. We listed fruits and vegetables that we could blend into smoothies. We then listed different flours to give the meals more taste, texture, and nutrients, like the coconut and almond flours I'd used for Jane's potpies and Peter's cake. We decided to alter the egg dishes and quiches that I'd been making for her into cleaner, simpler hashes and scrambles.

We developed vegetable dishes—poached, roasted, fresh and lightly seasoned.

"Put thin bread or tortillas on the list. He can get more calories by topping or wrapping almost anything we make."

"Great idea."

Jane sat up straighter. "What about a mole?"

"Never found one in Hemingway; it's more Mexican really. But what about a picada—it's like a pesto. There's a great one from the Cataluña region that uses roasted almonds and hazelnuts rather than pine nuts. And with only garlic, olive oil, and parsley, it should have great flavor and no real spice."

"Calories too."

"An added bonus." I grinned. We were on to something. I could feel it and was completely exhilarated by it. Cecilia surprised us when she came to unhook Jane.

"We're done?" Jane jumped at her touch.

"You two have been busy. The whole room changed over."

I looked around and realized that I recognized no one. I had become used to the "patrons" of my dystopian library and had enjoyed saying our farewells at the end of Jane's sessions. "Hey, I never saw Andy today. I'd hoped we could play a hand or two. Did he come and go while we were working?"

Cecilia stepped away and pulled her mask

down. "Not today. He's not doing so well."

I felt Jane grow still beside me, but I couldn't turn to her. I kept my eyes on Cecilia. "He'll be back, right?"

"I don't know."

"Will you . . . will you let us know? You can do that, can't you?"

"Of course I can. Courtney asked me to keep you posted." She looked around the room. "Donna and Tony are on break, and I need to go hook up a patient, but I promise to call if I learn anything about Andy." She turned back to Jane. "You did great today. Welcome to Taxol."

Jane tried to smile. "One more down, huh?"

Chapter 24

The news of Andy quieted us both, and soon after we arrived home, Jane headed upstairs for a nap. I wondered if she was tired—after all, the steroids were still surging through her—or a little depressed. They can feel the same. I, too, felt sluggish and heavy. But Tyler's food, the anticipation of making him something wholesome and sustaining, enticed me with a sense of hope and purpose. It was beyond food. It was that magic—that illusive magic—that turned a meal into a feast.

As I was checking her kitchen for spices and

supplies, Jane's landline rang. I raced to catch it in case she'd fallen asleep. *Health Services* flashed across the caller ID.

"Hello?"

"I'm calling for Ms. Elizabeth Hughes?"

"This is she. Are you calling from New York?" Surely Tabitha could handle inspections. My mind raced, calculating if any permits were due and wondering how anyone got Jane's number.

"From Seattle, Washington. We received a complaint that you are running a commercial food service from a private kitchen."

"No, I'm not." *Tyler's meals.* "I did . . ."

"All food service businesses require a permit. Can you give me your permit number?"

"I . . . I'm visiting my sister. I don't live here." My voice sank. Rules governing permits in New York were incredibly strict and carried severe penalties, especially for professionals working outside commercial kitchens.

The man listed a series of permits I either needed or had possibly violated. I heard little of it. My head swam with the implications for me and for Feast.

In the end he took pity on me and did not issue a citation. It was perhaps my high-pitched notes or the truth: I was leaving town, cooking for my ill sister, trying to help a new friend and he, too, was ill and isn't cancer horrible . . . I won't do it again.

"Thank you. May I ask who complained?"

"I can't give you that information."

I hung up the phone and looked at all the ingredients I'd pulled out in preparation for Tyler's meals. The effort felt silly and useless—a few simple meals for a guy I hardly knew, and I'd jeopardized Feast. What made me think any of this was going to work? Pairing books and food? Who'd ever heard of such a thing? And what had I truly accomplished? I'd upset Tyler and Brian, gotten Cecilia in trouble with Donna—and for what? So that I could feel fulfilled? Find some silly idea of *magic* I probably dreamed up in my own head?

Without thinking I started to wipe down Jane's counters and sharpen the knives, closing down the kitchen. Closing down hope. Kate's sweet face as she sifted flour for Peter's cake crossed my mind, as did Danny's laughter as he watched the fine coconut shreddings fall like snowflakes across the icing. On the third knife I caught myself and laid it down. It did matter and it wasn't about me.

"Now or never." I grabbed my notes from the trash and spread them across the counter. The meals were to be gifts—I'd told Tyler that already —so I wasn't violating any rules or permits. I was going to prepare them. I was going to finish what I'd started. For him.

I grabbed a bunch of parsley and started chopping. Soon my self-recrimination turned to anger as I realized that someone had tried to get me in trouble. Someone had purposely sought out a way to stop me. Brian? Donna? Another patient?

The doorbell interrupted me. I stalked through the front hall and threw the door open. "Yes?"

"Whoa. What's that?" Nick took a step back.

I looked down at the nine-inch chopping knife still clutched in my hand. "Sorry. Chopping parsley. Come on in." I flicked the knife toward the kitchen.

"I—"

"Shut the door behind you." I'd already turned back.

Nick followed me. "What's up?"

"Someone called Health Services and reported that I was running a commercial kitchen out of a private home. Tried to get me in trouble."

"Who?"

"I have no idea. Who knew? Who cared? Do you think Brian did it because he was angry?"

"Why was he angry?"

I resumed chopping the parsley. "He said I got Tyler's hopes up, then failed to deliver. Tyler didn't eat . . . But maybe it wasn't him. It could've been that Nurse Ratched. Cecilia said she was angry that Brian caused a scene. I guess some other patients got really upset."

"From *One Flew Over the Cuckoo's Nest*?"

"Yes, but she works in the Infusion Center now."

"Can you stop and tell me what happened?"

I slid the parsley off the cutting board and lined

up the carrots. "I'm trying to, but I've got to get this done. It's important, Nick."

"What are you doing?"

"Chopping carrots, clearly. I'm making Tyler another batch of meals, on me." I flew through the carrots and lined up another two. "I listened. I really listened—"

"Elizabeth."

"I'm trying to explain if yo—"

"No, Eliz—"

Blood flooded the cutting board before I felt anything. The knife had stopped. It shouldn't have stopped. I pulled and looked down. It had caught on bone. My bone. I yanked to wedge it free. "Nick?"

"Stop." He raced toward me, grabbing a wad of towels from the counter. I looked down and the world spun. Nick reached around my shoulder. "Don't look. Come here. Sit. Hold your arm up."

"What are you doing?" I watched him frantically looking around the cutting board, the floor.

"Do you have them?" he cried out.

"What?"

"All your fingers?"

I blanched and pulled my hand down, ripping the towels from it. "I don't know. I don't— Yes, they're here. Oh—"

"Wrap it up. Don't look." Nick raced to the freezer and grabbed a handful of ice. "Come on."

"Where?"

"The ER."

"Jane—"

"I'll call her after you get seen. Come on." He pushed me out the front door and shoved me into his car. He buckled me in before running around to the driver's seat. I sat numb.

"Hold it up. Cradle the ice against it."

I started to cry. "I can't feel it. It doesn't hurt. That's bad, Nick. That's really, really bad."

"You don't know that." He reached over. "Hold it up."

"What have I—"

"No crying."

"Why is that such a bad thing? Jane always says that too. Crying is not wrong! Do you see this?" I yelled and held up the deep-red-soaked towels.

"Stop it. Cry all you want later. I've got to get you to the ER. Please. I need to think. I'm trying to drive."

Within minutes he pulled into the hospital's emergency bay. "Come on. I'll get you inside and then move the car."

He propelled me straight to the desk. "She sliced her hand. All the fingers. The knife caught on the bones."

The nurse took one look at me and dashed from her desk; within seconds two people came out and led me to triage. Nick followed.

"Let's set you up in here." Another nurse pointed to the exam table. "Hop up there."

I attempted to climb up but couldn't manage with my hands clasped together. I felt a hand wrap around my upper arm, steadying me, and looked up to find Nick's face close to mine. I hadn't noticed the lines around his mouth before. I liked them. They made him look real and reliable.

"You're pale," he whispered and kissed the top of my head. "Paler than usual."

The nurse started unwrapping towels when an orderly entered. "Sir, you need to move your car."

"I forgot." He turned back to me. "Are you going to be okay?"

"I'll be fine . . . but you're coming back, right?"

Nick stared at me a moment. "Yes."

I closed my eyes while the nurse examined my hand and another took my blood pressure and asked me questions. She wrapped it again and left. My mind drifted, not to my hand, but to the food I'd left on Jane's counter and all that was wrapped up in it—my conversation with Tyler, hearing him, listening to him, and understanding him. And the hope I'd felt . . .

A doctor walked in.

"I'm Dr. Jackson." He propped himself on a stool and rolled over to me. "What have you got here?" He reached for my hand and unwound the mass of towels. He looked up at me. "How'd this happen?"

"I was chopping carrots. I always do that." I glanced down to see the bones exposed across the tops of my four fingers. "Oh . . . not that." The world turned blue.

"Take a deep breath and lean back. Here." He pressed a button, and the back of the exam table came up. "Rest while I examine this."

I obeyed and closed my eyes again, and then it started—the pain. Unbelievable throbbing, burning pain. I scrunched my eyes shut, squeezing out hot tears.

"It hurts."

The doctor twisted my wrist back and forth. "I can imagine. This is significant."

"You can stitch it up, right?"

"No." *Twist, twist.* "This requires a little surgery."

I could hear him opening drawers, then I felt something cool across my skin that turned warm after the first touch. I opened my eyes to find my hand covered in gauze, black mixed with the red.

"What is that?"

"Iodine. Sit back and rest. I'm going to call the surgeon on staff, and we'll get you taken care of."

"Thank you." I ran my other hand across my nose and eyes, clearing the tears.

"Here." He handed me a tissue.

"Thanks." I sniffed.

I closed my eyes and lay there. My hand felt separate from the rest of my body—as I felt separate from everything that mattered.

"Hey."

Nick. I didn't open my eyes as more tears welled up. "I hate hospitals. I'm always in hospitals."

Nick kissed my forehead. "I think only doctors like them." He perched on the edge of the exam table and took my other hand. "You're going to be fine."

"What have I done?" I whispered.

Nick didn't answer. He just sat there and held my hand. *I'll be there.* I squeezed it tight, wondering if I could ever let go.

Chapter 25

I awoke in a bright room, disoriented and thirsty. My left hand lay across my chest, wrapped in white and the size of a football. Nick stared at me.

"It's about time you woke up."

"How'd it go?"

"They stretched the skin across one finger and needed a small graft from the side of your hand for three, but everything went perfectly." He brushed my hair off my forehead. "In fact, you can go home tonight if you want."

"I don't have to stay?" My voice sounded like dried, flaky dough.

Nick lifted a cup of water and ice chips to my lips. "Do you want to?"

I sipped and tried to sit up. "Definitely not."

Nick steadied me. "Easy there, New York. Go slow. We have plenty of time."

"What time is it?"

"Nine o'clock."

"You've been here all day? What about Matt?"

"He's with my parents. Jane's been in constant contact. She wanted to come, but I told her no. She said your dad will be here in the morning."

"She shouldn't have called him." I leaned back. "Can we just go?"

"As soon as the doctor checks you out."

The doctor came and described the graft. Uninteresting and basic to him, but to me it sounded complex and unbelievable.

"Will it work?"

He laughed. "Of course it will. It's all you. And it's tiny. You'll be stiff for a while, but you shouldn't have any trouble. You'll need to change the bandages every day. I've written out a prescription for some painkillers, and here's a tube of antibiotic cream. Keep the suture lines moist with cream for the next several days, and call my office if there are any problems." He handed Nick his card. "We'll see you at the end of next week to remove the stitches."

After he left we sat for another couple hours as the staff discharged me. The questions, forms, information, protocol . . . It seemed endless. Finally an orderly came with a wheelchair to escort us to Nick's car.

"I can walk."

"Hospital policy," he commented dryly.

We reached the doors, and Nick helped me stand and wrapped me securely under his arm. I started to cry. Perhaps it was being tucked into his arm, or the general anesthesia, or the Health Services call, or the cooking, or Feast, or Jane . . .

Nick pulled up in front of Jane's house. "Do you want to sleep here or on my couch?"

I slanted my eyes toward him and rubbed my nose with the back of my only working hand.

"I'm not trying to seduce you."

I sniffed. "Are you sure? This is me at my most enticing."

Nick chuckled. "I told Jane if it was really late, I'd take you to my house and watch over you. I didn't want to disturb her or the kids. Did I overstep?"

"It was thoughtful of you."

He nodded to the house. "Do you want to go in?"

"I'd rather go to your place." I looked up at the dark windows. "They're asleep, and they have enough on their plates."

"Don't think like that." Nick pulled his car out of the driveway. "You can lie on my couch and rest. Or we can watch a movie. Talk. Whatever you want."

"I'd like that." I glanced over at him. "Will Matt be okay with that?"

"He's staying at my parents'."

"I think you said that. Sorry."

"Why? They adore him and he loves to stay there. It's fine."

I held my arm up, like a surgeon who has just washed her hands, as Nick opened my car door. Every time it dropped, the throbbing pain sent it right back up. Nick unlocked his front door and then stood back, letting me enter.

"What can I get you?" He started plumping the cushions on his couch. Even in pain, I couldn't help but smile. "Water? Food?"

"Nothing right now."

"Let's start with water."

The man needed to get me something. He came back with a glass and a cookie, and built a pyramid of pillows on which to prop my left hand. He then gently sat on my right side so as not to bounce the couch.

"I won't break."

"Not on my watch, you won't." He leaned back and clamped his eyes shut. "That was really scary. I saw you chopping and I knew. I tried to say something, but . . ." He scrubbed at his eyes.

"I was stupid. I know better than that." I looked at my hand. "I've been using knives since I was about five. I've never cut myself like this." I chuckled. "Obviously."

He rolled his head across the back cushion. "What do you want to do? Talk? Watch a movie? Sleep?"

"Can we watch *Persuasion*?" I heard my small voice and couldn't believe I'd asked that. Suddenly I understood my mom and my sister—but not quite.

"I'll see if it's on Netflix."

"Wait. Don't." I reached out to stay his hand on the remote. "It's my favorite book, but it's not me. It's not what *I* want."

"What do *you* want?" Nick leaned over and tucked my hair gently behind my ear.

I let myself absorb his question. *I want to love what I'm doing. I want to not feel heavy all the time. I want to laugh like I used to—to be that kid in the picture on my nightstand with a smile so bright it could light the world or at least one heart. I want to heal and cook and be with Kate and Danny and actually enjoy my sister, the beautiful Jane, whom I've secretly adored and openly antagonized. I want to be whole. I want to be thankful . . .*

"Can you find *Babette's Feast*?"

Nick started scrolling through Netflix and Amazon, searching. "Is it a movie? A show?"

"It's a movie—a Danish movie about a small, remote village that gets caught up in petty squabbles. Then Babette, a formerly famous Parisian chef, comes to work for the two main characters. It's about a glorious meal that brings forgiveness and . . . love. It brings love."

"That's some food."

"It is the food—it's quite a meal—but it's more their hearts. The food is just a medium . . . You'll love it."

He pushed Play, and words filled the screen. "Are there subtitles?"

"I forgot about that."

He snuggled close to me. "You're worth a few subtitles."

I watched, mesmerized, until the scenes in which Babette began to prepare the feast. No one in the village knew what she had sacrificed to make that splendid meal—one meal to open their hearts to friendship and forgiveness, one pure effort. Instead, they saw the food as an indulgence and agreed not to savor it or enjoy it. They planned to shun the gift.

I had shunned the gift.

"Hey, what's this?" Nick tilted my chin up with his finger and brushed a tear away. "Do you want to turn it off?"

"No, it's beautiful."

He leaned over and kissed me gently. "Watch your movie."

I absorbed every detail of the meal. First the wines, an 1860 Veuve Clicquot and an 1845 Clos de Vougeot, which the diners sipped surreptitiously, but then enjoyed as the feast's sensory and transformative experience moved them and they finally accepted Babette's offering without question, as a gift of grace. Then came the sublime Cailles en Sarcophage, "entombed quail," Babette's signature dish—the brilliance, the care, the offering, the love . . . *When did I forget?*

I nestled into Nick's side as he wove his fingers through my hair . . . and I soon fell asleep.

At least I think I did . . . part movie, part pain, part painkiller . . . images flooded my mind at an ever-increasing rate. The timers were set too short, the ovens too hot, the spices too old, the wine tasteless, the vegetables rotting. I raced around the kitchen seeking perfection, seeking life, but none was there. I couldn't find it. I worked harder, spun faster as it decayed around me like Miss Havisham's wedding feast in *Great Expectations*.

I heard a voice. "Are you okay?" And I felt a hand on my hair. "You're safe. Just sleep."

Was it the movie? Was the voice in my dream? It felt real. I turned back to the kitchen, and it was light, and although it looked empty, it was full of voices, happy voices—a kitchen full of people creating, sharing, enjoying, loving. Where were they? I searched; I couldn't see them, but I could hear them . . .

The next morning I woke to find myself lying across Nick's chest. He was fast asleep, his head slanted at an awkward angle. I lifted myself off, embarrassed that I'd blabbed, cried, droned too long, and fallen asleep. As I sat up and tried to sneak from the couch, Nick's eyes popped open.

"Sorry. I woke you up."

He rubbed his neck while pulling himself up. "That's okay. I was awake earlier. I must have drifted off again." He stretched his back. "How's the hand?"

"It's throbbing horribly."

"I should've woken you last night. It's bad to get behind on managing the pain." He brought me a glass of water and a big white pill. "Are you hungry?"

I shook my head. "Thanks, Nick . . . for everything."

"Shall we get you back to Jane's?" His voice dropped. "Your dad may even be there if he left super early this morning."

I nodded, unable to speak.

"You okay?"

I nodded again as he pulled me into a hug. "It's okay to need people, you know?"

I shook my head minutely within his hug.

He softly chuckled. "Yes, it is."

I stepped back and swiped at my eyes. "I'm not sure about that. Another week and you'll be gone too."

"We can still be friends. Miles don't have to change that."

I shrugged and headed toward the door. If I knew anything, it was that I didn't want to be "friends" with Nick.

Chapter 26

I sat on the bed, resting my hand on a pillow, and tried to explain the injury to Paul. "Sliced through the tops of all four fingers along the second joint, right where you fold your fingers to chop." I held up my hand as if he could see it over the phone, but I refused to offer up FaceTime.

"How bad was it?"

"The surgeon needed to graft some skin from the side of my hand, but he says I'll only be stiff, no permanent damage."

"That's good."

"I know, but it means I'll need another week at least."

"I figured as much." Paul's voice sounded resigned.

"I'm sorry, Paul. You're being so generous, and I'm so close. I mean I was close. I could feel it. Designing those meals, planning for them . . . I was alive. It's what I've been after for—"

"I miss you, Elizabeth." Paul cut across my words. "I know you don't want to hear that. I know you're focused on Jane and Feast and now your hand, and I certainly don't want to divert you from that, but I need you here."

"Why?" It slipped out before I could stop it. Part of me wanted to know his agenda even if it pressed an awkward moment.

"Myriad reasons. We won't go into them now." Paul didn't have awkward moments.

"I'll be back soon. Game on, I promise."

"Good. Go heal, Elizabeth." His quiet, firm tone surprised me. "Heal. Then come home." And he was gone.

I clicked the phone off and closed my eyes, leaning back on the bed. Suddenly life felt complicated, and it had nothing to do with my injury.

I woke up four hours later, startled that I'd slept so long. I wandered to the living room and found Jane reading.

"I've been waiting for you. Dad looked in on you and said you were sound asleep."

"Where is he?"

"He's running some errands, then grabbing the kids at school. I think he sat by your side a full half hour before I could get him to move."

"Why didn't you wake me?"

"He said not to, and I understand. Sometimes I like to watch the kids sleep, knowing that in sleep they are safe and their bodies are healing." Jane smiled more at the memories than at me. "He'll be back with them after Danny's soccer game." She pointed to my hand. "Does it hurt?"

"Even on painkillers it hurts." I plopped onto the couch, bouncing it—which hurt more. "I still can't believe it."

"What happened? I mean I know what

243

happened, I got to clean it up, but why did it happen?" She curled up next to me, folding her knees to her chest.

"Someone, Brian or Donna perhaps, called Health Services on me. Reported me for running a business from a private kitchen. As a chef, that's a big deal—at least in New York it would be."

"Are you okay? Will you lose Feast?"

"No and no. And it's all okay, really. The guy didn't ask about my work, so I didn't lie, and he let me off with a warning because I live across the country. So that's that."

"Then what happened to your hand?"

"I wasn't so calm about it yesterday. I was angry and careless. I just felt lost and alone—again." My stomach growled.

"What can I make you for a late breakfast?"

I raised an eyebrow at her.

" 'I can cook, you know,' " she mimicked as she pulled me off the couch and dragged me to the kitchen.

I leaned against the counter and watched her pull out the eggs, green onions, salt, milk, a bowl . . .

"I want to finish Tyler's food."

"They'll understand."

"I need it, Jane. I'd already told him these meals were gifts. I need to see them through."

"But you can't cook now."

"You could help me?"

Jane looked at me and paused. "Does it matter that much?"

"It does. I feel like I'm wrapped up in this, and for once I'm not trying to prove my worth as a chef or even as a human. I just want to give Tyler something from me, something that can help him. Not much matters more right now."

"I understand that," she said. "Tell me what to do."

I felt deeply and inexplicably thankful. "First, let's call Cecilia. It'll be too much for you alone."

I reached for my phone, dialed Cecilia, and launched. "Hey, it's Elizabeth. Are you working today or do you want to cook?"

"I'm off in a few hours. I'll come right over."

Cecilia's enthusiasm washed over me. "Excellent."

I turned back to find a plate of scrambled eggs sitting next to me. Jane waited. I picked up a fork and took a bite, chewing with a slow, exaggerated motion. "Hmm . . ."

"Hmm . . . ?"

"They're excellent." I smiled.

"I know. What do we do now?"

I looked at her, then down at myself. "Get dressed."

After I inhaled Jane's yummy eggs, we headed upstairs. Within minutes she was dressed and standing in the guest room doorway. I'd pulled on

245

a short-sleeve T-shirt but couldn't button my jeans.

"How am I supposed to go to the bathroom?"

"I'll get you a pair of sweat pants."

"Not yet. I can't do that."

"What's wrong with sweat pants?"

"What's right with sweat pants?"

"Forget it. Let your fly hang open long enough and you'll give in." She pulled me toward her by my waist and buttoned the jeans.

When we reached the kitchen, the task ahead of us overwhelmed me. "Maybe this is a mistake."

"No second thoughts now. Cecilia's coming, and I'm excited about this. It feels dangerous—almost Robin Hood-esque."

I chuckled. "Here are the lists for the dishes. Let's pull out all the ingredients and divide them into piles."

Soon Jane started deconstructing a chicken, and I continued to sort greens and fruits for the smoothies and salads. The doorbell rang.

"How can she be here already?"

I went to answer it and found myself uselessly fumbling with the knob and lock. "I'm getting there." I finally swung it open to find Nick, camouflaged by a huge bouquet of flowers.

"These are for you." He stepped through the threshold and kissed me—no brush of the lips, nothing tentative—a full-on multisecond moment of bliss. "How's the hand?"

I buried my face in the flowers to hide my shock and delight. "Okay for now. Come on in. Jane's in the kitchen and Cecilia is on her way over."

Nick narrowed his eyes, clearly asking, *What are you up to?*

"We're finishing the meals for Tyler."

His eyebrows shot into a lock of hair hanging over his forehead.

"Jane is helping me. Cecilia too. It's import—" I felt my lip tremble. Nick noticed and touched it with the tip of his thumb. I stilled.

"What can I do?"

"Cook?"

" 'As you wish.' " Nick winked at me.

Princess Bride? I shot him a look, but he'd moved on. I rolled my eyes, sure I was attributing more to those three little words than he could possibly mean.

"You've come to join our lunacy?" Jane commented.

"I have."

"Great. Start chopping these, and I'll brown this chicken." Jane pushed the cutting board toward him.

"Should you be doing this?"

"The sum is greater than the parts, buddy, which is good. We have very defective parts." Jane flashed me a smile.

Exactly.

Nick looked as if he couldn't quite discern

Jane's meaning, but I got it. It simply meant we were in this together and could conquer anything.

He picked up the knife and started chopping. He glanced over at me, twice. "I'm sensing something's wrong."

"Your form isn't right." I bit my lip, certain I sounded dictatorial. "Can I show you?"

He held out the knife. I stepped within the circle of his arms and rested my bandaged hand on his left arm, pinning it in place. I then used my right to curl his left fingers under, so the tips touched the board rather than the pads.

"In theory, this is safest. Now take the knife and cut near the curl; use it as your guide."

"How's this?" he whispered behind me. I felt a blush creep up my neck.

"You're a natural." I ducked out from under his arm and found Jane staring at us, her mouth slightly ajar. "What?"

"You never taught me how to chop vegetables like that."

"Get back to work."

Jane grinned, Nick chuckled, and I turned away. Soon we settled in to a rhythm, and it felt comfortable. It felt like home. I looked over at Jane; she was a touch pale.

I reached into the refrigerator and pulled out a small pressed ham loaf with mustard I'd made a couple days earlier. I cut a slice and laid it on a plate with a few dried apricots and cornichons.

I passed it to her. "Sit and have this. I made it a few days ago. Think Mary Musgrove's 'cold meat' from *Persuasion*. I think you'll like it, and you're a little pale."

Jane nodded once, mouthed, *Thank you,* and sat.

"Now when we get to this dish"—I pulled a messy printout from the chaos and turned back to Nick—"follow the red marks rather than the original recipe. I changed it after remembering some food in *A Farewell to Arms*. Really, Frederic Henry is either eating or thinking about food throughout the entire book—and drinking. The man doesn't stop drinking. This is an Italian lentil dish with tomatoes and Gorgonzola, but I want to add parsley and chives along with the dill, and I've marked to double the thyme. Use fresh and lay it on the tomatoes for roasting, then we'll throw it away and—"

"Slow down a sec. I'm reeling that you remember who ate what in *A Farewell to Arms*."

"And I want to know what we're throwing away," Jane added.

"Nothing. We quarter the tomatoes, put them on parchment paper, drizzle olive oil and balsamic, and then lay the thyme on top. That's how we'll get the flavor. Nothing is—"

Nick touched my arm. "She's messing with you."

"Oh . . ." I watched him turn back to the cutting board as Jane dropped her plate in the sink. She then returned to her onions in the Cuisinart, Nick continued to cut, and I laid out more ingredients. Nick threw Jane a comment, and she shot it back and then looked to me. I laughed and caught her quick smile. *Banter*. This was what banter in the kitchen felt like. This was what cooking with others, offering yourself to them, as well as to the food you created together, sounded like—and felt like.

"Thanks, you two. I can't tell you what this means to me." My voice cracked.

"Don't cry about it." Jane smirked.

I flashed my eyes to Nick, remembering that I'd yelled at him that crying was not bad. He caught it and raised his eyebrows. A shadow crossed his face. "Does your hand hurt? Your face just pinched."

"How'd you— It just started throbbing again. I'll go get a pill." I headed upstairs to grab the bottle.

Jane trailed me. "I need to lie down a bit."

"It's too much."

"Don't say that. I love it and I'll be back down; I just need a little rest. Are you okay?"

I shifted my eyes from her gaze. "I'm fine." I glanced toward the stairs. "He's a good guy, isn't he?"

"He is. Peter and I have tried to set him up a few times. I've never seen him this relaxed. Who knew?"

"He considers me a member of your family. I'm safe—at least that's what he said."

"Interesting definition of safe." Jane walked to her room.

I grabbed the bottle and headed back downstairs.

"I'll open that for you." Nick gently took the bottle while surveying the counter. "The chicken is done. I put it there to cool. And I followed your notes for the tomatoes. Check them, then I'll put them in. You should also check the smoothies and some of the other salads before I seal them, but the quinoa and kale one is still too warm to seal."

"That's one you'll love too. Its flavors are clean, and it's got some olives and red peppers. It's Hemingway's Italian rather than Spanish work. Let's pull a bit out for you and Matt." I paused. "This was fun today, wasn't it?"

"It was the most fun I've had in a long time." Nick came around the counter and handed me a glass and a pill. After I set the glass back on the counter, he put his hands on my waist. "I'm sorry you're hurt, but I am so glad I got to be here and do this. It felt like the movie, didn't it? You as Babette?"

I smiled, feeling my cheeks burn with the width of it. It touched my ears. "Wouldn't that be nice? To be so skilled, so poured out that you blessed others? Changed others?"

"That's you."

"Doubt it. I'll have to wait to see what Tyler says."

"This isn't just about Tyler, and the outcome doesn't even matter. Look at Jane. You said you two don't relate, but that's not what I saw today."

"I didn't cook today, and it all looks great. I'm not at Feast, and it's thriving. Maybe that's my takeaway."

Nick narrowed his eyes. "I didn't mean that and you know it. Enjoy it, Elizabeth. Enjoy what happened here today. Don't run from it."

He pulled at my waist, drawing me to him. "I learned something else from that movie last night: Babette used her gifts all the time she lived with them, getting the best produce for the best prices, working hard, but it wasn't until she completely poured herself out for others that her past and her future came full circle."

"I think I missed some of that."

"You were asleep. I'm just saying . . ." Nick closed his eyes and took a deep breath, slowing and articulating each word with a meaning I couldn't grasp. "I don't want to hide." The words were significant for him, the movie significant, in a way I couldn't grasp.

"What does that mean?"

"It means I know you. I can't explain it, but I do—even more now, and I don't want to hide from that."

"What do you—" The doorbell rang. "That's Cecilia . . . but . . ."

"Later." Nick pulled me close, gently laying a brief kiss on my lips before releasing me.

There were no pleasantries when I opened the door. Cecilia caught sight of my hand immediately and gasped.

"What happened?"

"I killed it. Dr. Wharton operated on it yesterday."

"And you didn't call me?"

"I was pretty out of it."

She hugged me gently. "Of course you were. Have you changed the bandage?"

"I've been avoiding it."

"I'll do it."

She ushered me into the kitchen and stopped upon seeing Nick.

"Cecilia, Nick. Nick, Cecilia. Cecilia is Jane's fantastic nurse and my friend." I smiled as I added the last part. "And Nick is . . . a close friend of the family."

He winked at me and crossed the room. I turned back to Cecilia. "What do you need?"

"Did they give you an ointment? Cleaner?"

"All of the above." I reached for a brown paper bag on the counter.

"Sit here and we'll get this done."

I sat down as Cecilia pulled up a chair across from me and started unwrapping my hand.

Nick came to stand beside me. "You are in capable hands, and I need to get some work done." He leaned down and kissed the top of my head. "Rest well, okay? Call if you need anything. Nice meeting you, Cecilia."

I looked up. "Hey, but . . ."

"Don't worry. There's plenty of time to talk." He touched a finger to my cheek and turned away.

Cecilia stayed quiet until the front door clicked shut. "He's cute."

"He is."

"You don't sound convinced."

"I'm only here another week or so."

"Why does your leaving mean he can't be cute?"

"Something that cute I might want to keep." I clamped my right hand over my mouth.

Cecilia laughed and looked back to her work.

"Isn't that odd? Tons of men in New York, years of unsuccessful, tepid relationships, and some single dad who wears flip-flops in Seattle sets my pulse soaring. I can't explain it. You know what he said to me just now? 'I know you.' Like he saw me, the real me, and I was just what he wanted . . . And what's worse? I felt that way about him the moment we met and shook hands. That's pathetic."

"I think it's sweet." She twisted my wrist much as Dr. Jackson had done in the ER. "This is great work, Elizabeth."

I glanced over. It was a blotched, purple, swollen mess. "You've got to be kidding."

"Not what you did, but your stitches. Dr. Wharton is a fantastic plastic surgeon. Was he on call or did they bring him in?" She didn't wait for an answer. "You aren't going to have any problems with this."

I told Cecilia the entire story and my suspicion that Brian or Donna had called Health Services on me.

Cecilia bit her lip. "It might have been Donna. Brian's outburst really upset her because it upset other patients. I gather one woman was so distraught she left without treatment. Donna's tough and curmudgeonly, but she loves her patients and they trust her. I suspect she thought we'd both crossed a line."

"Did we?"

"I don't think so. I didn't ask you as a nurse to cook meals for Tyler. I asked as a friend."

"Can she hurt you?"

"No, not really, and she's not like that. She's more like a protective mother hen. I'm supposed to protect her chicks, too, not cause commotions."

I realized I was no longer angry about the call or my hand—the life of the kitchen over the past several hours had chased it all away. "Could just as likely have been Brian. He was mad at me too. Thought I'd set Tyler up." I touched one of the Pyrex dishes. "I hope these are better and help him."

255

Cecilia looked around the kitchen. "I think what you're doing is amazing. What can I do?"

I noticed the unsealed smoothie mixtures. "Nick was going to seal those, but he left."

We fell silent while she sealed the smoothies and I put the final items away and labeled the meals.

She wiped the run-off from the last pouch. "I read an article last week about an executive chef in Minneapolis who quit his job to run a Salvation Army soup kitchen. He said, 'Faith is part of the recipe. The main ingredient.' That's not that far from what you're doing."

"I wish I could take credit like that, had faith like that, but this is a blip for me. I head back to Feast soon, I hope."

Cecilia shrugged and laid the last packet in the box.

"Thanks, Cecilia, for doing this."

"Are you going to be okay?"

"You said it looked good."

"I wasn't talking about the hand."

"Am I that easy to read?" I chuckled.

"Yes, but I understand. I've been on both sides —afraid of where I am and where I'm going to finally feeling comfortable with the journey." She leaned against the counter, as if settling in for a long chat. "If you'd met me fifteen years ago, about the time your mom was dying, you'd have found me in a teenage residential rehab facility in

Arizona. God showed me a lot of grace when he put me there and then brought me out whole."

"Whoa."

Cecilia laughed. "Yeah, you and I wouldn't have been friends back then." She waved a hand toward her outfit. "That's one reason Donna watches me. She sees the clothes, the hair, the ink, and I told her about rehab. I make her nervous."

"Why'd you tell her?"

"I never want to hide."

"Have you thought about changing?" I realized how arrogant I sounded and rushed on. "I didn't mean it like that. I just meant that if she's making life tough on you . . ."

"I have. Life would be easier, but it was that kind of thinking that landed me in rehab in the first place. I'm not staging a coup or protesting the status quo, the government, my sweet folks in Nebraska, or small puppies. I just like it. I love hair so black it turns blue or purple in the light. I love that my arms record the experiences that have formed me. I love that when someone is hurt or aches, my look startles them past their defense mechanisms and they talk to me, listen to me—actually listen to me *because* of this, not despite it."

"Wow . . . I feel silly. You have no idea how much I spend on clothes to do just the opposite—to look so pulled together and in control that I'm afforded respect, and distance."

"Not now." She motioned to my blue Mariners T-shirt and ratty jeans.

I looked down and realized that I'd started raiding Jane's closet days before, because her clothes fit and were comfortable . . . because I was comfortable.

"And what you're doing here? This is not for respect or to maintain distance." She laid her hand on the smoothie box. "This is deep in the thick of it."

"It all feels different somehow." I smiled and surveyed our work. "I haven't felt this good in a long time, even with this hand. And that's the great irony—I prepared nothing today. I simply directed Jane and Nick and you, and you all did the work."

"Leading is also giving." She walked around the island and grabbed her bag. "Do you want help delivering tomorrow?"

"Jane or Dad can take me. I don't want to cause any more trouble for you with Donna. You can watch us from the window again."

"If it was Donna, I'm sorry she hurt you."

"It could've been Brian. I may never know." I looked down at my hand. "And it'll heal." I whispered it, more to myself than to Cecilia.

After she left, I stood looking around the kitchen. It did feel good and right and whole. And it was equally true: I'd done none of the work.

"You're awake." Dad's voice startled me.

"I am. Where are the kids?"

"They're out talking to Jane's nurse, Cecilia."

"Did you meet her?"

"I did. She was trying out the porch swing as we drove up. I think Kate likes her hair."

"Don't tell Jane that. She'll have a heart attack."

"What happened here?" He motioned to the boxes on the counter.

"We finished the food for Tyler. I wanted to see it through. Can you carry them to the basement fridge for me? I'll deliver them, with your help, tomorrow."

"Sure." He grabbed two boxes and we headed to the basement. "Is this why Cecilia was here?"

"She helped, but so did Nick and Jane. They did most of the work."

"Jane did?"

"I think she got a little worn out. She's napping."

Dad shot me a look.

"I didn't push her, honest. We had fun. It was nice. I think she was having so much fun that she got tired before she knew it."

"I wish I'd been here too." He sounded wistful.

"I'm sorry we haven't always been like that."

"Don't be. It's never too late to learn that the *love* needs to be greater than the *like*."

"Where'd you hear that?"

"I made it up. I've thought a lot about where I

went wrong over the years. I let you two believe the 'like' mattered most and that it was okay to drift and hold grudges."

I let the words soak deep. The like and the love *are* different—and I'd confused them for a very long time.

Chapter 27

The next morning Dad and I made the kids breakfast together.

"Just scoot the bacon aside and pour the eggs right onto the griddle."

"They'll run all over."

"That's the point, Dad. This can't be new to you. At the fire station guys have to cook like this; it uses fewer pans."

"They do."

"Okay, pour."

He poured the eggs on and scraped them quickly, not letting a single portion dry or burn.

"You cooked those perfectly."

"I know heat."

I laughed. "Of course you do."

We hadn't enjoyed each other's company like that in years—maybe ever.

Dad helped clean up, then carried his bag down to the kitchen. I was sad to see him go, even for a few days, but I think Jane and I were once again proving too self-sufficient. He needed to feel needed.

"I'm going to bring back that generator," he said.

"A generator?"

"There's a cold snap expected, and I don't want Jane to lose power and be without heat."

I smiled. Only a dad could come up with that one. "She'll appreciate that."

"You'll be okay?"

"We will." I held up my hand. "It's stopped throbbing, and as long as I don't bump it on anything, it doesn't hurt. And we prepared all the meals we need yesterday. You don't mind dropping those at the hospital? I had planned to come with you." I pointed to Tyler's boxes.

"Not at all. It's on my way out of town, and I've got Brian's cell phone number. If I leave now I'll be right on time."

"Thanks, Dad."

"You're welcome. These men are pretty lucky to have you cooking for them."

"Let's hope they enjoy it."

I hadn't told Dad any of the back story around Tyler's meals, and I hoped Brian wouldn't say anything either. Dad was so proud of me—and that felt good.

I headed up the stairs to dress for a lunch date with Nick. It was hours away, but I refused to wear sweat pants, and if Jane didn't wake up I wasn't sure how long it might take me to dress. I finally wrestled into a wool skirt, flat brown boots, and a cream-colored sweater. No zippers involved.

Nick arrived right on time, and we drove in comfortable silence downtown. We parked and walked toward what seemed to be a grocery store loading dock. I almost backpedaled. After working in restaurants for years, I knew what lived under and behind those crates.

But I was wrong. We came to a beautifully carved wooden door at the edge of a small garden—a hidden oasis.

Nick opened the door. "I hope you like this," he said, as he ushered me in to a softly bustling restaurant full of tables, crepe lighting, and an indoor bubbling fountain. It was lovely and felt special—almost outside reality.

We ordered way too much food, but Vietnamese is a cuisine I don't try often, and I wanted to absorb every taste and texture. We started with the signature Tamarind Tree Rolls—salad rolls with fresh herbs, fried tofu, peanuts, fresh coconut, and jicama. We then moved on to the Crispy Prawn Baguette—a lightly fried prawn and baguette served with hoisin and fresh chili sauce. I was impressed at how light and crisp the batter was—it was no more than a dusting.

For a main course Nick ordered a curry chicken braised with potato and served with fresh lime and chili sauce. I couldn't help myself—I ordered the beef stew. I do this almost anywhere I go, because the cultural permutations are infinite. This one was fresh and citrusy with a dash of carrot, lime, pepper, and salt. I mentally developed some changes for my next stew. We also ordered green beans stir fried with garlic, and Shrimp Patty Noodles—a frothy bowl of vermicelli noodles, tomatoes, fresh bean sprouts, shredded morning glory, and banana blossoms.

"I feel like I'm keeping you from a lot of work lately," I said.

"This is special, and I needed the break. As I said, I don't get out much. There's Matt, but there's also no time. Being a one-man show at work has been tougher than I thought possible."

"Jane said the same thing. It was one reason Peter encouraged her to step back."

"Neither of us charges enough for how involved we get in our projects. I feel like I'm building someone's dream rather than just a business, and who can stop when the time's up on that?"

"Dream building. I like that." I took another bite of curry. "I'm beginning to think the best dreams need others to help build them."

As the waiter collected our plates and provided containers for the leftovers, Nick glanced at his watch. "If you've got time, I need to grab Matt at Uwajimaya; then I'd like to take you somewhere special."

"Waja whatta?"

"It's an Asian grocery store down the street. Amazing place. Matt's off school today, and Dad said they'd meet us there."

"I'm all yours."

Rather than turn toward the car, Nick reached for my hand and starting walking down the street. He gently pulled me as the streetlight turned yellow, and we raced the last few steps into the store. It was huge, lit with bright lights and stocked full of eclectic packaging, fresh produce, fish—it was another world, vibrant and colorful.

"Hey, they have those sodas where you pop the marble in from the lid." I tugged my hand free.

"Do you want some?"

"I love those."

Nick reached for a case as I raced on. "Hey, slow down, New York."

"You keep calling me that."

"It fits you—tough, frenetic. Not everything needs to be such a rush."

"That's so Sea—"

"Dad!"

Matt came running up an aisle. "We saw you walk in, but you didn't hear us yell."

"I'm sorry, buddy. I've been chasing Miss Elizabeth." Nick slanted a glance at me, letting me know his double meaning had been intentional. He picked his son up into a hug, then released him. Matt didn't miss a beat as he threw his arms around my waist.

Nick's eyes flickered before he pulled his gaze to an older version of himself. "Dad, this is Elizabeth Hughes."

Nick's father reached out his hand. "Nice to meet you. Nick says you're helping your sister."

We shook hands as I lifted my left one. "I don't know how much help I've been."

"He mentioned that too."

Matt tapped my arm. "What happened?"

I squatted down to describe it as Nick chatted with his dad. When I finished, the three of us stood alone. "I didn't see your dad leave."

"No big deal, he headed off to meet Mom. Besides, you were clearly telling Matt a great story."

Matt still held a look of disgust mixed with complete awe.

"I have a plan. Miss Elizabeth has never been to Old School Custard. Shall we?"

"What's the flavor?"

"Has that ever stopped us?" Nick pulled out his phone and started tapping. "It's our lucky day, kiddo. Salted Caramel." He turned to me as we headed out the door. "It's a frozen custard shop that makes only one flavor a day, but they always have chocolate and vanilla for backup."

"I've never had frozen custard."

"You're in for a treat—tons more calories

than ice cream, but much creamier. Complete yum."

Old School Custard was a small shop with walls covered in pictures of all the local high schools. I found Garfield and imagined Tyler in that huge building, teaching his beloved math. I then noticed an amazing chalk calendar with the flavor for each day listed, with creative drawings, and I understood why it was addicting—who could resist flavors like Malted Milk Balls, Carmel Macchiato, Espresso, or Banana Nutella?

I ordered The Turtle sundae—two scoops of Salted Caramel custard, pecans, hot fudge, caramel sauce, and whipped cream. Nick ordered The Recess, pretty much the same thing, but with Reese's Peanut Butter Cups instead of pecans. And Matt's Playground came complete with crushed Oreos for "dirt" and gummy worms.

We sat digging in like schoolkids.

"Please don't tell me you do this often. I'm going to be sick." I finally laid down my spoon.

"No way. This is a twice-a-year type treat, but it's so worth it."

"We were here last week, Dad."

Nick took another bite. "Busted."

Matt was the only one who showed some restraint and was unable to finish. We pitched his, saying a few sad words of farewell, and headed back toward the car. I felt Matt slip his hand within mine. I smiled and squeezed it. The kid had won his way into my heart, and it had nothing to do with Salted Caramel.

"Matt, we've got one more stop. I bet Miss Elizabeth likes food markets."

"You kidding?" I interjected.

"We've got a neat one here, small, high end, on Melrose. You'll love it."

We drove a few blocks and parked near a yellow brick building, unassuming from the outside, but inside it was a completely refurbished warehouse with small shops selling crafts, artisan cheeses, wines, and meats. At the back was a gorgeous small restaurant, Sitka & Spruce. Its kitchen was completely open to the dining area, even utilizing one end of a large table at which customers sat.

"I definitely want to eat here," I whispered to myself.

Nick overheard and leaned in. "Let's come next week."

"I wasn't hinting."

"I didn't think you were."

Back at Jane's, Nick got out of the car and walked around to the passenger door to help me out and gather my small packages—a wheel of Trufflestack goat cheese and olive oil soap.

"Thanks. This was a wonderful day, and I'm so glad I got to see Matt."

Nick darted a glance back into the car. "He really likes you."

I headed up Jane's porch steps.

"Wait. I was serious about Sitka & Spruce. How about Monday?"

"That'd be nice."

"If I don't see you before then, I'll call Monday morning." He bounded up two steps and kissed me, lingering. "But I can't imagine not seeing you all weekend."

"It's three days."

"That's a lot when you've only got about seven left." As he turned away, I caught Matt's stare through the car window. Nick seemed to question it when Matt hugged me or held my hand, but then he kissed me in front of him? And was counting days?

"You're probably going to have to explain that kiss."

"That's the point." He didn't turn around.

Chapter 28

Inside I called out to Jane but heard no reply. I headed up the stairs and found her lying in bed. "You okay?"

"I ache, but I'm fine."

"I brought you cheese and soap. Smell them."

"Which?"

"Both. They're wonderful."

She held each up to her nose. "They're nice."

Personally, I thought the earthy, musty smell of the truffles layered over the sharp tang of the goat's milk and the beautiful simplicity of the olive oil soap deserved more than "nice."

"Thanks for making me the sandwich," she said. "I ate it during my lunch date."

"Dad made it before he left. Your date?"

Jane's face softened. "Peter called to ask about the Taxol, and we had a good, long chat. It felt . . . really nice. You were right, Lizzy. He knows a lot about all this, but there's stuff he doesn't know too." Jane's face blanched, then pinched. "I'm going through menopause. I've had hot flashes for weeks."

I almost made a quip, then sobered. She was serious. "You're forty-one."

"A friend called it chemopause. My cancer is estrogen positive—so estrogen feeds it. Killing the estrogen helps kill the cancer."

I sat on the edge of her bed. "Did you want more kids?"

"I wanted the choice."

"Does Peter?"

"He doesn't have the choice now either . . . And I won't have breasts, at least not my own, and I'll get wrinkles faster because my skin is so dry and now I won't have estrogen. And who knows what my teeth will be like. Taxol can do a number on them too. And sex, forget it. I'm like a dry, shriveled prune."

"Good to know." I thought my eyes were about to burst out of their sockets.

"I'm serious."

"I believe you."

Jane pressed her fists against her eyes as she had done a few mornings before. I shifted to sit next to her and leaned back against her headboard as well.

"I didn't know."

"I don't think anyone does until you go through it. Friends mentioned it, but I didn't know it would feel like this."

"I'm sorry, Jane."

We sat for a moment. And I understood Dad. Vulnerability was hard, and I wanted to push it away. I sat for a moment more before venturing to safe ground.

"You know, the whole upsized breast thing might be an advantage. I wouldn't mind going from a B to at least a C . . ."

"I'm thinking about that myself." She threw me a lopsided grin. "There's got to be some silver lining, right?"

"And . . . Peter might not mind, you know? About more kids? I got the impression he thought your family was pretty perfect."

"True, but I still feel like I'm robbing him. Like it's my fault."

"You can't think like that. Why do you do that?" I took a breath. She didn't need my exasperation.

"What?" Jane raised her eyebrows—her eyes, actually. For the first time, I noticed the startled expression she wore, bare of both eyebrows and lashes. She now had a permanent deer-in-the-headlights look.

"You always act like you can control things and if they go badly you're to blame. You were like that as a teenager. I remember watching you with your schoolwork, your friends, dating. You were so perfect—except when you weren't—and then you were devastated and tough. The only time you were truly relaxed was when you came home from one of your trips with Dad."

Jane was quiet for a moment. "I loved those trips. Fishing, hiking. Nothing to worry about, only to enjoy. I'd love to take a trip like that right now."

"Gardening wouldn't do it, would it?"

"What?"

"Nature. I was thinking about your garden, wondering if playing in the dirt would relax you because you loved those trips, but I think not." I looked at her. "Real nature's too big to worry about or control. You just have to enjoy it . . . I don't really know you, do I?"

"Perhaps not."

"Well, I do know this. This isn't just happening to you. Peter's in it, too, and I suspect missing out on the possibility of more children won't matter. He gets you and your two wonderful kids." I straightened the pillows under my back. "Did you know Dad and I took them to the park yesterday?"

Jane shook her head.

"You were asleep . . . Anyway, a boy with a leg brace showed up, and a bunch of kids stared at him and even pointed. Kate walked right up to them and told them to stop—really nicely too. Not a single kid looked sideways at that young boy again. Do you understand the gift of that?"

"That's so great." Jane's eyes filled with tears.

"Don't cry about it."

"I'm not." She smiled, but she was still crying.

"I know something that will cheer you up." I scooted off the bed and raced to the hall bathroom. "That whole dryness thing?" I called out as I grabbed my toiletry bag. "Wait till you see what I've got."

I rounded the corner back into Jane's room to find her eyes bulging out of her head in a curious and horrified expression.

"What?" I stopped. "Your face—the dryness and wrinkles. What'd you think I meant?" I plopped the bag on the bed and opened my favorite jar of cream. "Put some on the back of your hand." I reached for another. "And feel this eye cream. You'll never get crow's feet." I pulled out six little jars of creams.

"How do you have all this? You're like what, thirty-three?"

"I have a weakness for great-smelling face creams. Smell this."

"You buy these for the smell?"

"I assess everything by smell. The only place I don't like it is in the kitchen, but that's because—" I stopped. I didn't want to discuss Mom. This was about Jane.

"These smell for only a moment; then it's gone. That's part of what's so special. Smell this." I reached for my Dr. Hauschka Moisturizing Mask. "Roses. Who wouldn't want that spread all over her face? I got it at Whole Foods the other day. I'll get you one too."

"You crack me up." Jane shook her head at me, grinning—in a somewhat superior, older-sister manner—but it still felt good. She picked up a night cream. "Buy me this one too. It smells like berries."

I beamed. "Doesn't it? And it tingles when you put it on. Have no idea why, but it feels *so* good."

"When I was first diagnosed, I thought of Mom, and it scared me to death." Jane paused. I wondered if the smells had triggered memories in her too. "Then I got a good prognosis and thought I could beat it. It'd be one more thing I conquered, and we'd be okay."

She handed me back a jar. "It isn't happening. I've fallen down, and nothing . . . nothing about this is good."

I dropped the jars into my bag and sat still, waiting.

"When Mom was sick she wrote me a letter. I

wish I still had it. It said a lot of things, good things, and she quoted some Bible verse. It said something about God working stuff out for good for those who love him. I don't remember it exactly, but I found comfort in it. I figured if she believed it, then it must be true. Do you believe that's true?"

"I want to."

"Well, I need to believe it, but I'm scared. What if I never see my kids grow up? Katie in a wedding dress? Danny as a father? And Peter? We talked today, but it was more like friends catching up than talking to my best friend, my lover, and my husband. What if this is the end, and that's how I leave him?"

"Whoa . . . Don't you think you're getting ahead of yourself?"

Her eyes hardened. "I don't deserve this." She fisted a chunk of blanket.

"No one does. Mom didn't." I sighed.

"This is about me."

I shifted so I could face her. "Not entirely. It's about cancer and bad things happening to good people. And you can't beat yourself up because you can't control it. I get that you don't understand and that you're angry. It's okay to be scared, too, but you're not responsible. Let yourself off that hook."

Tears gathered in Jane's eyes and her lip trembled. "It's terrifying, Lizzy."

I closed my eyes because that was the one thing I couldn't truly say I understood. There was no getting around it—I was still the healthy one. I was not the one staring cancer down and wondering, wishing, hoping, and praying to be the one standing at the end.

I reached my arm around her and held her tight. "I only see it from the outside. But it's pretty scary out here too."

She whispered into my shoulder. "Thank you."

"For what?"

"Talking with me. Listening." I absorbed her compliment as she ran her fingers through the ends of my hair. Tears pricked my eyes.

"I'd kill for your hair right now."

I smiled but didn't move.

Jane took another deep breath and changed the topic, but not too far. It felt as if she was emotionally cleaning house. "It was good to talk to Peter today . . . but I still picked a couple fights with him, Elizabeth. I can't seem to stop."

Elizabeth, not Lizzy. She had collected herself, and somehow it made me feel like I'd reached the end of a good book or a lovely movie—a soft sadness crept over me. We weren't children anymore.

"He's not the enemy, but I feel like I'm in a war and if I let any side down, all sides will crumble."

"Think of him as reinforcements then. Drop one side and let him pick up the battle on that front."

"What if he doesn't?"

"He will."

She rubbed her eyes, mussing the hair on her forehead. A clump tangled in her fingers and pulled away.

I looked at it and chuckled. "That's not good."

She joined me and our laughter turned to tears. "It's not funny. But it is. Oh my . . ." She untangled her hair from her fingers and stared at it. "How is there any left? You were supposed to shave it off."

"Come on." I pulled at her hand. "Let's get this over with."

I pulled a small bench from the end of her bed into the bathroom. She found Peter's shaver and settled herself in front of the mirror as I draped a towel over her shoulders.

"Do I need one of these comb-y looking things?"

She attached one with half-inch long teeth to the shaver. "Use this one. It'll shorten it; then we can shave it smooth. Can you do this with one hand?"

"If you sit very still and switch it on while I hold it." The loud buzz and vibration startled me. It felt more dangerous than I'm sure it was, but I still felt nervous about scraping it across my sister's scalp.

Her hair caught and tangled the comb before it hit the blade. "It's not working. It's pulling out your hair and tangling it."

"Here." She grabbed for the razor, switched it off, then reached in a drawer and handed me a pair of scissors. "Cut it first, then shave it."

I started cutting her hair close to the scalp. I then shaved from her forehead across the top of her head. It took an inordinately long time with one hand, but eventually I made one straight line.

We both stared in the mirror. "The horse knows the way . . . ," I sang out.

"That's not funny," she laughed. "Don't stand there staring, keep at it. You can't leave me like this."

"I don't know . . . ," I started to joke before noticing her eyes. They were round and vulnerable. Her laugh had not reached them.

"Shave."

It took me about ten minutes before I handed her the razor to turn off. She held it in her lap, perfectly still and perfectly bald. She laid it down, never breaking contact with her image in the mirror, and rubbed her hands over her head. "I didn't know what to expect."

"You're good bald." I circled her.

"Oh God, what's happened to me?" Tears streamed down her face as she pleaded with God, not with me.

I knelt before her and swiped them away with my one hand. "You're beautiful. Can't you see that? You've always been beautiful. Your hair didn't make you that way. You just always were—

inside and out. I loved watching you as a kid."

"I'm ugly and broken. There's nothing beautiful here."

"Please, Jane. You're scaring me."

She took a deep breath and swiped at her eyes. "I'm sorry. It's probably the Taxol."

I sat back on the floor and started gathering her hair.

"You okay?" She tapped the top of my head.

I couldn't look up. "You're the one who matters."

"You matter to me."

I sniffed in reply, and when I'd collected the hair, and myself, I sat on the floor against the wall. Jane sat on the bench watching me.

She took a deep breath. "I need to tell you something. I took that BRCA gene test and it was positive. You need to get tested."

"I wondered about that. Cecilia brought it up. She asked if you'd taken it, but she also told me that only five to ten percent of the population carries one of those gene mutations."

"Lucky us." She sat up straight. "Which means I'll have to talk to Kate someday, maybe soon, and even Danny."

I gasped. "Your kids . . . my kids . . . I hadn't thought . . ."

"When Dr. Chun trailed through the implications, I almost fainted."

"I'll put it on my to-do list." I had suspected it was coming. It had played in my thoughts, and I didn't want to talk about it anymore. "I've got something for your list, by the way."

"What?"

"You and Peter should go out for dinner when he gets back. A date night."

"Because I look so sexy?" she retorted, but her voice cracked.

"You need an evening out and you need to lay down your arms, on his side of the battlefield at least." I looked up at the bathroom window and watched the light play through the sheer blinds. "He can't fix this, Jane, and it's killing him."

"You said that before."

"And I'll keep saying it, because it's true. Dad couldn't fix Mom and it wrecked him. Every day he got more frustrated, angrier, more withdrawn. You saw Peter last weekend, how he hovered around you."

"He certainly didn't say or do much."

"He's lost."

"What brought Dad out?"

I wondered if I should tell her the truth. After all, it was only my truth. Perhaps Dad held another. "Mom's death," I said. "There was nothing to fix. But I don't know if he ever came completely back. He didn't seem to notice that I lived in the same house my last months at home. And his world seems smaller to me now. Not that I've seen much of it."

"It is." Jane remained quiet for a moment. "You're not there."

I looked up at her and squinted my eyes, trying to assess if it was a statement or an accusation.

"That was a mistake . . ." I wrapped a last bit of hair in a tissue and tossed it into the trash can. "But you get a chance to make your story different. You can come out stronger. Just like you said, God can use it for good. All Peter's notes suggest you might."

"What notes?"

"*His* notes." She still didn't know. "Wait here."

I hoisted myself off the bathroom floor and ran to the guest room. I gathered up all the papers Peter had given me and returned to her bedroom, spreading at least a hundred pages across her quilt while she stared.

"What is all that?"

"Your diagnosis. Interviews with other doctors. Internet research. Lists of symptoms, homeopathic cures, medical alternatives. Drawings, though he can't draw. You name it and he's looked it up, assessed it, and recorded it."

"Peter?" Tears streamed down her cheeks.

"Your Peter."

She sniffled, a horrible, snotty noise, and sat on the edge of the bed. "Why didn't he show me these?" she cried.

I turned back to the bathroom to grab some tissues when I heard the front door slam.

"Mom! Aunt Elizabeth!"

"Up here, kids," I called out, my eyes never leaving Jane's. She grabbed the tissues from me and blotted her eyes, widening them to force them bright and dry.

We heard two thumps, backpacks hitting the floor, as Kate and Danny rushed the stairs.

"I got a solo for the spring concert next month," Kate called as she rounded the corner into the bedroom.

"That's fantastic." I pulled her into a hug.

She stiffened and stared at Jane. "What happened to your hair?"

Jane smiled, small and weak. "It was all falling out, so we shaved it off." She rubbed her hands on her scalp. "Do you like it?"

Danny stepped around his sister. "Cool. Can I touch?"

"Of course."

Kate didn't move.

"Katie?"

"How . . . how could you?" She burst into tears and ran from the room.

Jane's face crumpled and tears coursed down her cheeks again.

"Jane, we had to do it. I'll talk to her."

"I should go . . ." Her eyes looked huge and hurt.

I pressed my hand into her shoulder. "Let me see her first. You let Danny rub his hands all over that bowling ball."

They both laughed, forced and watery, and Danny leaned in to hug his mom as I headed to Kate.

I tapped on her door. "Kate?" There was no answer so I let myself in. "Kate?"

She had two closets, one to hold her clothes and the other full of books, with pillows on the floor—her childhood sanctuary. I opened that door and found her holding her knees to her chest, crying.

I crawled in next to her. "You okay?"

"Why'd she do it? She looks sick now. Everyone knows. Everyone talks about it. And now she looks it."

"I know."

She sniffed. "My teachers ask all the time, my friends and their moms, and they look at me like they're sad, and like I should be sad every minute and that she could . . ."

I hugged her tight. "Don't go there. And people aren't trying to be mean or insensitive. It's hard to know what to say. But no one expects you to feel sad all the time . . . You can't. Besides, your mom can be super annoying. You gotta be mad at her sometimes. I am, often."

I felt rather than heard Kate's breath catch between a sob and a laugh. "She's different, and now . . ." The sobbing started again.

"Now it feels very real." Kate nodded into my chest as I continued. "Your mom needed to do this. Her hair was almost gone, and now she feels like she did something positive. Almost like a fighter shadow boxing before the match begins. She needed to be a conqueror."

"I want to go back to how it was."

"But we can't. That's gone forever." I squeezed her tight. "I don't know what life will be like when all this is done. It may be better. Your mom reminded me today of something your grandma believed, and it gave me the hope that good can come from this."

"Like what?"

"Like knowing that we're not alone and that God's got us. Holding each other tighter. And the joy in discovering that something this dark can turn into light . . . And that we're a team, Kate. We're a team and we band together—no matter what."

"That nurse who was here the other day said something like that. The one on the porch."

"Cecilia. I'm not surprised. I'm beginning to think she's pretty smart."

"I hurt Mom's feelings."

"I think she was more hurt for you."

"But I'm okay!" Kate pushed herself up and dashed out of the closet. I heard her running down the hall, calling, "Mom, I'm sorry." And as I headed down the stairs, I caught a glimpse of them hugging on the edge of Jane's bed.

I stood still at the bottom of the stairs listening

to Jane's consoling murmurs, my heart racing. Another time flashed before my eyes, another moment, another girl, and another regret . . . And no chance to ever say "I'm sorry."

Chapter 29

Jane was asleep when it was time to prepare dinner, so I called the kids to the kitchen to develop an alternate plan.

"I thought we'd change it up tonight. I feel so virtuous with all the healthy stuff we've been eating, and I can't do much chopping right now. Can we have bacon and pancakes?"

"Yay!" Danny pumped his fist in the air, and Kate nodded like a bobblehead.

"Good. Give me twenty minutes, unless you want to help."

"I've got a spelling test" popped out at the same time as "I'll help."

Kate stayed while Danny trudged back down the stairs.

As we pulled out all the necessary ingredients for perfect pancakes, I watched Kate. Her face seemed lighter than it had in days.

"You have a good talk with your mom?"

"Yeah." She cracked two eggs and stuck her fingers in to pick out the shells. I shuddered and looked away.

When I thought it might be safe, I glanced back at her. She was watching me, almost as if making a decision. "She still tucks me in at night and sometimes we snuggle, but it doesn't feel the same now. She's thinner, and sometimes she falls asleep."

I smiled; she'd been wondering if she could trust me. "I still love a good snuggle."

"I miss how it was." She turned back to her eggs, and we worked in silence for a few moments. "Aunt Elizabeth? I wasn't going to have a birthday party next month, but Mom says I should. She said I should invite a few friends and she'd take us bowling. What do you think?"

"Do you want to?"

"I didn't, but . . ." She stirred, possibly sorting a thousand scenarios.

"I think you should. You're turning thirteen, and it's a big deal that should be celebrated. Your mom wants to do it, and bowling is awesome."

"I'll send out an e-mail tonight."

"Good. I think you could all use a celebration. It'll be fun."

After dinner the kids headed down to the basement to watch a show, and I went to see if Jane wanted something to eat. Her room was dark and felt stuffy.

"I'm gonna open a window."

"I just shut it. It's so cold."

"It is?" There was no way anyone could be cold

in that room. I leaned over and put my hand on her forehead. "You're warm. Is that normal?"

"I ache." Jane's voice caught. "My bones hurt. They actually hurt."

"That's not normal. What do I do?" I looked around the room. "Forget it. I'll be right back." I ran downstairs, grabbed my phone, and pushed Cecilia's number.

She was calm and direct. "Come to the hospital. I'll call Dr. Chun and the nurse on duty."

"Okay." I ran back to Jane. "We're going to the hospital."

"We've got to get the kids somewhere. Oh, Dad will be so upset about this . . ."

"Focus, Jane. Come on, sit up." I put my arm around her shoulders and tried to lift her.

"But they can't come with us." She sounded breathy and panicked.

"I'll call someone from your list. Can you get dressed?"

Jane dropped her feet to the floor and pushed herself up.

Once I saw she was stable, I raced to the kitchen and called the first three names. No one picked up. I then called Nick—the only person I knew.

"Can Danny and Kate come to your house? Jane's got a whole list of people here, but no one is answering. I need to take her to the hospital."

"I'll come get them right now."

"Thanks." I was stunned that he hadn't asked any questions. *I'll be there.*

Nick's car pulled in to the driveway just minutes later. He met my eyes over Danny's head, but neither of us said anything. He just mouthed, *Call me,* and took the kids to his car.

Jane was quiet, pinched, and pale as I escorted her into the hospital.

Cecilia waited by the door. "I've already arranged a room. Come with me." She ushered us down several hallways to a suite of offices and examining rooms. "Dr. Chun is on her way. I'm going to draw blood for a workup."

"Thank you," I answered for both of us.

About half an hour later Dr. Chun appeared with Cecilia. "You've got neutropenia," the doctor said.

"What's that?"

"It means your white blood cells are too low, by a long shot, leaving you open to infection. We're going to admit you, give you a booster shot and some antibiotics. If you look better tomorrow, we'll send you home."

"I can't stay here."

Dr. Chun reached for Jane's hand. "I need you to stay tonight—in isolation. Can your sister take care of your kids?"

"Of course." I cut off Jane's protests.

Another nurse came in with a shot.

"What's that?" Jane asked again.

"A variant of the Nulasta you take, but it's quicker. I'm going to inject this into your femur."

Jane blanched. I blanched.

"It'll hurt," Dr. Chun confirmed.

Tears started running down Jane's cheeks. I grabbed her hand.

"Okay. I'm ready."

Dr. Chun injected the needle into Jane's thigh. I expected her to cry out, but she didn't. I'd forgotten how tough my sister was. Instead, she gripped my hand so hard I thought she might break a bone—mine—and that was the only hand I had left.

Dr. Chun pulled out the needle as Cecilia prepped Jane's central port for an IV. "We'll see how this works." Dr. Chun squeezed her shoulder.

Jane's lip quivered. "You won't stop the Taxol, will you?"

"Let's discuss that tomorrow." She nodded to the IV. "There's a mild sedative in there that will make you sleepy. Rest here for a few minutes while Lori admits you and finds a bed."

As everyone filed from the room, Jane leaned back on the exam table and was asleep within minutes. I questioned Dr. Chun's definition of "mild." I paced the room. Three steps turn right, two steps turn back, and two steps turn left . . .

"You have to be okay," I whispered. Jane was asleep and I knew she couldn't hear me, but I couldn't hold my fear in. "I don't want to be here again, in this moment. Do you hear me? So you have to stop this. You have to be stronger. You can't leave too."

I pressed my lips together, hoping that would stop my tears, but it didn't and my whole face became a soppy mess.

"Please. Please be okay. You don't understand. I don't want to be alone. I'm always alone. You never got that. I tried to tell you today. I only wanted to be with you as a kid . . . even now. I'm alone. Please . . . Jane, please."

"Elizabeth?"

I swung toward the door.

"Are you okay?"

I shook my head, not caring how much Cecilia might have heard or how awful I knew I looked. She crossed the room and hugged me. "I'm sorry about this."

I leaned back and sniffed. "Why are you sorry? You got us back here, and you got Dr. Chun here so fast. I didn't know what to do. You did it all." I noticed Cecilia was wearing black tights and a plaid miniskirt with cool chunky boots. "I love your boots," I said and then laughed at the absurdity of the comment. "Hey, are you off duty?"

"I got off about an hour ago. I thought I'd stick around."

I pulled her into another hug. "Thank you so much."

"Do you want me to sit with you?" She pushed

me back and studied my eyes. " 'Cause if you're okay, I want to go make sure Jane gets admitted quickly. We're busy tonight."

"That'd be amazing. Thank you."

"Okay then. I'll be back soon."

"I'm not going anywhere."

When she left the room, I pulled the chair over to Jane's examining table and rested my forehead on its edge.

"Make her strong. Make her strong. You can do that. I know you can." I whispered it over and over—and over. "I can't be the only one left. Please don't make that happen. Make her strong." It was part mantra, part prayer, and I kept saying it until I felt my heart calm. I didn't feel so abandoned, and the words became prayer alone.

"Are you done yet?" Jane whispered.

I sat up, surprised. "With what?"

"Our Elinor-Marianne moment. I'm not dying, you know."

"That's not funny. This is serious." I pressed my lips together and sniffed. "I was actually praying for you."

"I noticed. Mom used to do that."

"I know." I scrubbed at my eyes to eradicate all signs of tears.

"I'm sorry."

"For what?"

"For scaring you . . . for teasing you . . . and I

like the prayers." Jane turned her head and watched me. I knew my face revealed more to her in that moment than all my verbal sparring or emotional outbursts. I felt completely bare.

"Come here." She hooked her arm around my neck.

"Why?"

"Because you're my sister and I love you."

I rested my head against her side in a semihug position. I never wanted to move.

After a couple minutes she pulled her hand back. "I feel better. Maybe it's the painkiller, but I don't think so. Deep in my bones, it doesn't ache like it did."

"That must be a good thing."

Cecilia pushed the door open, tapping on it as she entered. "Are you two okay?"

"No," we whispered simultaneously.

Cecilia perched against the counter. "I've got a room, so we're going to wheel you up there now. Do you want to come, Elizabeth?"

I glanced to Jane and knew where she'd want me to be. I reached for her hand. "I'm going to go take care of Danny and Kate."

Jane squeezed my hand, then let go.

I reached down and kissed the top of her head. "You sleep. The kids will be fine."

I turned away, but Jane grabbed for my arm. "Don't call Dad," she whispered.

"Why not?"

"This'll kill him. We can't do that to him. He left because he thought we were fine."

"We're never fine," I quipped.

"But he needs us to be."

"I won't call. You can, tomorrow, when you're out of here."

Cecilia gently smiled. "We'll take good care of her."

As I walked to the car, I knew Jane was right. Dad needed us to be okay. He hadn't ever "come out of it" as Jane had asked this morning. He still carried some misplaced guilt or blame for Mom's death and for the estrangement in our family. And for him to have left this morning, right when he was most needed—it would be a failure too painful.

I headed to Nick's house and rapped softly on the door. He answered immediately.

"I didn't ring the bell in case the kids were asleep. I'm sorry it's so late."

"No worries. I tucked Matt in a couple hours ago, and the other two are curled up on the couch in the basement. They were a little shaken, so I put on a movie. Danny fell asleep right away." He held the door open. "Do you want to come in for a minute?"

"I should just grab them."

Nick shut the door and led the way to his basement stairs. "I'm glad you called me."

"I'm glad you answered."

"Is Jane okay?"

"I'm not sure. She got toxic, so the new chemotherapy might not be possible, but I also gather that toxicity doesn't necessarily last, so it may still be possible . . . I only know she got a shot in her femur and she hurts."

"How are you?"

I looked at him and wondered if he wanted the real answer. So many people don't. "I hurt too."

He nodded and turned to go down the steps, but as he touched down on the first step, he bounced back up and grabbed me. He pulled me in to a tight hug, his arms around my back, pressing me fully to him. I was too stunned at first to react, then sank deeper in to the hug, curling my arms around him.

After a few minutes he pulled away and brushed my hair back from my temples and held my face in his hands. "I'm sorry you hurt." He then pressed his lips to mine, not in a romantic way but firmly, as if trying to absorb my pain. It was so solid, so melting, and it lasted long.

He touched his lips lightly against mine once more and turned to lope down the steps. It took me a few heartbeats to follow.

The movie had ended and both kids were asleep on the couch. I gently woke them and ushered them out to the car.

"Thanks again." I turned to Nick as I shut Kate's car door.

"You're welcome. I'll check in with you tomorrow." He leaned down and kissed me again—short and brief, but not a brush. Again, I found myself pondering the comforting, exciting solidity of it.

Chapter 30

I tossed all night and finally got up early and poached eggs in a thick puttanesca to serve over polenta.

"Why no oatmeal?" Danny asked.

"I've been up a while . . . Hey, I thought you didn't like oatmeal."

"I got used to it."

"I'll put it back on the menu tomorrow and get it just right."

My mind drifted to *Cold Comfort Farm* again and how the cooking of oatmeal reflected the heat and tension of the story—ours would be cold and uncooked if I tried it today. The whole house felt flat. I offered a smile alongside the eggs and ushered the kids out the door. On time—another sign things weren't right.

Soon after the kids left, Nick called. "Any word from Jane?"

"She called early and is doing well. I'm to pick her up around two, which will get us back before the kids get home."

"Then you're free for lunch?"

"I'm always free for lunch."

"Good."

"It's beautiful out and I'm making chicken salad right now. Do you want to have a picnic at the park?"

Nick paused.

"Don't you like that idea?"

"I love that idea and I love chicken salad . . . I'll walk over around noon and help carry the food."

At a loss to convey all I wanted to say, I simply said, "Thank you."

I hung up and thought more about all the ways Nick had stepped in to help my family. *My family.* Turning back to the chicken salad, I instinctively knew how to relay my thanks. *Mr. Hemingway. Mr. Greek Tragedy.* I smiled and relished the little brightness that simmered inside as I put away the tarragon and the mustard.

I had just finished packing the basket when the doorbell rang.

"I'm all set."

"We can't leave yet." Nick stepped through the doorway and headed to the kitchen. "I have a gift for you and a couple plants for Jane's garden."

I shut the front door and trailed after him. He'd placed a small box with plant cuttings and a white bag filled with pink-and-green tissue paper on the island.

"Did you wrap this?"

"I did."

I pulled out the tissue and stared into the bag. "How'd you know?"

"You said Jane didn't have one."

"Jane doesn't have a lot of things."

"Your tone said this one mattered."

I took a deep breath and blinked to hide my emotions as I pulled out the heavy marble mortar and laid it on the counter, running my hand all over it. It was cool, smooth, and perfect—and used. I reached back in and found the pestle wrapped at the bottom of the bag—an oversize wood one, my favorite kind, worn soft and smooth.

"This is yours."

"It is. The woman at the store said it takes weeks to properly break one in, and she only had marble pestles anyway. I don't like those. So I figured perhaps mine was best."

"Won't you miss it?"

"It's in good hands."

I stared at him.

"What?"

"Wait one sec." I held up a finger. "Don't say a word." Hope and excitement bubbled inside. I reached for a box from Jane's cabinet and sifted through some spices that I'd collected at Whole Foods, Melrose Market, and Pike Place Market over the past couple weeks. It was difficult to open the pouches with one hand.

"Can I help you?"

"Shh . . . I can get it." I pinched cumin, coriander, and sweet paprika. I laid my left arm across the mortar to hold it in place and ground the mixture gently. I smelled it and added black pepper and salt. *So close.* I tore a few leaves of thyme and cilantro and rolled them in gently.

"What are you—?"

"Stop talking," I whispered. I closed my eyes and lifted the mortar, smelling. I added a touch more coriander and rolled the tip of a mint leaf in my fingers to release only the oils. I then touched the spices and stirred again. "Done." I held the bowl to him.

"That smells good. Earthy, spicy. What gives it that clean scent?"

"The cilantro you brought for Jane with the slightest hint of mint oil."

He smelled it again. "What's it for?"

"It's you. That's what you smell like, to me at least." I shrugged, embarrassed. Only Tabitha knew I did this when I was trying to figure someone out. When I had attempted one for Trent, it had morphed into an angry diatribe that burned my eyes.

I gently pulled the mortar from Nick's hands and carried it to the compost bin. Nick reached for me.

"What are you doing?"

"Pitching it. I'm not going to use it." I rested it in the sink to brush the spices from it.

"Stop." He grabbed for my hand. "Don't. Please . . . Put it in a baggie. I want to keep it."

"You can't use it." I shook my head. "It'll clash when heated, especially with the fresh leaves I added."

"I won't. Promise. But I want to keep it."

I handed him the mortar and found a baggie. He quickly brushed the mixture in and tucked the bag into his back jeans pocket.

"Have you ever blended what you think represents you?"

"I wouldn't know how."

"What's your favorite spice?"

"Hmm . . . It changes all the time." I dug around in my box. "I found a blend the other day I really liked. Feast has no cultural root, but even so, I never cook Indian, so I don't come across this every day." I pulled out a pouch and opened it for him.

"I like that." He sniffed again.

"I think it reflects my mood lately. It's a regional blend called Garam Masala, so you can find endless permutations, but they're all earthy, subdued, almost sad—a mixture of peppercorns, cloves, cinnamon, black-and-white cumin seeds, and black, brown, and green cardamom pods. This is the brightest iteration I've found. It pushes the green cardamom more and has a fresh kick at the end. Maybe that's what I want to happen in me."

"I like the fresh kick." Nick smiled and dropped

a quick kiss on my cheek. "Shall we go enjoy our picnic?"

I pointed to the basket resting on the table.

"You have a basket and everything." He laughed.

"Jane did."

We walked out the front door and headed to the park. It was in the midsixties and perfectly sunny. Huge white clouds puffed above, and Lake Washington lay still and serene.

"I thought it rained here all the time, even more than in Hood River."

"This is unusual. Look, the Big Man is out." Nick pointed across the lake.

"The Big Man?"

"Mount Rainier. That's what I call him. When he's out, he dominates the landscape." Nick led me to a bench and set the basket between us. "What do you have in here?"

" 'Today I'm a mean beast and I cut it very fine.' " I reached in and grabbed two bottles of San Pellegrino and the tubs of chicken salad, handing one of each to Nick. "It's a line from *The Wind in the Willows* about a particularly splendid picnic."

I reached back into the basket and dug around. "There's also a box of crackers, some really nice cheeses, apple slices . . . and cookies. Save room for the cookies."

"You did all this?"

"Of course."

"One-handed?"

"I didn't say it didn't take all morning."

Nick stared at me a moment, then shifted his eyes out to the lake. After a moment, he turned back to me. "This is really nice."

"Let's hope it tastes as good."

Nick popped open the lid of his Pyrex container and waited for me to do the same. I handed him a fork and motioned to him to take the first bite.

"What's in this? It's my favorite chicken salad ever." He shoved in another bite.

"I thought you'd like it. It's got cherry tomatoes, chickpeas, red onion, radish, cucumber . . . salt, olives, olive oil . . . feta cheese . . . and lemon juice." I dug around in mine. "And red bell peppers. I couldn't remember those. And some herbs."

"It tastes Greek. I love Greek food."

"I figured as much."

Nick slanted his eyes at me. "I know I never mentioned that."

"Your books. You love Greek tragedies, and the walls of your house—they're all clean, white. You art is modern, southern European, even Greek, in its colors. It all goes together." I took a bite and continued. "Cecilia helped me think that through. I was cooking for Jane, then Tyler, and I mentioned their books. She basically said that all our interests form our totality. We can't be divided up. And even though I'd been leaning that direction, it became clear. I began to know how to cook for them when I focused on the whole person—what made them smile, what they clung to when scared or insecure, even what paintings are on their walls or books on their shelves." I shoved another bite into my mouth, embarrassed that I'd started to babble.

Nick smiled at me. "I love it when you do that."

"What?"

"Get all excited. Your face turns pink and your eyes light up. I've only seen it when you talk about food. I may need more time to find other topics that cause that reaction."

I ducked my head and shoved in another bite—and almost choked.

"Seems I found one."

Reality stepped in front of me. "I wish you did have more time, but Peter comes home tonight."

"What's Peter got to do with it?"

"I need to go. Peter hopped the first flight after I texted him about Jane last night—and they need to be together as a family." I lifted my left hand up, now wrapped only in a thin gauze. "I can get these stiches out in New York."

"I thought we had more time."

His "we" surprised me. "I have a few more days off, but it's time now."

Nick grabbed my forearm. "Stay. Take those few days. Cook. Be with Jane and Kate and Danny *and* Peter . . . and me. Stay."

"But you said yourself that—"

"Forget what I said. Forget it all. Please." He caught my eyes and held them. "Just stay. As long as you can."

Without breaking eye contact I heard myself answer. "Okay."

Chapter 31

Three nights later found Jane and me standing in her closet debating clothing. She was on her fifth outfit.

"Why don't you wear the first dress?" I held it out to her.

"No one wears dresses, and I've lost weight. It doesn't hang right. I'll stick with these jeans."

"It looked wonderful." I threw the dress on the bed. "At least put heels on."

"Flats are more practical."

"Then the leggings will be cuter with the flats."

"I think I like the jeans."

"Absolutely." I rolled my eyes. "Can I make any more suggestions?"

She finally decided on jeans, a light blue blouse with a fitted cardigan, blue ballet flats, and a silver necklace of mine that I forced around her neck. It played beautifully against the navy scarf on her head.

We moved on to makeup, and her first attempt

was terrifying. We stood shell-shocked before the mirror.

"I hardly put any on."

"Without hair or eyebrows or eyelashes, I guess blush stands out more."

"I'll say." She laughed.

I detected a note of hysteria. "No, it's funny. You will not cry."

She snorted. "Now you sound like me."

"That's why I should've gone home by now."

"I'm so glad you didn't." She looked back to the mirror and rubbed off the blush. "I wish I had a wig."

"Ugh . . . Really? That would look odd."

"I look odd now. I'd escape notice in a wig."

"I doubt it. I think it'd be horrid. Besides, you look good."

"You look better."

"It's the skirt. I'm telling you dresses and skirts never lead you astray." I twirled. "I got this at a fantastic consignment store. You wouldn't believe what women in New York sell for pennies the next season. Tory Burch."

"Who?"

"Never mind."

Jane turned from the mirror and stared at me. "I'm nervous."

"You've been married for sixteen years. You've been on a few dates with Peter."

"It's not that. I don't want to be the person I'm

303

becoming. I'm angry all the time. I want to go out tonight and laugh and have fun and feel alive. What if I can't?"

"You will." I touched her head. "Let the rest go. Mom once said God was there to hold what was too heavy to carry."

"I never heard that."

"She said it at the end." I leaned against the sink. "She said a lot at the end that's only coming back to me now . . . Going through this with you brings it back."

"That's no fun."

"I didn't mean it like that. I'm remembering that time, but in a new way. I can recall how she used to curl up with me on the couch and tell stories and share her thoughts, her faith, her perspective, really—and her joy. She had joy, Jane. I'd forgotten that. I never carried that with me. I only carried the pain."

We turned at a knock on the door. Kate opened it and peeked her head in. "Dad said to hurry up."

I laughed. "Tell him we're coming." I looked back at Jane. "Take a deep breath and let's go have fun."

As we headed down the stairs, Peter smiled up at Jane, and her face lit up at the expression in his eyes. Kate and Danny were somewhere else in the house. I wished they'd been there to see that moment.

"You sure you two don't want to go out alone?"

There was a moment of silence before Peter spoke up. "While that would be great," he said, with a glance over at Jane, "I'd like to see Nick and thank him. He really helped me out this time. And you? I can't tell you what it's meant to have you here."

I savored Peter's compliment as we drove to Nick's.

He met me on his porch. "Perfect timing. The sitter just arrived."

"Sorry it's earlier than we planned and there are more people."

Nick reached for my hand. "This is great. Peter and I haven't hung out in a while. I'm looking forward to it."

We climbed in to the backseat, and Peter turned around. "Where to?"

"I made reservations at Luc, but I think we should head to Capitol Cider on Pike instead. Elizabeth's been telling me about what Jane likes to eat, and their menu has a lot of gluten-free, slow-cooked food. And they have good ciders. And shuffleboard."

Jane twisted in the front seat. "Shuffleboard?"

"Exactly." Nick turned to me and winked.

At the restaurant, we found a booth and piled in. Peter and Nick started bantering about old friends and work happenings while Jane and I listened.

Jane grew quiet, her face drawn. I wondered if

she hurt or was too tired, or if this was a mistake.

"It was ballsy going out on your own," Peter commented.

"Agreed, but all in all, the timing was good. The economy put everyone in flux, and folks| were looking for new, more modestly priced work. It opened the field."

Peter rubbed his chin. "True. I couldn't have done it, but in-house is sure different. There's no getting around that."

Nick chuckled. "Microsoft is different."

"That too."

The waiter came to take our orders, but Jane simply shook her head.

I reached for her hand, which rested on the table. "Can I order something for you? There are a few things I think would taste good."

She shook her head again. I turned to the waiter. "Can you give us a minute?"

"Is this too much tonight?" Peter put his arm around Jane's shoulder. "What's up?"

"It's just . . . You get to talk about work. I liked my work too. I'm stuck, I hate it, and you . . ." Jane waved her hands, letting the gesture finish the sentence.

"I shut down your business." Peter sank into the booth.

"I—" Nick opened his mouth.

"—play shuffleboard," I interjected and pushed him out of the booth. He caught himself before falling off the edge as I hurtled after him and corralled him to the shuffleboard.

He stopped and turned into me. Our faces were inches apart. "I'll give them back. I don't need the clients. I thought she wanted this."

"Offer it later; this isn't about her work." I looked back. Jane sat with her arms crossed, her head down. Peter slumped next to her. "This is about a whole lot of stuff and maybe nothing more than fear. Social media is the least of it."

"I feel really bad."

I reached for the puck. "Don't. Let's play a game, and then we'll go back."

Nick glanced back and forth from the booth to the shuffleboard for a few seconds before committing.

We returned fifteen minutes later to find a subdued but happier couple. Peter was holding Jane's hand in his lap, and she was leaning toward him, no longer away. I could tell there had been tears, but she was smiling and looked beautiful.

"Have we held up the ordering?" I asked as I slid in.

"Not at all. Fish and chips all around. Is that good with you two?"

Nick sat down. "Definitely. Did you order the special sauce? I think Elizabeth will love it."

"What is it?"

"I read it's a pickled sauce. Getting great reviews." He smiled, slowly and deliberately, before turning to Jane. "Jane . . ." He spread his hands across the table in offering. "Your clients are yours. They miss you. I'm doing my best for them, but the minute you say you're ready, I'll step away."

"I shouldn't have said anything. I couldn't handle them right now, and you've kept me in the loop on my schedule and my terms. That's more than I could've asked for." Jane bit her lip and threw a glance to Peter. "This wasn't really about that. I simply don't like where I am right now."

"But you won't be in this place much longer." Nick's voice asked for an answer, a commitment.

"I won't. You're right."

When we arrived back at Nick's, I decided to play the proper date and walk Nick to the door, but as we got out he took my hand and leaned back in to the car. "Do you mind leaving her here? I'll get her home."

"Not at all." Peter waved and drove away.

"I figured they could use a few minutes, and it's a gorgeous night. Can I walk you home?"

"I'd love that."

After half a block, Nick pulled me to a stop. "Okay, what is it? You're grinning ear to ear."

"Isn't that the craziest thing? I never do that."

"Never?"

"Never. I don't think I've felt this light since I was sixteen. There's a picture on my bedside table—I saw it when I was home a few weeks ago, and my smile stunned me. It was so bright. I think that must have been the last time I felt that way. But as tough as this month has been, I've got that same feeling and I'm cooking and my hand doesn't hurt and . . . I'm smiling."

He took my hand and resumed walking. "I love that you feel that way. Don't let it go. Most of the time, I'm so busy I can't tell how I feel. But not these last few weeks. They've been really special." He looked down at me and smiled. "How *did* we become friends?"

"It was all your fault," I laughed. "I wasn't interested."

"I doubt that."

I could hear the smile in his voice and decided not to reply, just hold his hand, walk, and enjoy the night.

Chapter 32

Dr. Chun postponed Jane's chemo by three days to let her body heal. At first she was quiet and sullen, then came the Decadron tablets and she was sizzling. In a single day we cooked up a feast that would have put Miss Havisham's to shame—the one on her wedding day, not the rat-infested mess we find years later. We also planted Nick's cuttings, cleaned the garage, and organized Peter's study. I wasn't certain he'd appreciate that last effort. And, now, having gotten the green light from Dr. Chun, we were headed back to the Infusion Center.

"Why isn't Peter here today?"

"He asked, but you leave in a few days so I gave him another day off."

"Fine. Don't go toxic again."

Jane let out a small laugh that ended in a breathy hiccup. "I'll try not to."

The Infusion Center sign looked larger today. I'd thought so when we came for the blood draw earlier and conceded it was probably because I now appreciated the power of these drugs and this place. I glanced away and found Cecilia striding across the room.

"I've been waiting for you. Welcome back."

"Let's do this thing." Jane's voice reminded me of baking chocolate—dark, flat, and flaky.

Cecilia smiled. "I'll suit up."

Jane crossed the room to our chairs. Her energy from yesterday had vanished, and I sensed that as soon as the Taxol began she would fall fast asleep. She was shredded, but her house gleamed—and she had a garden.

She let out a huge sigh and snuggled in to the recliner. I reached for my bag and felt the weight of the book in my grasp. I pulled it out.

"*Persuasion*?"

"I grabbed it this morning. Can we read it next?" Jane's eyes were still closed.

I ran my hand over the cover. "Why not? I could use a happy ending."

"Austen always gives us that."

"True, but she gave us more in this one. This one's the real deal."

And for me it was. Without ever losing sight or diminishing Anne's reality and social limitations, Austen gave her and all of us the soft, steady hope of second chances, happiness, true love, and the promise that life might be better close to thirty than it was at eighteen. It was also an ending that didn't arrive with a ball and bow, but shot straight to the heart with the accuracy and power of a tipped arrow. And, as I visualized my face cream collection, we got to look better too. After all, Anne was a "very pretty girl" at eighteen. I contend she looked even better when her "bloom" returned.

I started reading and soon lost myself in the story. We quickly arrived at Uppercross Cottage, where Anne had come to care for her sister, Mary, who was always suffering under the weight of her own complaints. I stumbled over a passage.

Anne had always thought such a style of intercourse highly imprudent; but she had ceased to endeavor to check it, from believing that, though there were on each side continual subjects of offence, neither family could now do without it.

Anne had been observing the oftentimes antagonistic relationship between Mary and her in-laws, the Musgroves, but I saw my relationship with Jane and even her relationship with Peter. Could any of us survive without our "continual subjects of offence"? Or did we need them to remain strong? I bit the corner of my lip. I had held those offenses close and fed them over the years, but now I felt the harm they'd done and the emptiness they'd left.

"That's a new book, isn't it?"

I turned to find Andy sitting behind me.

"Hey, you're back—and today?" I checked myself, wondering if that was wrong to say. I held up the book. "It is. We finished *Emma* a couple days ago."

"I took ten days off and here I am." He gestured to the book. "I like this story better."

"You do?"

"She's thoughtful. That other girl was annoying. She was like my sister."

I chuckled. "Are you saying your sister is self-absorbed?"

"Yeah."

I glanced to Jane who had, in fact, fallen asleep. "Mine is too," I whispered. "Where's your mom?"

He nodded to the end of the room, where she stood chatting with Cecilia. "It's not working."

I refused to ask what he meant; I knew.

"This may be my last time. And even this is hardly worth it; I've been dosed down so much. My team is devising a new plan." He glanced back to his mom. "She's freaking out. I think Cecilia's trying to make her feel better."

I offered an "I'm sorry" that fell limp between us.

He shrugged.

"Do you want me to keep reading? You'll meet the hero soon. You'll like him."

Andy's eyes darted above my head. "Hi, Mr. Griffin."

I sprang out of my chair. I hadn't noticed Mr. Griffin, the grumpy older man with the sweet-looking wife, pushing his IV across the room. I glanced around. There were no available recliners.

"Do you want my seat? Here." I pushed my plastic chair toward him and grabbed another from a grouping a few feet away.

He sat and grinned. "Thought I'd come listen. Ruthie's gone to get coffee."

"Did I wake you? I tried to whisper."

"I wasn't asleep. I just close my eyes to make me look peaceful. Don't tell Ruthie. I'm practicing." Mr. Griffin winked at Andy.

"That's not funny," I gasped.

"Tell her it's a little bit funny." He turned to Andy, who nodded, agreeing with him.

"Fine. I'm going to keep reading."

Anne's hike to Winthrop helped me forget their gallows humor. The tension was exquisite as Captain Wentworth realized that Anne had refused another's hand in marriage. He needed to show

313

her he still cared, but in a way she would accept—
an invitation from his sister for a ride home. He
offered a hand into the carriage. They touched
and the horses walked on . . . *Swoon!*

I stopped reading and fleetingly wondered how
I had ever put Austen away. It was like Feast's
olive oil cake—simply perfect.

"How does she do that?" Jane opened her eyes
and stared at me. "She says virtually nothing and
I'm having a hot flash." Her face shot beet red
as she realized we weren't alone. "It could just be
the chemo."

I laughed. "It's all Austen. She's a clever lady."

"She never goes for the obvious. Her hero puts
you in a carriage because that's what we want—
someone to love us like that, to woo us even if our
egos or our fear makes us resist . . ." Jane's voice
drifted away. She wasn't talking about Austen.

"I bet you do that, don't you, Mr. Griffin? Woo
your wife?" I tried to redirect Jane.

"Call me Herb. I try, but Ruthie makes it easy."
His eyes softened as he followed his wife's walk
through the room.

"I didn't expect to find you here." She squeezed
his shoulder and pulled over another chair.

"I wanted to listen to their book." He nodded at
me to continue. So I did . . .

As we drove home, my eye caught the orange
awning on Madison Street. The empty sandwich

shop had been dancing in my imagination. I could see how I'd decorate it, what I would serve, how it would smell. I shook myself. Vacation was almost over; that would have to be someone else's dream.

Jane tapped my arm. "Can we stop for a coffee?"

"Don't you want to take a nap?"

"I'd rather stay up and join you all for dinner tonight. It's become the celebration it used to be. Kate's better, don't you think?"

"I do. She's smiling more. Do you remember how Mom called us to dinner?"

"No."

"She used to yell, 'The feast is ready.' I named Feast after that, after her. I'm beginning to think she meant more than just a meal."

"I'm sure she did." Jane sighed. "And I never noticed."

I turned in to the Starbucks, and, while Jane found us a table, I ordered and waited for our drinks. I ducked my head into the next room, thinking a seat by the fireplace would please her, and I found one—next to Nick.

"Hey, Nick. Can Jane and I come—" I stepped to him, but as he turned his head, I stopped. "You okay?"

He ran his hands over his face. "I didn't sleep last night." He motioned to the spot on the couch. "Join me?"

"Jane's here too. I'll go get her."

Nick didn't reply.

I grabbed our drinks and motioned to Jane to follow me. I sat on the couch next to Nick, and Jane took the chair to the side, tucked right up to the fireplace. He barely lifted his eyes from the fire as we sat.

"What's up? You look like death warmed over," commented Jane. I smiled. The steroids were still working.

"I feel like it." Nick looked between us. "Can I ask your opinions?"

We nodded.

"Rebecca called last night." He shot me a glance. "She's here in Seattle and she wants to meet Matt. I don't know what to do." He ran his hands down his quads, leaving them resting on his knees.

Jane and I shared a long, wide-eyed stare. She spoke first. "Out of the blue? Just called up and said, 'I'm here'?"

"Basically." Nick reached over and touched my hand. "I wanted to call you last night, but it was late and I knew what today meant." He looked back to Jane. "It went well?"

"Yeah, I feel good. Even this early in the day, it's different from last time. Now back to you. What'd you tell her? How long is she staying? What does she really want?"

"Whoa, slow down, Jane. We're not all firing that fast." I squeezed Nick's hand.

"I told her I'd think about it, but I don't think I have a choice."

"Of course you do." I leaned forward.

"Not really. Last time she came she simply called, and when I explained I was losing my job, Matt was sick, everything was in chaos, she immediately withdrew. She said she was busy, staying with friends, and would touch base the next time she came to town. End of story. But this time is different; she's here to meet him. She pushed hard, and she could too; she could meet him on the street or show up at my door. She says she wants to be in his life and that I can't deny that. And she's right. Right? She's his mom. If I somehow keep her away and Matt finds out, how could he ever forgive me?"

"He might not."

"Jane!" I called out, then looked around and lowered my voice. "That's hardly helpful."

"But it's the truth. She's Matt's mom and that's powerful. And if she's determined, really determined, Nick can't stop her. Not really. You're not a mom, Lizzy."

"I know, but—"

"She's right." Nick cut me off.

"What?" I let go of his hand.

"She's right. Rebecca's not going away. I could hear it in her voice. I've got to manage this as best I can, but it's happening." His voice came out flat and defeated.

I accepted it too. "Anything we can do to help?"

"I wish." He took a deep breath. "I need to call Rebecca, then head to the school to pick up Matt." He stood and pulled his phone out of his back pocket.

"We'll go." I stood and motioned to Jane. She stood silently and walked past me. I stood in front of Nick but could tell he'd already gone, and I instantly missed him. "Call me, okay?"

He glanced up from his phone. "Huh? Yes, of course . . ." His eyes focused. "Sorry about all this. Of course I'll call. Later tonight?"

"Whenever is fine." I stood on my tiptoes and kissed him on the cheek, then followed Jane out the door.

Chapter 33

As we drove home, Jane turned to me. "Whoa. That's a mess. Hope he doesn't lose focus at work."

"That's what you're thinking about? Your clients? Did you see his eyes? And what about sweet Matt? What's going to happen?"

"They'll be fine. Maybe Rebecca's really changed and is back for good, I don't know. It might be good for Matt."

I was good for Matt shot across my mind. I

pulled the car in to Jane's driveway and sat for a moment, stunned.

"What's wrong?"

"I really liked him," I whispered, mostly to myself.

Jane snorted. "Don't be dramatic. You're here for a moment. You'll head back to New York and never think about him again. This is about Nick and his son and what's best for them. Did you seriously just criticize me about worrying for my clients, and you're upset about a spring fling?"

I didn't think. I attacked. "I will think about him again because I actually liked him. A lot. I'm not wired like you. 'Out of sight, out of mind' doesn't work with such ruthless efficiency in my life." I pulled myself out of the car, balancing my coffee and my bag in one hand.

Jane was silent for a few steps before I heard a soft, chilling, "It all comes back to Mom, doesn't it?"

"It all comes back to you."

"Don't you think I've paid enough?"

I turned to face her. "Enough? What have you ever paid? I paid, Dad paid, and Mom certainly did. You didn't come visit your dying mother, Jane, or your family who was suffering. So, yes, it will always come down to that." I'd never said the words aloud, and now they came out—clear, clipped, and biting.

"Peter and I were living in Shanghai then. We

319

were a world away, and Dad would call and say, 'She's stronger today,' 'Her color is good,' or 'I think we'll come visit you when all this is over.' I wanted to believe him, so I did. You can't blame me for that."

"Yes, I can. You know Dad. You can read him better than that. You two are so alike. He ran away in the same house and you . . . you never came back. Yet you've ridden me for a decade about not coming home, not showing Dad enough respect. Well, you only pay it now because it's easy. You weren't there for the hard stuff. I was. I was the only one. And when you're now the one going through it, who's here again—me. And you belittle me by saying my feelings don't matter. How dare you."

We dropped our bags in the front hall and faced each other.

Jane's face fell. "I was scared, okay? I couldn't help, and I felt guilty, guilty for not being close, not like you were. I was deficient. I should've done more, felt more . . . And then it was too late and the shame overwhelmed me. I let her down. And it was too late." Tears ran down Jane's cheeks.

"You didn't even stay for the reception."

"I couldn't stay . . . All those people. It's such a small town. They all knew I hadn't come home." Jane's eyes filled with tears, but none fell.

"It wasn't about you, Jane. When can it stop being about you?" I looked toward the stairs.

"I'm done here. It's past time." I trudged up the stairs, calling halfway up, "If you need me, I'm packing. I'll get a room near the airport tonight." I reached the doorway of the guest room and realized I couldn't pack with one hand, and suddenly I felt too tired to try.

Someone tapped on the doorframe behind me. "Are you okay?" Peter asked.

I swiped at my eyes. "You heard all that?"

"The kids and I were in the kitchen."

I flopped on the bed. "I'm so sorry. They don't need that right now. None of you do. I'm messing all this up."

"You're not." He sat next to me. "You've been a godsend, and we had all this going on before you came."

"Will you get through it?"

"Of course. Jane will heal." He chuckled. "I've done enough research to know that. Her doctors have told her, too, but she can't hear it. I think she's replaying your mom's illness and her guilt like an old movie."

"Maybe we both are." I held my head in my hands.

"Tell you what . . . Spring break started today. I was going to take the family to the Great Wolf Lodge next week; it's a goofy water amusement park about an hour away. But Jane wants to leave today. She told me to give the kids a half hour to pack and we're out of here."

"She can't do that. She could go toxic. She's not strong enough."

"Your sister? She's as tough as they come. Besides, if something happens, we're less than an hour away. She knows what it feels like now."

"But why?"

"I think she's doing it for you and . . . I think she wants to fight. There was a light in her eyes just now. I don't care what put it there, I'm just glad it's back."

"Excellent. That's what I'm good for, firing up Jane."

"I think she doesn't want you to leave, not like this. You won't come back if you do." Peter leaned forward onto his knees. "We all know that." He tapped my hand. "Besides, you still need to get your stitches out."

"It's time. We all know that too. If I'm going to salvage my career, I'd better get to it."

"Paul gave you the time, Lizzy. Please don't leave. Jane isn't the only one who's afraid that you'll never come back. I can't have that."

"Why not?" I snorted.

His eyebrows sank as he met my gaze. "You're my family too."

I leaned my head against his shoulder and rested. "I like that, Peter. I really do."

He patted my leg. "Give us a half hour. If you want to be useful, help Kate and Danny pack. They're going to freak out in about five minutes and probably forget their swimsuits."

Peter was right. I heard Kate and Danny scream somewhere in the house, and then they charged the stairs like elephants to their rooms.

"Dad says we have to be ready in twenty minutes. What do I pack? What do I pack?"

"Whoa. I'll help. It's a water park. Start with a swimsuit."

"Right." Kate pulled her dresser open. "This is so fun. We never do stuff like this." She stopped and stared at me. "You're coming, aren't you?"

"Can you imagine this at a water park?" I held up my hand.

"Will you be here when we get back?"

For a fleeting second I thought about escaping. No good-byes, no strings. They wouldn't even know for a couple days. "I will."

I passed between the kids' rooms and got them packed in less than fifteen minutes. Peter was true to his word, and within the half hour the family headed to the car.

As they walked out the door, Jane found me picking up coats in the back hall. Her face was closed and her eyes still held tight anger, yet she asked, "Will you be okay?"

I nodded.

And they left . . .

I spent my next day wandering Seattle, numb and alone. I didn't call Nick. I wanted him to call me.

He didn't, so as a form of self-torture I walked by many of the places I'd visited with either him or Jane. I saw all the flowers at Pike Place Market, the ferryboats down at the water, the carousel ride near the aquarium, and the cheese shop at Melrose Market—and Sitka & Spruce. And all I could think was *Kate would love this; we should bring Matt here; Danny would laugh at that; that color would look great on Jane.*

But that's all I did, dwell on the thoughts. I didn't call, text, or reach out to any of them—only to Dad.

"Jane and Peter took the kids away for a few days."

"Is she strong enough for that?"

I hesitated. "She said she was."

"Why didn't you go?"

"I said something I shouldn't have and I upset her. It's such a mess, Dad."

"I'm going to drive up. Let's go to dinner."

"No, it's four hours. Jane's not even here. Wait till she gets back."

"You're worth the drive, Lizzy. I'll see you soon."

Now I waited in the small alcove at Palace Kitchen, one of Tom Douglas's famous restaurants. I didn't want to talk at Jane's house—I didn't even want to return to Jane's house.

I saw Dad walking down the sidewalk before he noticed me. His shoulders were slightly slumped, and I accepted the weight—I had added yet another burden to our fragile family. We sat down, and I found I had nothing to say. After far too many moments of silence, I asked, "Did you talk to Jane?"

"Of course not. I'm not getting in the middle. This is between you girls."

"Dad, you've always been in the middle. You could at least call her."

"Not anymore. Maybe that was part of the problem. You never needed me there, and I certainly never helped. If you did something wrong, you need to fix it."

Oblivious to my annoyance, he opened his menu and reviewed the dinner choices: three different types of beef, two pork preparations, and two chicken choices. Food was always a gift to Dad, and he thoroughly enjoyed every offering. He thought my mom's cooking was as close to heaven as he could get here on earth.

I watched his eyes flicker from one choice to the next, and my anger abated. I thought yet again about Cecilia's comment on perspective. How clearly had I seen my dad? Who was he in his own right versus who I constantly tried to construct? Or who I wanted him to be?

"If I were you, I'd go with the pork tenderloin."

"Why's that?"

"Coal-roasted kale rabe, garlic and chili with pickled ginger, and caramelized ham broth . . . What more can I say?"

"It does sound good. I had mashed potatoes and meatloaf at the station last night. Perkins was on detail. It was not very appealing." He chuckled, and I knew he had probably secretly relished every bite.

"I can imagine." I laid down my menu. We sat there looking at each other, each waiting for the other to begin. I dove in. "My stitches come out Tuesday. Then I'll head home."

"Was it all bad?"

"Not all. I made some friends." I smirked. "Lost some, too, but it still wasn't all bad."

"And Jane?"

"I thought it was better, and at times it was, but we're too far apart." I spread my hands across the table. "We are who we are, Dad. You may have been in the middle because without you Jane and I can't connect."

"Why not?"

"We're too different. There's too much between us. We'd never choose each other as friends, and as adults that's what we need to be."

"No, you don't. Remember what I told you? The love needs to be stronger than the like. We're family."

"I know you want to believe that, but it doesn't always work."

"It does if you make it; it's just not always easy."

"Well, I'm going to disappoint you, because I don't have the energy."

Dad put his menu down and mimicked my posture. "You never disappoint me. Whatever you say or do, I love you." He paused and studied me. "Do you know that?"

"I do." I leaned back in the bench. "And I'm sorry, Dad. I was wrong to leave for New York like I did, and I stayed away too long . . . I didn't know how to come back, how to stop feeling angry with you for stuff beyond your control." I pressed my lips together, gaining courage. "I missed Mom and I couldn't handle that. I still miss her."

He nodded, up and down, up and down, up and down, and I got the impression he was weighing our years of estrangement and my endless quarrels with Jane.

"What are you thinking?"

"About how much I've missed you and how much you look like your mother. You're beautiful."

"Dad . . ." And the tears started.

Chapter 34

Monday morning arrived, and I padded around the kitchen, feeling lonely. There was no point in making oatmeal, no point in making breakfast at all. I held my coffee and leaned against the counter as I did every morning in New York, but it felt different.

I pushed away and ambled into the living room. The light danced through the windows, the warm walls burnishing to saffron as the sun peeked from behind the clouds. I could see Lake Washington over the house across the street. The water looked dark and deep, the sun throwing diamonds across its surface.

I contrasted it with the shallow, dull waters I'd played in for so long—taking care of a cat I refused to name, a staff I never embraced outside my own needs as their boss, friends I kept at an affectionate but cool level . . . even Paul, who now hinted at a desire I couldn't fulfill.

But now I was in deep, way over my head. There were Nick and Matt, Kate and Danny, and Peter with his starched-up vulnerability, and the secret knowing that if Jane would look up, really look up, she'd see him. She'd see me—always waiting, never pulled in.

This desire to connect scared me—for, as I curled in to the couch, I recognized that I'd always held it close, secreted it away because I knew there was more behind this want, this need—and it could sink me. My mind drifted to my last birthday. I had concealed the day away, hoping no one would find out. I realized as the sun flashed across the room that I had done that to escape disappointment. What if someone had known but still found it unworthy of celebration? What if, in fact, I really didn't matter outside my cooking?

Each day I justified my life through purpose.

And now it felt like a burden and an awful lot of work. I sensed that this shift in perspective was like the fairy dust floating around me that needed light to illuminate it. One strong burst of wind or one quiet, true thought would make it clear and I could be free. I chased the thought, wanting it and fearing its illumination simultaneously. My phone rang.

"Elizabeth, it's Tyler. I called to say thank you. I ate. I ate everything. I gained two pounds this week."

"You did? That's fantastic."

"Can you make more? I know these meals were because you felt bad, and you shouldn't have, but they were everything I didn't know I needed." Tyler's voice was light—pure, dancing, and clear.

"I can make a couple, but I'm heading back to New York in a few days. Are you at the Infusion Center this week?"

"Tomorrow as usual."

"Jane switched days, but I get my stitches out tomorrow. I'd love to bring you a few dishes."

Tyler was silent.

The light around me dimmed as I absorbed his disappointment. "I wish I could do more, Tyler."

"I wasn't thinking that at all. I was thinking how incredible you are to help me out like this. You hardly know me and . . . I can't tell you what this means."

"Really? It's been good for me too. I've enjoyed it."

"Can I do anything for you?"

"Thank you. That's such a nice offer, but I'm fine."

I hung up the phone and looked once more around the room, thankful I'd been able to help, thankful he'd called. *Thankful.* It was something. A true thought. I took a last sip of my coffee and, without thinking, dialed Nick.

He answered before I mustered the courage to hang up, so I rushed out the words. "Hey, Nick, it's Elizabeth. Tyler ate. He gained weight."

"That's great." But it didn't sound great. Nick sounded subdued.

"I'm sorry. You're busy." I lowered my phone to disconnect the call and heard a yell.

"No, hang on . . ." There was muffled talking, then silence. "I'm so glad to talk to you. It's been a rough few days."

"Where are you?"

"Home, but I needed to step out of the kitchen. Rebecca was around all weekend."

"How'd it go?" I heard the tension and coolness in my voice and tucked my lips in, as if to tamp it down. This was about Matt. And he needed a mother.

"Pretty good. They built a Lego castle; we went to the zoo, took him downtown to a movie and out for dinner, read books, went to the park. Tons of stuff. He was slow to warm up and hasn't said much, but he seems okay. Right now he's eating breakfast."

"It's Monday. Why isn't he at school?"

"Spring break."

"Forgot that. Jane's family is gone for a few days."

"What have you been doing? Have you been alone?"

He sounded like he'd missed me. I savored it a moment before answering.

"Dad drove up last night and we had dinner. He drove back home this morning because he's volunteering at a school."

"That was short."

"It was, but I'm glad he came. We had a really good talk."

"What are you doing now?"

"Tyler called for a couple more meals, so I'm going to make those and bake a cake for the Infusion Center. Sort of a good-bye gift."

Nick paused. "Can we come help? I've got some work this morning, but with Matt out of school it's a light week."

"What about Rebecca?"

"I don't want to even think about her right now. Can we come over?"

"Of course."

Within minutes the doorbell rang and my lonely

morning evaporated. Matt charged through the door, anxious to see Kate and Danny.

"I'm sorry. They're all at a water park for a few days. It's just me."

"That's okay."

He passed me and headed to the kitchen. Nick shrugged. "Totally nonplussed."

"That's good." I motioned to Matt, who had already left the hall. "Maybe he'll talk while cooking. That's where my mom and I talked most."

"You two seem to have some connection, so I don't doubt it. He hasn't opened up to me at all."

We trailed Matt and sorted the ingredients into piles around the counters. I pushed a recipe in front of Nick.

"Why does he get to make the cake?"

"He's my favorite." I winked at Matt and showed him how to grate coconut and chocolate. "You can have a taste, but try to leave some."

When I turned back to Nick, he'd started chopping the vegetables: onions, mushrooms, carrots, celery, and broccoli.

"The recipe says Chicken Potpie, but these are more vegetables than I remember. I thought it was chicken, sauce, and peas."

"Not anymore. And this one won't have a sauce either. I'm keeping it simple, with cilantro and only a touch of honey and olive oil as a binder."

"Yum." Nick stopped chopping.

"Don't worry, I've already manipulated the recipe in my head. We're making two. One for you—hence the broccoli. Tyler's won't have that."

"Really?"

"I figured you'd like it."

I reached over him to help Matt and was surprised by a kiss on my cheek. Matt looked up at me and scrunched his nose. I mimicked his expression. Both of us were asking each other, *What's he doing?*

"Thank you." Nick stood staring at me, oblivious to Matt's and my interplay. "How'd you know?"

"I told you before, it's not rocket science. You like warm food, nothing sharp, and clean tastes, like everything else about you. Tyler reads Hemingway, too, and that's where I got the idea for no sauces and drier, more direct fare. The honey came from you, but it works for both. What's with Hemingway, by the way? Is it a guy thing?"

Nick resumed chopping. "I guess, disregarding the suicide part and some of the general disillusionment, we want to be him: larger than life, fisherman, hunter, bullfighter, go to war, come out alive, and be forward, direct, no fluff."

I studied Nick, appreciating no fluff, directness, and the fact that he was standing near me. My mind flashed back to the day I'd stepped within his arms and showed him the proper chopping motion. A blush crawled up my neck.

He glanced over and smiled as if remembering too. "Am I doing this right?"

"You had a good teacher." I flicked my hand toward his knife. "Stay focused."

He laughed, but instead of returning to the carrots, he laid the knife down and stepped toward me. I froze as his fingers brushed my cheek. "I love it when you blush. And you've got flour all over you. Do you know that?"

I scrubbed at my face.

"You made it worse. Stand still." He took a dish towel and brushed away flour on my chin and cheeks. "You must be a mess in your kitchen."

"I'm not. My coat and apron are always spotless," I whispered, still standing very close.

"Do I make you nervous?"

"No . . . A little," I admitted.

"Good." He kissed the tip of my nose.

I felt, rather than saw, Matt staring, so I stepped back and dotted his nose with flour as well. The three of us worked together for almost an hour before Matt grew bored. By that time the cake was in the oven and the pies almost constructed, so we sent him to the basement to watch a movie while we cleaned the kitchen.

"Why didn't you go to the Great Wolf Lodge too?"

I held up my wrapped hand. "But it was more than this. They need time together, without me . . . Jane and I had a fight, and then suddenly she wanted to leave. I think she didn't want me to go home." I scrubbed a spot on the counter. "That's new, but we still can't seem to get past our 'mutual inconveniences.' "

"Your what?"

"It's from *Persuasion*."

"Your favorite book."

"Yes." I stopped scrubbing and smiled. "I'm reading it to her while she gets her chemo. We are so like a couple of the characters in there. We can't let our annoyances go, understand each other, or forgive each other. It's hard to even be around her sometimes. We relate to each other best when I'm reading to her during chemo."

"It's your common ground."

"We're sisters. We should have more than that."

Nick shrugged. "It's a place to start."

I leaned against the counter. "I love that phrase . . . My dad once said that the minute he saw my mom, he did everything he could to find 'a place to start' with her. He made it sound intentional, romantic . . . and he's not that kind of guy."

"You'd be surprised how intentional a guy can be when he finds someone special."

Zing.

After a wonderful dinner, a small time of dish duty, and an episode of *Jeopardy*, Nick and Matt headed to the door.

"Wait, I have dessert. Take it home with you?"

Nick raised an eyebrow. "I'm not using you for the food, you know."

"I know, but I made this with you in mind." I shrugged. "I was bored this weekend."

He stilled. "I'm sorry I wasn't here with you."

His look and slow, deep tone made his words take on more meaning than could exist between mere friends, at least in my mind. It was an attractive and desirable thought—and an impossible one. "Don't apologize."

I hurried back to the kitchen and grabbed a glass container of ice cream.

"What flavor?"

"Tell me when you try it."

He held up the container, trying to discern the flavor by the color. Then he smelled it. "I know this . . . honey?"

I smiled. He closed his eyes and smelled again. "There's something more. It's . . . it's lavender?"

"Very good. You sound like me."

He smiled; then his eyes morphed to serious. "I've only got a few days left with you, so . . . when can I see you again?"

"I'm getting my stitches out tomorrow; then I deliver this food and the cake to the Infusion Center. I can call you when I'm done."

"I'll take you." He lightly touched my hand. "I was there at the beginning."

"Yes, you were." I let the *and this is the end* remain unspoken.

Chapter 35

The stitches came out smoothly, and even though my hand was pale and wrinkled with huge purple-red lines over and across every finger, it worked. Stiffly and with slight pain, but it worked.

"Be gentle with it." Dr. Wharton turned it over, looking at it from all angles. "I am so pleased with how this came out. It looks great."

"Your idea of great is different from mine. It looks like Frankenstein's."

"Just wait. All this will settle down, and you'll have only a hint of pale lines here and here." He pointed to the worst of the slashes.

"Thank you."

"You're welcome, and thank yourself too; you used a very sharp knife."

I laughed. "I'll have to tell my sous chef that."

He held up his hands. "All of us who work with our hands in such precise ways know exactly where they are and how they work, which makes harming them all the more telling."

"I was pretty angry."

"Figured as much."

We shook hands and he left us. Nick stood without looking at me and held the exam room door open. He didn't speak as we pulled the food from the car and crossed the parking lot toward the cancer center entrance. His silence began to unnerve me.

"You don't have to come. Do you want to wait in the cafeteria or somewhere, and I'll text you?"

"I'd like to come, if it's okay. It is, isn't it?"

I took a breath. "Is that why you're not talking? You're nervous?"

He looked down at me. "A little. And your stitches are out."

"That's a good thing."

"You'll leave, and that is not a good thing. Things are so messed up right now, with Rebecca and life and . . . they feel good when you're near."

I opened my mouth to say something, anything, even though I didn't know how to reply, but the elevator door opened and our moment broke. Something was wrong—a stillness pervaded the lobby. I caught sight of Cecilia adjusting Mr. Griffin's IV bottle. She wasn't in her protective garb, so I knew she was flushing his lines or taking his initial blood draw. She looked exhausted, and Mr. Griffin was rubbing his forehead bright red.

I stopped at the counter. Nick stayed beside me, silent.

Cecilia finished, noticed me, and hurried over.

"Donna here?" I quipped, knowing it wasn't true.

"It's Andy." Her voice dropped.

"No."

"He was admitted yesterday, and Courtney called a little while ago. Barring a miracle . . ." She pressed her lips together.

My eyes stung. I glanced toward the cake and hated it. Hated its optimism, its naïveté, its sugar. Hated that I'd baked it thinking it would bring joy, bring a form of healing. Hated even that I'd enjoyed baking it and had felt true delight in guiding Matt and flirting with Nick. It was so trite. *A cake is just a cake.* I looked at Tyler's potpies and felt no better about them.

Cecilia pulled me into a hug. It took me a moment to lift my arms; then I grabbed her tight.

"It's so sudden," I whispered.

"Not really."

"But why?"

"I don't know that one."

"I should go." I gestured to the food. "Please give Tyler these pies. They're for him, but the cake was for everyone. I'm embarrassed it's here. Can you take it to a staff room somewhere?"

"Of course."

I turned to go when I caught Herb Griffin in the corner of my eye. He waved me over.

"I'll be just a sec." I brushed Nick's arm. "You can come." I crossed the room as Herb motioned to two chairs.

"Pull those over."

We did and sat. I introduced him to Nick and then sat without more words.

"Cecilia told you about Andy?"

I nodded.

"Are you all right, dear?" Ruth leaned forward.

"He's so young." I rubbed at my eyes.

Herb tapped my hand. "Don't do that. It's okay to cry. It's good."

I snorted and flashed a look at Nick, who gave a slight nod. A tear plopped down my cheek. "And poor Courtney . . . I think of Jane. She said that as mad as she was to be here"—I motioned around the room and dropped my voice—"that watching your child suffer would be infinitely worse."

"It is." Ruth nodded slowly, and I sensed she understood from firsthand experience.

"Please." A beat of sarcasm stopped our conversation.

We turned our heads as Tyler jabbed his brother. "Brian, don't."

"You people know nothing about that family or what they feel about any of this." Brian didn't look up from his magazine, as if addressing us directly wasn't worth his effort.

"Stop." Tyler gripped his upper arm.

Brian shrugged free. "Get off me."

I cringed away from his anger, but could say nothing. It was like watching a train wreck. Cecilia hovered on the edge, fully suited to administer Tyler's chemo, but she stood frozen too. Others around the room looked up, and the whispering grew louder as people turned to Brian.

I remembered that he'd had outbursts before—ones that upset people, caused harm.

Brian glanced around, savoring his audience. "Don't presume to know that family. You have no idea what they feel—or don't feel."

"Son." Herb cut him off with such an authoritative tone the entire room paused midbreath. "Andy's family is in a lot of pain." Herb held Brian's stare. "And while you're right, there's a lot we don't know, we do know they love their son and this is hard."

"No one knows what goes on behind closed doors."

"I'm sorry your family isn't here. I'm sorry if they hurt you . . . or Tyler."

Herb's words felt so real and so clear. It was about love and our definition of it, our striving for it. And it was about how that love gets accepted, returned, or rejected. Or even the pain loved ones, our families, can cause.

It felt as if in that moment, no matter the outcome between life and death, it was love that mattered and the only thing that could bridge a link between the two. For Andy. For Brian. For me. There were my shallow waters. The cakes? The potpies? Those came from my heart. The clothes, the face creams, and even Feast? None of it bad, but none of it worthy of defining me or worthy of defining love. And yet those were the objects of my affection, my time, my work, and my life. I felt Nick's hand slip into mine.

Cecilia started Tyler's treatment, then stepped back. She looked at Brian with soft eyes, an expression of empathy and acceptance. She'd seen him clearly from the start. I was the one who wanted him to change and be different, be brought down a peg or punished for his arrogance—all so that I wouldn't look at myself too closely. She stripped off her gloves and lowered her mask, dropping into the chair next to him. She reached for his hand; he tried unsuccessfully to pull away.

Brian stared at her. "What?"

"It's okay to be angry, even scared."

He wrenched his arm free.

"We're all scared, and we should be. Angry too. We should be stunned and shaken when something so fundamentally wrong happens. And it's hard, especially if family isn't there to shoulder it with us. And worse when they contribute to it."

"Don't—" He stopped, as if he'd run out of words.

"Please, Brian." The steady peace in Cecilia's voice and eyes stunned me. I'd classified her as a sidekick—a quirky, amazing nurse, but one with growing up yet to do, not ready to lead the show. Now I saw the true Cecilia, and she was spectacular—completely comfortable with who she was, to whom she belonged, and what she was called to do. She was a heroine.

"You know, I had to forgive my parents for not being who I needed them to be. I'm sure my situation was different from yours, but I got hurt and I needed them and they weren't there."

"This isn't about my family." Brian's face twisted. "It's about Andy . . . It's about . . ." He shut his mouth and nodded slowly, not to us, but as if to some thought or understanding.

"She never came," Tyler whispered.

Brian looked at his brother, and the slow nod morphed to a slow shake. I saw them in that moment, and I saw them in the past—the older brother always trying to carry the burden, lift the load, protect the younger, and having all efforts rain down on him useless and futile because the younger still shouldered the load, recognized the hurt, and now carried a burden that could kill him.

"I'm at peace with that, Brian," Tyler whispered.

"No. No." Brian turned and held out his hand to his brother, his palm pushing forward with each word. "This isn't peace." He turned and raced from the room.

Tyler closed his eyes, and Cecilia went to pull off her protective gown. I sat still and felt the pressure of Nick's hand within mine. I looked down. My knuckles were white. "I'm so sorry." I let go, embarrassed by how hard I'd been gripping him.

He reached again. "Don't be," he whispered.

"Are you okay?" Herb addressed Tyler.

"I'm not his responsibility. I can't be his burden anymore."

I jumped from my seat. "Stop it, Tyler. Stop it. He loves you. He doesn't know what to do, and he's scared. We all act badly when we're scared. At least I do, so I know what it looks like. And he loves you." I hugged him close. "You aren't a burden. Please don't ever think that."

I stood up, completely embarrassed by my outburst. I swiped my sleeve across my nose, laughing a sobby, choked noise at how ridiculous I must have looked. "I brought you potpies. Helping you made me so happy because you're important." I pointed to the counter. "They feel really stupid now, but they're there. At least take them when you go today."

Tyler laughed, in a similarly wet fashion. "That's really nice. Thank you."

"You're welcome." I pressed the heels of my hands into my eyes. The left was tender, but the sting felt right. I took a deep breath. "I'm sorry. I'm sorry for Andy and his family and I'm sorry, Tyler. I hope Brian's okay." I turned to Ruth, then to Herb and hugged him. "Thank you. You've taught me so much, and I bet you don't even know it. I've so loved meeting you."

I turned to go as Ruth reached out for Tyler's hand. I knew they'd keep talking and that somehow Ruth and Herb would now be involved, would help Tyler and even find a way to reach Brian. It was simply love.

As I headed for the elevators, with Nick silently trailing me, I realized how unique that room was and how unlikely it was that I'd ever pass this way again. In my "dystopian library" we were at our most basic, stripped of inhibitions, and we exposed our very selves—be they scared, angry, peaceful, faith-filled, or despairing. True emotions shone out of each one of us, sometimes many emotions conflicting at once. There was no hiding. I understood Brian's anger, I felt Tyler's vulnerability and burden, but I wanted Herb and Ruth's conviction. I wanted Cecilia's peace.

The elevator doors opened. "That was more than you signed up for." I entered and leaned back against the wall. Nick's expression was tight and closed. He reached for my hand and squeezed it tight.

"How old is Andy?"

"Probably fifteen. Hard to tell because he's smaller than Kate, but I suspect he's older. I think he has leukemia. He's the one I played cards with."

"I figured that." Nick clenched his eyes shut until the door opened onto the ground floor.

"Where to now?" I asked.

"Do you mind if I take you home? There's some . . . I need to get some stuff done." He lifted our hands to his lips and kissed the back of mine.

"Not at all."

We drove home with few words. Our lightness and banter were gone. My stitches were gone. And I missed Jane's family.

The day turned cloudy and chilly. It fit my mood. I thought a walk would help, but my thoughts only turned in on themselves and made everything feel worse. After about an hour of wandering Madison Park, I turned the corner to Jane's house to find Cecilia rocking on the porch swing. "Have you been here long?"

"I just arrived. I was about to call you, but I got sucked in by this thing. It's relaxing." She tapped her foot to the ground, perpetuating the gentle sway.

"Then I should be out here daily." I plopped next to her, sending the swing in a sideways rock. "I went for a walk."

She didn't answer.

"You okay?"

She sighed and glanced at me. "I was going to ask you the same thing."

"I was a mess, wasn't I? I can't believe I leapt on Tyler like that . . . I saw Jane and me and our mess and their misunderstandings and how we all screw everything up and how I'm still screwed up, but I don't want to be . . . and poor Andy and Courtney and his siblings and how they're handling this . . ."

I looked over. Cecilia stared straight ahead. I'd never noticed how pale her eyes were under all that black eyeliner. I poked her arm. "Hey . . . I'm not a patient, Cecilia. Talk to me."

She sucked in a huge, halting breath. "Thank you." She pressed her fists into her eyes and screamed, "Agghhh . . ." Her yell filled the moment with more power and emotion than I could scoop out of a decade.

I looked around, but no one was outside to witness or listen.

"Sorry about that." She lowered her fists. "It's just that I have to hold it together there, and usually I can. Then something like this happens." We rocked for a few moments. "And you were fine today. Honestly, you helped Tyler more than you know.

"When I was young," she continued, "everything felt so real, so final, scary even . . . That's part of the reason I started using. Emotions ballooned into big, black demons that bit and overwhelmed me. That's how it felt today. In rehab I learned I was wired that way. I feel things deeply—too deeply. It's even got a name beyond high sensitivity . . ." She glanced over at me and shrugged.

"Anyway, an amazing counselor taught me to watch others, but to create borders and protect myself while still being able to give. He helped me make my world bigger, forgive myself, my parents, too, and to be thankful—to believe that God gave me these odd sympathies, empathies, and emotions that are always in me, to be a blessing and even a gift. It was a shift in perspective, and it's good, but on days like today I'm falling again . . . and it's too hard."

I reached my arm around her. "Your counselor was right about perspective. I learned that from you. You have a beautiful one. Hope is a good perspective. Faith, a good lens."

"I don't feel it right now."

"But isn't that the point? That God is still there, reality is still there, no matter how you feel?"

She turned to me and sighed. "You've reminded me of a lot I'd forgotten."

I shrugged and we swayed. Back and forth. Back and forth.

"I'm going to miss you." She spoke into the silence.

"New York isn't that far away."

"It is, but thanks for saying that. We can keep in touch. Are you on Facebook?"

I chuckled. "I will be."

She leaned back and pushed us harder. "What about you and Nick?"

"Will we stay in touch? No, I don't think relationships work over long distances, and our lives are on opposite coasts."

"That's a shame." She smiled at me. "In the Infusion Center you're stiff, and you're stiff with

Jane. You get this tight expression in your eyes." She narrowed her eyes in an unflattering imitation. "But when you cook, you're funny and you're part of your work, not separate; you're almost bubbly. When I walked in and saw you with Nick the other day, you were lit up to a whole new level."

"Yikes. Am I really that transparent?"

Cecilia quirked an eyebrow and nodded. I interpreted it to say, *Sucks to be you.* And she was right. On so many levels, that is exactly how I felt, and it didn't help that the whole world seemed to know it before I did.

"Nick and I were a blip, and while it was nice . . ."

She pinned me with a glare and raised the eyebrow again—so much more daunting when dyed jet black and firing twice in a moment.

"Fine, it was more than nice, but still just a blip. He's got a lot going on in his life right now, and I'll go home, get back to work, and, I hope, keep that bubbly feeling you described. That's all I need."

I told her about Paul, Chef Dimples, and trying to recapture my "gift" for cooking. As I told my story, I began to believe that I'd done it, that I'd regained what was lost and that I'd even found something new. After all, we created the magic that day in the kitchen for Tyler, even for Jane. And I had created food that meant something to each of them and to Nick—the chicken salad, the potpie, the ice cream. All these gifts were relevant, and they mattered. I kept telling her more and more, with a generated eagerness, until I believed it myself. And I rested there. Feast would be mine again.

An hour later, as she headed down the steps, Cecilia blew it away with a single question. "What if it was never about the food?"

Chapter 36

Nick called the next morning. I curled up on the couch, expecting a warm chat.

"I'm sorry I basically dumped you at Jane's yesterday. I needed to call Rebecca."

My heart skipped a beat. "What about?"

Nick sighed over the line. "I think . . . I realized . . . I'm making it all too hard. She's not what I expected, but she is Matt's mom and she wants to be in his life. She talked about moving here and finding a job. I was pretty hard on her and . . . I needed to call and apologize."

"You want her to move here?"

"I want my son to have his mother. That's more important than what I want."

I wanted to keep the conversation on Matt, but I couldn't help myself. "Do you find her attractive?"

"What?"

"She's the mother of your son, Nick. You clearly found her attractive once, and if you two got together, you'd have a family. Matt's family would be complete."

"That's not on the table right now. I doubt she's even thought about it. I certainly haven't." When I didn't reply, Nick's voice took on an edge. "What's going on here?"

"Absolutely nothing. Just thinking aloud." I took a breath and remembered, *I'm going home.* "I think it's great if she moves here. Mothers should be with their kids. I'm happy for you."

"Thanks. I think."

"Nick, I lost mine at seventeen. It's a big deal. This is good . . . Listen, I gotta go. Jane and family will be home at three, and I haven't exactly kept this place clean. I also want to make some soup. Will you be around later?"

"Sure, but I—"

I cut him off. "I'll give you a call." I hung up. There wasn't much to clean, but there wasn't much to say either . . .

And at three p.m. on the dot, the front door slammed. My family was back.

"Elizabeth? Elizabeth?" Peter called into the house.

"Up here." I laid down the laundry on my bed and headed toward the stairs.

"It was so much fun." Kate grinned up at me.

"You should've come," Danny joined in. "Hey, your hand."

I held it up. "All fixed." He bounded up the stairs and grabbed for it. "Tender," I squeaked.

The kids raced through every moment at the water park with Jane and Peter chirping in. It sounded full and fun and bright. Exactly what they needed. And Jane looked lighter and softer —the version I always imagined at Peter's side. There were moments that pain, emotional or physical, flittered across her face, but she chased them away. I recognized it in her because I was engaged in the same exercise.

Jane caught my expression during one of those moments and widened her eyes at me. "Later," I whispered. She nodded.

Later never came, so I knew the next morning we needed to talk. Peter walked into the kitchen right as I finished making coffee. "I'm heading to work, but I wanted to warn you, Jane took her Decadron tablets for tomorrow."

"Seriously? It's Thursday already?"

"Yeah. You may want to stop loading that dish-washer. Give her something to do." He chuckled and pulled open the door. "Have fun today."

I took his advice and stopped cleaning the kitchen. Instead I headed to my room to get dressed. When I came down, I found Jane with her head in the oven again. "We've cleaned this already. It can't be that bad."

"What did you cook in here?"

"Get out." I tugged at her shoulder, shut the oven door, and pressed the self-clean button. "There. What's next?"

"I thought we could—" Jane looked at me. "You're laughing at me, aren't you?"

"I'm not." I stood before her, and the emotions of the past few days caught me. I wanted to be different. "Tell me how I can help you today."

Jane bit her lip.

"Don't cry."

"That's just so sweet." She gave me a quick hug, then flashed me a determined look. "I need to do the laundry from our vacation; then I want to go through Danny's closet. The homework area needs sorting . . ." She paused. "The kids just went next door to play, so we can . . . Forget all that, I don't want to do any of it . . . Peter put his computer away over our trip."

I smiled.

"We talked, probably not enough, but it was a start . . . I want to keep feeling that way."

I wilted inside while holding my expression blank. I needed to tell her about Andy.

"Let's go to Snoqualmie Falls. It's about a half hour away, but it's beautiful and we've got sun. Let's just go. The kids won't be home until after lunch."

"Okay then."

She grabbed her keys. "I've thought about

what we said last week, right before we left."

"That was my fault—"

"It wasn't. It's always been there. I left to avoid it, but I also left to buy time. If you'd gone back to New York, I wouldn't have this chance." She grabbed my upper arm to command my attention. "I'm sorry. I was selfish back then—still am—and I was scared. Those aren't excuses, but it's the truth."

"I understand. Believe me, I wasn't much better."

"Dad says you were magnificent."

"I was there." I paused for a moment. "But I only saw what I wanted to see . . . and at the end, I left too."

"What do you mean?" Jane pulled onto the street.

I looked out the window, wondering if I could confess what I'd never told anyone, and to Jane —the one who, armed with such information, would know how to use it to her advantage. "At the end, I knew she was dying, I mean the exact moment. She wanted to talk, it was a whisper really, and there was something in her voice and in her eyes. It's strange, in that moment, how much you can see. I pulled my hand free and left the room . . . I never went back. And then when I graduated high school, I did the same to Dad."

I looked to Jane but couldn't see her expression. She didn't pull her eyes from the road.

"You were a kid. How could you be expected to stand there?" Her voice caught.

"I never said good-bye. I didn't let her say good-bye," I whispered, and it was done.

We said little until we reached Snoqualmie Falls—our hearts elsewhere. And when we did stand at the railing, our destination reached, neither of us could find words. Instead we watched the sun ignite each droplet, making diamonds rain around us.

"It makes you almost feel that everything can be made new." I broke the silence as I took in the sights, the smells, and the sounds of the roaring water. "Can we be made new?"

"I'd like that." Jane reached for my hand and squeezed. Then she closed her eyes and let the spray fan her face.

She was thinner, her skin seemed hollowed beneath her eyes, and small wrinkles spread from their outer corners. One crossed a vein near her temple. "Are you tired?"

"Not today." She grinned, her eyes still closed. "I'm sorry, Lizzy. I'm sorry that happened to you, but she wouldn't want you to carry it. I say that as a mom, not a sister. I would never want Kate to carry that."

I stood silent for a long while, then exhaled. "Thank you."

"Doesn't the air smell great?" She pulled off her scarf and laid it on the railing. "I love this. I love getting out in nature where it's so big I know I can't control it. It's so big and glorious and I feel peace."

"I need to tell you something."

"What?" She must have caught my tone, because she turned away from the waterfall and faced me directly.

"Andy is dying. He was admitted to the hospital a couple days ago, and he's held on longer than anticipated, but Cecilia called this morning. It could be any time."

Tears flooded Jane's eyes. "He's a kid."

"I know." I pulled her into a hug.

"How's Courtney?"

"Cecilia said she's managing. She and her husband are staying at the hospital, and her sister has come to be with their other kids."

"That poor family. I . . ." She stopped talking and buried her head into my shoulder. We simply stood and gripped each other.

After a few moments she picked her head up and stepped back. "People are staring at us."

"You're bald and we're standing here hugging and crying. Of course they're staring."

"I need a wig." She touched her head, now glistening with mist. "I really want one now."

"That wouldn't save this moment, and for goodness' sake, this is Seattle. Do you know how much ink, piercings and weird clothing, strange hair and baldness you see in this town?"

"Not in Snoqualmie."

I looked around. She was right. Maybe it was all the water spraying up and around us, maybe it was the tears, but it felt like a fishbowl and we were the shiny attraction. I swiped at my eyes. "Let them stare."

We stood for a few more minutes, trying to focus on the water and not the stares or the pain.

"Come on, let's get a bite at the coffee shop before we head back. We'll be in time for the kids, and if you're very good I'll let you mop the kitchen floor. You can even clean the dishwasher filters."

Jane gave me a fleeting smile. "You say the sweetest things."

I grabbed her scarf off the railing and followed her to the coffee shop.

She stopped inside the door and pulled a baseball cap out of her bag. "It was like this at the Great Wolf Lodge too," she whispered.

We sat at a table in the corner as she continued, "The kids didn't notice it, but Peter did. I think it was the first time he understood how hard this is, on multiple levels."

"Well, there you go. Something good."

Jane threw me a wry smile.

"This time I'm not joking." I leaned forward to make my point. "It's what I meant about being new. Peter learning empathy and understanding . . . That's a good thing."

Jane laid her hands on the table. "So I should enjoy these stares?"

"That's not what I'm saying."

Jane looked around. "I think about that story you told me, the boy at the park? The one Kate told the other kids not to stare at?"

I nodded.

She sighed. "I get that it's good for them to learn that stuff, it's good for Peter, for me . . . And I'm glad I knew Andy." She caught herself. "Know Andy. But I'd have chosen to skip all these lessons if given the option."

"I don't think God works that way."

"Then you tell me why this happened to me? Why it may happen to my kids someday? Or to you?"

I waited a few beats, considering the cost of my next statement. "I guess my answer is why *not* you, or me? Why not any of us?" I paused. Was I really willing to say "even me"? Did I believe in a God who could turn such pain to good? That love really did matter and could heal hearts? And that none of it was based on performance?

Jane stared at me.

"What can I say? You left me alone for five days, and between Cecilia and my own thoughts, I got deeper than usual." I shrugged. "I don't think we get exempt from the pain because we live good lives. Some circumstances we can't control—in fact, most are truly beyond our abilities. Instead maybe it's how we get made new; it's one of the only times we slow down enough to listen and receive grace, real grace."

"Do you believe that?"

"I'm beginning to. I've been running a long time and I'm empty. I felt good cooking with you and Nick and Cecilia, and I wasn't even doing the actual cooking. You all showed me grace. But now I'm looking to home, back to New York, and I'll be cooking again and I don't want to lose that. I don't want to lose you all and the gift and this feeling of grace."

I dropped my hands into my lap and pulled at a cuticle. "I'm living larger now, somehow. Cecilia gave me a book last week. You know its opening line? 'No one told me that grief feels like fear.' That's how I've felt—for almost fifteen years. And now it's falling behind me. I can't express what that feels like." I took a deep breath and crept forward. "When I go back . . . can we keep doing this? Talking? I can't go back to the way it was."

"Why don't you stay?"

"Here?"

"Find a job out here. Get an apartment."

"Feast is my restaurant, my life really. I've worked years to build it, and I'm not ready to walk away. In fact . . ." I pulled my phone out of my bag and glanced at the screen.

"Why do you keep checking that?"

"I got a text from Paul this morning to keep my evening open. Something's up. I'm afraid he's going to call and say Murray's taken my job."

"Fire you?"

"He could. He's been generous to me, Jane, too generous really. Business started slowing months ago. I wasn't cooking the same, and any owner except Paul would've tossed me."

"Well, he didn't, and now you're cooking great, so don't assume the worst."

"You're right." I laid the phone down, putting Paul and Feast away from me, and gave Jane my attention.

On the drive home my phone rang. *Paul.* My stomach clenched.

"Hey, Paul."

"Elizabeth. Good to hear your voice. I just landed and would love to meet for dinner. Are you available?"

"Excuse me?"

"I'm in Seattle meeting with a company we're thinking of acquiring, and I thought we could grab dinner."

"Of course. I can't believe you came to see me."

Paul laughed lightly into the phone. "I came for work; you're a bonus. So, dinner. I'm in meetings all day tomorrow, and I fly out tomorrow night, so tonight is my only chance."

"Just tell me when and where."

"I'm at the Four Seasons. Why don't you meet

me there and we'll grab dinner close? Someone told me Matt's in the Market is a Seattle favorite, so I had Lois book me a reservation for seven thirty."

"I'll be there."

"Come to the hotel first. Seven o'clock? We'll have a drink and walk over. She sent me a map link; it's only a few blocks away."

I smiled. Lois, as always, had covered every detail. "See you then." I tapped my phone off.

"Paul is here?" Jane kept her eyes on the road.

"He wants to take me to dinner."

"You sound excited."

"I think I am. I feel more whole than I've felt in a long time, and I feel like I have something to offer Feast again."

"What are you going to offer Paul?"

"What do you mean?"

"I've heard talk about Paul for years. A man doesn't send flowers to an employee's sister and fly across the country to check on said employee, especially one who's already returning in a couple days."

"He's here for business."

"If you say so . . . What are you going to wear?"

Chapter 37

I pulled Jane's car into the Four Seasons round-about and smoothed my skirt. I smiled as I remembered her comment. *You're so New York tonight. I forgot how intimidating it is.*

She was right; I'd gotten awfully comfortable in jeans and a few borrowed sweaters and flannel shirts. Granted, they were J. Crew, adorable and slim-cut, but the shirts were still flannel. Not tonight. Tonight was *game on* in high Manolo black heels, a long patterned Armani skirt, and a sleek, carpaccio-thin navy cashmere sweater.

Paul crossed the lobby upon my entrance and kissed my cheek. He gently took my hand. "How is it?"

I slowly bent the fingers within his, then held it out. It was still pale, crisscrossed in red, and vulnerable looking. I had wanted to wrap it, but Cecilia said it was time to move it and expose it to the world—carefully. "Working well. See? Stitches out and everything."

"Physical therapy?"

"No need. I didn't do much nerve or muscle damage. Went straight for bone."

Paul cringed. "I keep forgetting that none of that bugs you."

I laughed because he was right. A chef can't be

squeamish around blood and bones. If you want fresh meat, poultry, or fish, you're part butcher, part surgeon. "This almost had me on the floor, I'll admit. It wasn't pretty." Nick immediately came to mind. I heaved him away.

"Let's a have a drink, then walk to dinner."

Paul directed me toward a barstool. I stopped before sitting. "You always prefer tables."

"You always prefer the bar."

I blinked. "I do. Thank you. I like to be near the action."

"There you go." He pulled a stool out for me. "I can't believe you've been away so long. How are you?"

"How's Feast?"

"It's doing well and waiting for you."

"Really?"

"Of course it is. I was never trying to push you out, Elizabeth; I was trying to save your dream. You lost your step."

"I did, but it's back." I smiled and relaxed.

We chatted a bit more before walking over to Matt's in the Market. It was on the second floor of a building right on the edge of Pike Place, looking straight at the iconic red-lit sign. We sat by the window, looking out on a darkening gray evening sky with sun igniting the tops of the clouds and only breaking through here and there like spun sugar beams. But it was the menu that absorbed my attention.

My mind started generating menu changes for Feast as I looked at all the fresh options, the bold pairings, and the construction of their menu. I started with the octopus with kimchi, daikon radish salad, and chili vinaigrette. Paul ordered the seared foie gras. When he held up his fork, offering me a taste, I froze—Paul never shared his food. He gently put the bite inside my mouth. Rather than comment, I closed my lips.

"I bet yours would be even better."

"I used to make a seared foie gras. I haven't in years."

"You should." Paul smiled warmly.

I then moved on to sturgeon, with fava beans, English peas, mint pesto, radishes, and wild greens. The plate was green and fresh. I smiled as I thought of all the wonderful produce in season—the spring vegetables that were just coming in when I left New York would now be in full bloom. I'd incorporated lots of greens and fresh purees in the food I'd cooked for Jane, but had hesitated to freeze some of the fresh local favorites.

What if I did? Pestos? Purees? Peas? Kales? Smoked, grilled, braised? Then frozen? Perhaps in separate containers as I had done with Tyler? I could even couple them with toasted seeds or grains. The starch would help them withstand freezing. And dividing meals into more discrete elements would not only allow for crossover and greater variety, but people with different side effects from chemo, different needs and tastes, might be able to pull from many of the same dishes. That was the element necessary to take the catering idea larger, to help more people and make it a commercial venture. Nick's idea had consumed my imagination for days, and, while more precise consulting and individual catering work to patients would be the focal point, a provision store could help it float financially and broaden its base. That's what Nick hadn't considered—I stopped myself and flicked a glance to Paul, sure my face had betrayed that I'd completely left him and Feast, if only for a moment.

"You know, Elizabeth, you seem good here. You were right to take the time." I simply nodded. Paul's inflection told me there was more. "But . . . I'm delighted you're coming home. I have a surprise for you."

"You do?"

"I wanted to tell you months ago, but you were so distracted and I didn't want to add pressure. But that's not the case now. This is the Elizabeth I know. The beautiful, confident chef ready to take on the world."

Part of me reveled in his description while another part wanted to protest that I was no longer that woman. I didn't want to take on the world, just to make a difference in one small important corner, but the idea was so new, so fleeting, that I said nothing.

He pushed a small blue box across the table. I opened it and found a gold charm, a delicate chef's hat.

"This is the charm you gave me when Feast opened, but mine is silver."

"Gold for the next restaurant."

"The next . . . restaurant?"

"I secured the lease on a small space in the Village about a year ago and took possession in November. Work is almost complete and it's ready to go."

"Another kitchen?"

"That's the way this business works, Elizabeth. It's not just about the food; it's about a name and a presence. Murray was vital to that, but you're the muse and it's your food. That was one of the reasons I encouraged you to take the time here and recoup before we fired up the next one."

"What's it called? How big is it? What's the menu? What's—"

"Slow down. It's small. Half the dining room of Feast. Very intimate. No name and no menu. That's for you to decide."

"I . . ."

"Don't say anything. Just fly back with me tomorrow and I'll show it to you." Paul reached out his hand and covered mine.

"Tomorrow? I have reservations for Sunday."

Paul leaned back, withdrawing his hand. "Surely two days can't matter."

"No . . ." I shook my head, trying to clear it. "Of course they don't, not really. But I want to say good-bye to the kids properly. I need to leave well, Paul. I've changed . . . I need to . . ." I drifted into silence. I didn't know what I needed.

"Of course, I'm sorry I pushed. Take until Sunday. As I said, two days can't matter. You can dream up names and the theme during that time. I'll e-mail you some pictures. It'll be fun for you." He reached again. "And it will be, Elizabeth. We'll have fun with this."

"I know we will."

Paul's eyes flickered concern, and I knew I hadn't offered enough excitement. "You've completely overwhelmed me, you know? I've never been good at surprises; I need a moment to process this."

"I know, darling. It's a lot, and I never meant it to be a surprise. Well, I did. I wanted to give this to you, but I thought I'd share it long before now. You seemed so lost and struggling. And now . . ." He leaned forward again, his eyes searching and eager. "It's our time."

"Our time." I repeated the words, and my heart faltered. I knew what Paul was asking. I knew what he now expected. A business. A partnership. Me. Maybe it was time; maybe it was right. And yet in the past weeks I'd played with those same words, those same dreams—but they hadn't included Paul.

I turned to the window. Night was falling but I could still see beyond the market. One huge shipping barge dominated the waterscape. Seattle drummed to a different beat than New York, and I understood it now. I had thought there was only one speed at which I could live, but there was a tenor to life here that resonated with me. Nick's nickname for me flashed through my mind. *New York.* Was I still that too? I had to be. It was time to go home.

"You look miles away."

"I was just thinking about my time here. It's been good."

"But you're ready." A statement, not a question.

"I did what I needed to do. I'm ready."

Soon the conversation drifted to Paul's other investments, his kids, and his ex-wives who were chirping with annoyances. I drifted back into my own world, where I hovered on the meals I'd created and the time I'd spent with Nick. It was like watching the good-parts version of a movie in your head after the show ends.

As we walked back to the Four Seasons, Paul put his arm around me. "I've missed you, Elizabeth. More than I think you realize."

I looked up at him. "I needed this time." I laid my hand on his cheek. "Thank you." I reached up and replaced it with a small short kiss.

He turned in to me, capturing another before I

stepped back. He clasped my hand, laying a kiss in my palm. "Anything."

I looked beside us and found the hotel valet hovering. Without breaking eye contact with me, Paul handed him my ticket.

Chapter 38

The next morning I watched Jane eat dry toast and a soft-boiled egg.

"Do you expect my white blood cells to drop off me?"

I blinked and looked to the floor. "Can they do that?"

"No, and they aren't going to." She carried her plate over to the dishwasher. "I can't explain it, but everything doesn't feel so stripped and burned. I'll be okay again."

"If you're not, you have to tell me faster; that was too scary."

"This time we'll make Peter carry me to the ER."

"I keep forgetting I'm off duty." I looked around the kitchen, suddenly feeling irrelevant. Paul's new ideas for a restaurant and for *us* had played in my mind all night, yielding little sleep and odd, frenetic dreams. Dreams where I raced and raced and found nothing at all.

"You are, but come today and say good-bye to everyone."

"I did a little of that when I dropped off the cake, but I'll come. I'd like to see Cecilia. We haven't talked much in a couple days." I turned to Peter. "How about you take the first half and I'll trade places at lunch?"

"Why don't you just com—"

"Perfect," Peter interrupted her. "Taxol *is* a time commitment."

I flashed a glance at Jane, thinking she might throw daggers at that, but she looked placid—and I'd dodged a bullet.

I entered Dr. Chun's office with every nerve spliced and seared. After a few minutes in the waiting room and an informative article on auto-immune diseases, a nurse ushered me to her office.

I took a deep breath and forced myself to sit tall and straight. Dr. Chun tapped on her chart, bringing up my data. "This is a hard test to take. Did you tell Jane?"

"Not yet."

"I understand. It has implications—for your body, finances, emotions, your children someday, your whole life. But I can't say that I'm not pleased you took it. I do believe that having the information, as painful as it may be, is important."

"And?"

"You tested positive." Her voice dropped low and monotone.

"I figured that."

"I'm sorry, Elizabeth." She waited. I sensed I was expected to say something more, but when I didn't, she continued. "I will forward the results to your primary physician, and we can talk about some options right now."

The world felt black and I struggled to hear her through the tunnel. "Can you just forward them?"

"This does not mean you will get cancer, Elizabeth. You had your last mammogram just a couple months ago and it was normal, right?"

"It was, but my chances just skyrocketed, right? It's only a matter of time."

"Not necessarily. Studies show they did increase, but there are so many options now."

I breathed slowly. I'd played this scene in my head a million times, but the cold blackness surprised me.

"Stay and talk."

"No . . ." *Act reasonable.* "I need to digest this, and I have a wonderful doctor in New York. I'll make an appointment next week."

She hesitated, then acknowledged defeat with a small nod. "All right, take this." Dr. Chun handed me a pamphlet. Part of me wanted to laugh, but I felt the tears building and feared I might not be able to stop them—ever.

She continued, "This is actually a very good pamphlet. There are some websites also listed on the back you'll find helpful. It's a place to start."

A place to start. "Thank you." I stood to leave.

"Make an appointment to talk to your doctor, Elizabeth."

I pulled myself together with a deep breath and rigid shoulders. "I will, and thank you, Dr. Chun, for letting me take the test. I did want to know."

"It's hard to live so close to Jane and not know. I understood that. Will you be okay?"

"Of course. As you said, I'm fine right now. I simply have some decisions to make."

She raised her eyebrows as I turned away, as if saying there was nothing simple about any of it.

I walked out and stopped at the elevator. I wanted to head back to Jane's house and curl up under the covers, but I'd agreed to trade places with Peter. I pushed the button for the sixth floor and took another deep breath, trying to convince myself that nothing was different. The truth of my situation had not changed, only my understanding had, and that was good. Now I could act and not react. I almost reached equanimity when the doors opened—at least enough to fake it.

As I stopped at the room's entrance and scanned for Jane and Peter, Cecilia stepped from behind the desk.

"I have to finish a few things, but I need to talk to you."

I drew my eyebrows in. *Not today.*

She squeezed my arm, oblivious to my tension.

"Jane's off to the right. Give me a few minutes and I'll come over."

The room was quiet. The Griffins weren't there. No Brian and Tyler. No Andy. It was Friday and they were the Tuesday crew. It was time to go. There were new faces, new people. I didn't want to know them, hear their stories, or even look into their eyes. I crossed over to Peter. He was typing on his laptop and Jane was asleep.

"I don't think I read with as much inflection as you do. She fell asleep about an hour ago."

"She does it to me too. I think she gets so jacked up on the steroids and then is so relieved she actually makes it here that she passes out."

"I can stay if you want. I'm certainly getting a lot done."

"You go. We'll stick to the plan."

"If you're sure." He gathered up his briefcase and papers so quickly I almost laughed.

Cecilia passed him on his way out and they spoke briefly. His shoulders drooped and he glanced back, first at Jane then at me. The moment our eyes met, he darted his away. Something was wrong; I couldn't read his expression. I stood to chase him, but Cecilia was already beside me. She dropped into a chair and pulled me down into mine.

"Andy died last night."

"No . . ."

"His whole family was there. He wasn't in pain."

"Why didn't you call me?"

"I couldn't make that call. I wanted to tell you in person, and it was so late. Would you really have wanted that?"

I reached for her hand. "No. I'm sorry." I hiccupped. "Did you tell Jane?"

"I couldn't. Tyler and Brian came by after an appointment and I told them. Tyler was so upset; he dropped into a chair and sobbed. Brian punched a wall, then swiped his arm across a couple tables and sent magazines and a lamp flying. I had to call security. It was horrible." Tears filled Cecilia's eyes. She rested her elbows on her knees and pressed her hands to her temples. "It was my fault. I thought . . . It wasn't my place. They need help and I hurt them. Oh . . . I messed up so badly."

"Don't take that on. You can't control Brian, and you had to tell them. Tyler would want to know, even if it hurt."

"Donna was right to be so protective of them. I thought I could help, listen, do something, and I made it worse. And poor Andy . . . and Courtney." She pressed a fist into her heart and lowered her voice to the faintest whisper. "This place is too hard. I've made a mistake, a horrible mistake. I worked so hard to earn a place in this department."

I leaned in and rubbed her back. "This has got to be the toughest part. As your counselor told you, keep the focus on others, but don't absorb their pain. It's not your own. You can't carry it."

She clenched her eyes and shook her head.

"Look at me." I leaned down to my put face next to hers as I pressed my hand into her back. She looked up and we stared at each other, steady and unblinking, until the panic in her eyes calmed.

"Thank you." She nodded. "I'm okay. I'm sorry I made this about me. But I didn't expect that to happen . . . Will you be around later?"

"Absolutely. Just give me a call."

"I thought I was strong enough . . . Later. We'll talk later." She stood and took a shaky breath. "Will you pray for Andy's family? That's what we should focus on. His family."

I reached up and squeezed her hand. "Of course."

"Ben is almost finished over there. I need to go. I'll be back . . ." She looked to Jane.

"I'll tell her."

I spent the next hour staring at page 30 of *Me Before You* until Jane woke up.

"When'd you get here?"

"Awhile ago . . ." I told her about Andy and all that Cecilia had said. Jane flipped her recliner into sitting position as tears flooded down her face— then she started hyperventilating and gasping.

"Stop, Jane. Stop it."

I dug in her bag for Kleenex and flashed my eyes around the room. Cecilia's warnings about hearts stopping pounded in my ears.

Cecilia was suddenly there, leaning over Jane. "Take deep breaths. That's right. Calm down. Take this." She handed her a paper bag and Jane began to calm, first her breathing, then her eyes. Cecilia held out a piece of mint gum. "Can you chew this without choking? Are you calm?"

Jane lowered the bag and reached for the gum.

"Not yet. I want to see you calm. Deep breath . . . Another." Cecilia glanced at me. "Mint calms people."

"I know, but I never would've thought of gum." I reached out my hand. "Can I have a piece?"

Jane lowered the bag. "I'm sorry. Maybe it's the steroids. I just . . . I just . . . Oh . . . poor Andy . . ." She rocked back and forth, whispering and weeping.

Cecilia drew up a chair and rubbed Jane's shoulder. "Deep, slow breaths . . ."

On the way home Jane leaned against the window. "I can't help but see Kate and Danny when I think of him. That's so horribly selfish."

"It's pretty natural. I think of them too." *And me. I now think of me.*

My phone beeped again.

"Who keeps calling and texting you?"

"Nick."

"Why aren't you answering?"

"I can't talk to him . . . and it doesn't matter. I'm

headed to New York, Rebecca's back, and as you said, it was just a vacation fling."

"I didn't—" She stopped talking as I pulled in to the driveway. Nick was sitting on the front steps. "I guess you should've answered."

I didn't reply as we got out of the car. Jane walked up the stairs with a simple hi and walked inside. I stood in the driveway.

"Why won't you call me back?"

"I've been busy and you've got your hands full."

"I thought we were friends, Elizabeth. More than friends." He dug his hands in his pockets. "I thought I could be honest with you about her. This is a big deal for me and my son."

"I get that, but it doesn't involve me." I tried to walk past him.

"Doesn't involve you?" Nick's face closed. "So the line's drawn now, is it? You're leaving and we're done."

"What do you want me to say? That's always been the reality of this." I waved my hand between us. "And you'll end up with her anyway."

"What are you talking about?"

I walked past him. "She lost her job, Nick, and suddenly she wants to move here. You're stable. Doing well. What's not to love? Nothing you've told me makes me believe any of this is about Matt; it's about her. And you? You'll give it to her thinking you're giving it to him." I turned around at the porch steps and faced him.

"That's not true, but she's his mom and he's thrilled. I won't deny him that. I've thought a lot about this since . . . Is his name Andy? . . ." Nick's voice rose with each word.

"Don't bring Andy into this." I spit out the words, suddenly angry with him—angry that I was leaving, that I'd "failed" that gene test, and that Nick had the gall to use Andy to justify his choices, that he'd even mentioned Andy's name. And to top it all off, I didn't know anger—it felt foreign and slightly scary. Anger required caring, and not much of that had permeated my life in recent years. I took a breath and detached a heart-beat more. "You know nothing about him, and you're not doing this for your son."

I stepped forward. "You don't tell your dates about Matt's birth, your great one-night mistake, because you want to be honest. You tell them because you need to punish yourself. You haven't forgiven yourself and you revel in a public thrashing. You built him a sanctuary, a home and a garden, where you can hide and do everything right, never feel, never let anyone in. I know that one, Nick, and I've been at it a lot longer than you. But you let me in. I don't know why or how, but you did; yet she's back and I know you, you think she can make it whole, and deep down you want that because it will erase your mistake."

I looked down the street and knew where to find

comfort. I knew where to stand and I knew I needed to go home.

"You're wrong." Nick stepped back.

"Well, it runs two ways . . ." I dropped my voice to mimic his. "I know you. And you're a fool."

I watched his face harden. "Good-bye, Elizabeth."

"Good-bye." I climbed the few steps and my anger evaporated. "Nick?" I turned around. "She'll go. She's not trying to be Matt's mom. Protect him."

He said nothing, but simply turned and walked away. By the time I crossed the porch and looked around again, he was halfway down the block, his long legs eating up the sidewalk. And everything I felt, good, bad, ugly, and everything in between, dropped away and I was alone.

I turned the knob and walked inside, right into Jane. "Were you listening?"

"You were kinda loud."

"Only if one is standing with her ear pressed to the door."

"So Rebecca is back for good."

I leaned against the door. "Doubt it, but she's his albatross. Always will be."

"His what?"

"His weight. The weight hanging around his neck. Rebecca is his. Mom is yours. And mine? Mine is that I feel nothing. I'm done."

"That's not true."

"It is. I am what I am. I don't know what I thought might happen here." I pushed my hands against my eyes. "But I need to go back to what I know. There are doctors in New York, my work is there, I need to go."

"Why do you need a doctor?"

"Forget it." I sighed.

"Forget what? You? I can't do that. You're my sister."

"I'm your sister who stayed with you because I had nowhere to go. Just like Rebecca. I needed to cook and you had a warm kitchen. That's all this was."

She stared at me. "It was more than that."

"I'm never more than that." I turned to walk for the stairs.

"What's happened? Why are you doing this?" She took a deep, shuddering breath. "Is it about Nick? Go after him."

"It's not Nick."

"Then what? Tell me. You told me to stop fighting with Peter and I'm trying. You stop fighting with me."

"I just did. Send me one of your passive aggressive e-mails next week complaining how I abandoned you and the children, and we'll be back where we started. I'll never fight with you again. And tell Peter to send me an e-mail with how all this works out." I took a step on the bottom stair before my brain caught up with my mouth. I turned back as my jaw dropped with the recognition of what I'd implied . . .

And that is what made the slap sting all the more. In three bounds Jane was in front of me and her hand flew so fast and connected so hard that I fell onto the stair behind me. I grabbed my cheek, on fire and swelling before she drew back her hand.

I looked up, expecting to see her livid and towering over me. Instead I found her cradling her hand, tears spilling over her lower eyelids. Her bottom lip trembled. "Get out."

I held my cheek. "I'm so sorry. I didn't mean it like that."

"Pack your bags and get out. Anything you forget, I'll mail. You've got thirty minutes."

"Please, Jane—"

"No. I choose to spend my energy surviving this for my husband and my children . . . I don't need you. Not like this." She walked out of the room gripping her hand.

I pulled on the banister to stand, then trudged up the stairs. I threw everything within reach into the suitcase, berating myself with each item I tossed. Within minutes, I noticed a cab pull up outside the house. I shut the suitcase and headed down the stairs, noting the silence. I suspected Jane had left or was hiding somewhere to avoid me.

Before my thirty minutes were up, I was pulling away in the cab and making a phone call.

"Paul, I'm heading back with you after all."

Chapter 39

My key slid in the lock and I pushed Feast's front door open. Something that a month ago had felt warm and vibrant now seemed cold and foreign. My eyes lingered on the picture of Jane and me above the hostess stand, and I remembered that afternoon as if it were only yesterday. Jane was seventeen and I was nine. A friend had come over and was bullying me, and Jane came striding into the room.

"Don't talk to my sister like that. She's your friend, and if you don't know how to be a friend, you can leave."

I recalled how Lisa's mouth had dropped, and I had noticed a silver filling in her bottom molar.

Without missing a beat or drawing a breath, Jane had continued, "Are you going to be nice?" Lisa nodded. "Good. Grab your coats and I'll take you to town for ice cream."

And that's what we did. We went for ice cream and then drove Lisa home, all vanilla smiles and cookie-dough laughs. When we pulled in to our driveway, Jane and I were still laughing and singing at the top of our lungs. Mom was outside taking pictures in her garden and caught this shot of Jane wrapping me in a hug, both of us smiling bright. It was one of the best moments of my life.

Tears filled my eyes and one plopped down my cheek before I could catch it. I swiped it away and glanced around the room, making a note to purchase a few large color photographs or maybe a couple modern paintings in bold colors. I huffed away the notion that it would look more like Nick's home.

Something caught my attention. The alarm hadn't gone off. The room was silent. Someone was probably in the kitchen prepping. I stepped away from the photograph and ran my fingers along a linen tablecloth. It felt rough. Jane wouldn't like that. Her fingers were sensitive right now. Textures mattered. I reached out and touched the cloth with my left hand, imagining her tender nerves might feel like my recovering ones. The cloth scratched and I shivered. Jane was right.

I looked toward the steel door to the kitchen, wishing I could find it silent and dark. I had anticipated that moment when I turned the lights on and saw my kitchen again for the first time. I needed the confirmation that Feast still flowed through my veins and remained my sanctuary. I held my breath and leaned in to the door.

"What are you doing here?" Paul pushed himself up from the counter and tapped his phone several times before pocketing it. He narrowed his eyes, as if trying to solve a puzzle. "I thought you'd call this morning."

"I wanted to come in on my own, like I always do."

"And?"

"It feels the same, but different."

Paul stepped toward me. "Before you settle here, let's go see Spread."

"Spread?"

"The new place. I've been calling it that in my head. One of my marketing guys came up with it, but I'm not sure it works."

He wrapped his arm around me and propelled me back through the dining room, out the front door, and into his waiting town car.

Spread was a tiny place—a gem of one, actually—and I was enchanted the second I opened the door. The location, right on Greenwich Avenue, the charming front, the tiny dining space—I loved it. It felt more intimate and personal than Feast could ever be. It embodied everything that I now valued.

"Murray's been directing the interior design." Paul glanced at me. "I hope you don't mind, but we needed to move forward."

"Not at all." I stepped over a stray board and surveyed the space. I envied Trent Murray—I knew he got it. The changes I saw, the new work being fashioned, clearly enhanced warmth and relationship—he was actively creating more than food in this space.

He was refinishing the woodwork to bring out

honey and blond tones, not Feast's deep, semi-intimidating mahogany hues. A piece of protective floor paper had torn away, revealing large vintage tile ready to be buffed to a high polish. There was wrought iron detailing around the bar that had already been restored. Circa 1920? The small space could seat no more than thirty to forty, but what an evening those patrons would enjoy. It brought to mind the excited glamour of *The Great Gatsby* tempered with the tranquility and warmth of a private dining room.

We heard a crash from the kitchen. Paul beat me to the door.

"Murray?"

"Hey . . . Chef Hughes? You're back. I just dropped the oven grate. Sorry." Trent slid the heavy grate into the oven as we walked into the room. The kitchen was half the size of Feast's, but well designed. A new range took up almost an entire wall.

"Wow." I froze.

Trent looked over. "Isn't it gorgeous? I thought Paul was going to kill me when I insisted on it, but we'll love it."

I absorbed his *we* and saw the future span before me. Paul had worked it perfectly. I glanced over at him. He surveyed the room with a proprietary air. Two chefs, two restaurants. Trent and I now needed each other and had no cause to complain. I ran my hand across the warm stainless steel. Marketing, Trent's. Culinary vision, mine.

There were questions, but I knew the future. As Tabitha had said, I was "on Paul's list," and he had made his intentions clear—as clear as he ever did, always putting business ahead of personal concerns. But he had expectations, and I wasn't naïve enough to believe that two restaurants didn't come with a price.

My hand ran off the edge of the warm stove and turned to ice. The cold of the stainless steel counter was a sharp reminder of what life felt like, would feel like. I glanced to Paul and Trent quietly chatting in the corner.

Paul caught my eye. He stared, reading something. Without breaking contact I heard him articulate slowly and carefully, "Chef Murray. Please give us a moment."

Trent darted a glance between us and left the kitchen with no words. As soon as the door swung behind him, Paul stepped forward. "You're not staying, are you?"

"I'm not, but I didn't realize it until just now."

"I did." At my expression, he raised his brows. "I could always read you. Determined, hungry. I loved your fire. I knew you'd get it back and I thought I'd get you back." He looked at me hard. "We've been heading to this point for years."

"We have," I assured him, knowing it was true whether I'd planned it or not.

"While you were gone, listening to you, I sensed

the 'fire' had nothing to do with Feast or with me. Then Thursday night at dinner, and yesterday on the plane, it was clear."

"I'm sorry, Paul." I stepped forward and rested my hand on his crossed arm.

"Don't do that." He laid his hand over it. "Don't feel sorry for me, Elizabeth. I simply made a miscalculation." He closed his eyes for a beat— then opened them and zeroed in on me. "You'll return to him, won't you?"

"Who? Nick?" I stepped back. "That's over, and this isn't about him. It's about Jane and my dad, Peter and the kids . . . I need to go home. My family's in Seattle."

"And Feast? This place? Me?" Paul's voice cracked and his eyes softened, but no moisture, no tears. "Are we so easily forgotten?"

"Never. But I can't be who I want to be here. I don't want to work to justify my existence, Paul, in every aspect of my life. I can't anymore." I looked around. "Trent and Tabitha will make these restaurants shine and you know it. Tabitha is a gifted chef. They'll thrive, and you'll make money."

Paul chuckled lightly. "I should be offended by that, my dear." He added the last words pointedly.

I reached up and hugged him. "But you aren't, not really."

Paul gently pushed me from him. "Best not to presume too much." He gestured toward the door. "Go."

I stepped forward and kissed him on the cheek, lingering to smell his cologne. Expensive, floral, a touch of moss and sunshine. I turned and walked away.

Chapter 40

Halfway down the block I realized I had no one to call and nowhere to go. My roommate was out of town with her boyfriend, visiting his family in DC, and I had no desire to tell Tabitha she now had her own kitchen. That was Paul's job. And she deserved it.

I turned into a coffee shop. It was small and dark. No armchairs, no fireplace, no antipasto platter. I felt my shoulders slump. With all I'd lost in Seattle and now all I had given up in New York, it was the coffee shop that made my lip quiver. I ordered a latte and sat at a table in the window, staring at my cup and missing the fireplace and the little brown Starbucks sleeve.

I had never once in my wildest dreams imagined giving up Feast, not really. Sure, I'd flirted with vapors—other dreams, musings, and what-ifs—but I knew perfectly well what ingredients bound my life. Yet as I stood in that kitchen, my hand running from the warm to the cold, I knew. I knew I could no longer justify my existence. No work could accomplish that. And if it couldn't, then it meant that I was more. I could be more, live more, give more—live large and thankful and with no regrets.

I wondered how such revelations could dance within me without a lightning bolt accompanying them. Hadn't I just turned all I knew upside down?

I needed a list . . . There was nothing to write with. I glanced around, trying to force a next step. The lack of a fireplace in the coffee shop bothered me . . . and the uncomfortable chairs . . . and the . . . the shop across the street . . .

I finished my drink, disposed of the cup on my way out the door, and waited impatiently for the light to change so I could rush across to the door beneath the sign: *Wigs for Cancer Patients.*

The salon was small and well lit, and wigs covered the shelves floor to ceiling. A saleswoman, Saskia, introduced herself and politely gave me space to roam. I needed it. I was overwhelmed by the styles, the colors, the quantity—and the need such variety implied. I had scoffed at Jane's request, equating it with putting a Band-Aid over an amputation, but these wigs looked real, soft to the touch. They were as complex and varied as the spice mixtures I created with my mortar and pestle and could be as unique and comforting to her as my spices are to me. I closed my eyes, sorry that in this small way, too, I had belittled my sister.

"Are you shopping for yourself?"

"For my sister . . . I had no idea." I grasped a long swath of hair, thicker than my own ponytail.

"That one is made of real hair, but the synthetic wigs over here are easier to style."

"She lives in Seattle."

Saskia nodded, perhaps agreeing but not understanding the relevance.

"Let's just say she won't spend time styling it. She won't find that enjoyable."

"Was her hair that color?" Saskia motioned to the ponytail I still held.

"Blonder."

"Come look at these tones. Many patients want to match their former color because it feels familiar."

"Former?"

"Hair often doesn't come back the same. Some blondes become brunettes, some straight hair comes back in ringlets, some perfectly white or a shade of red. There isn't a rule, but it's never precisely the same."

"Nothing is," I muttered and looked at her color samples. I picked one. "Can I have it wavy, though? She had straight hair, and I think she'd prefer some waves."

Saskia pulled out an order form and began recording my choices. "I just need the circumference of her head."

"I don't have that."

"Can you call her?"

I shook my head and sighed. It was over—my starting point, my opener in a plea for forgiveness. "I can't. I don't think she'd even answer the phone."

I shoved my wallet back into my handbag and brushed across a swath of fabric. I pulled it out. It was the scarf Jane had pulled off at Snoqualmie Falls. I balled it into a fist. "I'll just get her more of these; then she can tie them where she chooses . . ."

I stepped from the counter, fingering the scarf. "Wait . . ." I turned back, spread it on the counter, and folded it into a diagonal, noting the firm wrinkles where the knot had been tied. "Look. Look where she tied it. That's the circumference of her head. Can you use that?"

"Show me how she wore it."

I put it on my head, clasping it behind where the knot formed.

I laid it back on the counter as Saskia pulled out her measuring tape and carefully measured from the center of each wrinkled pock. "If you're willing to take the risk, I estimate we'll add a quarter of an inch to compensate for the angle. It should work, but I can't guarantee it, and the sale is final."

"I'll take that risk." I reached again for my wallet. "It'll work, right?"

"It could."

I took a deep breath and let it out in a huge puff. "I wasn't really talking about the wig."

"I didn't think you were."

Saskia finished recording all my details and assured me that my custom wig would arrive within three days.

Chapter 41

I stood in the doorway of my apartment and shook my head. I had never really looked at it, had never stopped and fully absorbed the space I called home. There was little within that was mine. Even in the kitchen, I had contributed only some fantastic knives and a set of All-Clad pots. It felt as if I'd withheld myself, even from this place. Or perhaps I had simply been that little— that unattached and absent.

I walked into my bedroom, knowing if I wanted to find *me,* there was only one place to look. I lay down on the floor and reached my arm under the bed, making huge sweeps that pushed everything out: Jane Austen novels, a high school scrapbook, birthday cards, and a box of photographs. *The box.* I took a deep breath and opened it. There it was—the peach linen envelope with a small, precise *Lizzy* scripted across the top.

Jane had mentioned hers, the final letter Mom had written to her, but she'd thrown it away. Two daughters, two letters—and neither of us had reached across our divide. One threw it away. One buried it.

I opened the envelope and ran my hand over the fine, careful script. I could practically smell her perfume.

Dear Lizzy,

Your smile will return soon. I know you hurt and I wish I could hold you, dry your tears, and tell how much I love you, but your smile will come back, and your sense of humor, and your bright eyes. I want to remind you of that right now because I suspect you feel alone. Please be patient with both Jane and your dad. Those two are so alike—sometimes I wonder about their analytical brains. They forget the soft emotions occasionally, but that doesn't mean they don't feel them. Your father has loved me well and has taken such good care of me during our marriage and this illness, and I love him with my whole heart. We are a team and he will miss me.

You may need to be his glue for a while. I'm sorry to place such a burden on you, but it is who you are. You are a servant and a seeker of hearts, love, and truth—a true chef. I've seen you mix together the very best that sustains us and offer it up with a piece of your soul on the side. God works through you, sweetheart, and I am only sorry it took me this long to understand the power in that. I hope you will learn from me, now while you are still young and not in the eleventh hour of life.

My eleventh hour is not without joy. Please know that. All is not sadness. And even more joy will come in the morning. Always choose the Feast, my love.

God bless you, my Lizzy. I will love you always . . . Mom

I held the letter in my hand and cried. Cried not because I missed her, but because I'd been less than what she saw and less than what I knew I could be. I hadn't been glue. I hadn't been a seeker, a servant, or even a good friend. I'd turned my back on my gifts and regarded everything as burdens. I'd built a strong defense and a hiding place.

Feast. I knew this was where I'd gotten the name, thinking that naming the restaurant after her would keep her close, make all she wanted for me real. But it hadn't. It hadn't because I only chose the name, never the journey. I hadn't known how—until now.

I grabbed my cell phone and called our building's doorman. "Dominic, are there any packing boxes in the basement?"

By the time he came up with a dozen flattened boxes, I had torn through my room and created five piles: throw, move, donate, Suzanne, and Tabitha. There was little I wanted to take. There was little that mattered.

"Are you packing or spring cleaning?" Suzanne stood smiling in the doorway.

"You're home!" I raced across my room and hugged her.

She laughed at my unexpected enthusiasm. "You are, too, and that's the more amazing thing."

"I'm not, Suz. Not yet."

She nodded into the room. "I see." She stepped in and moved a pile so she could perch on the bed. "Back to Hood River?"

"Seattle. I'm going to open a catering business. I'm going to be a sister and an aunt and a chef. I'm going to start that business I told you about, cooking for cancer patients with a provisions store on the side."

"Good for you. What about a girlfriend, maybe a wife?"

"Ah . . . I just said good-bye to that."

Suzanne looked startled.

"Paul . . . it wouldn't have worked . . ."

"I was talking about Nick."

"He's gone too."

"You sounded like you really liked him. I assumed he was part of this." She spread her hands around the room.

I plopped next to her. "I did really like him, but

he's moving in a different direction." I covered my eyes with my hands. "And oh . . . you should've heard what I leveled at him on my way out of town. I was horrible."

"Elizabeth—" She started to reprimand me, but her eyes caught the letter. "What's that?"

"It's from my mom." I handed it to her. "Please. Read it."

She sat silent a few moments, reading. "I always wondered about your mom. It's beautiful." She carefully folded it and placed it back in the envelope.

"She was beautiful. And she knew much more than I gave her credit for. I've messed up, Suz."

"You're going to have to tell me the whole story."

"That would take all night."

"Then we've got some talking to do. I'll order in."

She ordered Thai food and we sat on the couch eating, talking, laughing, even crying. I told her more about Nick, Jane, the kids, and my final blazing farewell. I told her about Paul, Feast, Trent, and Tabitha, and the catering business that was coming more alive in my head with each moment.

"How are you going to fund it? Paul backed Feast, and I don't think he'll be interested in this."

"I'm going to call Palmer and get his advice, and I'll take out a loan."

"I'll run some numbers for you. You'll need a business plan."

"Thank you."

Suzanne stared at me a moment. Her expression wasn't that of numbers and business. It was softer, like the expression she held when Grant's name flashed across her phone screen.

"What?"

"You have to tell him."

"He's not the reason I'm going back." I shifted my legs under me. "I'll admit he got under my skin. I don't know how or why. Looking at him, you wouldn't see it. Not my type, nothing like Paul, but we understood each other." I shrugged. "This business was his idea, and maybe that's what knowing him was really about. There are some friendships that you need in a season, others in a life. He was a season."

"Don't you want a life?"

"That's what I'm chasing. My life."

She held her hands up. "You're right. I'm clearly feeling romantic, but I'll say this—don't go at everything alone just because that's what you've always done. Dare to imagine something new."

My mother's words, *We are a team,* flashed through my brain. "I'll try . . . I'm trying. I've got a family to rejoin . . . if they'll have me."

"And if she won't?"

I sank back in to the chair. That was what I

hadn't fully sorted. I could ask for forgiveness, but there was no guarantee Jane would grant it. "She hasn't got the most malleable or forgiving personality, but I need to try."

After a couple wonderful hours of sharing, our natures got the best of us and we started making lists. We pulled out our laptops, paper, and pens, and noted moving companies, the Salvation Army and Goodwill, real estate companies, car dealerships. We looked up the small storefront on Madison Street, printed our apartment's release forms, canceled my gym membership, researched Seattle professional societies, and finally and most painfully, we canceled all the reservations I'd booked for haircuts, color jobs, massages, facials . . .

"This is unbelievable. I had no idea how organized you were."

"When you go through it like this, it doesn't have much texture, does it?"

"You were busy. It's orderly. I almost envy it." She checked the pad of paper beside her. "Do you really think you can make that flight?"

"Three days. I want to pick up the wig and head straight to the airport."

"Let's keep at it then. What else?"

Chapter 42

Somewhere over North Dakota I smiled, completely stunned by my to-do list. I'd lived in New York for fifteen years, and all I left behind me was one measly item. Suzanne had made it too easy.

"The movers arrive Saturday, and Grant will be here to help direct them."

"You've left me nothing to do."

"You'll need to transfer the utilities into my name. I e-mailed you the forms yesterday; you have to print, sign, scan, and e-mail them back. That's something."

"It's only one item. I need a better list."

"You may need to watch a movie or read a book." She shoved a small book wrapped in brown paper into my hand. "Here, I got you one."

I shut my laptop and reached for the book in my lap, *One Thousand Gifts.* On the inside of the cover she'd written, *Enjoy the Feast! Love you, Suz.* I sighed. She understood, probably always had, what my mom had meant. I wasn't in my eleventh hour, and I was ready to learn.

From the airport I took a cab straight to Jane's house. The wig box bounced on the seat next to me. Would she understand? Could she forgive? The questions bounced in tempo with the box.

By the time I arrived, I felt fully shaken and unnerved.

Heart in throat, I rang the doorbell.

Jane opened it and stared at me. She looked thinner and paler and sported a black Neff ski cap on her head. I stood silent, waiting for some sign, some word, but she only pressed her lips together, as if holding something in.

I took a deep breath. "I'm truly sorry, Jane. Can you please forgive me?" I held out the box. "I brought you something. It's not much, but it's—"

She grabbed the box from my hands, plopped it on the floor, and pulled both my shoulders into a hug. She didn't push back to look at me. She didn't pat my back. She didn't say anything for a full minute. We simply held tight.

Eventually I heard a small, soft whisper. "I love you."

"I love you too."

We both laughed, sobby and joyful—until one of us snorted.

We spent the afternoon talking and laughing and crying. I had brought my letter and for the first time, we shared rather than fought over Mom. I also told her about the test.

"How could you do that and not tell me? When did you do it?"

"After you mentioned it, I got obsessed. Dr. Chun took pity on me and did the blood draw. You were napping one day." I pulled at a cuticle. "I couldn't tell you. I'm not used to sharing, Jane. I was . . . I was scared."

"Of course you were. What are you going to do?"

"I have an appointment with Dr. Chun next week to discuss my options. I've read over all the websites on a pamphlet she gave me and there are lots of options. It sounds dramatic, but I'm leaning towards a double mastectomy—get rid of the risk, if I can." I took a sip of tea. "Could you come with me and help me think it through?"

"Absolutely." Jane leaned over and gripped my hand. "Let's just not have surgery together."

"Too much sister bonding?" I laughed.

When the kids came home, we moved into the kitchen and continued our talk, a twenty-three-year download, while baking cookies. She pranced around the room and kept the kids in stitches tossing her new hair over her shoulder. And I watched her, studied her, and tried to lay down my assumptions and see my sister for exactly who she was.

When we heard Peter come in, she lit up. "He's here. Hide." Jane pointed under the kitchen table.

"Why?"

"Shh . . . just do it." She turned to the kids. "Sit down and don't say a word." They grinned and pulled out chairs, bumping me with the chair legs and knobby knees.

I tickled Kate's ankle and she giggled.

"Shh, stop it," Jane hissed as Peter opened the door. Footsteps shook the floor beneath my hands and knees. Jane spun around at the sink, offering him her back.

"Lizzy?"

She flipped her hair as she swung around. "I got you! I got you!" She bounced on the balls of her feet. "Lizzy, I got him."

I crawled out from under the table in time to catch Peter's stunned expression. "You've got hair."

Jane twirled her fingers through it. "Isn't it fun? I've always wanted wavy hair. Lizzy brought it."

Peter caught my eyes and smiled, but crossed the room to kiss his wife. "I love it."

"But not more than my real hair, right?"

I bit my lip. It was not the time to tell her what Saskia had told me.

Peter laughed. "This is a nice substitute, but yes, your real hair was and will be more beautiful." He looked over at me and winked. "You're back." It was a statement, not a question.

"I am."

"It's about time." He pulled me into a quick hug. "Good to see you."

"You too."

"She's moving here," Danny added.

"So I gathered." Peter turned back to me. "Seattle's a great food town, plenty of restaurants."

402

"I'm thinking something smaller, more personal. A catering business and a provisions shop."

"That's exciting. Are you going to work with cancer patients, like you did with Jane and Tyler?"

"That's the central plan, but I'd like to take it a little bigger with a storefront too. I contacted a Realtor a couple days ago. We look at spaces tomorrow, including the one on Madison Street down from Starbucks."

"We'll get to see you." Peter smiled as if the very idea made his family complete.

He and the kids soon drifted out of the kitchen while Jane and I finished dinner. She'd planned broiled salmon, quinoa, and spinach.

"I wouldn't have thought this sounded good to you."

"It doesn't." She bit her lip. "I couldn't think of what else to make. I haven't eaten anything in days and—"

"What?"

"Last night I couldn't do it. I let them fend for themselves." Tears gathered in her eyes. "I found the kids' plates in the basement this morning."

"Stop it. It's okay."

"I can't go back there . . ."

I squeezed her shoulder. "That's what I'm here for."

"Oh, Lizzy— Sorry. Elizabeth."

"Don't. It doesn't hurt . . . I like it." I shook my

head. "Move aside. In fact, go sit over there. I'm taking over your kitchen."

Jane smiled and obeyed. She sat silently for a few moments while I figured out what to do with her dinner plan.

Stillness filled the room as I started to chop. "You can talk, you know."

"I was thinking." She crossed back toward me to get a glass of water. "What about Nick?"

My knife stalled and I looked down at my hand. I was flexing it, a muscle memory, not of the injury, but of his care during that time. "Nothing doing. I'm sure I'll run into him. In fact, if you see him, will you let him know I'm back? But I'm not going to seek him out."

"You could at least be friends. He could help you with your marketing. I don't think I can."

Her hand tightened into a fist, and I reached out and grabbed it. "Stop." I rubbed her fingers.

She looked down and huffed an impatient breath. "I didn't even feel it."

"It will all come back to you, Jane. Just like your hair. It'll be different, but it'll come back. Relax and wait."

"It doesn't always change. It could still be blond or—"

"I love you." I smiled indulgently like Mom did during our whiny tantrums.

"Yes, but . . ."

I flashed her my stern look.

"Fine." She huffed again and took a sip of her water. Her voice then came out singsong and perky. "Elizabeth, I'm not taking on new clients at this time. May I suggest a capable colleague with whom I've entrusted my own clients?"

"Much better, but no, you may not. Nick and I couldn't work together. That'd be too tough for me."

Chapter 43

The week rolled by quickly. The Realtor was frighteningly aggressive, but after fifteen years in New York I was used to the sharks. And she was *my* shark, so I let her do her job. She got me a lease on the Madison Street storefront that was so favorable I signed a two-year contract. I was committed. She also found me a small, two-bedroom house in Madrona, about a mile south of Jane. Again, the lease was favorable, and I signed within a couple days. I couldn't believe how fast life changed. I almost asked her to visit the car dealership with me.

Soon I was unpacking my scant furniture and few boxes from New York and had my head shoved into my own oven.

"Lizzy?"

"Back here." I pulled myself out and sat on my heels.

Jane pushed through the door of my tiny storefront and stared at me. "Funny finding you there."

"You want in?"

"No. This is all yours." She looked around. "It's interesting."

"Code for small, dirty, and dark?"

"Something like that."

"See the potential. Flip that switch over there."

Jane flipped the last switch on a bank of six, and the room flooded with light. "Oh, it's just small and dirty."

I stood up and straightened my back. "Cute. Dirty I can fix, and it's actually the perfect size for what I want. It's got a great layout and plenty of counter space." I pointed to a bag she'd rested on the counter. "What's that?"

"A welcome home or new business gift, I can't decide. Open it."

I unwrapped the small box inside. "I never wear perfume."

"I know, but the girl who smells everything needs some good perfume. Open it up. It's fresh and has a little bite, just like you."

"Funny." I pulled the cap off the bottle of Jo Malone English Pear & Freesia and sprayed a little on my wrist. "I love it. It *is* me! How'd you do it? It's actually me."

Jane laughed. "I thought so." She glanced around again. "What are you going to do out front?"

I took a last sniff and then dragged Jane to the front of the store. "I ordered a huge double-glass door freezer for here, and I'm going to put shelves of provisions, maybe a small display cabinet with locally cured meats and cheeses and prepared salads, all through here." I spread my arms around the room, much too grand for its size, but appropriate for my dreams. "I'm flirting with the name Feaster."

"You can't be serious. That's ridiculous."

"I don't want to use Feast. This is something new, but I like what Mom said, I like the idea of choosing the feast, being thankful, being present, coming to grace, and celebrating the freedom—being a 'feaster,' always. I want to live large, Jane, and help bring the feast to others."

"You can't." She shook her head. "I mean, you can do all that and you'll be wonderful, but you can't use that name." She paced around the small space. "What about Evergreen?"

"What's that?"

"It's always alive, growing, changing, choosing life, thriving—all the same stuff you're after without the completely awful name."

"It's not bad, but—"

Peter pushed through the door. "Peter, I picked a name," I told him. "Feaster."

"Fester?" His brows drew together.

I turned back to Jane. "Evergreen it is."

The following Friday I invited Kate and Danny to walk to Evergreen after school so Jane and Peter wouldn't have to rush home from her final chemo session. As the kids ate cookies in the kitchen, I waited for them, leaning against Evergreen's doorjamb and feeling almost completely and thoroughly happy. The business hadn't opened, but I was cooking, prepping, babysitting my niece and nephew—and relishing each sight, smell, taste, and moment. I held my wrist to my nose and breathed deeply. Maybe that was what I'd been missing all along—a good perfume.

The moment of peace felt well earned after a frenetic Thursday and a dinner at Jane's house for ten of my dad's firefighter buddies. They had come all the way from Hood River to clean my kitchen and refurbish the storefront—a huge home-cooked feast was their reward. I leaned against the doorjamb and recalled the work, the dinner, and the miracle it had brought.

"I can't believe you're opening your own catering business."

I had turned to Tubs yesterday (if he has a real name, I've never heard it) and replied, "Technically one could call this a demotion, you know. I ran a restaurant in New York for years."

Tubs shook his head, clearly not hearing me. "Your very own business." He drove in a nail, chuckling to himself. "Who'da thought when your dad kept calling that school that it would come to this? I thought he was crazy to think you'd make it big."

"What calls?"

"That school where you cooked."

"Dad never called me there." I felt my shoulders slump as I remembered that I hadn't called my dad either—not once that entire summer. I had sent an occasional e-mail letting him know I was alive, but had made it clear I didn't want more. As far as I was concerned, there was nothing between us.

"Not to talk to you," Tubs said. "He and that director talked all the time." Tubs shook his head again and walked away, carrying a stainless steel sink to the back Dumpster.

I stood there for a beat, then beelined to the front of the store. "Tubs said you called the Institute." I knelt down next to Dad, who was painting the baseboards.

"I'd forgotten that . . . John. Good man. What brought that up?"

"Tubs was waxing nostalgic." I sat back on my heels. "Why'd you call Chef Palmer, Dad?"

He stopped painting and turned to me. "You were young. The school didn't want to accept you, so I called. After a long chat, John agreed to not only let you in but to keep an eye on you. We probably talked twice a week that summer. And when you came to work for him during college, he'd call and give me updates. We only stopped chatting a few years ago. He was so proud of you."

"And when were you going to tell me this?"

"Never." Dad shrugged.

"Why?"

"I failed you then. I still do, I think." He caught my narrowed eyes and continued, "You wanted to leave, but I needed to make sure you were safe. John did that for me when I couldn't do it myself."

"You're a good man too, Dad." I leaned forward and hugged him.

"I love you, too, Lizzy." He squeezed me and pushed me back to look into my eyes.

I smiled. *That's my dad.*

I stood out on the sidewalk in the afternoon light as the memory danced in my head much like the sunlight in the tree above me. I lifted my wrist again and inhaled. I'd gotten so much wrong—for so very long.

"Elizabeth?"

I took a quick breath and looked up. I heard his voice in my dreams; it was only a matter of time before it invaded my reality. My first glance struck upon Matt. His small face was pinched and wary. I crouched down to his level, wondering if I had hurt him, if I'd caused those hazel eyes to tighten and shadow.

"What? No hug, big guy?"

He looked up at his dad, and I followed his gaze. Nick had once mentioned that Matt was not affectionate with others, but that had never included me. An almost imperceptible nod gave Matt permission, and he slowly stepped into my arms.

A quick hug and I released him. "I think you've grown." That brought a small smile. I tried for another. "Kate and Danny are sitting at a counter through there." I tapped the top of his head. "Could you please make sure they don't eat all my cookies?" I stood quickly and looked at Nick. "If it's okay with your dad?"

Without breaking eye contact, Nick replied, "Bring me one, too, kiddo."

Matt set off at a run while Nick and I stared at each other.

"Hi," I said.

"What are you doing here?" He wasn't angry; he was dumbfounded.

"I leased the store. I'm opening a catering business, focusing on cancer patients, and a provisions shop, exactly as you suggested . . . I thought Jane would've told you."

"I haven't seen her. What about your restaurant?"

"It's still standing, but I'm not the chef." I caught myself fidgeting with my hands and clasped them still. "I found something more out here, and when I got back to New York, I realized I couldn't let it go."

Nick gripped the back of his neck and stared at me. "What'd you find?"

"Forgiveness. Family. A life. Things I was too obtuse to know I was missing." I couldn't stand there any longer. "Come see."

He followed me inside, and I showed him the storefront space. "A huge double-door freezer arrives tomorrow morning. It'll go here." I spread my arms across the wall. "And I have a butcher-block top for this space. I'm leaving this counter stainless—And I have my first client. You remember Tyler?"

"Hemingway."

"Hemingway." I chuckled. "He ordered a whole bunch of meals and told me he'd pass my name around."

"Andy?"

I stopped. "I thought you . . . He died the day . . . the day I saw you on the porch." I took a tentative step toward him. "About that day, I am so sor—"

"Don't apologize. It doesn't matter anymore." Nick ran his hand through his hair and stepped back.

I stood for a moment, not knowing what to say. I wanted to clear things between us so that we could bump into each other and not feel awkward. Now I felt foolish.

"I made something yesterday. I think you'll like it. Wait here." I ran back to the kitchen and grabbed a small square of pastry, catching the honey on a paper towel, and shot back out to the front. I handed my small bundle to Nick.

"Baklava?"

"I've been practicing and finally think I got the pastry right."

"Greek tragedy?" His voice came out in a deflated monotone.

"Just Greek. No tragedy."

Nick held the pastry in his hands but didn't take a bite. Instead he stared at me a moment, then nodded. "We should go."

He passed me and pushed open the kitchen door, calling to Matt.

I rested my hand on Matt's head as he passed me. "It was great to see you. You can come back for a cookie whenever your dad says it's okay."

He wrapped his arms around me and held, just a degree too tight and for a second too long.

Although the next couple of days were hectic, I found Nick creeping into my thoughts—while planning menus, wiping the counters, cutting parsley, rolling out crust for savory pies, and especially as I sat stymied by my nonexistent marketing plan. I called Jane.

"Do you have another capable colleague who could help me?"

"I've got a few, and Peter knows the entire industry here, but I think you're being stupid about Nick. He's a gifted marketer."

"I don't doubt that."

"I'm sorry. I know you wanted more from him."

"I must really be transparent . . . to everyone but me. Looking back, I suspect you're right, but I need to let him go now, and I can't do that if we're leaning over spreadsheets."

"Ah . . . I miss a good spreadsheet."

"Jane, I'm being serious." I looked out my window. "Hey, I gotta go." I hung up the phone as Matt pushed open the door. "Hey, buddy, where's your dad?"

"Behind me. He's slow."

"Okay . . . Do you want a cookie?"

Matt nodded and I grabbed for a tissue and reached into the jar, occupying myself with the boy and his cookie as the dad pushed open the door. "There you go. I added walnuts. Tell me what you think."

"Why don't you take that to the bench right there?" Nick pointed outside the window.

I froze as my little shield shuffled outside.

Nick turned back to me. "You shocked me the other day. I had no idea you were back. Were you not going to tell me? Not call me?"

I could feel my eyebrows scrunch together. "I said some pretty awful things, and with Rebecca here . . ." I took a deep breath. "No, I wasn't going to tell you."

Nick nodded. "Rebecca's gone. She left a few days after you did to get her stuff from San Francisco. She didn't come back. I got a text telling me to say good-bye to Matt, that

414

she'd decided to head down to LA with some guy."

"Now I feel really bad. Is Matt okay?"

"No." He swung around and watched his son outside the window. "He cries. He has nightmares. He's never had those." Nick shoved his hands in his pockets and faced me again. "You were right about me too." He shrugged. "I never meant to use him. I honestly thought I was protecting him."

"I'm so sorry. Are *you* okay?"

He stood for a moment, staring at me. I wondered what he saw. Rather than answer, he turned the question back on me. "Are you?"

I looked around. "I am. For the first time in years, I feel peace. I'm not just working, I'm living. It's different and it feels great."

"I understand that. Something changed in me when I got Rebecca's text, and that's a good way to describe it. I'm ready to live."

I looked at him and thought it might be true—that he, too, had gone through his own crucible and had possibly come out different and new. "I bet Matt helps with that."

"He does. As did you."

I ran my hand over my eyes. "I still can't believe I lashed out at you. It wasn't even about you—"

"Elizabeth." Nick stepped to the counter and reached for my hand, which still rested on the cookie jar. He squeezed gently, brushing across the scars with his fingertips. "It's forgotten. Forgiven, if you want. It's gone. Let yourself off the hook." He let my hand go.

"Thank you."

"Now I should take my son to the park or he might be back for another cookie. Do you want to join us?"

"I've got a delivery coming soon."

"I'll wait." He said the words low and slow. They carried weight.

"For the delivery?"

"No. For you." He lifted his hand and waved it in front of me as if wiping away any confusion between us. "I'm not sure what's going on here. You're usually so easy to read, and now . . ." He paused. "But I know what I want, New York, and I'll wait till you want it too." He blew out a deep breath. "Just so we're clear."

Chapter 44

"Do you want this piece?" Cecilia pointed to the last slice in the box. We sat on opposite ends of my couch—feet tucked under us and an entire large pizza, minus one scrawny slice, inside us.

"It's all yours."

"I'm done too." She closed the box. "I got a couple new clients for you, by the way, or I should say Tyler did. They asked me to pass their numbers to you and for you to call them. They're pretty overwhelmed, so I agreed."

"I remember that. You can be so stunned you can't reach out, even to help yourself." I rested my plate on the coffee table in front of me. "As I've cleaned and built stock for Evergreen, memories keep coming, stuff I haven't felt in years—like that one. Dad and I were zombies until . . . quite recently."

"Very funny."

"But you know I'm right. Jane, too, in her own way." I bit the side of my lip, considering Jane. "Has she changed?"

"You both have." Cecilia smiled and tapped my foot. "You two aren't so different, you know."

"I know." I smiled back. "Will you miss it?"

Cecilia grabbed a pillow and squeezed it. "I think so. It sounds odd, but the Infusion Center is a special place. I enjoyed my time there, but that's the thing about healthy boundaries—you've got to keep checking them. I need to move on."

"Babies could be hard too."

"I haven't settled on neonatal yet. I'm talking to HR and a good guidance counselor. My reviews have been strong, and Donna gave me a wonderful reference. Who'da thunk?" She smiled. "I'm taking this one step at a time, as they say. But in the meantime, make up some business cards. People are asking about Evergreen."

"I have to design them first. I tried to do that

today and could only get one image to upload. My name was on the back and the front with nothing else." I ran my hands through my hair. "Ugh . . . I can't take it. I have to hire someone. Did you know Twitter only lets you use one hundred and forty characters, and if you use the name @chefelizabethhughesevergreen, you've used twenty-nine already and said nothing at all? Stupidest name or handle or whatever you call it. I've got to change that too."

Cecilia laughed. "It'll all work out."

"That's what you say, but it doesn't feel like it. No wonder Paul hired Trent. This stuff matters."

My cell phone rang. I glanced at the screen and mouthed, *Nick,* to her before answering. I couldn't say hi before he launched.

"Elizabeth, I'm sorry to call. This isn't your problem, but . . . can you come over?"

"What's wrong?"

"It's Matt. I don't know what to do. We go through this every night. He was always so comfortable with you, and I thought since you lost your mom—I know it's not the same, but please . . . could you come see him?"

I looked at Cecilia, my eyes wide with surprise and a good dose of panic. "Sure, I'll be there in about fifteen minutes." I hung up the phone. "Matt's upset and Nick thinks I can help."

"I'm sure you can." She got up and gathered her stuff.

"Stay. I won't be long."

"I don't want you to think of me waiting here. You should be all there. Call me tomorrow."

"What could I possibly say to him?"

"Just be there. Maybe that's all he needs."

I nodded and gave Cecilia a quick hug before searching amid the boxes and mess for my keys.

Nick must have been watching for me, because the front door opened as my foot hit the first porch step. "I'm really sorry to bother you. I just . . ." He dropped his hands to his sides.

"I'm glad—that you called, not that Matt's struggling." I put my hand on his arm as I moved past.

He caught it and pulled me around. We faced each other for a moment before he whispered, "Thank you."

Nick stayed in the kitchen as I headed upstairs to find Matt. I peeked into the first bedroom, clearly Matt's, and found it empty. The door next to it was open, so I ventured there. Nick's room. It had white walls with a huge single painting between the windows. No rug, just a dresser and a large armchair. It was so Nick. In the queen bed, tucked in to a white comforter and practically lost in fluff, I found Matt.

I sat down on the edge of the bed. Nick had left his bedside table light on. He had several books and magazines, a photo of Matt, an alarm clock, and . . . I reached down and touched the plastic bag. My spice mixture.

Matt was lying with his back to the light. I lightly ruffled his hair. "Hey, buddy, your dad says you're having trouble sleeping."

He rolled over. Tears rested on his long lashes, and his lip quivered. He nodded against the pillow. I wanted to scoop him up and hug him tight, but instead only pushed his hair off his forehead.

"Are you sad?"

He nodded.

"I felt that way when my mommy left. I was a little older than you are now, but it was scary and sad and I felt lonely. It took me a long time to realize that those feelings were okay and that they wouldn't last forever." *Like a couple weeks ago* flashed through my brain. I left out that detail.

"Where'd your mommy go?"

"My mom . . ." I almost lied, afraid to make things worse by telling the truth, but knew no good could come from that. "She died, and I felt very alone. Los Angeles can feel pretty far away, too, can't it?"

Matt nodded.

"It is. I was in New York a few weeks ago, and that's even farther away, but I thought about you a lot, and I bet your mommy does the same from Los Angeles." I smoothed his hair again. "Do you know what I miss most about my mom?"

Matt shook his head.

"Her hugs. She really squeezed you tight. She gave bear hugs. None of that silly back patting, arms-only stuff that people do these days. Here, sit up."

Matt pushed himself up.

"This is what most people try to get away with." I squeezed him, then pushed him out, pulled him in, patted his back, pushed him out . . . I repeated this a few times until a tiny, soft giggle escaped.

"But not my mom. This is how she hugged." I pulled him in and held him tight, talking as I squeezed him securely. "See, no pushing and pulling. It feels safe. This is a hug that lets you know you are loved, completely and forever. When I miss my mom, this is what I need."

I let him go but kept my hands on him. It felt important to keep contact. I rested one hand on his shoulder and used my other to brush a tear from his cheek. "When you miss your mom, go to your dad, and I bet he'll give you one of those. Did it help?"

Matt nodded but said nothing.

"Do you need another?"

He nodded again.

"Come here." I pulled him across my lap and felt his arms loop around me. I closed my eyes to hug him tighter and give him that elusive feeling of unconditional love and complete safety. The feeling we seek but, in this life and in this world, perhaps never quite find.

I whispered over his shoulder, still holding tight. "You're good at this, kiddo. In fact, I may come to you next time I need one."

He squeezed my neck. "I love you, Miss Elizabeth."

Tears sprang to my eyes and my heart broke the tiniest bit. I hoped I hadn't, in my attempt to help, offered too much and set him up for more loss. I closed my eyes and held him and tried not to travel a road not set before me. I could be Matt's friend now, and maybe that was enough. "I love you, too, buddy." I gently released him. "It's late and you've got school tomorrow. Are you ready to sleep?"

He nodded again, this time surer and stronger.

"Shall we go to your room?"

I reached for his hand and closed mine around each short, warm, and wonderfully small finger as we walked to his room next door. It was full of Thomas the Tank Engine and dinosaurs and emergency vehicles. The rug was a road map, and trucks and ambulances were scattered across it like there had been a horrid wreck.

I stepped over a fire truck to get to his bed and tucked him in. His eyes were already closing. "God bless you, Matt. He will watch over you tonight and every night. You are loved and you are safe." I kissed his forehead and left.

I walked down the stairs.

I found Nick sitting at the kitchen counter, papers scattered all around him. He looked as undone as Matt had felt. "I tucked him in. Maybe he'll sleep."

"I heard you."

"I hope I didn't say anything wrong." I squeezed my hands tight to stop my fidgeting.

"You said everything right." He turned to look at me, his eyes so full of sadness.

"You're a good father, Nick. He's going to be fine." I shrugged and turned toward the door. "Call me again if you need me."

"Wait."

I turned with my hand on the knob.

"This is for you." He shoved an envelope into my hand.

I held it up. "What is it?"

"A note." He pushed his hands in his pockets, straightening his elbows. "Read it now, read it later, but read it. Please."

I looked at the envelope, then back to Nick. His face revealed nothing so I turned and left, but I only made it a couple blocks before I pulled over under a streetlight and tore open the envelope.

"I can listen no longer in silence. I must speak to you by such means as are within my reach . . ."

Please don't say I'm too late and that the

damage I've caused is irreparable. I'm sorry for pushing you away and for not seeing you, the real you, and for not hearing what you were trying to tell me before you left—and for not begging you to stay.

Now you're back and I will not make those mistakes again. I told you I'd wait for you and I will, but I'd give anything for a sign, some sign that you'll open to me, as you have to Jane and Peter and the kids. I won't hurt you, Elizabeth.

I loved seeing the light in your eyes as you talked about your work and the life you're chasing. I want to be part of it. I'm chasing you, Elizabeth. Please see that. Please see me . . . "A word, a look, will be enough . . ."

I love you.

Nick

Without thinking, I turned the car around and drove back. I reached for the doorbell and hesitated. Afraid to wake Matt, I knocked.

Nick immediately answered. His eyes were shiny, and a red mark covered his forehead.

"Were you leaning against the door?"

He rubbed his forehead. "I hadn't moved yet."

"What is this?"

"A letter."

"I got that, but . . . you read *Persuasion*? This is basically plagiarism, you know."

Nick chuckled lightly. "I thought you might let that slide."

"But why? Why'd you read it?"

"It's your favorite book. I would have made that meal from *Babette's Feast*, but I can only make a good chicken rub."

"And I've got your mortar and pestle."

"That too." He reached for my hand, crumpling the letter between us.

I jerked away, pulling the letter from his grasp, and caught his flinch in my periphery. "Don't crumple it."

Nick let out a soft laugh. "So you did like it?"

"Who wouldn't? It's what every girl dreams about—an arrow straight to the heart."

"But?"

"I think . . . I gave you up." It was all I could say. It had taken courage to come back to Seattle, envision a new life, and chase it. It had taken courage to ask for forgiveness from Jane and my father. Did I have enough courage for Nick? He could crack me open and leave me gutted for a very long time if he walked again, if Rebecca grew bored of LA, or if someday Matt decided he didn't like me. I'd seen the real Nick while he cared for me after I hurt my hand and while we cooked—and he was wonderful, clever, and giving, with his crinkly eyes, his smell, his patience . . . all of him.

"I can read you better now."

I lifted my chin up, challenging him. "What do you see?"

"Fear," he said, so simply and so softly.

"There you have it."

"Then let's start with something easy." He flicked his head back toward his house. "I baked you chocolate chip cookies. Not nearly as good as your baklava, but I know they're your favorite. Come try one?"

"I can do that." I smiled and stepped forward.

He stepped back through the door, letting me step inside. As I passed, he leaned down and kissed my cheek, right below the ear, and whispered, "It's a place to start."

Chapter 45

I held off opening day for six days after Evergreen was ready in order to honor the day Mom had died. I planned to rebirth the day I had nursed and cosseted in misery for sixteen years. And so I opened a bottle of Champagne—at nine in the morning.

"Feels a bit early for the bubbly," Jane giggled.

"Gotta toast now. Thanks to your marketing campaign, I have clients coming in right when I open at ten o'clock."

"Ah . . . and my one client may actually pay me soon."

"With food and my warmest personal regards, dear sister."

Jane huffed, but I could tell she was pleased. "Pour."

"Bossy." I poured five glasses. "Grab one."

Dad reached across and handed one to Nick and another to Peter. I stood there. Speechless. Nick broke the silence with a small laugh. After evenings scrubbing the store until it glowed and sharing every thought, feeling, memory, fear, and dream in the process, I think only he fully understood how far I'd come to reach this day and how I was now completely without the words to christen it.

He reached out and squeezed my hand. He may have meant to let it go and allow me to stand alone to usher in my business, but I didn't give him a chance. I held tight.

My dad stepped into the silence. "I want to make a toast." He raised his eyebrows, asking my permission. I nodded.

"I'd like to toast my beautiful daughters. Your mother would be so proud of both of you. On this day, long ago, we got lost, but today . . ." He stopped and scrunched his nose to stop tears from forming. He took a deep breath.

"Today, we are found."

Reading Group Guide

1. As the story opens, Elizabeth is struggling at Feast. Paul and Tabitha say she is "divided." Have you felt times in life when your focus is divided?

2. Elizabeth and Jane seem to want to connect but always have something contentious between them. Can you relate? What keeps you from connecting with family and even friends, despite sincere efforts?

3. Illness—or change—of any kind can put pressure on a family. Have you experienced such pressure in your family? How did it play out in daily life?

4. Have you seen the movie *Babette's Feast*? Or read the book by Isak Dinesen? It's a wonderful story of forgiveness, grace, and gorgeous food. What changed in Elizabeth after she saw this movie? What changed in Nick?

5. What do you think of Cecilia's desire to "never hide" but rather use her unconventional look to reveal her true self? Versus Lizzy, who does the opposite, using her appearance to hide herself from the world?

6. Jim, Lizzy and Jane's dad, says the *love* must be more than the *like*. What do you think he meant? Do you agree?

7. At the beginning, Lizzy and Jane seem to have forgotten or shut out their faith. Through their

trials, memories and questions start to surface. Do you find this is how faith works in your life? If so, why might that be?

8. Lizzy notices her "gift" returning in parallel to her loosening control. She even comments that she did none of the cooking one day—and yet she felt joy over it. What might she be experiencing?

9. Jane, while sitting in the booth with Peter, expresses anger and frustration at where she is in life. She resents being "stuck." Have you felt that way? What propelled you forward?

10. Before Jane's family goes to the water park, Peter states that if Lizzy leaves, he is certain she'll "never come back." Do you think that is true? If she left, would the pain between the sisters remain unresolved? Would Lizzy be running again?

11. "No one told me that grief feels like fear." This is C.S. Lewis's opening line in his book, *A Grief Observed*, and was one of the starting points for Lizzy and Jane's story. If you've experienced grief, do you agree or disagree with Lewis's statement?

12. Paul arrives in Seattle ready to make all of Lizzy's dreams come true—or at least, what she once thought her dreams were. How has she changed? Was she foolish not to accept what the world would consider a good deal?

13. At the end of the story, Jim declares the family "found." What do you think he meant? Do you agree?

Acknowledgments

A blank page is an intimidating thing, and this blank page is the most daunting of them all. Not because there is no one to thank but because so many hands, hearts, and heads join in this journey, I fear not saying enough . . .

I'd like to start by thanking all the women who shared their experiences with breast cancer with me—especially Pam Muir, Katherine James, and Lisa Youngblood for going deep. I also thank Julie Jarema, Annie Gunderson, Sandy Sampson, Amy Juneau, Dawn Behling, Peter Armstrong, and all the nurses and doctors at McLaren Northern Michigan Regional Hospital, for their amazing work, patience, and generosity. Any mistakes—and the many changes in treatment to fit a very *fictional* case—are most definitely my own.

And to the incomparable team at Thomas Nelson—Daisy Hutton, Katie Bond, Becky Monds, Elizabeth Hudson, Jodi Hughes, Ansley Boatman, and the fantastic Sales Team—you all make me smile each and every day. Kristen Vasgaard, thank you for yet another beautiful cover, and LB Norton, for being the best Word Master I know. There are so many others who work tirelessly—I sincerely thank you all.

I also want to always remember my dear friend

Lee Hough who helped create *Lizzy & Jane*—and to thank Andrea Heinecke and Bryan Norman for guiding it on.

And to my family . . . Mom and Dad, thank you for— Well, there's too much to list isn't there? I'll start with my "desk away from my desk." It, and all that comes with it each summer, is an outpouring of your love. Thank you.

As always, thanks Team Reay—especially you, SHM, for always believing and digging in beside me each and every day.

Finally and especially, I thank the Elizabeths. Each of you has your fingerprints all over this story and my heart. I hope you will always know, deep in your soul, how much I love you.

About the Author

Katherine Reay has enjoyed a lifelong affair with the works of Jane Austen and her contemporaries. After earning degrees in history and marketing from Northwestern University, she worked in not-for-profit development before returning to school to pursue her MTS. Katherine lives with her husband and three children in Chicago, Illinois. *Dear Mr. Knightley* was her first novel.

Visit her website at www.katherinereay.com
Twitter: @Katherine_Reay
Facebook: katherinereaybooks

Center Point Large Print
600 Brooks Road / PO Box 1
Thorndike, ME 04986-0001 USA

(207) 568-3717

US & Canada:
1 800 929-9108
www.centerpointlargeprint.com